THE
HALF-LIFE
EMPIRE

THE HALF-LIFE EMPIRE

BOOK ☢ 1

SHAMI STOVALL

Podium

Podium

THE
HALF-LIFE
EMPIRE

CHAPTER ONE

I had been shot, beaten, attacked by aliens, and once left for dead . . . yet *this* was the second most stressful day of my life.

Today I had to sneak into a silver mine.

Guards watched the entrance, their rifles held close. If they found me, they'd throw me in with the rest of the *forced labor*. That was the lucky outcome. If I were unlucky—and I usually was—I'd be given the "worst player of hide-and-seek" award, which consisted of a dozen bullets buried deep in my small body.

Instead, I headed for a hidden fissure in the rocks, far from the main entrance. It led into the facility, in a part of the mines rarely visited.

I slid from one shadow to the next, avoiding the guard towers posted on the side of the mountain. With careful movements, I crept inside the silver mines, scooting through the narrow crack-like tunnel until I arrived at a metal panel built around one of the mine's rooms. I had to remove the panel to get inside, but it was the perfect hidden hatch for my operations.

Months of meticulous planning had brought me to this point.

If I failed, my life would be over.

But if I succeeded, everything would change—for the better. I'd get out of this godforsaken wasteland. I'd be free. I just had to stay focused.

Once I entered the main portion of the mine, I hustled through the corridors. The place was huge, but only half of the mines were in use. I effortlessly made my way through the empty areas. As I got closer to the heart of enemy operations, I had to slow myself and wait for the guards to pass before continuing my way deeper into the facility.

Shouts echoed off the far walls, coming from the belly of the mine. It was the miners—the imprisoned enemy soldiers.

A chorus of smashed rocks and grinding metal hid my footsteps. Halfway to my destination, my hip flared in pain, making it difficult to walk without a limp. I was only twenty-three years old, but without a proper doctor, some injuries never healed quite right.

I continued regardless, even if I was slower.

Nothing would stop me.

Finally, I reached my goal: an alien computer terminal that controlled the doors to the storage rooms. Rust stained the outside, but the technology on the inside could last hundreds of years without degrading, even in the face of the world-ending bombs and radiation. That beautiful technology, crafted by those disgusting space monsters—*A-tech*, as everyone called it—was worth more than every slave in the nation of Ex Cathedra.

Which was why I had to steal some.

My plan to cross the border would take resources, and if I ever wanted to reach the coast, to escape Ex Cathedra for good, I would need more than a handful of trinkets.

After a few quick keystrokes and reading through the alien-text instructions, the computer let me in. I shut the door behind me and took stock of my surroundings. The storage room had all the warmth of a cannery. Grated floors, steel walls, and a ceiling chiseled from rock itself. The fluorescent lighting flickered.

On the opposite wall stood a battery box, a thin aluminum container nearly the size of a locker. Everything I wanted was within that box.

But I wasn't alone.

Two young women huddled together in the far corner, dressed in dirty, ripped clothing. They trembled when I entered, but their eyes grew wide when I stepped farther into the room.

They were captives.

Neither said a word, no doubt fearing they'd draw the attention of the taskmasters, but they motioned me toward them, their frantic hand gestures betraying their terror. They were tethered to the wall with a set of cuffs and a thick wire, no better than animals.

Did they think that, since I was also a woman, I had come here to rescue them? I didn't even know who they were.

It took me a moment to register a man sitting against the side wall, his hands chained above his head. He still had his clothes—cargo pants and a shirt—but that was a sorry consolation prize considering his injuries. Bruises, burns, and small cuts marked all visible portions of skin, like he had been dragged through the radiation and back on a sled made of barbed wire. He took in ragged breaths, rivulets of blood seeping from his mouth and onto his lap.

I had a layout of the mines, a schedule for the taskmasters, and the passcodes for specific computer terminals, but I hadn't planned on people being inside the storage room.

I hesitated. There wasn't much time between shifts in the guards. And what if these unknown people attacked me after I set them free?

The women pleaded with their glossy eyes.

Broken by empathy, I hobbled over to them and knelt, my right leg burning in agony. I withdrew a set of lock picks from my jacket pocket. I had worked as a thief for years, and simple cuffs posed no difficulty. I undid their restraints.

"Do you have a gun?" one woman asked in a hushed voice as she crossed her arms tight over her chest.

I shook my head.

The two women exchanged panicked looks, and then they turned their attention to my stiff leg. A piece of me felt their judgment, and I knew they'd leave me behind. Before I could even voice an alternative plan, they both bolted for the door.

Of course they saw me as a liability—a hindrance to their escape. Everyone did. I'd grown accustomed to being the one left to slow the pursuit of wolves.

At least they hadn't thought to take the prizes locked away in the room.

I limped over to the battery box and picked the lock. The container was large, like a closet, and I swung open the aluminum door to get a better look at the contents.

Although the box was mostly empty, the first shelf held two atomic batteries, can-sized squares filled with radioactive isotopes. The decay of the isotopes generated electricity, and the atomic batteries could last for generations. They were perfect for household power problems, and once I reached United California, I could sell them for a small fortune.

But they weren't what I was looking for.

I felt around the inside, pushing aside wires and storage containers. My heart rate increased with each barren shelf and dry power cell. It had to be there. It *had* to.

A rumble shook the tiny room, and I struggled to stay on my feet. Somewhere within the facility, the mining machines flared to life, executing their deep drilling procedures despite the fact that no one manned them. Autonomous and self-reliant, the A-tech mining equipment would continue digging out the mountains until it gathered every last scrap of silver this side of the Colorado River.

New A-tech machines couldn't be built, not after the bombs devastated the world, so the imprisoned soldiers—slaves, really—were kept as pack animals, meant to carry the metal and stone out of the mines, helping the machines with the mundane tasks to save time.

The man chained to the storage room wall watched me as I steadied myself. His intense gaze startled me. He was much more alert than I would have expected for someone in his condition.

Once the rumbling stopped, I spotted his dog tags. They marked him as an Ex Cathedra soldier. It meant he was an enemy—Ex Cathedra owned the mines, after all. I had been trying to escape Ex Cathedra for damn near seven years. I couldn't risk releasing him if it meant he could turn on me.

I returned my attention to the battery box.

At the bottom, underneath a stack of yellowed paper, I found my true goal for the operation: a fission battery. My hands trembled as I uncovered it. The battery was my ticket out of Ex Cathedra.

And unlike the atomic batteries, which powered small buildings or equipment, the fission batteries worked on a much larger scale—capable of powering a small town, maybe more—with nuclear fission as the power source. They had universal adapters and could be fashioned to connect with damn near anything. They lasted for centuries, perhaps longer. I never heard of one dying.

Fission batteries weighed close to fifty pounds thanks to the special shielding of the case and heavy elements contained within, but it was still only the size of a dinner plate. I dragged it out of the battery box, but my injuries would make carrying it through the silver mine a bitch of a task.

"Woman."

The soldier's gruff voice startled me. He hadn't moved.

"Undo my restraints," he said. "Please."

I slung a small backpack off my shoulders and shoved the fission battery inside. Getting mixed up with anyone else would only hurt my chance of escape. And he didn't look well. He probably wouldn't make it.

He exhaled, his breath ragged. "I'm a traitor. Why do you think they locked me in here? I want to escape as much as you do."

Traitor or not, helping him meant taking extra time in the mines. Best not to risk losing it. I made my way to the door.

He pulled against his cuffs. "*Please.*" He hung his head. "They'll do worse than kill me."

I stopped, knowing he was right. But the peril weighed heavy on my mind. The extreme heat of the mine shafts, coupled with the occasional flesh-hungry arthropod the size of a dog, created a catalog of horrors to challenge Dante's tour through hell. I didn't want to get trapped in here.

Indecision killed more than risks out in the wasteland, however. I needed to commit one way or the other.

He saw I had taken the battery. What if he wanted it for himself? So many factors to consider and not enough time. I had a knife, and his injuries would hinder him if he tried to overpower me.

With a quick exhale, I turned and hobbled to his side. The soldier lifted his head as I knelt to undo his shackles. Although his gums were bloody and his skin wan, none of his wounds would prevent him from walking.

Once finished, I swung open his cuffs and stood. He pushed himself to his feet slower than I did—which was never a good place for someone to be in—and I had enough time to back away as he gathered his strength. Would he try something stupid, like attacking me? I slipped a hand into my jacket and fingered my weapon.

"Thank you," he muttered. Then he motioned to the door. "We need to go now. The guards will be back through this hallway any minute."

I pulled my hand out of my jacket and nodded.

His apparent familiarity with the schedule meant I wouldn't need to explain everything, and I waited for him to go first out the door. Better to stay behind someone, in my experience. Most of the lights in the hall were dim or flickering, as if we had stumbled onto the set of a horror movie. At least the lighting worked in our favor.

The soldier turned right.

I turned left.

He glanced over his shoulder and hesitated a moment before hustling to my side. I gave him a quick glance, confused by his continued presence. He could leave, I wasn't stopping him, and he obviously knew the layout of the mines well enough to find an exit.

Although he could still walk, he doubled over for a moment and held his side, his fingers twisting into his shirt. He didn't complain, though. With gritted teeth, he forced his posture straight. "This way is a dead end."

"I know what I'm doing," I whispered, my voice rusty. I rarely spoke. For years I'd lived alone, worked alone, and hid myself away at all times.

"If you know a way out, please take me."

Hadn't I already helped him enough? He moved with an awkward jerk, as though every bit of movement pained him.

The soldier walked to the next door over and leaned against the wall. "I know they have more supplies." He punched a passcode into the A-tech computer terminal. When the machine beeped in rejection, I cringed. The echo of the harsh sound traveled down the hall.

"What're you doing?" I hissed.

"They must've changed the codes." He exhaled and shook his head. "Give me a moment. They cycle through a set of standard passcodes."

I motioned him aside and tapped at the keyboard. Trying out several codes wasn't a viable option. The beeping would alert the guards to our presence.

Although I hadn't gotten the passcodes for all doors, I didn't strictly need them. The coding for the silver mines was old—some of the first alien computer code given to humanity—and I knew it well. There were back doors in the command systems, and I typed away at the terminal, changing the passcodes manually to something I made up on the spot.

"You can read the alien language?" the soldier asked.

"Yes."

"And you know how to bypass A-tech systems?"

I finished my hacking job and then stepped aside, allowing the unlocked door to answer for me.

The soldier regarded me with his eyebrows knit as he stepped into the room.

Not many people were familiar with alien computer codes, especially not after the war. A vast number of people had died, and all the major cities were destroyed, leaving humanity with few sources of actual pre-war knowledge. It didn't surprise me this soldier knew nothing of the language.

The man went straight for a gun rack mounted to the wall. When I glanced around, I realized we had opened an armory.

He grabbed a couple rifles, opened them up, and checked the fragile parts, making sure time hadn't destroyed them beyond functioning. He slung one with a strap over his shoulder and picked up two .45 handguns—HK45s, nice models, and in good condition. Once he had a small arsenal's worth of ammunition, he limped back to my side.

Before exiting the room, he grabbed himself a backpack and dumped an armful of bullets inside.

I clenched my jaw, half tempted to leave him, half tempted to use him as a decoy for my escape. Ironic to consider someone else for the role of scapegoat, but desperate times always turned my thoughts dark. If one of these weapons discharged, the echo would surely draw unwanted attention. I couldn't bring myself to do it, however, I already knew. The few times I had been left behind haunted my thoughts.

"My name is Dallas," he said as he zipped up his pack.

"I'm Kita."

Dallas coughed into his hand, coating his palm in fresh blood. He wiped away the crimson with a quick swipe of his arm.

"Take this, Kita," he said as he thrust one of the handguns to me.

After a long moment of hesitation, I took the weapon. With my hand shaking, I tucked it into my jacket. He kept the other gun for himself and shuffled into the hallway. Although I didn't plan on using it, having the gun would at least act as a deterrent. Dallas would have to think twice about betraying me if he knew a bullet could come from my end.

We made our way through the mine shafts, but I fell farther and farther behind. Dallas walked back to me and reached for my backpack.

"No," I growled as I flinched away.

I couldn't let it go. I couldn't.

He stepped up close and motioned to our narrow surroundings. "You'll get us both killed. Let me carry it. I swear you can have it back once we're safe."

I didn't trust him. How could I? I'd drag myself through this place with one broken arm before I let anyone take my battery. I held on to the straps of the backpack, my knuckles white.

"I can do it," I said.

Several seconds of silence passed between us before Dallas replied with a curt nod. It would no longer be an issue, but I knew it meant I would be at a higher risk of getting caught.

A siren screeched throughout the facility. I slammed my hands over my ears. What had happened? Who discovered us? The guards would converge on us at any moment.

"We have to run," Dallas shouted.

Despite his injuries, he took off down the hall. I ran after but only for a few hundred feet. After turning into another hallway, all I could hear were my own hissing breaths. They performed the perfect impression of a torn bellows as they stoked the cold fire of my chest. My leg injury affected more of my health than I'd ever admit. Cardio wasn't something I had focused on while in hiding.

I'd never be able to keep up. Never.

And then my leg gave out, and I hit the steel grating forearms first. The flare of pain momentarily blinded me. The extra fifty pounds from the battery didn't help, either.

Dallas must've left, which meant I was going to be a scapegoat yet again. Of course he had left me to a slow death at the hands of the Ex Cathedra judges. Anyone would.

Damn, it hurt.

Not the fall or my labored breathing, but the rest of it. I had lived through so much! Isolation, the wasteland, hell radiation, the aliens—but I would finally die in the hallway of a random silver mine. My obituary could read the same as a cockroach's.

Someone grabbed the back of my jacket and yanked me up. I snapped my attention to the individual, shocked to see Dallas. He unceremoniously pushed me forward, and I staggered to get my footing. With my backpack still in place, I took a few deep breaths.

"Hurry," he said. "If you can't walk, lean on my shoulder."

"I—"

Dallas shoved me again, but he kept his hand twisted in the fabric of my jacket, keeping me upright even when I stumbled. Together we raced toward the exit, and any time I might have fallen, he was there again to keep me going.

When we reached an intersection of hallways, he stopped and gulped down his breaths.

I pointed down the darkest corridor. "There. We're not far."

The sounds of boots stomping on the grated floors got my pulse running faster than before. Dallas didn't move. Did he think I was leading him into a trap? This time, I shoved him.

"Hurry," I said. "Or go your own way."

Dallas must have weighed the pros and cons of trust because he hesitated for half a second. Then he continued with my route, half laughing to himself.

"Let's get out of this hellhole."

CHAPTER TWO

We entered a narrow room before any of the taskmasters ran into our hallway.

Dallas shut the door while I pulled out a small flashlight from my jacket pocket. The room was once a lab for testing metals, but the computers and machines weren't made with A-tech components and had ceased to function decades ago.

A fine layer of dirt covered most surfaces. I worried we would leave an easy trail to follow, so I took a moment to scrape my boots along the floor and brush my sleeves over the walls.

Dallas didn't question me—he probably guessed what I was doing—and he waited at the door, listening.

The siren alarm and hustle of movement echoed in the hallway, but the thick steel dulled the intensity. The harsh sound of every door in the hall opening and slamming shut was evidence that the taskmasters didn't know where we were, but it wouldn't take them long to find us. After a deep breath to clear my thoughts, I pointed to a metal panel on the far wall.

"There," I said. "It opens, and there's a fissure through the rock. That's how I got inside without getting caught."

Dallas pulled at the edges of the panel until it popped off, revealing the narrow crack through the rocks. While there was enough room for me to slide through, Dallas took a step back and examined the entry, his eyebrows knit together in healthy skepticism.

"You sure it's big enough?" he asked.

"Positive."

I eased myself into the dark crevice, keeping my backpack close, and scooted along sideways, the rocks pressed against my back and chest. Dallas removed his backpack and rifle and held both by the straps in one hand. He grimaced when the jagged edges of unworked stone scraped across some of his injuries, though he kept quiet.

Once fully inside the fissure, he lifted the metal panel and propped it back in place. I doubted it looked convincing, given his haste, but it didn't matter.

We slowly moved along until the mountain rumbled again from the stress of the machines. Dallas bumped into my side, his breathing strained from the lack of room to inhale, and he grunted something in an apparent attempt to urge me forward. It wasn't long before the crack widened and I could walk normally once again.

I exited onto the mountainside, comforted by the glory of a burning sunset. The fresh air and my victory invigorated every cell of my body. I wouldn't be able to sleep for a good twenty-four hours, not while riding my triumphant high.

So many months of planning had finally paid off! With the fission battery, I would be able to escape Ex Cathedra and make it all the way to the coast; there was no doubt in my mind.

Dallas stumbled out of the darkness and into the muted radiance of the setting sun. Overcast clouds did their best to drain the world of color, but the sun broke through, basking us in the glory of a few simple rays of orange and gold. Dallas ran a hand through his auburn crew-cut hair, dusting off the dirt.

I unconsciously did the same. I hadn't much considered my appearance while living alone. The uneven ends of my black shoulder-length hair were a result of thinking haircuts to be a waste of my time. I shook the thought from my head. Better to continue with my high than dwell on trivial details.

Dallas squinted up at the sky.

Most days were overcast, the clouds pregnant with leagues of black water. Every once in a while, sunlight seeped down to the earth. Perhaps it was a sign that destiny was on our side. A pleasant thought, if one believed in such illogical concepts as destiny.

The silver mine's siren sounded, even on the outside. Dallas flung his backpack and rifle back over his shoulder. He took in wet breaths as he did so, his breathing becoming ever more ragged.

"You have radiation poisoning," I said.

"It's worse than that," he replied with a forced chuckle. "But we don't have time for bullshit. Where are we going?"

My plan had involved escaping without getting caught, but I did have contingencies. My hideout for the past six months wasn't far, and we could walk along the broken highways to avoid leaving tracks through the dirt.

The silver mine sat atop a large slope on the side of a mountain. The facility was closed off and surrounded by a wall. The guards on the posts couldn't see us from our angle, and if we slid around the side and down the slope, we could avoid them altogether. I motioned to a path between rocks.

As if the universe had a dark sense of humor, a lone patrolling guard hustled up between the rocks, sweat dripping from his face as he glanced around. He held an M16A1 rifle in both hands, his finger already tight on the trigger.

I stumbled back, attempting to head for the fissure, but my weak leg gave out, and I hit the dirt. The guard snapped his attention to me, rifle up. A loud crack of gunfire echoed off the mountain as Dallas shot the man with little hesitation. It took me a second to shake off my dread. Now they would know we were outside.

"Thank you," I murmured as I got back to my feet.

Dallas offered me a hand. "I've seen these bastards kill enough people in my lifetime. I'm done with it."

Ex Cathedra always had war on her borders, and everyone knew of their scorched-earth practices. If soldiers like Dallas were turning traitor, maybe it had become too much.

But we didn't have time to dwell on the state of the world. We headed down the mountainside at a steady clip, staying hunched in the harsh shadows as we passed lookout towers. People yelled and barked orders. It made it easier to scramble across the rocks.

The half-collapsed highway at the base of the mountain still carried a hundred deserted cars from before the Forever Winter. Rust bled onto the road and painted the concrete brick red. The wind rushed by, peppering the sky with scraps of urine-yellow paper. Everything else, from the broken buildings to the charred trees to the walls of the mining facility, haunted the scenery with shades of lifeless gray and dull black.

Some said the sights were bleak, but they were all I had known. The desolate landscape was infinitely better than anything in the mine shafts, at least in my book.

I lost my footing a few times on the steep slope. I didn't gasp or cry out—being silent was my natural state—but my heart leapt into my throat each time. Killing myself on a rocky Slip 'N Slide would be the worst way to end my day of success.

As we reached the base of the slope and the beginnings of the highway, the gates to the mining facility opened wide. They had finally assembled their search team. Dallas and I hustled between the discarded vehicles and hunkered down, chancing only occasional glances.

Guards stepped out of the facility, but I wasn't worried about them. It was the judge that came out after. Even as the light faded, leaving us with the evening darkness, the judge stood out among the rest, bits of glowing power cores radiating from his armor.

Judges in Ex Cathedra held a rank equivalent to captain in most other surrounding countries, but they were given the title *judge* because of their A-tech exoskeleton power armor. The JUDGE-X0 exoskeletons had been one of the final military innovations before the world ended, and they were produced en masse at a factory located in the heart of what was now Ex Cathedra. It was how Ex Cathedra got so much influence after the Forever Winter—their judges dominated the battlefield.

And now the silver mine's judge headed our way.

Why had the alarm gone off so quickly? In my original plan, I had anticipated several days before they realized what happened—more than enough time to escape Ex Cathedra altogether. Had it been Dallas? Had he somehow alerted them?

Then it struck me. It wasn't Dallas.

It was the two girls.

They hadn't escaped. They were caught and no doubt mentioned me to alleviate their punishment. Which also meant the storage room would've been investigated and the fission battery reported as missing.

Of course they would send a judge to retrieve the battery. Those batteries were incapable of being reproduced after the world ended. Hell, I would send a whole army to retrieve one if I were in command.

The judge leapt down the mountainside with ease. The exoskeletons vastly improved a soldier's strength, speed, and mobility, and the steel alloy plating shielded them from bullet fire. The judge would be upon us in no time.

"Fuck," Dallas said under his breath.

With unsteady hands, I reached into my backpack. "I prepared for this."

My heart pounded hard enough it rang in my ears, deafening me to distant noises. I had thought of every possible contingency plan before setting foot inside the silver mines, but that didn't mean I wanted to use them.

Closer and closer the judge came to the bottom of the mountain. His exoskeleton covered him from head to toe, and the HUD system that made up his face mask could use thermal imaging to detect nearby people. Hiding wasn't a viable option.

"You *prepared* for this?" Dallas repeated, disbelief and sarcasm mixing in equal amounts in his tone.

I pulled out my last EMP grenade from the large pocket of my backpack. Dallas flinched away, his jaw clenched tight.

"It's okay," I said, holding it close. "It's not a normal grenade. This one uses an electromagnetic pulse to disrupt electronic systems and—"

"*I know what they do,*" he hissed. "It won't work on the judges."

"It won't work on Mark III exoskeletons or later, but the judges here are wearing Mark II variants, which are still susceptible to EMP grenades."

Dallas opened his mouth and then closed it, like he had an argument ready but it derailed faster than he could think of a new one.

The judge jumped and landed hard on the end of the broken highway platform, the boots of his power armor cracking the concrete from impact.

Dallas slinked behind another vehicle, putting more objects between him and the approaching judge. I moved after him, quiet but slower. The carbon steel of the dilapidated vehicles would hide our heat outlines, but it wasn't perfect. My panicked breathing would also elevate my internal temperature, though there was little I could do to control it.

"How do you know what model of armor they're wearing?" Dallas asked.

The judges of Ex Cathedra painted their armor with all sorts of intimidating images or words, often covering the serial number and model variant since such designations were worthless within their new order. Even our pursuing judge had painted his armor black and red—the red in the shape of blood splatters across the gauntlets, boots, and chest guard.

And he also had a name written with the faux blood across the shoulder of the suit.

Judge Gascoigne.

"The air filtration vents," I whispered. "The Mark II air filters are a different shape than the Mark III, IV, and V variants. This is definitely a Mark II suit."

Dallas regarded me with a quick glance. "Goddamn, you know a lot about A-tech machines."

"Thank you?"

He replied with a single laugh, though this wasn't the time for jokes.

"When the judge gets close, I'm going to set this grenade off," I whispered. "After that, we run."

The guards of the silver mine wouldn't travel far, not at night. Twenty of them headed down the hill at a slow pace, which meant as long as the judge couldn't follow, we would be able to run back to my hideout.

"No," Dallas said. "You can't. I can't be in the radius of the grenade."

"It won't harm flesh, only electronics. The voltage is—"

"*I can't be in it.*"

His dire insistence shook me. We didn't have time to argue. We didn't have time to plan. My heart beat twice, but that was all the time Judge Gascoigne needed to turn in our direction and effortlessly flip over a vehicle in the way.

The car crashed off the side of the road, sending shattered glass across rocks and dirt.

"Run," I said. "The pulse radius is fifty feet. I'll go in the opposite direction."

"What? No. The judge will tear you apart and—"

Ignoring him, I stood, the grenade held tight in my hand. My impromptu plan to draw Judge Gascoigne away from Dallas was reckless, but it *could* work, and that was all I needed.

"*Kita*," Dallas hissed under his breath. "Kita!"

I weaved through the vehicles, using them for support since my leg wouldn't hold up, and headed for the side of the highway. It was collapsed enough that I could climb down to the ground below.

Judge Gascoigne stepped onto one of the cars and leapt toward me. He smashed down on a four-door town car, blowing out the windows and knocking me over in the process. I hit the concrete as the glass showered down around me.

And the EMP grenade flew out of my hand.

My heart stopped. I watched it bounce away as though in slow motion.

I leapt for it, but the oval-shaped weapon slid under a large shard of the car's windshield. I wasn't fast enough. I scrambled to move the glass, cutting myself with each wild motion.

Judge Gascoigne landed on the street next to me, shaking everything with each heavy step. Those damn exoskeletons were suctioned close to the driver's body, making them sleek and person shaped, but they were still two hundred and fifty pounds of deadly metal, and they all stood an impressive eight feet tall, no matter the height of the person inside.

"You must be the thief," Judge Gascoigne said.

Not a man, but a woman. Her feminine voice, warped by the armor's mask, echoed a bit. It had a harsh metallic tinge that sent a shiver down my spine.

She reached down and grabbed my shoulder with the vise grip of a robot. In my last panicked moments, I reached the grenade and snatched it from the wreckage. The grip of her gauntlet cut off blood flow to my arm. She could kill me—she could rip me in fucking half if she were so inclined.

"Where is your traitor friend?" Judge Gascoigne asked. "You will tell me."

For a moment, all I could hear was the beating of my overworked heart.

I triggered the grenade.

The only visual component was a quick flash, but the click and pulse that ran through my body left me tasting copper and my ears ringing. The instructions for EMP grenades said not to be *right on top of them* when they went off, but I didn't have much of a choice.

Judge Gascoigne's exoskeleton sparked and hissed. She took a step back, but then the armor froze in place, creaking as the metal plates jammed together, not moving properly without the assistance of the onboard computer. The brightly lit power cells flashed a warning that something was wrong internally. After that, Judge Gascoigne didn't move or speak. No doubt she was raging on the inside, though.

I struggled to my feet. The clouds overhead thickened, adding an extra layer of gloom to the atmosphere. But it couldn't dampen my mood. I laughed—even though it hurt like a bitch, my stomach aching for the sweet release of death—and I hobbled off, smiling the entire way, despite the pain.

My nose bled, and I wiped it away with the sleeve of my jacket.

Without much visibility, I continued forward until I heard the sound of boots on concrete. Although I normally avoided such noises, I perked up and looked around, wondering if I would spot Dallas amid the odd shapes of a broken world.

Sure enough, he hustled back to get me, his own injuries slowing him a bit. I offered him a half smile and wanted to give him a *you're still alive?* remark, but too much speaking would strain my already taxed body, so I opted for brevity.

"I stopped her," I said through a wheeze.

"It's a goddamn Christmas miracle," Dallas quipped. "I thought for certain you'd be in pieces."

Bullets plinked off the broken vehicles. I threw my hands over my head as Dallas pushed me behind a vehicle. Was he looking out for me? It had been so long since anyone was on "my side," I had almost forgotten what it was like.

Silver mine guards slid down the last bit of mountainside toward our location, slower and clumsier than the judge. Dallas returned fire as he motioned me in the opposite direction.

"Let's hurry," I said. "They'll probably stop to help the judge."

Dallas picked off a few of the faster guards before turning and walking alongside me. Although my body ached and my eyelids hung heavy, I knew I couldn't rest until I reached my hideout. We traveled along the dilapidated highway until the guards stopped their pursuit, no doubt to conserve strength and ammunition.

Silence fell over the world.

I stopped and bent over, my hands on my knees, the weight of the fission battery heavy on my back. Dallas stood next to me, his eyes downcast.

"You can go," I said. "It's unlikely they'll send anyone until dawn."

"I'll never make it," he muttered. "I need . . . someplace to rest."

He wanted to stay with me. But it wasn't part of my plan. I closed my eyes and took a minute to mull over the situation. Although I didn't have much food or water, I did have a small workshop hidden in the hills. He could rest there while I prepared for the rest of my trek.

"I know a place," I said.

Dallas nodded. "Thank you."

I kept quiet and pointed him to the narrow path that led away from the highway. We were the only two souls out wandering the wasteland in the dead of night.

My hideout consisted of two rooms underground. One I called my workshop—I kept my tools and boxes piled around the walls—and the other I had made into a shabby bedroom. I took Dallas to the workshop and showed him the door tucked away between rocks. It was impossible to find from the road and completely separate from my personal quarters.

We stepped inside, and I turned on the sole light. It hung from a wire, swinging back and forth, casting shadows that darted around the room like frightened animals. Then I motioned to the surroundings as if giving a tour. One wave of my arm was all it took, but even that sent pain shooting through my system. My stomach was bruised from the base of my ribs to my belly button.

Dallas walked in, set his backpack by the door, and gave the place the once-over. I couldn't bring myself to say anything, so I shadowed his steps as he glanced around.

My workshop—my only comfort in the world, if I were being honest—was an old cellar. Nothing impressive, but at least it kept me safe. And, unlike most cellars, which were found around houses and easy to spot, my workshop had been created by a man named *Joel* in order to save himself from the apocalypse. He hid the place, camouflaged the door, and kept it in good shape, even throughout the Forever Winter.

I never met Joel, nor do I think we were alive at the same time, but he left a good deal of messages carved into the wooden support beams around the cellar. I felt like I knew him better than my own parents. Some of his writing stuck with me. He wrote, *We all strive for good times, but they create weak men, and weak men are the source of great evil.* On another he wrote, *Honesty, duty, and hard work are dead.*

His last message, the most disturbing, simply said, *Today I lost another finger. God is taking me home one bit at a time.*

Dallas glanced down at the sad-sack accommodations. A few empty battery cells littered the corners, and I kept my food in a box by the door. I used to think the cellar was spacious, but with Dallas's company, the place seemed unbearably cramped.

He turned his attention to the opposite side of the room, where I kept my work desk and planning materials. Before I could think of anything to say, he ambled over and stared at my figurines.

I made buildings, people, and props out of junk I found around the wasteland. I used them for planning purposes, as I built most objects to scale with their real-world counterparts, but a few were merely for my own pleasure. I made a cat and dog out of twisted coat hangers and a couple of birds crafted from old bottle caps. I even had a little house with furniture,

like in all the old-world magazines I'd read over the years, so they would all
have a place to live. Childish musings, but it passed the time.

Dallas grazed his fingers over the figurine of a mother and her child.
"You made toys?"

"Th-They're not toys," I said, flustered. "And I'd like to see what you do
with your extra time, thank you very much. At least this is constructive."
The world had too much destruction in it already.

"I never said it was bad."

I rewound the conversation in my head, feeling foolish for the effort
when I realized he was right. I had taken offense at a specific word, but he
hadn't yet cast judgment.

"You're talented," he muttered.

"Er, well, thank you."

Without warning, Dallas doubled over and slammed a hand on my
table. He gripped his gut with his other hand and took in a breath through
his clenched teeth. When he coughed, he splattered fresh crimson blood
all over the floor of my cellar.

I rushed over and placed a hand on his back. "Are you okay?"

He growled something I couldn't understand.

"There are treatments for radiation poisoning," I said, trying to keep
my voice steady. "I could take you to the edge of a city. The doctors will
charge you for the treatment, but you could get it."

Dallas shook his head. He took in a deep breath and steadied himself.

"I need to lie down."

I motioned to a bench positioned between boxes. I technically had a
bed in my other room—if you counted a dilapidated cushion as a mattress—but I needed someplace to rest if I was going to make the long trek
anytime soon. I didn't have any chairs or luxuries. Dallas could have the
bench or the cold cement of the floor.

Dallas rested back on the wooden bench, sweat glistening over all visible portions of his skin. I fetched him water from my food box, but he
only took a single sip before closing his eyes and falling asleep.

I limped over to my work desk and finally took off my backpack.
Although I had gone through a gauntlet of effort, energy burst from my
pores, my heart rate never settling back into an even rhythm.

I could use the battery to escape. And waiting around only invited
failure.

Someone could find my cellar or other judges could come calling.

I had to leave. And soon.

I gave Dallas another glance, narrowing my eyes as I examined him.

Again, I wondered why he was here. He could be a liability, especially given his radiation poisoning. Then again, I could guide him to a town on my way out of Ex Cathedra. I chuckled to myself as I glanced away. For months—maybe a couple years—I had been alone. Very alone. Even having someone over, even if he was just sleeping on a bench, reminded me how much I missed interacting with others.

Conflicted, I hefted the fission battery out of my backpack and looked it over.

It was in perfect condition. Once satisfied everything was ready, I tucked it back into my pack and left the workshop. My limping grew worse as fatigue settled in. The hatch to my bedroom, hidden under dirt and rocks, wasn't far, but the walk felt like an eternity. Once inside, I slid down the stairs and hobbled to my dilapidated mattress.

With my fission battery close, I laid my head down and the butt of the handgun jabbed into my side. I pulled it out and tossed it away. Even touching one brought back unpleasant memories.

CHAPTER THREE

I didn't sleep well.

My gut hurt, and excitement coursed through my veins. I woke a couple hours after I closed my eyes, sweat dappling my skin. When I sat up, my head spun. Dehydration was an ever-constant companion, like a second shadow, but I couldn't guzzle down water whenever I wanted, not when I made my home away from the cities.

After a drink, I checked my battery, gathered up what little supplies I kept in my bedroom, and then limped to the door. I listened before exiting. No unusual sounds. Then I made my way outside and straight to the workshop. Again, before I entered, I waited and listened.

Nothing.

Had Dallas left? It would solve my dilemma on what to do with him.

I slowly opened the door. Dallas rested on the bench, his back to me. His chest expanded in a slow but constant rhythm. I breathed easy knowing he hadn't died. No one liked handling corpses, and dragging a full-grown man from my workshop would be a hassle.

I couldn't eat, not with the pain in my intestines, so I hobbled over to my work desk. The little figurines sat perfectly still in line, and I decided I'd think about my situation while I made a new one. Crafting things helped me think straight, since it gave my hands something to do.

I grabbed a pair of pliers and half an aluminum can, my focus on the mother and child I had made months ago. I hadn't thought about it until then, but maybe they could have a father as well.

I used my measuring tape to examine the figurines. Half an inch represented a foot, so the mother was two inches and three quarters—my own height—which meant the father should be three inches.

Such details mattered to no one, especially given my hermit lifestyle, but I couldn't help it. I wanted things to be exact. I wanted them to make sense with numbers and planning. It bothered me sometimes when things weren't in order. I lost sleep when the floor plans to my model house didn't match the dimensions I estimated from the picture in the magazine.

Just as I finished twisting the aluminum into a humanoid figure, the bench squeaked with movement. I held my backpack close and turned around in my chair.

Dallas sat up, his elbows on his knees.

"Good morning," I said.

It wasn't morning, but I enjoyed the ring of the phrase as I said it. I hadn't greeted someone good morning in years.

Dallas ran a hand down his face. "I need to piss."

I pointed to a bottle in the corner of the room. The ammonia in urine could be used for all sorts of useful things. It helped plants grow and could remove rust from iron. I had Joel to thank for such wisdom. His survival guide etched into the cellar's posts had helped me greatly over the years.

Dallas stood with a grunt and ambled over to the bottle. There was a funnel nearby, and I almost mentioned it, but I stopped myself before looking foolish. Obviously men didn't need a funnel. Obviously.

With almost no modesty, Dallas unzipped his cargo pants.

I quickly turned away and clutched the fission battery tighter. Just as I hadn't wished someone good morning in years, I hadn't felt the burning heat of social embarrassment for years, either. I hadn't missed that sensation, however.

Once he finished, he screwed the cap back on the bottle and returned to the bench. I turned back around in my chair and studied him for a moment, neither of us saying a word.

To my shock, Dallas looked better than before he went to sleep. No, not just *better*, but free of injury. The small cuts, burns, and bruises were nowhere to be seen. His skin had no blemishes; only his clothes held the evidence of blood that proved he was once wounded.

"What happened?" I asked, motioning to his body. "Those kinds of injuries don't go away that fast."

"I told you. I just needed a rest. I wasn't that injured."

"But the burns . . ." My gaze shifted to the bench. Flakes of dead skin littered the wood. Then I glanced down at the blood that stained my floor. The copper tinge that lingered in the air would take weeks to go away.

"It was dark," Dallas snapped. "Trust me. It wasn't that bad."

Being quick to anger was a sign of lying, and I knew it well. But I didn't have another explanation for why his injuries had cleared up, so I left the issue.

"Did you have any dreams?" I asked. I knew it was a bizarre question the moment I asked, but I wanted some sort of connection. Speaking about dreams felt like something I had done a lifetime ago, when I was happier.

"Dreams?" Dallas asked, glaring at the floor. "No."

"Pleasant dreams refresh me. Mentally, I mean."

"I . . . usually have nightmares," he murmured, almost too quiet to hear.

"Hm." I understood the sentiment, so I opted to change the topic. "If you're a traitor, why were you in the silver mines?"

"I tried to steal some of the A-tech components. The ones in the major machines."

"Why?"

Dallas took in a deep breath and then exhaled. "I needed the money to get out of Ex Cathedra."

His answer struck a chord. I stared at the cement floor, my breath held as I debated telling Dallas about my plan. Giddy excitement bubbled up in my chest. I had never told anyone, and now that I was so close, everything felt surreal.

"I also want to get out of Ex Cathedra," I said.

He turned and narrowed his eyes. "With a leg like yours?"

I clenched my jaw. Did he have to mention it like that?

He looked away again. "I'm sorry. I'm just curious how you thought you'd make it all by yourself."

"There are old-world military bases all over Ex Cathedra," I said. "Some are destroyed, some are infested with alien drones, but there's one nearby that's simply sealed."

He didn't respond. He stayed still and quiet, like he was curious and afraid to interrupt.

I continued, "The military base's fission battery isn't working, so all the doors and security measures are locked in place. People have tried to break in, I've seen it, but the compound is too secure. And according to these inventory listings"—I swiveled around in my chair and grabbed a stack of pre-war paperwork—"the base should have a couple all-terrain vehicles."

Then I turned back around and grabbed an old-world map from my research pile. It had the lines of past nations marked across it, along with the rivers and mountains, but most of that was irrelevant. Those nations didn't exist anymore.

"I want to use one of those all-terrain vehicles to cross the border into United California."

I pointed to the map, specifically to my own markings designating the new-world territories.

Ex Cathedra controlled the flatland territory between the Rocky and Appalachian Mountains. There were only two viable ways to leave Ex Cathedra on the western border, and that was either through a stretch of land south of the Rocky Mountains or across a portion of the mountains themselves.

Unlike whenever the maps were made, the land had changed after the war, creating new obstacles besides rocks, rivers, and deserts. Everything north was too hostile or inhospitable, and traveling too far south would result in getting caught in the radiation mire. And the leftover alien drones were a plague in some areas, killing anyone who entered.

Dallas stared at the map for a long moment. "This military base . . . Do you think it has other A-tech equipment?"

I nodded. The facility had been locked down for years.

He breathed easier than before and half smiled. "Clever. Real clever. You thought of this yourself?"

"Yes. I've lived here alone for some time now."

Dallas glanced around my hideout as if seeing it in a whole new light. Then he turned back to me, his eyebrows knit together. "How long?"

The pity in his voice stabbed at me. I couldn't find my voice, so I simply shrugged.

Perhaps Dallas could sense my pain because he quickly tapped on the map, refocusing the conversation. "What route will you take to get to U-Cali?"

I pointed to the stretch of land south of the mountain—some place once called *Arizona*.

"There are old-world roads that lead through this territory," I said. "By my estimates, it would only take a couple days to reach United California. A week at most."

Dallas turned away and chuckled. "You can't go that way. It's a fucking war zone."

"But the vehicle can reach top speeds of—"

"It won't matter," he interjected. "Obviously you haven't seen the border. Those U-Cali bastards use land cannons to keep the Ex Cathedra soldiers at bay. There's nothing but a scorched strip of land there. Anything that moves—anything large enough, like your vehicle—will get annihilated."

I stared down at the map, my chest tightening as my carefully laid plans ran across a snag. Traveling six hundred and seventy-five miles didn't look far on paper, but it would feel thirty times longer to try and maneuver through battlefields and no-man zones.

"The mountain path is longer, but safer," Dallas said. "If you had an all-terrain vehicle you could use the busted roads there."

It would require traveling eight hundred and fifty miles if I took the mountain path, but I was sure the vehicle could make it, given the batteries I had amassed. That wasn't a viable option, however.

I shook my head. "The Iron-Blooded have infested most of the mountains. Everyone knows they're insane."

Unlike Ex Cathedra and United California, both new-world nations who were trying to rebuild something out of the twisted corpse of Earth, the Iron-Blooded were lunatics hell bent on serving the cause of humanity's demise—those fucking space monsters. They worshipped the aliens like only end-of-world zealots could. I had never heard of the Iron-Blooded being reasonable or levelheaded, and they used what A-tech they found to undermine the roots of civilized society.

And while most people were ignorant of A-tech, the Iron-Blooded knew how to make the devastating weapons work to their advantage.

"I'll just have to think of something else," I said as I grabbed a new piece of paper and one of my homemade pens. I could write out a plan and work from there.

"Why are you so desperate to get to U-Cali?"

That was the part of the plan I couldn't tell him. I wasn't interested in U-Cali, per se. I needed to reach the docks and ships. I wanted to go north, to a place beyond the snow line. Some said people buried themselves in an icy coffin when they went too north, but I knew something they didn't.

There was a facility hidden in the snow. I glanced down at a brochure I kept at my desk. The colors had long since faded, and the edges of the paper flaked off occasionally, but I knew the information well.

It advertised an underground greenhouse, one capable of growing vast amounts of plants. It was the largest in the world—or so the ad boasted—built before the war. It ran off fission batteries and could feed a quarter million people a year by its lonesome. And there were machines, like in the silver mine. Machines that ran by themselves.

They called it the BC Oasis.

It would be the perfect place to live in a world ruined by war, especially for a hermit girl like me. I couldn't imagine it being uninhabited, but if the fission batteries had been taken or damaged during the fighting, there was a chance it would be deserted. And I could get the facility up and running again, in theory. The brochure had a map to its location. I was willing to take the risk.

I knew it was a pipe dream, but leaving Ex Cathedra was the first step to take regardless.

I couldn't tell Dallas about the BC Oasis, though, so I mulled over his question—*why go to U-Cali?*—and I decided to lie.

"I hear it's better over there," I finally said.

He slowly nodded. "I see."

I returned to my planning. I had to take the route south of the Rocky Mountains. The Iron-Blooded were too dangerous.

"The cannons must use ammunition or have a power source," I said. "I will move to a place closer to the border, and then I'll gather information on the weapons. In a few weeks' time, if I'm lucky, I can devise a strategy to get—"

"Kita," Dallas said, his tone melancholy.

I stopped and glanced back at him.

"I didn't tell you the whole truth. I needed the money for more than just getting out of here."

"Okay."

"I'm dying."

The statement caught me off guard. I waited for the punch line, holding my breath until it hurt to do so.

"The Iron-Blooded have lots of A-tech," he said, "so I went to them to see if they could help."

What a terrible idea.

Dallas continued, "I got to know some of them. They . . . helped me . . . but I need to go back to get the last of my treatment. That's why I needed the A-tech from the mines. Nothing else could pay for what they'd give me."

Treatment? The word sounded intentionally vague. What kind of treatment? For what?

Dallas stared at me. "If we go together, I'm sure they'll let you pass through the mountains."

His claims went against everything I knew about the Iron-Blooded. They didn't help random people. As a matter of fact, I heard they sacrificed people to the aliens, like a fucked-up ritual meant to keep the sun in the sky. Those weren't the actions of empathetic and understanding people—of people who gave someone "treatment" because they were sick.

"I can't risk it," I said. I returned my attention to my to-do list. "I'll find some other way to leave Ex Cathedra."

I crafted plans that involved myself and *only* myself. I knew what I was capable of, and relying on others could be a gamble. No one could fail me if I worked alone. No one could betray me. No one would leave me . . .

I stopped writing, my mind lingering on haunting memories.

It was best to do everything myself. Trusting Dallas to get me through the mountains was only inviting trouble. What if he died in the middle of the trek? Or the Iron-Blooded decided they wanted my vehicle? Those were circumstances I couldn't handle.

"I want to reach U-Cali as well," Dallas said, an edge of pleading in his voice. "If you go through the mountains, we can go together. Please. I don't know if I can make it on my own."

His dire expression and tone dug into my thoughts. It had been a long time since someone needed my help. After I lost my sister, I had been so alone.

I glanced at the little family of figurines.

Dallas stood, his motions slow and careful, like an old man with arthritis. "We could help each other. I know all about Ex Cathedra's border defenses, and you're intelligent enough to make it on your own—someone dependable. If we run into any renegade A-tech, I'm sure you could handle it."

The BC Oasis was far away. Having someone with me for half the trek wouldn't be so bad, and he obviously had military training. If he worked as my gun and I worked as the brains, we could get far. And if he was dying, there wouldn't be much reason for him to delay our trek.

I didn't want to mill about any longer. Not when Ex Cathedra would be sending judges to retrieve their battery.

I grabbed a paper at my desk and flipped it over, ready to make a list of things I needed in order to make it across the mountains.

"All right," I said. "We'll see the Iron-Blooded, but we need to have a few contingencies, just in case. I still don't trust them."

Dallas smiled. "Thank you, Kita."

"In the morning, we'll head for the military base. Until then, we should get some more rest."

We walked along the cracked roads, moving at a slow pace due to my limp.

Dallas carried everything but my battery. I wouldn't be returning to the cellar, so everything I could fit into our two backpacks was the totality of my possessions. I feared the seams would rip, but once we got a vehicle, I wouldn't have to worry.

The deathly quiet of our surroundings was a requiem to the millions who died decades ago. I had a portable radio, but Ex Cathedra controlled the broadcasting towers. Wartime propaganda wasn't my favorite genre of music, so I opted for silence instead.

Dallas wobbled a few times on his feet, his eyes half-lidded. I didn't ask. He always managed to shake it off and continue forward, no matter how pale he got.

When he shoved his hands into his pockets, I heard the jingle of metal. I glanced over and lifted an eyebrow. He pulled out my figurines—the mother, father, and child. I had left them all behind since they weren't needed. Plus, I could always make more.

"You took them?" I asked.

"Do you mind?"

"No, but why?"

"I like these. They remind me of happier times."

I walked a bit closer and nodded. "Do you have a wife?"

"I did," Dallas said, curt. "She died. End of story."

And then I returned to my normal distance away from him. As far as I was concerned, it might be easier to find a sugar cube on the moon than craft an engaging conversation. I searched my memories for any clues to make the discussion between us meaningful.

Dallas exhaled. "Where . . . is your family?"

I was glad to hear the awkward strain in his voice. At least I wasn't alone in my conversational deficiencies.

But I didn't want to talk about my family. "They're all dead," I intoned. "End of story." I touched my injured hip, flaring the pain for a moment just to stop my mind from wandering down memory lane.

"No children?" Dallas asked.

"No. I've never had children."

"Yet you made so many toys."

I huffed and said, "They're not toys, they're—" but I stopped myself the moment I got a good look at Dallas. He smiled and chuckled, as though amused by my reaction to such a trivial statement. He was fucking with me, basically.

I stifled a laugh and turned away. I had almost forgotten what it was like to joke with someone.

The clack of rock on rock caused us both to stiffen and fall silent. Although the harsh cloud cover blanketed the area in gloom, I could see movement in the distance. A swarm of flies and birds hung around an outcropping of rocks, a visible cloud of death and illness.

Dallas pulled out his .45 handgun. "Stay close."

I did as he said and gripped the straps of my backpack. The birds in the region were aggressive and riddled with diseases—a terrible combination. Two cawed and took to the air. Dallas positioned himself for the confrontation, keeping himself between me and the birds at all times. Normally I avoided animals, but we didn't have that luxury if we were going to get him to the Iron-Blooded for his mysterious treatment.

The two birds swooped close, pecking and flaring their talons. They were great-tailed grackles—black and shiny like spilled oil—and their yellow eyes pierced the darkness, honing in on us with bloodlust.

Dallas fired twice. I flinched with each shot, my pulse high and my breathing shallow. Both birds hit the dirt, feathers everywhere. The remaining flock took off after the first shot, their companion swarm of flies following them as they went.

The ring of the gunshots traveled for some distance.

Dallas didn't hesitate. He grabbed some ammo out of the backpack and slotted two more bullets into the magazine. The HK45 only had a ten-round capacity, so it was probably for the best. Running out of ammo at a crucial moment could spell demise.

"Are you okay?" he asked.

I nodded.

I pointed into the distance, beyond where the birds flew. "Do you see that building? That's the military base."

"I've seen that place before. It's Fort Molena."

His familiarity invigorated me. We made our way to it, eagerness in our step. Even my limp wasn't as bad as we traversed the rocks and cracked earth. The only sight that slowed my pace was the corpse the birds and flies had been scavenging on.

Not a human corpse—one of the aliens.

I turned away, holding back a sneer. As long as we didn't run into one, it wouldn't matter.

We reached the gate of Fort Molena faster than I expected. The cement wall was adorned with rusty barbed wire and covered in decades-old graffiti. The place had the aura of a ghost town.

"You know how to get in?" Dallas asked.

I nodded. "We can slide open the gate and head to the reserve power box at the back of the building."

The thought of getting my hands on an all-terrain vehicle excited me more than anything had in the last few days, even getting hold of the fission battery. It was another monumental step, another key to the puzzle of taking control of my life.

Dallas shoved the gate open and motioned me inside.

CHAPTER FOUR

We crossed a crumbling parking lot littered with broken vehicles in various shapes and sizes. Unlike the military-grade all-terrain vehicles, the cars scattered around the wasteland were useless. Their tires had long since died and the fuel expired, corroding the insides. The all-terrain vehicles didn't use gasoline—no combustion engine—and instead could be completely powered by a large enough atomic or fission battery.

Before we reached any of the buildings, my leg grew stiff and painful. I slowed, despite my excitement. Although Dallas could have continued on, he stayed close to my side.

We walked around the back side of the first building. Dallas reached for the door. I grabbed his arm and pointed to a damaged area. The wall was cracked open, exposing a portion of the reserve power room. The small opening—a tight squeeze for someone like me—had edges lined with jagged pipes and metal bars, but it worked as an entrance. I had gone through it several times before during my investigations.

It was futile to try any of the base's doors. The security system had been placed in lockdown before the power cut out, resulting in all doors being shut with dead bolts and triple locking. It wasn't something I could lock pick, and my only hope was the battery.

I slid into the power room, keeping my backpack close. I had my battery and my tool kit—everything I needed for minor adjustments on the machine.

Dallas waited outside while I shone my flashlight over the power reserve system.

According to the paperwork I gathered, Fort Molena's primary power source had been a civilian power plant before the war. But the base had a backup system complete with its own fission battery. For whatever reason, the fission battery wasn't functioning. It powered nothing, even the testing devices I tried hooking up to it. Everything pointed to an internal problem, but since I didn't know how to fix it, replacement was my only option.

I detached the old fission battery, hefted it out of the machine, and placed it on the floor. Breathing hard, I placed the new battery inside and went to make the attachments.

But I stopped when I noticed something out of place.

The new fission battery already had something plugged into one of the input ports. At first I thought it was a cover meant to keep the port protected, but the longer I examined it, the more I realized it was a device.

A tracking device. It said so on the faded lettering: US GPS MDL-196.

I tried to rip it off the battery, but it was secured with screws to the casing. My heart rate increased as adrenaline dumped into my veins. With unsteady hands I used my screwdriver to detach the device. Once off, I shoved it in my pocket. Perhaps it would continue to transmit my position for a short period while power still coursed through it, but not for long, not when it was designed to be connected to a power source.

How had I been so careless? I cursed myself under my breath as I connected the new battery to the power system.

"Dallas," I said.

"What is it?"

"Did anyone in the silver mines know how to use the computer systems?"

"I don't know. I never saw anyone use them besides cycling through passwords. It was rote memorization, though. They couldn't read the alien words."

Of course. That was common. Technology had become more of a magical force in the world—a thing people knew about but didn't understand—so there was still a chance no one in the silver mine would even know of a tracking device on the battery. At least, that was my hope.

"Why did you want to know?" Dallas asked.

"I"—I took a breath and held back my words, half embarrassed by my own mistake and half rushing to get everything done—"was thinking about the mine's capabilities."

Once the battery was in place, I took a step back and turned the whole thing on.

A groan issued from the machinery and echoed throughout the room for a good thirty seconds. A flood of lights shone for a moment before two sparked out, leaving me in the shadows of a partially dim environment.

Another groan, this one laced with the grinding of metal, rumbled somewhere in the base. I knew everything wouldn't be in working condition—it had sat idle too long—but I hoped I would have enough access for my plans.

I walked to the inner door in the reserve power room and checked the handle. It unlocked, and I entered the main hallway. Before I went for the computers, I limped over to the front door and unlocked it.

Dallas stepped inside and offered me a smile. "Impressive."

I didn't know how to respond to the compliment, so I rubbed the back of my neck and nodded.

Together we made our way through the empty base, our footsteps our only companions. The moment I spotted a computer perched on a desk, I made my way over.

Dallas glanced around, his gaze lingering on the shadows.

The computer booted up when I hit the power. Words flashed on the screen about the Fort Molena base, something about being property of the USA and other such statements. I ignored them and instead went into the command prompt to bypass any of the passwords. The base worked on pre-war coding. I knew that the best.

Once I had full access to the contents of the computer, I immediately went for the site map and storage facility information. But while I looked through the information, a notice popped up from the computer.

A video message.

Curiosity got the better of me. I opened it.

The video started in a room not unlike the one where we stood. A man in his pre-war uniform stared into the camera. There were soldiers and officers running around in the background, but I couldn't get a good look at them. A siren sounded outside, muffled by the base's walls.

"This is Base Commander Daniel Robins," the man said, his voice rusty, but firm. "Moments ago, we lost contact with Fayetteville, New York, and Jacksonville. As per emergency protocol, the soldiers stationed here at Fort Molena will evacuate to Chanute Space Force Base."

Dallas glared at the screen. "What're you doing? This doesn't matter to us."

Something about the pre-war world intrigued me. It was like I lived in a world of perpetual night, and the pre-war world lived in the day. They were the same yet so very different.

Base Commander Robins continued, "Humanity was betrayed. Hobbled by our indecision and blinded to our enemy's desperation, we didn't foresee—"

A soldier ran up to the base commander, out of breath and covered in sweat. "Sir, it's all over. We lost contact with the last of them."

"Then this message is for anyone who—"

I turned off the video.

Dallas was right. What did it matter what happened all those years ago? No one in the video could help me. I continued to poke through the computer until I found the map. Once memorized, I released the emergency settings and unlocked all the doors.

Dallas and I exited the main building and headed for the special operations garage. An odd mixture of excitement and dread plagued my thoughts as Dallas slid open the doors.

For months, I had planned this. For years, I had yearned to escape. Every piece of the puzzle to my freedom had been constructed through persistent struggle, willpower, and determination. I dreamed of the moment I would see the steps of my plan checked off one by one, even going so far as to name the vehicle in all my imaginings. I'd name it *Joel*, so I could pretend I was taking him with me when I left Ex Cathedra.

But all emotion in my body spoiled like milk the instant I got a good look at the inside of the garage.

The place was empty. The vehicles gone.

My mind ground to a halt, and my heart beat up in my throat, preventing me from breathing. It took me a few moments to regain control of myself.

Of course. *Of course!* If they evacuated, they would've taken the most valuable equipment—there had only been ten vehicles here. And it's not like they would've updated their inventory listings after they left the base. Why would they? The world was ending all around them, and bureaucracy was the first casualty.

Dallas walked in and gave the empty space a quick glance. "Is this the only place they would've been?"

Unable to speak, I nodded.

"So there's nothing here for us."

I nodded again.

Dallas ran a hand through his hair, his jaw clenched tight. Afterward, he doubled over and rubbed at his stomach. I had almost forgotten about his impending death, and I was certain he didn't appreciate the empty garage. It meant we'd take even longer to escape.

I was accustomed to setbacks. No matter how carefully I prepared ahead of time, no plan ever went 100 percent the way I wanted. There was always a chance I didn't find an all-terrain vehicle, and my contingency was to go to another military base.

"We'll find something else," I said as I took a deep breath. "There's another base not far from—"

"I don't have time. I need to return to the Iron-Blooded."

His curt statement left no room for deviation. He needed his treatment, and I didn't have any medication for him. I had said I would help him, but already it felt like I had failed. What if he died because of me? He had already gone out of his way to assist me, yet I couldn't seem to do anything in return.

I would need to find a workaround. Perhaps the Iron-Blooded weren't the cutthroats I had heard about before. Perhaps we could get help from them. Genuine help.

"Let me search the rest of the base," I said, grasping at possibilities and hypotheticals.

Dallas lifted an eyebrow. "We won't be able to carry much without a vehicle."

"Maybe we can use something else."

"Please make it quick."

As if the universe wanted to impose a harsh timer, a cloud of dust in the distance caught my eye. I stared, wondering what could cause such a disturbance considering the lack of wind. Dallas turned to follow my gaze.

"*Someone* has a vehicle," he stated.

The wall around the base obscured my vision of what caused the disturbance, but in my heart, I already knew.

The tracking device on the battery had led someone to us.

Judges. No doubt in my mind.

"We need to go," I whispered.

Together we made our way back to the reserve power room. I turned off the machine, and the lights flickered and faded. I removed the battery and returned it to the backpack without a wasted second, but my hands trembled a bit, adding to my stress.

Neither of us was in good shape, and the judges wouldn't hesitate to kill us this time around. And I didn't have a way to deal with them. Not anymore.

Without the security measures in place, the doors opened with little trouble. We slipped out of the building and hid along the side wall until we made it to the gate. A truck headed toward the base along the destroyed road—a transport truck, the kind with a tarp-covered back and all the colorless joy of a graveyard.

"Ex Cathedra soldiers," Dallas said. "We can't leave this way."

"I don't think the other gates are capable of opening."

"Then we'll have to climb over."

We hustled away from the main gate and followed the outer wall. By the time we reached a steel ladder mounted into the side of the wall, the terrible screech of metal against concrete grated on my ears. A building sat between us and the main gate, so I couldn't see, but no doubt the transport truck had forced itself into the base by driving through the ruined defenses.

Dallas leapt onto the ladder and pulled himself up one rung at a time. I attempted to follow, but the moment I put my weight on my injured leg, it buckled and sent a wave of agony through my spine. I tumbled to the ground, my body shaking. I took a deep breath and steadied myself before standing.

Dallas used the butt of his rifle to smash away the rusted concertina wire still perched on top of the wall. Once he'd cleared a path, he slung a leg over and gave me a quick glance.

"Can you make it?"

I nodded.

Countless obstacles had tried to stop me over the years. I would not be defeated by a ladder. I refused.

"Search the compound," a harsh metallic voice echoed throughout the base. Judge Gascoigne's tone was cemented into my mind, and I knew she was the one giving the orders.

Steeling myself with determination, I grabbed the rungs and pulled myself up with my arms. The strain wore me out by the time I reached the midway point, but I knew if I fell, the Ex Cathedra soldiers were sure to catch me. Dallas waited at the top, motioning me to hurry with each rung I made it up. Once close, he grabbed the collar of my jacket and pulled, helping rush the last few.

The twelve-foot drop to the ground got my heart beating fast and my skin coated in sweat. My leg wouldn't handle the impact.

Without warning, Dallas leapt off the wall. When he hit the ground, he rolled and tumbled until the momentum had gone. It took him a few moments to stand properly, but once he did, he glanced up at me.

"I'll catch you," he said.

The sound of boots on dirt urged me to take the leap without any of my normal critical analysis. I tried to turn my body so my injured leg wouldn't hit first, but the fall happened so fast I doubted I made much of a difference. Dallas caught me, but we both hit the dirt when his knees buckled, the weight of the fission battery on my back not helping anything.

Winded, I took a moment to feel over my body before standing. Dallas's catch lessened the overall impact, and although he was dazed and coughing, he also appeared unharmed. Then I checked my backpack. The battery wasn't fragile, and neither were my tools. Everything made it through the fall just fine.

Dallas stood and helped me to my feet.

The slam and smash of doors from inside the base weighed heavy on my thoughts. The layout of Fort Molena was a simple one—five buildings, a special operations garage, a normal garage, and some forgotten training grounds. One of the buildings was an armory. Although the evacuating soldiers had taken the ten all-terrain vehicles, I suspected they weren't capable of taking the million units of equipment stored in the base. And since I had unlocked everything, I had basically given our pursuers even more firepower.

My only solace came from the fact I had detached the tracking device. Even if they had more weaponry, would it matter if we disappeared into the Rocky Mountains?

Dallas and I made our way away from Fort Molena.

Still shaken from the failure of the mission and the close run-in with Judge Gascoigne, I continued pushing myself to the limits of exhaustion.

Fifteen hours.

Six hours of walking, two for rest, another four walking, an additional two resting, and the last hour climbing rocks. I couldn't handle much more, and neither could Dallas. He coughed more and more, his wan complexion a terrible sign.

My blistered feet wept blood, and every time I sat down, I gave serious thought to never standing ever again. The icy evening winds didn't help, either. I kept my jacket tight around my body and secured a pair of goggles over my eyes. The dust kicked up by the breeze carried all sorts of harmful particles. I didn't want to injure the one part of my body that functioned at higher-than-average quality by allowing my eyes to get infected.

Dallas stopped when we climbed up to a small landing near a partially intact road. He took a seat on a couple rocks and breathed easier. I sat next to him, relief flooding my system.

While we rested, I took the last of the water and smoked meat out of my backpack for us to share. Dallas insisted the Iron-Blooded would have supplies, and right now we needed the nourishment. In the worst possible scenario, we could return to my cellar.

"They'll meet us here," Dallas said.

I glanced around. "Here? How do you know?"

He shone his flashlight on a dented sign sitting on the side of the road. In yellow and black, it had the picture of a car on a slope.

"This is where they told me to wait. They said they'd be watching this location."

I chewed my dinner and swallowed, my sandpaper esophagus making the process difficult. Once finished, I gulped down water and then said, "I'm sorry."

"For what?"

"The vehicle. I thought . . . it would definitely be there."

"Feh. It was too good to be true."

My feet pulsed with pain in time with my heartbeat. I reached for the large pocket of my backpack and withdrew bandages and gauze. Dallas watched intently as I removed my boots and cleaned the bloody soles of my feet.

"How are you holding up?" I asked, motioning to his boots. "Do you need any bandages?"

He shook his head. "You've done enough for me already."

"If you're bleeding, we should take care of it."

"I'm fine."

But I had seen the way he grimaced with each hard step on the rocks. It mirrored my own torture as we climbed. He really wasn't in good shape.

"I don't mind bandaging you up," I said as I finished wrapping my feet. The pressure on the injuries, while stinging at first, eased the ache. "I still have plenty of Cellucotton and gauze."

He turned away from me and said nothing. I didn't understand why he insisted on keeping distant, but I knew I would have to push if I were going to help.

"At least take off your boots for a little bit," I said. "The wounds can get infected or worse if you leave them."

Dallas clenched his jaw. At first I thought he wouldn't do anything, but then he unlaced his boots and kicked them off. His once-white socks were blackish-red with blood, and pieces of the fabric clung to the raw and damaged skin of his feet when he peeled them off.

Without asking—because I knew he would deny my offer to help—I knelt down and used a bit of my water to wash away the excess blood. Dallas ground his teeth as I wiped the injuries clean with the Cellucotton, his body tense. At first I thought he might shove me away, especially when he shifted his weight on the rock, but it never happened.

After a few moments, he relaxed.

But we didn't speak during the process. Anytime I glanced up, he would look away, unwilling to meet my gaze. I felt along the bone ridges of the tops of his feet as I bandaged them, making sure nothing was broken. Each time I touched his skin, he would flinch, but still, he said nothing.

Once finished, I took my seat back on the rock next to him.

"See?" I said, smiling. "That wasn't so bad."

Dallas silently stared in the opposite direction.

"Are you okay?"

Nothing.

"Did this upset you?"

"I wish you wouldn't," Dallas said under his breath. "It just makes everything harder."

Before I could ask him anything further, lights shone from down the road. We slipped our boots back on and moved behind a couple large rocks. The purr of an electric engine rolled down the mountain, and while I was content to hide, Dallas stepped out and waited in the middle of the landing.

He motioned me to join him.

Although I tended to hide whenever new people showed themselves, I limped out to his side. They had already seen me anyway if they had been watching the landing. What was the point of hiding now?

I waited on burning feet.

The vehicle had to belong to the Iron-Blooded. The darkness made it difficult to see much, which added to my unease.

The vehicle stopped twenty feet from us, the headlights shining directly in our eyes. Although I could hear the door, the crunch of boots on dirt, and the heavy heft of weapons, all I could see were three silhouettes. I moved a step closer to Dallas.

"*Looks like he made it back*," a man said—not in English, but the alien language, Tethlite. It had a thick use of the tongue in order to make the proper syllables, and I would've recognized it anywhere. "*I guess I owe Dannik a drink.*"

"*Who's the girl?*" another asked, also in Tethlite.

"*Don't know. She wasn't part of the agreement.*"

"*I don't like it when insects think they can run the show.*"

"*Want me to shoot her?*"

I gripped Dallas's shirt and moved half behind him. "Say something. They're talking about shooting me."

The three Iron-Blooded became quiet.

Dallas took a step forward. "I—"

"Can the girl understand Tethlite?" one of the men asked, his English not as good as his alien tongue.

"Yes."

Again, silence fell over the unseen Iron-Blooded. I tried to shield my eyes from the lights, but they were much brighter than anything I had dealt with before. No matter how hard I squinted, I couldn't make out much detail.

One of the Iron-Blooded drew closer. "Did you get the parts from the silver mine machines like we asked?"

Dallas shook his head. "I was caught before I was able to retrieve anything."

He had been telling the truth. The information put me at ease.

"You came here empty-handed?" the man asked with a chuckle. "That isn't going to help you or your daughter. And she's got a lot of internal bleeding. Maybe we should go back and shoot her now and put her out of her misery."

"No!" Dallas shouted. "I didn't come back empty-handed." He grabbed the strap of my backpack and yanked me forward. "I have a fission battery, along with a lot of other useful junk."

My mind and body locked up, the revelation blindsiding me with enough force to prevent me from breathing.

Dallas shoved me out in front of him. I stood next to the backpack, still unable to move, my heart frozen in my chest from the shock of the situation.

"And the girl," Dallas said. "You can take her, too. She knows everything about those damn A-tech machines, even how to read Tethlite. She can fix whatever you need."

"That's quite an impressive haul."

"You'll take it?"

"Well," the Iron-Blooded drawled, "it wasn't what we agreed upon . . . but I think it's a fair trade. Now load it up into the car. We have work to do."

CHAPTER FIVE

took a step back, my thoughts returning with each forced inhale.

How could Dallas do such a thing? Hot anger and icy shame mixed in equal parts throughout my system. I gritted my teeth, uncertain of a plan given my predicament. All that came to mind were spiteful tactics or throwing myself from the landing in the hopes I survived the fall.

I took another step back.

"She's gonna run."

Before I could whirl around and attempt a leap, one of the Iron-Blooded struck me across the face with the butt of their heavy rifle. Blinding pain dominated my senses to the point I didn't even register hitting the dirt. I gasped for breath through my mouth as blood wept from my nose. No matter how much air I got, the dizzy sensation wouldn't stop.

Someone grabbed my arm and hauled me along. They continued to speak, but I noticed none of it. Even the images I saw were suspect— shadowy shapes, lights, the backseat of a vehicle. Nothing made much sense, and the unknown scared me more than anything else.

I closed my eyes and couldn't open them again.

I awoke in darkness.

Right away I realized a thick cloth was tied across my face, covering my eyes, nose, and forehead. I tried to reach up and pull it away, but my wrists were secured at my sides, strapped to whatever I was lying on. A table, most likely. The flat surface irritated the sharp points of my shoulder blades.

Where was I? The question stewed in my thoughts. I grew restless and antsy. Despite my better judgment to remain calm and collected, I struggled against my restraints, attempting to break them. Even my ankles were secured to the table, and with each twist of my body, I hurt my hip more and more.

After taking in a few deep breaths, I stopped.

It was only then that I realized I didn't have my jacket or shirt. I wore bindings over my chest, still secured in place, but more importantly, I had my pants, even if my boots had been removed. A small consolation not to be naked, but it eased my dread.

I still couldn't believe Dallas had betrayed me so thoroughly. He helped me that entire time just to turn me in to the Iron-Blooded? He begged and pleaded for my help, just so he could lure me here? And for what?

The memory of the encounter stewed in my thoughts.

He had a daughter.

Did he do it all for her?

With my body tense, I remembered my father. He died protecting me and my sister. He could've saved himself. He could've left us to the aliens when they came to attack. But he didn't. He made sure we were safe inside our hideaway, protected from the carnage and out of sight.

Everything my father did was for me and my sister.

Everything.

So while I hated Dallas, another piece of me wanted to erase him from my mind and move on as fast as possible. I didn't care if he wanted to protect his daughter—it was a noble goal—but it was exactly the reason I wanted to work alone. None of this would've happened if I had kept away from him. If I had done everything myself.

The creak of a rusty door stilled my thoughts.

Footsteps drew closer and closer. With each click of boots against cement, I tensed up. The draft from the open door sent goose bumps prickling across my exposed skin.

"*You're awake,*" a man said, his Tethlite speech smooth and easy.

I took in a deep breath, my throat sore. "Where am I?" I whispered.

He didn't answer. Instead, he picked up something nearby. Something metal that scraped against the hard surface it had been on.

"*They said you were an expert with alien tech. Where did you get all that knowledge?*"

"I . . . learned it all from my father and grandfather."

It was true. I didn't have a reason to lie, and in my position I didn't want to provoke them. Besides, the Iron-Blooded worshipped those space monsters—perhaps they would be impressed with my lineage and release me.

"*Speak in Tethlite,*" the man said.

"I speak better in English."

"*I'm not here to argue. You'll speak Tethlite or I'll start removing body parts you don't need. Do you understand?*"

The situation registered with my subconscious before I could process the statements. Sensory-numbing hormones flooded my veins, seizing up my muscles and slowing my breathing. They planned on torturing me. And the man spoke with deathly seriousness, no mirth or sarcasm in his tone.

I rarely spoke Tethlite, so when I struggled for the words, I knew I'd speak with a terrible accent. "*I understand.*"

"*Good. Now, who taught you Tethlite?*"

"*My grandfather, Dr. Benjamin Yamasaki.*"

Silence followed.

Everyone knew of Dr. Benjamin Yamasaki. He was one of the first ambassadors to the aliens when they made contact with Earth. Within the three alien "clans"—the Teth, the Vay, and Frest—he helped establish friendly dealings with the groups most aligned with our ideals. He pioneered the translations and instruction of their language. He helped integrate the advantaged A-tech into our civilization. His whole life had been dedicated to understanding and unraveling the mysteries of aliens. He wrote twenty books, made hundreds of televised appearances, and became the face of human-alien relations.

"*Dr. Yamasaki died when the firestorm fission bombs hit,*" the man said.

My grandfather changed his name to avoid people who would blame him for the bombs, but he didn't die.

"*My grandfather was a Winter Survivor.*"

The Forever Winter came after the bombs hit, but the name was misleading. It lasted a few years, not *forever*, blanketing the world in storms and frost. Pockets of civilization survived—anyone who lived through the Forever Winter earned the title of *Winter Survivor*—and my grandfather was among them. He knew how to cultivate the alien vegetation, plants that grew in Earth's soil no matter the frigid temperature. His knowledge saved thousands, perhaps hundreds of thousands.

The man grazed his fingers over my bullet scars. I flinched, even at the gentle touch. "*Maybe you didn't think I was serious,*" he drawled. "*But I don't play games. Where did you learn to speak Tethlite?*"

"*I . . . told you the truth. From my grandfather.*"

The tip of a sharp object pressed into my injury. I sucked in air through my teeth, the pain already flaring. No doubt the object was a knife. Even imagining the blade carving through my injury got me trembling.

"*I don't believe you,*" he said.

What was I supposed to say? I could lie, but everything would pale in comparison to reality.

The man pressed the blade harder into my old bullet wound.

"*Please,*" I choked out, my volume high. "*I'm telling the truth.*"

"*You picked the most famous doctor of all time. Do you think I'm that gullible? Who are you trying to hide?*"

Outlandish claims were signs of lying. Perhaps I should've known better than to spout the truth when it sounded so preposterous.

The blade pierced my skin and slid half an inch into my flesh.

I screamed. Tears soaked into my makeshift blindfold. I took in shaky breaths and whimpered, but he didn't remove the weapon.

"*Please,*" I said, my voice unsteady. "*I . . . might not be able to walk if . . . if you do this.*"

I almost hadn't recovered the last time and it had left me with a terrible limp.

And what would I do if I couldn't walk? There'd be no place for me— no way for me to take care of myself in the harsh and unforgiving environment that was the wasteland. I'd never make it anywhere. Not out of Ex Cathedra, not across the mountains, not to the BC Oasis.

I would be unable to achieve anything I had worked for.

A fate worse than death.

I twisted my wrist around in the restraints until I could grab the edge of the man's sleeve. I clung to him, hoping to impart some of my desperation, hoping he would understand my dread. Hoping he would have a bit of humanity.

"*Please,*" I said again. "*Don't do this. I need to be able to walk.*"

"*I don't think you'll strictly need it for where you're going,*" he replied, a cold amusement in his voice.

"*I—*"

"*Tell me who taught you Tethlite or this will get worse.*"

"*I was a slave in Ex Cathedra,*" I blurted out, my mind scrambling a story together out of nothing. "*My masters taught me to help them work on the machines.*" If he wanted a lie, I would give it to him.

"*What were their names?*"

What were their names? Any name would do—it was all a sham, anyway—but the only name I could think of was Dallas. When I didn't respond, the man huffed and slid the blade in deeper.

All I could hear was my own screaming. All I could feel was the burn— the searing agony that rushed through my nerves. All I wanted was for it to end.

I couldn't breathe through the sobs. Why? Why would anyone do such a thing? I told him the truth! *I told him the fucking truth!* Why? Why wouldn't he end it? With each twist of the blade, I tried to get away, but the restraints held me in place. I wouldn't be able to walk again after this— I just wouldn't. The blade went too deep and the pain spread too fast. Knowing that hurt more than the physical torment. When I cried, it was for the loss of capability, like a piece of me was being murdered, and I couldn't do anything about it.

Thankfully, my body wanted it to end, too.

I didn't feel anything for a brief second before losing consciousness.

When I awoke again, I wasn't blindfolded.

I blinked back the light that invaded my eyelids. The fluorescent flicking of the overhead bulb was so annoying it could agitate the dead.

The constant ache from my hip reminded me everything had been real. With each beat of my heart, a new wave of agony coursed through my veins. I bit my lip until it bled, hoping to numb myself to the sensations of pain. It helped, but not by much.

Someone had applied a hasty bandage to the wound, and I dreaded to know what was underneath. Surely a mass of knotted, gnarly flesh. And that would be if I were lucky.

To my surprise, an IV stood near my prison table, the tube strung down to my arm. They didn't want me to die, but they didn't want to deal with me much, either. The medication attached to the IV line had the Tethlite language scribbled on the side.

"Is someone there?" a man whispered.

I tilted my head to the side in an attempt to look around. The tiny room, constructed entirely from cement, had no windows. Through the flickering light, I made out a second table with a rangy man on top, but the details eluded me. Another prisoner? I couldn't see properly—not through the ache and fuzzy state of my mind.

"Dallas?" I asked, though speaking hurt my raw throat.

"No. Sorry."

Why would I even ask about him? He was probably long gone. He left me to be tortured—or perhaps to be converted to one of the Iron-Blooded themselves. The man who tortured me said I was going somewhere, after all. If they weren't killing me, that was the only conclusion I could draw.

My fellow prisoner didn't move much, though I could hear his raspy breaths without much trouble. After a few inhales and exhales, he spoke.

"My name's Joel."

I laughed aloud.

"Are you okay?" he asked.

The universe had a bizarre sense of dry humor that never ceased to amaze me. Although I knew nothing about the other man, already I liked him, as irrational as it was. Joel. It felt as though I were destined to encounter that name for all eternity.

"Did you ever live in a cellar?" I asked, forcing a smile.

The man chuckled once, perhaps baffled by my strange reactions and questions. "No. My home is in Richfield."

Richfield.

Not a city in Ex Cathedra, which meant he came from the other side of the mountains. Where was I? I knew the Iron-Blooded had vehicles, but what distance had they taken me?

Joel shifted around on his table. "Do you have a name?"

I almost didn't answer. What use was it to make attachments with other people? But I trusted Joel—at least the one in the cellar—and I couldn't will myself to stay quiet.

"My name is Kita."

"Did you live in a cellar, Kita?" He spoke in such a soft voice.

"Yes."

"I hope you get back to it one day."

What an odd sentiment. I knew he was trying to comfort me, but the words rattled around my head like a bird trying to escape a cage.

"Joel," I whispered.

He moved a bit, but didn't say anything.

"I . . . don't think I'll be able to walk again."

The words caught in my throat. A few silent tears ran down the side of my head and splashed onto the table. Why did I tell him? I didn't know. My chin trembled, and I couldn't get any more words past the blockage of the previous sentence.

Joel held up his right hand as much as he could with a leather strap over his wrist. All four fingers had been removed at the first joint, leaving only his thumb.

"They don't like me speakin' the way I do," he said. He set his hand down. "You got an Ex Cathedra accent, though. Your cellar located there?"

With the way he asked—the levity he kept in his voice despite the metaphorical and literal darkness all around us—I couldn't help but regain the strength to speak.

"Yeah," I muttered. "I was born in Ex Cathedra."

"I heard it's rough. Lot of fightin'. Big, though. Everyone says they'll reclaim the land."

"From sea to shining sea," I intoned as I recalled Ex Cathedra's war slogan.

"You a soldier?"

"No."

"Did you ever get a look at any judges? I heard they were a sight."

I chortled. What a sight. What a damn sight. "Joel. Do you . . . know anything about United California?"

He mulled over the question for a bit before answering. "It's got cities."

"But does it have ports and boats?"

"Lots of those, or so the gossip mice say."

Perhaps I just wanted to fantasize, because there was no reason to think I'd make it there. But I liked knowing it existed. Someday, maybe, if life eased up and gave me an opening, I'd find myself among the boats at dock.

Or perhaps it was all a naïve dream—the hope that fueled my will to live when I obviously should've given up long ago. Either way, I kept it close and refocused on the present.

"Thank you, Joel," I murmured.

"No, thank you," he said with a chuckle in his voice. "You've got a voice that makes the birds jealous. And ever since they got my eyes, it's talks like this I live for. Though anything's better than their gutter-spit speech."

I wanted to thank him again—to tell him his mere presence made the whole ordeal bearable—but the door opened, killing all conversation between us. Footsteps echoed in the room until two men stood on either side of my prison table.

They wore matching outfits, no doubt some sort of uniform.

Black long-sleeve shirts. Bulletproof vests painted black. Bandoliers of ammo and plastic explosives. Cargo pants of matching color. They could be shadows if it weren't for the insignia stitched into both their shirts.

A human skull inside of an alien skull's open mouth.

The mark of the Iron-Blooded.

The aliens had elongated faces, like a horse or a dog, but their tooth structure was remarkably similar to Homo sapiens. Incisors, canines, molars. The Iron-Blooded had the incisors and canines right, making the whole mark a sick horror fest of branding.

"*They're both awake,*" one man said. The same man who stabbed my side. A man with an angular face, his expression devoid of emotion. Or perhaps it was disdain; I couldn't tell.

The other Iron-Blooded soldier gave Joel a quick glance. "*This one is a mess.*"

"*He doesn't know where the bunker is. He took all the equipment he could carry and promptly forgot the location, apparently.*"

"*Sounds like a liar to me.*"

"*I've done everything to jog his memory. He's more corpse than man now. He never remembered.*"

"*So he's useless to us?*"

My torturer nodded.

Before I could offer a word of protest, the other Iron-Blooded asshole pulled out a .40 handgun, leveled it at Joel's head, and squeezed the trigger. The loud bang reverberated in the room, stinging my ears and my sanity. Joel spasmed atop his table, his blood coating the far wall of the room.

The man half laughed as he tucked the weapon away. "*So much more satisfying than cleaning the bastard. Now I can just wheel him to the back with all the other corpses.*"

"*Make it quick.*"

The second Iron-Blooded took Joel's corpse away, the wheels of the table squeaking as they went. I couldn't control the pounding of my heart or the dark thoughts that ran through my head. The Iron-Blooded were every horrible thing I had heard and more.

Once the door shut, I stared up at the man who had stabbed me—the man who had crippled me.

"I need you to answer a few questions," he said. *"Can you do that?"*

I nodded.

"We found a few items we couldn't identify among your belongings. Tell me, what is this?"

He held up one of my soldering pens—a compact device used for electrical connections. It wasn't an A-tech device, just something humans made long before the bombs.

"It repairs electronics," I said, as I couldn't remember the Tethlite word for soldering.

"And what about this?"

He held up the tracking device.

My heart stopped for a second, and I held my breath. He didn't know? He couldn't read the letters on the side? No. He probably could, but he didn't understand the acronym. I was sure if it said *global positioning device* he wouldn't have asked me.

My thoughts came to a halt.

If I told him, he would destroy it. If he reconnected it to the battery, however, the judge would find this place, wherever it was. And judges were known for their personal combat capabilities. No way the Iron-Blooded would walk away.

No way I would, either. Not in my condition. Not strapped to a table. Summoning the judge was like summoning death itself for the whole compound.

But then I glanced over at the bloodstain on the wall. Did I want to end up like Joel, or did I want one spiteful parting blow? It might not even happen, even if I lied. If we were too far away, the judge might not make the trek. Still—the thought of a judge ripping through everyone here delighted me more than it should have. I almost laughed.

"Answer me," the man said with a sneer. *"Or do I need to remind you what happens if you don't?"*

"It's a cover for the fission battery," I said. *"It protects the access point when it's connected. Prevents damage from dust and other particles."*

Everyone in the wasteland knew about the dangers of hazardous particles. Fallout from hundreds of bombs didn't just disappear over-night. Most electronic devices had covers for the ports to prevent undue damage.

The man turned the device over in his hand. *"Is that so?"* He pocketed the device. *"That's all for now. When I come back, I'll expect more answers."*

I nodded, though in my heart I knew I hated the Iron-Blooded just as much as I hated the aliens themselves. They could all burn and I wouldn't shed a tear.

I closed my eyes and imagined the judge's arrival with half a smile on my lips.

CHAPTER SIX

How long had I been trapped? A few hours? A few days? I didn't know. Time and time again they came for questioning.

"The individuals who taught you Tethlite—where are they?" the man asked.

"They died."

My third rule to lying: avoid contradictions and easily verified facts. No one could ever trace my source of knowledge, not when they were rotting. Although it wasn't really a lie. Sure, I'd spun a tale of slavery and forced study of A-tech, which the Iron-Blooded appreciated more than reality, but whenever I could fit in the truth, I did. Easier to keep the facts straight.

"Have you ever opened an A-tech vault?"

The question didn't register with me for a long moment. My head hurt, and each wakeful moment was its own torture. More and more of me wanted to remain quiet and allow my end to come with the last of their patience.

Perhaps the man could sense my apathy because he placed his fingertips over my twisted hip wound.

I gritted my teeth and swallowed hard. Anything but that, but I refused to beg. Refused. I had asked already—pleaded with him to show me even a shred of mercy—yet he showed me none.

When he spoke again, it was with a softer tone. A faux soft. Artificial comfort like only a sociopath could muster.

"We have advanced medications unlike anything found out in the wasteland."

I turned my attention to him, my thoughts returning to Dallas. Their medicine was the reason Dallas defected in the first place.

"Once you're one of us," the man continued, *"it won't have to be this way."*

"You killed Joel," I whispered, my lips dry.

"Who?"

"The other . . . in the room . . ."

"Oh," the man said with a sneer. *"You're referring to that inbred garbage we caught carrying our belongings. We don't integrate filth into our ranks. But people like you—people who already know the master language and the technology—we want to rehabilitate. You should be elated to cooperate with us. We're nothing like the squalor writhing around the radiation."*

I didn't answer. Whispers about the Iron-Blooded's recruitment methods had reached me years ago. Forcefully converting people they thought compatible. How did they do it? Breaking people? Did they intend to torture me until I gave in? Or perhaps take away my will to live and then offer it back with their medication, like they wanted to induce Stockholm syndrome in their victims?

It didn't matter how much they tortured me or how much medical knowledge they had, I wouldn't join their ranks.

"We're looking for something. And I think you can help us find it."

I closed my eyes. The pulse of my headache made it difficult to care about the content of his speech, but the information did interest me. What could the Iron-Blooded be looking for? Perhaps they wanted to find more surviving aliens—not the brainless drones that wandered the wasteland, but the innovators and architects.

"Acknowledge me when I'm speaking to you."

I remained silent, the words fuck you on the tip of my tongue. I knew he could stab me again, but he'd tipped his hand about killing me. They wanted me for something, so he wouldn't go to the extremes. I didn't know if I could hold out during another round of torture, but I was willing to try.

"I've done this hundreds of times. None of you last."

The door opened, and I tensed further, if it were even possible.

"Commander Dannik," the new Iron-Blooded said. *"We have a situation."*

The man questioning me, Commander Dannik, narrowed his eyes. *"Can it wait?"*

"No. We don't have much time before they get here."

Without a second glance in my direction, Commander Dannik strode out of the room, following the Iron-Blooded messenger.

I waited. Nothing happened after the heavy door slammed shut. Alone in the tiny room, I stared at the ceiling. With a deep breath, I tilted my head to the side. The poor lighting made it difficult to see anything that wasn't directly above me, but the shapes made sense the longer I stared at them.

A small silver table sat next to mine. The shine of a scalpel caught my attention.

I held my breath, a plan for escape blooming in my mind.

The hope sent energy through my veins, pumping into each cell of my body.

With all the power I could muster, I jerked my body toward the silver table. My table had wheels—rusty, not cooperative, but still wheels—and with each successful motion I moved closer. When the two tables tapped together, I jerked upward, moving until my restrained hand was close to the gleaming scalpel.

Sweaty and winded, I stretched out my fingers, walking them along the aluminum surface, closer and closer to the weapon.

Had this scalpel been the one to pierce my hip? The blade had felt so much larger and duller than the scalpel on the table, but I knew it had to be the culprit. Still, it would be my salvation.

My middle finger reached the handle, and I spun the tool around until it came back into my grip. With a relieved exhale, I smiled. I scooped up the scalpel and brought it back to the leather restraints. As long as I didn't drop it, which was a real possibility given my track record, I could saw through the strap and get off the table.

Slow sawing motions. It was all I could muster. Fiber by fiber, I severed the restraint, but at no great speed. I counted in my head to keep time. Three minutes. Ten minutes. Half an hour. An hour.

The room shook and the wheels of my prison table squeaked from the jostling. Flakes of cement rained down from the ceiling. I scrunched my eyes shut and continued. I refused to be distracted.

Another rumble and I held my breath.

When I yanked my arm, the strap let up enough for me to pull my hand through. I held back a laugh. Then I turned over on my side and cut away at the other wrist, with ten times the vigor.

A third rumble captured my attention. They weren't seismic activities. The tremors were created by explosions. But why? Had the Iron-Blooded attached the tracking device? Was the judge attacking? If she was, I already regretted my spiteful decision. I wanted nothing to do with a fight between alien-worshipping zealots and an Ex Cathedra judge.

Determined to just make it out alive, I finished cutting through the last of my restraints. My right leg, the one most affected by the bullet injury, ached with every movement I made. Even flexing my toes was a torment I couldn't handle. When I slid off the table, I used my left leg, but even that didn't support me like it should have.

My whole hip hurt.

And, like I had suspected, walking was out of the question. The knowledge stung my chest, making it hard to breathe, but I pushed it from my mind. I'd have time to mourn later.

I refused to give up.

I used the table for support, its wheels squeaking as it moved, and I gently hopped on my left leg to make it over to the door. When the IV tugged at my arm, I ripped it out.

Once out from under the harsh blinking light, I realized I was in an underground bunker. The stagnant air hung like a spider web. I coughed a few times and opened the door into a narrow hall.

Another rumble and tremor threatened to knock me off my feet, but I remained upright. Since no one knew I was leaving, I could slip away during the fighting and—

"*Hey!*"

I looked up, my eyes wide.

Three Iron-Blooded soldiers stood in the hallway, each with their black outfits and double-skull insignia. Their faces were kept hidden behind goggles and bandannas, obscuring every bit of flesh and transforming them into interchangeable cogs in the machine of war. I kept my scalpel close, but each of them had heavy rifles ready in their hands.

One raised his weapon.

In the next fraction of a second, one of the Iron-Blooded turned his gun on the other two. After two rapid-fire shots, both point blank to the side of the head, the two Iron-Blooded fell to the ground, their bodies jerking in unnatural ways.

I flinched and stumbled back, but I couldn't get far without the aid of the table.

The last Iron-Blooded ripped off his goggles and bandanna.

Dallas.

It took me a moment to realize he was scarred. On his neck and jaw, right next to his ear, someone had taken a hot brand and seared in the Iron-Blooded insignia. The fresh wound half clung to the fabric of the bandanna as he removed it fully.

"Kita," he said as he jumped to my side.

I slashed at him with the scalpel, cutting his hand when he reached for me.

"Stay back," I hissed.

He retreated a few feet and kept his hands up. "Please. I understand what I've done, but I do want to get you out of here. We need to hurry. There isn't much time."

Every cell in my body wanted to tell him to go fuck himself. What if he turned me over to the Iron-Blooded a second time? I could make it out of here on my own. I already got off the damn table and made it into the hall. I'd rather take my own way—die by my own way—than get duped by him again.

When he didn't move, my attention fell to the two corpses in the hallway, their darker-than-average blood pooling all around my feet. He could shoot me, but instead he turned and pointed to a solid metal door down the hall.

Without another word, he ran off, leaving me alone.

I needed to escape—that was paramount. Determined to break free from the underground prison no matter what it cost me physically, I wheeled my table along, my gaze focused on my own dried blood staining the side.

Dallas threw open the door he had pointed to and rushed inside. As I was making my way past, he emerged, his hands shaking and a little girl by his side.

She stood three and a half feet tall, her long black hair like inky waterfalls that spilled over her shoulders and down to her elbows. She stared at me with bright blue eyes—such an odd sight—and I caught my breath.

My sister had had the same dark hair and light eyes.

But even remembering my sister churned my stomach. On the verge of vomiting, I turned away.

Dallas held out his hand. "Please, Kita. I don't care if you hate me. I'd do anything for my daughter."

When the next rumble came, it was accompanied by the terrible sound of an explosion not far off. The whole underground hallway shook, dirt sifting down from the ceiling. For a brief moment, the lights went out. The little girl clung to Dallas's side, her small hands twisted into his Iron-Blooded uniform.

She couldn't have been older than seven.

What did Dallas want from me? To help his daughter? How?

He picked up the girl and then jogged through the facility. While I wheeled behind him, I heard the echo of gunfire. Was he clearing the way? Perfect. I shook my head to clear the sweat dripping into my eyes and continued. Then I saw a door at the far end of the hallway, and I was greeted by the icy chill of darkness. Once I made it outside, I abandoned the table—it wouldn't wheel across rocks and mountain terrain.

Bursts of bright lights lit up the area. Rapid rifle fire, grenades, and claymore mines shook the mountain with the intensity of a war zone. I would've sworn we were being bombarded by a howitzer if I hadn't seen the source of the commotion with my own eyes.

Only eighty feet away, Judge Gascoigne fought with the Iron-Blooded. Her new exoskeleton, a Mark III variant, shone in the sporadic lighting thanks to the fresh coat of crimson blood. She didn't wield a rifle, even though judge armor could handle powerful weapons a normal man couldn't. Instead, she fought the Iron-Blooded at close quarters, leaping to the men fighting her with little trouble.

When she reached them, it was all over.

Judge Gascoigne grabbed one man by the arm and tore it clean from his body. Before he could catch his breath from the scream, she ripped out his throat with her metal-crushing grip, silencing him forever.

The bullets they used barely dented the outside of her armor, and the fragmentation grenades were nothing more than smokescreens as they attempted to set up a tank-buster gun across the open flat of the mountainside.

I silently rooted for her success, delighting in the death of the Iron-Blooded more than I should have.

"Where is my motherfucking battery?" Judge Gascoigne shouted, her metallic voice half washed away by the incessant rifle fire and heavy weapons.

Dallas pulled me away from the commotion when he placed a hand on my shoulder. I flinched away and collided with the wall of the facility. He didn't speak. Instead, he turned and ran down a small incline, toward an off-road vehicle.

My heart jumped into my throat the moment I spotted it. The damn jeep held the scars of a hundred battles, each door dented and scraped, all the glass long since destroyed. It was beautiful. Just what I needed to escape.

Dallas opened the driver's side door and hefted his little girl inside.

While the war with the judge raged on, I pushed myself to my limits and stumbled toward the slope. Unable to correct my balance, I half tumbled down the road until I came to the vehicle. I slammed up against the side, my hands shaking.

"Please take my daughter," Dallas said with a strained breath. "I'm begging you. I'll stay to make sure you get away."

I said nothing to him as I dragged myself into the car. He was going to let me just take it? With his daughter? Was he *that* desperate? I pulled myself into the driver's seat.

Dallas slammed the door shut and then leaned on the window, never making eye contact. "She means everything to me. If you help her—if you take her to Boulder City—I'll meet you there. I'll return everything I took from you. I swear it."

I didn't believe he'd make good on any promises, but the fact he was leaving me with his daughter spoke volumes. And the desperation in his voice struck a chord with me. My father had had the same tone when he pleaded with me to hide while he dealt with the aliens. Even if Dallas couldn't make good on his promise, I wasn't about to let a little girl become a victim to the Iron-Blooded or the judges of Ex Cathedra.

I started up the vehicle but kept the headlights off. Dallas pointed to a narrow road and backed away.

Another round of ear-stinging explosions, followed by the boom of a 75mm tank-buster shot, rocked the mountainside. The armor-piercing ballistic caps were capable of shattering JUDGE-X0 exoskeletons at close range, but the suits' incredible mobility made them difficult targets.

When the fighting continued, I figured they had missed.

With my shaky left leg, I applied pressure to the forward pedal. The jeep revved and my mind snapped to the many manuals I had read in preparation for the all-terrain vehicle. I switched it to drive and applied a little pressure. The jeep moved at a quick pace over the rocks and broken road, the suspension system keeping the ride relatively smooth.

Several other jeeps took off, driving away from the concrete bunker. At first I thought they were coming for me, but I relaxed the moment I realized they all headed in different directions. No doubt they were fleeing from Judge Gascoigne. Without the proper equipment to stop her, she could easily run amok inside their outpost.

I didn't drive fast.

Bullets plinked into the side of the vehicle, and I suspected it wasn't accidental. I picked up the speed, but without the headlights, the void of night made everything a nightmare. What if I tumbled down the side of the mountain? Unwilling to take the risk, I flashed the lights on for a short bit to get a lay of the land.

A fork in the road waited ahead of me. The electronic compass on the dashboard told me one road went east and the other west. One went straight back to Ex Cathedra, and one went to the other side of the mountain.

I could return to my cellar. I could make a plan. I could exhaust all my options with the surrounding military bases. It was the safer option, but the longer one. Would I ever again have the opportunity to make it over the mountain? I might never get another chance. It would be a risk.

Or I could keep going. I could finish the drive across the mountain and head to the cities that dotted the flatland between the Rocky Mountains and United California—the lawless territory that no nation claimed. With no plan, no equipment, no help . . . it was the riskier option, but the faster one. The only option that capitalized on my opportunity to escape Ex Cathedra immediately. I could make it over the mountain if I went straight for my destination.

My heart leapt into my throat as I came to the fork faster than I anticipated. I allowed instinct to make the decision for me.

With a hard jerk of the steering wheel, I headed away from Ex Cathedra and over the mountain.

CHAPTER SEVEN

The cool evening air washed into the vehicle. I shivered constantly, but I didn't stop driving. Hiding never worked. I learned that the hard way after my father hid me and my sister. We were eventually found, not by the aliens, but by the soldiers of Ex Cathedra.

So hiding wasn't an option. I had to keep going—moving forward—until I couldn't go any farther.

Where had my jacket gone? Without a shirt, and only my bindings, too much skin was exposed to the elements. Clothing was my top priority once we were somewhere safe.

I glanced at the girl from time to time. She stared at me, her dark hair fluttering in the wind. From every angle, she appeared like my sister. It made it difficult to maintain eye contact.

Sweat dappled my exposed skin, chilling me further.

"Do you have a name?" I asked, trying to ground my thoughts in the immediate. I didn't want to dwell on the past.

The girl frowned.

"My name is Kita," I said.

Still, the girl remained silent.

The jeep jerked back and forth over a cluster of jagged rocks. Pain surged from my injuries. Fortunately, nothing in the vehicle broke, and we continued on our way down the winding mountain path. I flashed the lights occasionally, keeping the image of the road in my mind's eye as I drove. Nothing too fast—without a windshield, my eyes couldn't handle the wind pressure.

After a long hour of driving, I turned to the girl again. "It's okay. I'm going to take you to Boulder City."

She forced a smile and scooted over in her seat until she was as close as she could get without sitting on the center console.

"You can tell me your name."

The girl patted her throat and shook her head.

She was mute.

Birth defects weren't uncommon. The radiation messed with human development, and pregnant women didn't have the luxury of avoiding the worst of it in most cases. But children with such problems typically had more in the way of physical deformities. Missing limbs, enlarged body parts, a cleft palette—something, anything. Dallas's daughter seemed healthy and fully formed, however.

Uncertain of how to handle a mute child, I returned my attention to driving.

Twice I almost went over a sharp drop-off, but each time I managed to correct myself before the last possible moment. My eyesight faded in and out, and my head pounded with the force of a thousand bombshells. Staying focused required all my willpower, and as I descended further and further into delirium, I knew I was ill.

Couldn't stop driving, though, lest I get caught.

Daybreak brought with it a minimal amount of light. Clouds dominated the sky, but the glory of the sun managed to pierce through regardless. Pillars of sunshine fell onto the flatlands beyond the rocks of the mountain. I spotted a tunnel up ahead. Once I got to the other side, I would be beyond the worst of the terrain.

The tunnel might as well have been a black hole. No light got in, and it looked like nothing got out. I switched the jeep's headlights on as I entered. Dallas's girl climbed across the center console and grabbed my arm, her warm body a pleasant sensation against my clammy skin.

"It's okay," I whispered.

Even speaking took a toll on me. It was then that I realized I was on the edge of losing consciousness. And if I fell unconscious, there was no guarantee I would awake again, not when the Iron-Blooded were in the area, not when my only companion was a seven-year-old girl whom I knew little about.

When we emerged from the other side of the tunnel, I took a deep breath. A cityscape sat in the distance, the shattered skyscrapers and twisted metal frames of old buildings a pleasant sight.

There were always old A-tech storage facilities in ruined cities that remained intact. Not many people knew how to open the vaults or safety storage units. But I did.

If I could just make it . . .

My vision faded for a moment and my foot slipped from the pedal. The jeep veered and hit a pothole, jerking us around and agitating my injuries. The little girl gripped my arm, her fingernails piercing my skin and drawing blood.

I stopped the vehicle and rubbed the sweat from my brow. The taste of salt and copper lingered at the edge of my perception. When had I eaten last? The question haunted me for a long moment.

Was this the sensation of dying?

I couldn't even feel the pain from the girl's fingernails, only the rivulets of blood that resulted. I didn't even have the capacity to press the forward pedal anymore. I opened the door to get out and rest, but the last thing I could recall was falling.

Water.

On my lips.

My eyelids fluttered open. A man stood above me. The situation reminded me of Commander Dannik, and for a short moment, I thought my escape had all been a dream. But it wasn't Dannik—Dannik had an iciness to his appearance and movements. This new man wasn't like that at all. He cocked a half smile.

"Oh, look," he said. "You woke up. Good. I hate diggin' graves."

He lifted my head and tilted the bottle of water enough for me to have a sip. I tried to gulp down more, but he kept the container steady, allowing only a few mouthfuls at a time. Once I'd gotten enough, he set the bottle down and brought a hardtack biscuit to my lips.

I turned away, uncertain of what to do.

"C'mon," he said. "You've got to eat. I can chew it for you, but I doubt you'd like that."

I reached up and took the biscuit for myself. Should I eat it? What more could harm me? I had already been unconscious and on the verge of death. The biscuit couldn't do any worse. I nibbled at the edge.

The man set my head back down on a soft surface, his smile persistent. "The name's Uriah Bishop Geffen. Just call me *Bishop*. You mute, too, or can you speak?"

After a long swallow of saliva-soaked biscuit, I tried my hand at speaking. "K-Kita," I managed to choke out between coughs.

"Kita, huh? Interesting name." He turned and motioned to someone. "Crouton, bring me some more water, will ya?" Once he had a new water bottle, he set it next to me. "Here. Drink it slow. I've got to watch the streets."

Then he walked away. Left alone, I took a deep breath and cleared some of the fog from my mind. It was amazing how effective a couple bottles of water and a hardtack biscuit were for the body. A sore ache pervaded my being, but I could now function. I took in my surroundings.

We were inside a building. Light poured in from a busted window—the type of large window used to display goods back before the bombs. This was an old storefront. The man, Bishop, knelt by the windowsill, a powerful sniper rifle perched on the edge and facing the streets, the kind that took 7.62mm ammunition. Dallas's daughter sat on a chair by the back wall, her attention consumed by three figurines she played with.

My figurines. The mother, father, and child.

I sat up, my hip still aching, and rubbed at my face. Without speaking, I ate the biscuit and consumed the rest of the water, taking my time as I did so to get a better understanding of the situation. The girl wore a pair of ratty overalls and a white shirt so dirty it had become gray.

Bishop licked his lips, a smile still affixed to his face.

He was larger than most I had met, and his muscular frame betrayed a diet steady in protein. With his unkempt hair slicked back, he had a wild look about him. The stubble across his chin didn't help. Had he found me collapsed outside my jeep? Or had Dallas's little girl led him back to me?

"Crouton," he said. "Pass me a water. It's almost time."

Dallas's daughter hopped off her chair, walked over to a duffel bag in the corner of the room, and then rummaged through it. She brought Bishop a bottle of water, and he patted her on the shoulder.

"Good job. You might want to stay down. Explosions shoot things all over." He made gestures with his hands, making a fist and then opening it quick, fingers splayed.

The girl nodded and moved behind the wall, away from the open window.

"What's going on?" I asked, my voice rusty. Did we need to run? Could I even move?

Bishop kept his gaze down the scope of his rifle. "Don't worry. I'm just dealing with a couple tally marks."

Tally marks?

When nothing happened, I slid my legs off the side of my makeshift bed. Someone had placed a bunch of blankets on a desk and made a pillow from fluffed cotton held together in a plastic bag.

Was it Bishop's doing?

"Thank you," I muttered, but the words didn't adequately convey what I felt.

"Don't worry about it," Bishop said. "You paid me for the food and water with your jeep."

"What?"

He motioned me over. "You'll see."

I couldn't walk. Somehow, Dallas's daughter must have known. She got up and hopped to my side. With my hand on her shoulder, I could move, though it was at an awkward pace. My left leg supported my weight, but the right wouldn't cooperate, not without a wave of agony.

Bishop glanced over and stared as I hobbled to the windowsill. His smile disappeared as he gave me the once-over, and for a brief moment, he had a calculating look about him.

But then he returned his attention to his scope.

"There," he said. "It's the Iron-Blooded."

The twisted cityscape surrounded us on all sides. Collapsed buildings, ruined cars, and oceans of shattered glass made up the scenery. Melted tires and permanent shadows told me this was once an impact site for a firestorm fission bomb. Which meant the fine coating of ash over the environment was a cocktail of incinerated corpses.

I shuddered.

It took me a few minutes to even register the jeep sitting out in the middle of the road.

"What are you—"

"Shh," he said as he steadied his gun.

Two Iron-Blooded goons exited one of the many destroyed buildings. They glanced up and down the street before motioning to the jeep. With careful movements they made their way over, rifles in hand. My heart beat faster the closer they got. I hated the sight of their double-skull insignia so much it had me grinding my teeth.

What were they doing here? Nothing good, no doubt.

The instant they opened the jeep door to get in, Bishop squeezed the trigger, the ammo shell flying off to the side in one powerful shot that stung my eardrums more than the explosion, no doubt due to our close proximity. I covered my ears, and so did Dallas's girl, but it didn't help much. The bullet slammed through the man's skull and brought him down. A half second later and Bishop shot again, laughing the entire time as the second Iron-Blooded hit the pavement, a hole in his head the size of an aluminum can.

"Your jeep makes good bait," he said, his voice barely audible over the ringing in my ears.

I went to stand, to get a better look at the destruction, but Bishop grabbed my shoulder and held me down. I remained kneeling.

"Don't move," he said. "They always travel in threes."

Sure enough, a third Iron-Blooded soldier emerged from a nearby building. Although I couldn't see his face through the bandanna and goggles, he threw his hands up behind his head in a show of frustration and shock, his crimson red gloves an odd sight. Before Bishop could fire again, the red-gloved man ran back into the building. Smart move.

We waited.

The seconds transformed into minutes. Bishop cursed under his breath.

"I'm gonna have to chase him," he muttered. Then he stood and walked out of our dilapidated shop.

I watched him walk out into the street—he wasn't worried about getting sniped back?—but there were no hesitations in his movements.

Bishop stopped at each of the bodies and shot them all again with his sidearm, riddling them with two or three more bullets. I couldn't look away. His sheer delight made the moment almost cruel, but I refused to feel sorry for the Iron-Blooded.

When Bishop returned, I took in a deep breath and asked, "Why are you wasting your ammo?"

He chuckled as he holstered his handgun. "I'm not wasting anything. Those Iron-Blooded lunatics can live through a lot, let me tell you. They've got machines in them that stitch up all sorts of injuries."

Bishop grabbed his sniper rifle—the whole thing three feet long—and disassembled it. It took me a few moments to register his claims.

"Machines in them?" I asked.

"Yeah. Little machines. In their blood. Where do you think they got their name? Aliens used to have the same damn thing. Tiny machines in their blood, healing them quick."

"You mean nanites?"

"Whatever they're called. The damn little machines will fix up a lot of injuries. You can't trust one of them Iron-Blooded is dead unless you riddle them full of holes."

Everything about the Iron-Blooded made a lot more sense. Bishop was right; their name, the fact their blood ran dark, it all linked back to an abundance of nanites in their blood. And nanites were something else—something amazing. Microscopic robots that fixed and repaired human flesh faster than it could naturally. I thought they were more a thing of history after the bombs hit, but the Iron-Blooded must have found themselves a supply, like the judges of Ex Cathedra found the factory of exoskeletons.

My thoughts jerked to a halt.

Dallas had been afraid of the EMP grenade. Had the Iron-Blooded offered him nanites in order to survive? It would explain how he healed so fast in my cellar and why he thought the Iron-Blooded could save his little girl.

EMP grenades messed with the function of nanites enough to disable them. And, according to my grandfather's stories, anyone with disabled nanites in their system would soon die from clots in their arteries—in a matter of minutes.

Once Bishop finished cleaning up, he pulled a tactical KA-BAR knife from his belt. I leaned away, instantly aware I didn't have a knife of my own. He flashed me a smile as he pulled out a lighter and heated the edge of his blade. What was he doing? I couldn't bring myself to ask, fearing the worst.

He rolled up the sleeve of his jacket, exposing his skin up to his elbow. Tally marks riddled his flesh, each scar neat in a group of five. He had at least twenty, but the marks continued up under his clothes.

Before I could comment, Bishop pressed the blade into his skin, carving two new tally marks into place. He grimaced with each mark, but his smile persisted, like he was some sort of masochist that enjoyed the sting of a cauterized wound.

"There," he said with a forced chuckle. "Two more."

He shoved his jacket back down, picked up his duffel bag, and slung his sniper rifle over his shoulder. He turned to leave, and I relaxed a bit. The little girl—who I had almost forgotten about—jumped to my side, her eyes wide and glued to Bishop.

"Wait," I said.

Bishop stopped by the door.

"Are you going to take my jeep?"

Was he going to steal it? A piece of me was already surprised he was just going to leave us. He could sell people, if he wanted. Small girls could get him a few batteries or a bag of ammunition. But instead he headed for the door without a second glance back. My foggy mind couldn't logic out a motive for all his actions.

Bishop shrugged. "I already have a truck. It would be too much of a hassle to drag your jeep around. Plus, you and Crouton need something to get back to town, right?" He glanced outside and then half laughed. "I don't know why you two have an Iron-Blooded vehicle, but I also have a rule I like to follow. No Iron-Blooded equipment."

"S-So you're going to leave it to me?"

"That a problem?"

I ran a hand over the back of my neck, the ridges of my spine easy to feel. "Do you think you could spare anything for . . . our trek back to town?"

Why would I ask such a stupid question? Of course he wouldn't. Why would anyone help a cripple and a little girl? Then again, if he was already being kind to us, I might as well milk him for everything he had.

And Bishop could leave. Nothing kept him here. But he mulled over my comment as though it were a dire question in need of an answer.

He pulled out his sidearm and tossed it to the floor. It hit the wood with a clunk, and my mouth went dry even staring at it.

"It's got a full magazine of ammunition," he said. "It'll keep you safe until you get to town."

"I . . . don't use guns."

Bishop laughed. He turned to me with his half smile, his teeth visible. "Weird sense of humor."

"I'm not joking. I can't."

"You can't be serious. You sound like you come from Ex Cathedra, and maybe they do things differently there, but I guarantee this place isn't similar. Might equals right. If you aren't gonna shoot someone, they're gonna shoot you, especially if you have something and you look like an easy target."

I didn't reply.

"Your best bet is to get into a city and stay there. Your injury doesn't look so good, either. Might want to see a doctor."

Bishop took another step for the door and then hesitated. When I said nothing, he continued on his way, leaving me and the little girl alone in the dilapidated shop.

I turned to the girl, and she pointed to the gun. Did she want me to pick it up? I shook my head, and she must've understood I wasn't going to do anything with it. The girl jogged over, picked it up, and stuffed it into the front of her dirty overalls. When she returned to my side, she had a look on her face that spoke volumes.

What do we do now?

The question weighed heavily. I glanced out the window to the jeep. "We'll take the jeep to a nearby town," I muttered aloud, hoping the girl would understand. "Once there, I'll exchange the gun for provisions and . . . anything else we'll need."

The girl nodded along with my words.

"Are you . . . good with a gun?"

Shifting her gaze to the floor, the girl offered a single nod in response. I took that to mean she knew how to fire a gun, but that she didn't want to. It would have a kick, and if she missed, especially in a terrible moment, it could cost us everything. Such responsibility was hard to put on someone as young as her. But I didn't have many options. Using a gun brought back too many memories—I couldn't do it.

"Help me to the jeep," I said.

The girl helped me up. Together we hobbled outside, my head hurting and my legs weak. She never said a word, and I dwelled on that fact until I took a seat and placed my hands on the steering wheel. Bishop had said she was mute. Once she took her own seat, I started up the engine and allowed the soft vibrations to soothe me.

Where would I go? I waited for the answer to come to me, but I still couldn't get a grip of my head.

The corpses of the Iron-Blooded men bled out around the tires of the vehicle. They deserved every bullet, in my opinion.

Gunfire echoed between the broken buildings. Dallas's little girl jumped in her seat. She reached out and took hold of my arm, her eyes searching the empty road ahead of us. Whoever was shooting had to be a few blocks away and around a corner—someplace I couldn't see. But I knew the Iron-Blooded had to be involved. Maybe Bishop? Either way, I would need to avoid it.

With shaking hands, I stepped on the pedal and drove down the cracked roads, avoiding the forgotten wreckage of vehicles from an era past.

The gunfire intensified. The echoing effect made it difficult to determine which direction it came from, but I kept at a slow pace, ready to punch the jeep into full gear should anything happen.

"Duck down," I said.

Dallas's girl did as she was told.

I drove through the city until I came to an intersection blocked with the rubble of a collapsed building. After I flipped the jeep around, another series of gunfire blasted throughout the city. My skin crawled. It sounded like a war zone.

I drove back a long way before turning down a new street. Then I found the source of the commotion—I had been right. The Iron-Blooded. I would recognize their black uniforms for the rest of my life. Four of them held their rifles pointed at a building, squeezing the triggers in short bursts. One of them wore crimson-red gloves, no doubt the same man from before. Had he gone and gotten backup? Their bullets tore through the broken windows and shattered walls. Who were they aiming at?

I slammed my foot on the brake and shifted the car into reverse. The Iron-Blooded didn't glance in my direction or even alter their actions. They continued firing at the building. Two of them spread out every few shots.

It hit me then. They were using suppressing fire. They intended to keep someone, or some group, pinned down while they inched around. And although it was difficult to distinguish gunshots over the sound of continual fire, I could see the occasional flare of red from the muzzle of a rifle inside the building.

Someone was firing back.

The Iron-Blooded inched closer to the building. When they reached the faded yellow lines in the middle of the road, my heart seized in my chest.

There was rubble and rusted husks of cars on the sides of the road, but there was nothing between me and the Iron-Blooded.

"Get out of the jeep," I said. It was difficult to breathe, but I knew what I wanted to do.

Dallas's girl let go of my arm and did as she was told, her eyes wide. I reversed the jeep until the bumper came up against a wreck of deserted cars. I had at least a quarter of a mile between me and the scumbags. They continued forward, their eyes down the sights of their rifles, still oblivious to my presence.

I shifted the jeep and slammed on the pedal.

In three seconds, I reached sixty miles per hour. In six seconds, I reached one hundred. At eight seconds, one Iron-Blooded finally noticed me. But the second's worth of reaction time wasn't enough. My jeep barely slowed when I plowed through the first guy. The second and third dented the bumper and jostled the vehicle. The fourth guy leapt up—*jumped to avoid me*—but still hit the frame of the jeep with a sick crunch.

I crushed the brakes, and the tires squealed in protest. When I hit the wall of a fragile building, a chunk of cement broke away from the rubble and crashed down on the hood. I came to a halt with a jerk and almost broke my face on the steering wheel. Dust and debris sprang into the air like a fog. It took me a few moments of coughing to clear my lungs.

Goddammit.

I had intended to stop sooner, but the fourth guy jumping up startled me more than I'd ever admit. My body, sore from bracing for impact, took a few minutes to relax. My head pounded, and I wondered whether I would ever feel normal again.

"Who's there?" someone shouted.

CHAPTER EIGHT

I rubbed at my temples and tried to open the door to the jeep. It wouldn't budge.

"Damn," the same person said with a chuckle. "I hope you ain't dead."

My coughing was answer enough. Although I wanted to crawl out and avoid all contact with people, I continued to shake the door of the jeep. It wouldn't open, and I was far too weak to get it to do anything.

Once the debris settled, a dusty Bishop emerged on the scene. He stepped over the broken chunks of cement and walked straight to the door of my jeep. With little effort, he threw it open. Then he motioned to the street.

"You're crazy, Viper," he said. Then he glanced back at the bloodstains left on the road. "You earned yourself four tally marks, though."

Who was this guy? I hadn't asked him much about himself when he was giving me water and biscuits. Was he fighting the Iron-Blooded? He had to be the one in the building—the one they were trying to kill.

Bishop tapped the roof of the jeep. "You really did a number to your ride." He slung his rifle over his shoulder and then offered a hand. "C'mon. We can't stay here. There's no end to those Iron-Blooded bastards, trust me. Best to get out of here as soon as possible."

"Y-yeah," I muttered.

Then he picked me up. I hadn't expected it, and I clung to him with trembling hands.

"Put me down," I snapped.

"It'll be faster this way, Viper. Trust me. We don't want to linger." He glanced upward, and I took in our surroundings with a more critical eye.

I hadn't realized how far I'd plowed into the building. Papers and cloth littered the area, so old and moldy they filled the air with a damp stench. I typically avoided large buildings because the air inside contained all sorts of terrible particles in high concentrations. Standing around in a small portion wouldn't harm us, but people died all the time from trying to make homes out of giant buildings with no airflow. Plus, the slightest thing could cause a collapse, and no one lived after getting caught under a thirty-story building.

Reluctantly, I nodded and allowed Bishop to take me out. Dallas's girl stood on the road, her eyes wider than I would've thought possible. She ran to us the moment we emerged from the cracked and unstable building. I breathed easy once we were away from the wreckage.

Bishop continued past the Iron-Blooded corpses, the little girl glued to his side.

"You need to eat more," he said as he lifted me up and down in his arms, as if evaluating my weight. "My mother would've never let you leave without four meals in your gut. No wonder you collapsed on the side of the road."

"I didn't have anything."

"Yeah, I noticed." Bishop glanced over his shoulder. "You keeping up, Crouton? I don't want to lose you."

Dallas's girl nodded.

"Crouton?" I asked.

"Well, I didn't know her name, and she didn't speak. What is her name, anyway?"

"I don't know," I muttered.

Bishop laughed aloud, his voice echoing against the surrounding city wreckage. "You're the mom, ain'tcha? Forgot your own daughter's name?"

"She's not my daughter."

"Really?" Bishop gave me a hard look and then turned his attention to the girl. He mulled over the statement until he finally said, "You two look similar enough. You're not fuckin' with me, right?"

I shook my head.

"Then who is she?"

"Who are you?" I interjected.

"I told you. My name's Bishop."

I shook my head again. "Put me down. I mean . . . who are you? What're you doing here?"

Bishop did as I requested. He gave me the same easygoing smile he did the first time I met him. "I do lots of stuff for money. Junk hunter. Mercenary. Ya know. Whatever."

Crouton ran over the moment I wobbled. I grabbed her shoulder and braced myself before asking, "What were you doing here?"

"Hunting some Iron-Blooded. You helped me with that, though." He shot me a pair of finger guns. "Nice work, too. I was startin' to think I'd never make it back. But now that everything's good, I'm feelin' pumped. You need to get back to town, right? Let me give you a ride in my truck. Your leg doesn't look like it'll make it."

Although I wanted to say *no* immediately, Crouton turned toward me with a smile.

I held my breath. It wasn't like I was going to walk any significant amount. And Bishop didn't seem like the type to murder me in cold blood. He did seem . . . different. Nothing like I had met before—nothing like Dallas. And if Bishop wanted to hurt me, he could've done it twice over without much trouble.

"You ready to get going?" Bishop asked.

I rubbed at my arms.

Crouton nodded, as if answering for both of us. Without warning, Bishop scooped me up again. I tensed, almost ready to yell at him for doing it, but I bit back the urge and allowed the assistance. Anything would be better than standing around in the middle of the road out in Iron-Blooded territory.

Crouton maintained a bright smile as we walked, her happiness as apparent as the devastation all around us. She continued to carry my figurines, her hands clenched tightly over them. It made me wonder how much she missed Dallas.

"You like the name *Crouton*, right?" Bishop asked.

She nodded.

"Crouton it is."

Since she couldn't articulate her name, it made sense to give her one. It rolled around in my thoughts as Bishop jumped over cracks in the road, effortlessly taking me with him as though I barely impacted his travel. Occasionally, his grip on my side caused me to suck in air through my teeth, but I never cried out.

"Are you taking us to your vehicle?" I asked.

Bishop snorted back a laugh. "Hell no. Neither of you gets to sit in my truck until you're cleaned up. I've seen sewer roaches in better condition."

Crouton slowed and stared down at her clothing. Her pair of ratty overalls had more holes than the Iron-Blooded corpses, and her once white shirt would forever be a shade of coal gray. She attempted to wipe away the dirt and grime, but every swipe of her sweaty palm resulted in another smear.

To my amusement, she narrowed her eyes into a glare and pointed at Bishop. Then she motioned to her chin and shook her head.

He lifted an eyebrow. "Are you giving me shit for my stubble?"

Crouton nodded.

"Kids these days," he said with a chuckle. "So precocious."

"Stop," I said. "Where are you taking us? I want to know the details before we go anywhere."

Bishop came to a halt atop a large pile of busted concrete. From our vantage point, I could see down all four roads that led away from the intersection. The howl of wind through broken glass reminded me of ghost stories I heard when I was younger.

Bishop rotated his shoulders. "I know a place we can wash up. And then get you two some new clothes."

"Where? Specifically? And where are we? I need to know."

"Calm down, Viper. This is just for washing and—"

"No," I snapped, my volume as loud as my raw throat would allow. "I don't want to go anywhere unless I know exactly what's going on."

I didn't want to be at the mercy of anyone else's schemes or tactics. It was my plan or nothing—Bishop would be a tool toward an end, not an ally I relied on in crucial moments and crisis. I wouldn't have a repeat of Dallas's betrayal because I would never allow myself to be put in such a position. I wasn't going to go to a wash area unless I was certain it was something I wanted.

Bishop set me down. I used my left leg to remain standing and kept my hands on his arm for balance. Before I could ask what he was doing, Bishop pulled out a paper map and unfolded it in front of me. He had writing everywhere—notes on locations, images drawn, like caves and plants—but the most important details were the cities.

He tapped the eastern side of the map. "We're right here. A few hours away is Dodge City. We'll get you two cleaned and then head there."

I stared at the map for a long moment, but my pounding head—no doubt a result from me crashing the jeep—prevented me from focusing properly. "Where is the city of Boulder?"

"Well, you can go from Dodge City to Richfield, then George Town, then Tomato Creek, and finally Boulder." He ended his finger on the western-most point of the map. "These spots here are ruins. Lots of those. All these lines are hazards. There's a hell radiation zone and a drone nest."

His map referred to our location as "Ruins C." The Rocky Mountains stood nearby, to the east, and Ex Cathedra just beyond it. For a moment, I reveled in a tangent thought—I had escaped. Even if it wasn't like I had imagined. I had made it to the lawless flatlands, free from Ex Cathedra. Soon I would make it to United California. I was getting closer and closer to my goal.

"I'm taking you to the ramen cups," Bishop said.

I stared up at him, confused to the point of silent bewilderment.

He laughed, flashing his teeth. "What's that look for? Those ramen cups catch water from the rains, and one of them has dirt and sand inside, so when they trickle down, they're somewhat filtered. I wouldn't recommend you drink it, but it's cool and it'll clean you good."

Ramen . . . cups?

Bishop closed the map and tucked it back into his pocket. "Dodge City has public baths, but I wouldn't trust that place if I were you. Lots of crazy shit goes down there."

Before he could say anything else, I said, "I want to go to the public baths."

"Tsk," Bishop said with a click of his tongue. He glared at me for a long moment.

"That's what I want."

"Fine. But you can't sit in the cab of my truck. You sit in the way back, where you can't dirty up my seats."

Bishop scooped me back up in his arms and turned around. Crouton stayed at his side, undisturbed by our discussions. Once we reached the bottom of the concrete pile, I squeezed Bishop's arm.

"I've changed my mind," I said.

He stopped and stared down at me. "Now what?"

"I want to go to the ramen cups."

He didn't protest, but he did huff before turning on his heel. "Women."

The change of plans was a test. If Bishop had insisted on anything— forced the issue through threats or scare tactics—I would've suspected him of scheming. But his willingness to alter course based on my flippant shifts meant he probably wasn't invested one way or another.

It put me at ease. I relaxed in Bishop's arms.

Perhaps he felt it. He held me a little tighter and offered another one of his easygoing smiles. It reminded me of the Joel inside the Iron-Blooded compound. Someone with a level of comforting charisma that chased away negative thoughts.

But I pushed the idea from my head. If Bishop were a tool, it was best not to think about it. Everyone I knew—literally everyone—had either died or betrayed me. With those statistics, why would I ever want to get attached to people? It was foolish to think anyone would be the exception. And loneliness was a better outcome than heartbroken loss or deep-seated anger.

We walked a few blocks of empty streets. When Bishop rounded a corner, he pointed with the jut of his chin. "There they are."

Three gigantic ramen cups, the kind for instant noodles if normally sized, were smashed into one another a good ten feet above the ground and attached to a building with steel rods. They had been an advertisement for something before the bombs hit. The word *restaurant* was painted in red and half faded away. Each cup could hold ten thousand gallons of water, by my rough estimates, and the top one leaked into the middle, which spilled into the last, filling it to the brim.

Bishop set me down by a lone standing wall and jogged over to the lowest cup of the three. He reached up and tugged at the chain of a metal gate built into the bottom. It was obvious someone had altered the cup to be a makeshift shower system, and the brilliance intrigued me.

"Bishop, did you do this?"

"Nah," he said as he opened the hatch and allowed a stream of cold water to pour down. "I just found it. These stupid cups have been here for years. Real handy when you're out in these dusty ruins, am I right?"

His laughter didn't change what the dust represented, but I buried the thought deep in my mind. Now wasn't the time for disgust and dread.

Bishop threw down his duffel bag and rifle. Then he took off his jacket and hung it on the tip of an exposed pipe jutting from the wall of a dilapidated parking garage. "We shouldn't stay here long. This is out in the open, and you never know what kind of tally marks are lurking around these parts."

I agreed with him. Outside of cities, it was a risk to interact with individuals. I preferred my hermit lifestyle to constant fear and jumping at shadows, but I couldn't retreat, not when I had come so far.

Bishop ripped off his shirt and threw it on the same pipe with his jacket.

I stared—not because a shirtless man was a rare sight, but because of the tally marks etched into his skin.

So many tally marks. Perhaps a hundred. Perhaps more. They were clumped in sets of five, not organized or level with each other, but all over. His shoulders, his chest, some along his sides, some near his belly button, some half covered by the waistband of his pants.

He leaned under the water and allowed it to splash over his head, hair, and neck. After a few moments of rubbing his scalp, he stepped back and rummaged through his duffel bag. "Here. I've got soap. You two make this quick."

He tossed a bottle, and I caught it, much to my surprise.

Despite my malnourished and weakened state, I could still manage a simple catch, it seemed.

Bishop dragged a small mirror and knife out of his bag. He hung the mirror on the side of the parking garage and stared at it, all the while running his hand over his stubble. I appreciated that he kept his back turned to us, but I also knew the mirror could be used to watch the surroundings at the same time. A polite and prudent gesture.

Crouton didn't wait for permission or instruction. She unclipped her overalls and threw off her grimy shirt before jumping under the water. Then she flailed around and leapt away, her whole body rattling from a heavy shiver. She rubbed at her arms as her teeth clattered.

Faded yellow and green bruises marred her complexion. One of the Iron-Blooded had mentioned internal bleeding, and the discoloration supported that claim. But the bruises were old. Had the Iron-Blooded cured her? Did she have nanites in her system, like Dallas?

I sighed. It wasn't the time to think about such things.

I wanted to walk over and hurry through the washing process, but my leg wouldn't cooperate. Instead, I got down on one knee and half crawled over to the water. It wasn't far—five feet at most—but it was a humiliating and painful five feet. The kind of five feet that stuck in my thoughts. The kind of five feet that made me wonder what it would be like to watch someone do what I was doing.

With my jaw clenched, I slid into the puddle of water pooling at the bottom of the fresh stream. I tried to ignore my newfound condition, I truly did, but my mind wouldn't let it go.

I removed the binding over my chest and placed it to the side. My pants, on the other hand, would be just as much of a struggle as the damn five feet.

I unbuckled my belt and struggled with my clothing. It wasn't that my arms failed me, but every move to slide anything over my left leg left me breathing shallow and holding back cries of agony. I had needed to piss for a long while, but I had held it back, fearing this exact moment.

Pathetic.

The word burned more than any physical pain. I scrunched my eyes shut, but it didn't stop the tears.

I couldn't let the thoughts consume me. Time and time again, people killed themselves in the wasteland—their hope extinguished by the bleakness of reality. I wouldn't be one of them.

I moved the last couple inches until I was under the water. The icy chill swept over me, and I welcomed it. After a few seconds of shock, the cold numbed my body. I didn't want to feel anything anymore. I just wanted to keep my eyes closed, pretend reality was different, and allow my dark thoughts to disappear with my warmth.

Someone touched my shoulder, and I flinched.

Crouton knelt next to me, her eyebrows knitted. I didn't know what to say, so I remained silent. She took the bottle of soap and opened it up. At first I thought she would once again leave me to my darkness, but she stayed next to me and smiled.

Without any words, she squirted the soap into her hands and placed her palms on my scalp. She scrubbed with gentle circular motions until my black hair hung heavy with suds. Then she ran her hands down my back and shoulders, clearing away the dirt and dried blood. Each time she met my gaze, she smiled again.

"You remind me of my sister," I said. "Her name was Tamura." I just wanted to tell somebody. It felt like forever since I had said my sister's name.

Crouton nodded along with my words. Then she walked to her overalls and withdrew the little figurines. She returned to my side, and after looking over the options, she handed over the child.

I almost chuckled. "Is this my sister?"

She nodded. She placed the father figurine back on the overalls, but kept the mother close. She pointed to my "sister" and then the mother.

I understood.

Her mother had died.

"Dallas told me about his wife . . ."

But I couldn't complete the sentence. The haunting look on Crouton's face said it wasn't a memory we should return to.

"Fuck me," Bishop said through clenched teeth.

I turned my attention to him. Blood dripped from a cut across his chin, mixing with the stubble he had managed to shave. But the injury didn't seem to deter him. He returned to shaving, like he was determined to finish what he had started.

Crouton, once finished helping me, gathered the figurines back up and cradled them gently until she returned them to her overalls pocket. Afterward, she scrubbed her own hair, washed away all the grime, and then pulled Bishop's duffel bag close. She withdrew a towel and dried off, never needing to be told or reminded.

Children had to become self-reliant at an early age, but her maturity still impressed me.

She walked over and held the towel out. I backed away from the numbingly cold water, the tips of my fingers blue, and I wrapped myself up in the stiff cloth.

"I know a great doctor," Bishop said as he started down the other side of his face. "She's done wonders. A guy I knew once got a nail stuck in his head." He stopped shaving, put a finger in his mouth, and popped it out along the cheek for the dramatic sound. "She got it out just like that. And it was a big nail, too. All the way in the fucker's brain. You'd think you'd die from something like that. What I'm tryin' to say is she might be able to help with your walkin'."

I dried off while I mulled over his story, still unable to stand without assistance.

Crouton put her dirty shirt back on, but not the overalls. The shirt must've belonged to an adult because it went down to her thighs, like a summer dress.

"You two are gettin' new clothes," Bishop said. "So don't bother, Crouton."

I glanced around us. Ruined cities were treasure troves of interesting items. "Bishop, do you know where we might find some tools? Soldering pens, pliers, screwdrivers . . . things like that?"

"Yeah. A lot of junk hunters have picked the place apart, but I've found some interesting areas forgotten by others."

"I need them."

Bishop rotated a shoulder. "Well, it's not too out of the way, and you did help me out. I'll get you some."

Crouton pointed upward. I tilted my head back to get a better look. A small swarm of birds and insects shot across the sky, all moving in the same direction, as though running from something. Bishop must have arrived at the same conclusion because he hastily finished his shave, picked up his clothes, weapon, and bag, and motioned for me to stand.

"We've got to go."

I struggled for a moment as I attempted to stand with my left leg. It proved difficult, but when Bishop started to walk over to help, I glared.

"I'll do it," I snapped. I had to.

Bishop turned back around and dressed himself. "Is now really the time for pride?"

I pushed through the flaring agony and forced myself up to one foot. I almost yelled, but I didn't. The tiny victory invigorated me enough that I allowed Bishop to carry me afterward. He closed up the ramen cup hatch and jogged in the opposite direction from which we'd come—farther away from whatever scared the birds.

Crouton easily kept up, her ratty overalls in her arms.

I just wanted to know that, if I had to, I'd be able to stand without assistance. Sometimes it didn't matter what people were actually capable of—just what they *looked like* they were capable of.

I kept my towel secure around my body as Bishop hustled down the street. He hid behind the first corner and then stopped. After a long moment of waiting and listening, a truck drove down the far road, kicking up dust as it went.

Bishop set me down and then withdrew a pair of binoculars from his duffel bag. After he got a good look, he handed them to me.

I didn't need the binoculars. I'd recognize an Ex Cathedra troop truck from a couple miles away.

"Do you see much of Ex Cathedra out here?" I asked.

"Never. Those damn soldiers never cross the mountain paths."

"Do they . . . have a judge?"

"Standing on the back bed. That's some mean-lookin' armor."

I drilled a hole in the ground with my gaze, my thoughts piecing together the situation into something understandable.

It had to be Judge Gascoigne.

But why? Was she chasing me? Had I injured her pride with the EMP grenade? Unlikely she'd travel this far for such a petty reason. More likely, she didn't recover the fission battery from the Iron-Blooded, which meant she followed them beyond the mountain and to the ruins.

Judge Gascoigne was still in pursuit of her stolen property.

"You said you would get us clothes?" I asked in a quiet voice.

"Yeah," Bishop said.

"Where?"

"There's a mall nearby with some clothing. I like the place—a little hidden from most. Not too many know about it."

"Take us there."

Bishop smiled, his attention glued to the Ex Cathedra truck. "Hm. Just give me a minute. I've never seen a judge up close. Looks like one hell of a tally mark."

CHAPTER NINE

"Do you kill everyone you run across?" I asked.

Bishop gave me a sidelong glance. "You're still here, ain'tcha?"

"Do you avoid killing women? If that's the case, the judge following us is—"

"Followin' you?"

"Er, it's not—" I bit my tongue. He could strand me if he thought the escort mission to Boulder City was more hassle than it was worth.

Bishop laughed and returned his attention to the Ex Cathedra truck. It drove down the far street, in the opposite direction. "I don't care if the judge is a woman, if that's what you're tryin' to say. I kill anyone who's gonna kill me, understand? It's like a contest, and I like to keep score."

"Judge Gascoigne is looking for a stolen fission battery."

Bishop whipped his attention back to me. "A fission battery? Do you know where it is?"

"I . . . stole it from an Ex Cathedra mine."

His eyebrows rose to his hairline.

"I don't have it anymore," I quickly added. "Obviously."

"Still. Fuckin' ballsy. Like running a jeep into some Iron-Blooded. I like that. Then again, you're not a very good thief." He flicked his middle finger on my upper arm. "You once had a fission battery and a jeep. Now you're down to a towel. Easy come, easy go, I guess."

I grew red and silent, not entirely sure how to rebut such statements. I *had* considered myself a talented thief, but perhaps my ego got away with me. Within the last week, I'd come close to dying multiple times, and I had lost all my equipment. I didn't have anything to show for my efforts.

Well, except for the distance traveled. That couldn't be taken from me. And I might've given everything I had to make it this far regardless.

"The Iron-Blooded took the fission battery," I said, trying to steer the conversation away from my mistakes. "I don't know where it is anymore. But that doesn't mean Judge Gascoigne will let me go if she spots me. I'm sure she'll kill me for my crime against Ex Cathedra."

Bishop rummaged through his bag and withdrew an A-tech gas grenade, the kind that melted flesh. "What if we use one of these?"

"The JUDGE-X0 suits have air filters that remove deadly gas. It won't work."

His excitement over facing a judge baffled me. He was going to use an A-tech gas grenade for this one judge? Perhaps he didn't understand how invulnerable they were? When he placed it back in the bag, I noticed he had two more. Interesting.

"I thought those judges didn't wander around much because they needed to recharge their power armor suits," Bishop said. "How is she out here, then? So far away from the Ex Cathedra power stations?"

"The Mark III variants can go a month before needing to be recharged. She's likely taking a gamble in order to retrieve the battery."

Which explained her attack on the Iron-Blooded and her continued pursuit into the lawless territories. If I had to guess, she was desperate to retrieve the battery and likely didn't want to return home to report a failure.

"What if we scared her?" Bishop ran a finger over the fresh cut on his chin. "I've got lots of explosives. People act real stupid when they get unnerved. It's easiest to kill them then."

"Don't bother. The JUDGE-X0 suits have special helmets that connect to the driver's head. They send electrical signals to the brain, stimulating certain hormone production in their adrenal glands. They keep the judges focused and . . . *angry* . . . for lack of a better term. So they don't buckle during combat."

The special connectors had to be embedded in the skull. It prevented someone from killing the judge inside the suit and then taking the suit for themselves. The damn power armor wouldn't function without the proper connectors.

"You sure do know a lot about judges," Bishop drawled. I remained quiet as he picked me up. "I'll have to dig up some more C4, just in case. Shit like killin' a judge requires a solid plan."

I chuckled. And, of course, I agreed with him. Whenever I had a firm grasp of the enemy's capabilities, along with enough time and resources, I typically came out on top.

Bishop carried me down three more streets, his steps careful not to disturb much in our surroundings. The stomp of his boots left a ghost of an echo, nothing that would be heard from a distance. Finally, he crossed a decimated parking lot, weaving between rusted cars, and only stopped once he reached the front door of a mall.

He glanced around, his eyes narrowed.

"What's wrong?" I whispered.

"I leave strings around the base of these doors. If they're disturbed, I know someone's been here."

With little effort, he knelt and examined the frame of the wide door. The strings—thin and translucent—would be difficult to see without direct light. But they were there.

"Good," Bishop said as he stepped over them. "Looks like no one has been this way."

"Are there other entrances?"

"Yeah. But I'm gonna drop you two off before I check them. If I have to deal with somethin', I don't want to be holdin' you."

I clung to Bishop as he headed deeper into the mall. Holes in the ceiling provided some light, but not much. Dust hung heavy in the air, and I coughed a few times before we made it to a shop with a door that kept most of the particles out.

Bishop flipped a switch, and four lamps flickered on.

"Light?" I asked.

"Yeah. I've hooked up a few atomic batteries." He pointed to a power strip with a portable power source. "I've been cleaning this place out. So much bullshit in here, ya know? There're enough supplies for an entire city, and this was just one mall. The damn city has, like, ten."

My grandfather had told me all kinds of stories about the world before the bombs. Vast seas of entertainment, food, and material objects. Sometimes he referred to such things as *bread and circuses.*

"That's what everyone wanted back then, my grandfather had said. Bread and circuses."

The shine of the lamps brought me back to the present.

I glanced around the shop. Nothing remained on the racks except tatters and threads. Large boxes filled the corners of the room, and a lone door in the back stood ajar. It was like seeing a phantom of the world before the bombs hit. My grandfather had been right. So many things, so many advertisements for sales and discounts. A world so peaceful it could focus on the wealth of the average person, yet they let it be destroyed.

"See those boxes?" Bishop asked. "They've got clothes. The bugs haven't gotten to them, so they're nice and clean. Go on, Crouton. You can change in the back room. There's a mirror and everything."

Crouton rushed off toward the boxes.

Bishop stared down at me. "What do you want?"

"Set me down. I'll do it myself."

"Like you did at the ramen cups?"

I didn't know what to say. Would he mock me for my pathetic display? I waited, but it didn't come. Still, I couldn't rely on him for something as simple as dressing myself. I had to have a baseline minimum of self-reliance.

Bishop set me down and waved at the boxes. "Suit yourself. I've gotta check those other entrances. Don't worry. This place will always be in my sights."

He left us to the shop, the hard crunch of his steps over broken glass a constant reminder he remained nearby. I turned back to the boxes. Using the counter, and then a few coat stands, I made my way over. Crouton had ripped open most of the boxes in a frantic search. I didn't know what she wanted specifically, but it was obvious she had something in mind.

To my amusement, most of the boxes were for women's clothing. Dresses. Skirts. Impractical shoes. Lovely items, no doubt, but nothing I'd want to wear out in the wasteland. There were bras and underwear—things I had, in the past, fashioned for myself out of other clothes, as both were harder to come by.

I tried a few on, not understanding the numbers for sizes, until I had something that fit. I repeated the process for a plain black shirt and a jacket. I needed them to fit, not only because I couldn't stand the thought of having something not sized perfectly, but because I didn't want my clothing loose enough to get caught on something, especially if I needed to move quickly or quietly. So I tried on several jackets—especially the kind with several pockets—until I found one that fit just right.

"Are you two done yet?" Bishop asked as he walked back into the shop.

Without pants on, and feeling rather foolish, I half hid behind a pile of boxes and shook my head.

Crouton, on the other hand, walked out of the back room, a smile on her clean face. She wore a pink dress. A frilly kind, with lace and shimmering material. It puffed out around the hips, and the hem fell to her knees.

Bishop snorted and laughed. "You can't wear that."

Crouton hugged herself and offered a glare.

"It's not practical. Look at your legs. We'll walk through one field of tall alien grass and you'll be chewed up by every insect and thistle. And I'm not gonna deal with cryin' kids, do you get me? So pick something else."

Mulling over his statements, Crouton rushed to the back. When she emerged a second time, she wore the same dress, but with a pair of thick leggings and large boots.

"Nope," Bishop said. "You can't wear it. Viper, tell her she has to change."

"What's wrong with the outfit now?" I asked.

"It stands out like a bloodstain on linen; that's what it does. The name of the game is *don't become a target of cannibals or marauders,* and she's ready to fail the first level."

Before I could weigh in, Crouton hastily grabbed a jacket and threw it over her dress. It hung long enough to cover the shimmery bits, and she could zip up the front. I didn't know why she was so desperate to wear the pretty outfit, but I could understand.

There weren't a lot of nice things out in the wasteland. At least, not for random travelers or rogues. Most cities had nicer things for those who could afford it, and I knew the judges and justices in Ex Cathedra lived easy so long as they served their government well.

"Are there many cannibals and marauders in these parts?" I asked.

"Of course. If you aren't in a city, there's a good fuckin' chance you'll run into someone lookin' to gut you. Where do you think I got most of my tally marks? And children have the worst of it."

Bishop walked over to Crouton and gave her the once-over. Crouton kept her jacket closed.

"We should at least cut your hair," he said. "It's still wet. Not good for you, and lots of assholes who lost their locks to radiation poisonin' like makin' wigs."

Crouton held her long black hair tight. She shook her head and instead tucked her hair inside her jacket.

With a huff, Bishop grabbed a beanie from a nearby box and covered Crouton's head.

"There," he said. "And it's blue. Matches your eyes."

Although Crouton was already in the process of ripping off the beanie, the one comment gave her pause. She hesitated, her fingers curled around the hat. After a few moments, she positioned it back in place, smoothing it over her head so it fit just right.

"And what about you?" Bishop turned his hard gaze over to me.

"Hm?"

"You know what will really get the marauders' attention? A young woman not wearin' any damn pants."

My face burned from the comment, and I struggled not to hide behind the boxes completely. "*Obviously* I'm not going to leave like this," I said, louder than I anticipated. "Obviously."

"Yeah, well, you said you could do it yourself, so let's see it." He stomped back over to the door of the shop. "It's a bad sign when Princess Crouton over here has her whole royal wardrobe picked out before you."

I grabbed the first pair of pants I came across in the box in front of me. They were cargo pants—multicolored green, like old-world military camouflage—and I managed to get one of my legs inside without much hassle. I had to lean against the wall afterward, but I managed to pull them on.

They were two sizes too big. An irritating itch filled my thoughts. I didn't like it. I wanted them to be the exact size. But Bishop motioned for me to hurry, and I didn't want to hold us up any more than I had already. So I grabbed a belt and secured the pants low on my hips—underneath the injury—and I promised myself I would fix it later, though that didn't stop my mind from dwelling on it.

I hobbled out from behind the boxes and made my way to Bishop. Before he picked me up, he pulled a necklace out of his pocket.

"I grabbed some tools, like you wanted," he said, "but I also got you this. You should have it. For good luck."

"You don't believe in things as irrational as luck, do you?"

Bishop placed the necklace in my palm. "Things happen that you can't explain. That's luck. And trust me, I thought of this the moment you said you'd try to kill me. It suits you."

I stared at the metal pendant hanging from the thin chain. It had the picture of a coiled snake with its fangs bared. Written around the circular edge were the words "Don't Tread on Me." Was that why he called me Viper?

It had been a long time since anyone had given me a gift.

I laughed. A nervous, uncertain laugh, but still. "Uh," I began, once again flustered from simple interactions. "Thank you."

"You also need to eat more." Bishop handed over another hardtack.

I took the food and chewed on it as he lifted me into his arms.

Crouton glanced from the necklace to Bishop, a tight frown on her face. He chuckled and motioned for her to follow with a tilt of his head.

"Not for you, Crouton. I'll try to find a tiara. You'd like that?"

She clapped the tips of her fingers together in a quiet show of appreciation.

Bishop carried me out of the mall and back into the heart of the ruined city. Crouton kept at his side and occasionally glanced underneath her jacket, as though in disbelief she still had her dress. It amused me more than it should have. Tamura had been an odd mix of tomboy and princess. Crouton's boots and dress combo reminded me of the details I had almost forgotten.

It didn't take us long to reach a parking garage.

Bishop grabbed a tarp on a nearby line of cars and pulled it off, revealing three rusty clunkers and one pickup truck. It was one of the fancy pickup trucks—the electric kind with an A-tech computer system and an exterior that resisted the elements better than most. It practically gleamed, even in the shadows, despite the cracked frame and nonexistent paint job.

I knew why Bishop liked it so much.

Crouton ran to the passenger side door. She threw it open and crawled in without any instruction. And much to my increasing surprise, she buckled herself in and sat ready with a smile.

Bishop got in the driver's side with me still in his arms. He set me down in the middle of the cab before throwing his stuff through the cab window and into the truck's bed. He kept his handgun close, which I appreciated, but his sniper rifle went in the back as well.

Most electric A-tech vehicles didn't have keys. Bishop touched the small computer screen. It scanned his fingerprints, and only afterward did the engine flare to life.

"Who programmed this for you?" I asked. Vehicles didn't just accept any fingerprints; they had to be registered in the vehicle's database during initial purchase.

"I did some work for a guy in Boulder," Bishop said with a smile. "He's one of the guys who runs the place, and they have lots of interesting stuff, let me tell you."

He pressed down on the forward pedal and drove out of the parking garage. The skeleton city passed by at a quick pace as I relaxed against the seat. The moment we left the ruins, desert flatland stretched out before us. Roads, signs, and the occasional field of alien weeds dotted the landscape. Mountains lined the horizon, but my eyes focused on the brown and gray of the terrain.

I was tired.

Could I sleep? Bishop could take us anywhere. Then again, if he wanted to do something heinous, he could've already. Of course, he could be taking me somewhere I didn't know about. The lawless territories dealt in the trade and sale of people all the time, either to Ex Cathedra as slaves or to roving bands of migratory people who needed an influx of "breeding stock."

Would Bishop do that? Sell us off?

The thought kept me awake. I forced myself to keep my eyes open, even when my body begged me for rest. I just couldn't take the risk.

Crouton slept with her head on my shoulder most of the ride.

The clouds grew dark, limiting our light, but Bishop drove with only one hand on the steering wheel, as though he'd taken the road a million times before.

"See that building over there?" he said, keeping his voice low. "Used to be a prison, back before the bombs. Now it's a damn mausoleum. Filled to the brim with corpses. Those prisoners never got released, apparently. Guards just took off after the world ended." He laughed, loud enough that Crouton stirred, but didn't wake. "Can you imagine? What a fucked-up way to go."

Bishop hadn't stopped talking since the drive began. He talked about our surroundings, the history of certain buildings, or how his truck got recharged, but next to nothing about himself. Made me wonder what kind of life he led.

"What about you?" I asked. "Tell me something about yourself."

He let out a long exhale. "I used to get sick around corpses. Damn things make you realize we'll all die someday. My grandmother would say this weird phrase. *All flesh is grass.*"

"What does it mean?" I whispered.

"Not entirely sure. But it made me think about death a little differently. It's all fleeting, ya know? Nations. Cities. Life. Everything has stages. Newborn. Adult. It's like we're living in Earth's *rotting corpse* stage of life."

Again, he laughed, though it was more melancholy than before.

I kept expecting him to talk about a wife or children—Dallas had been quick to mention them—but Bishop never did. Perhaps he didn't have anyone.

"Look." He pointed straight ahead. "There's Dodge City."

It wasn't hard to spot, especially given the dark clouds and gray surroundings.

Bright lights shone upward, like a lighthouse in the middle of the desert. I sat up, eager to get a better look. Most cities in Ex Cathedra had walls and soldiers. They kept the peace, but at a price. To disagree with any of the soldiers, no matter how absurd or disgusting their request, could cost people their life. Would Dodge City be the same?

"How long will we stay here?" I asked.

"The night. Tomorrow we'll head to Richfield. Technically, it's faster to go straight to George Town, but my doctor friend lives in Richfield. Shouldn't be too long a detour."

The closer and closer we got, the more details I absorbed. The signs on the side of the road read DODGE CITY—FOR ALL YOUR CAR NEEDS! and NO CREDIT, NO PROBLEM!

But those were the old-world advertisements. New phrases had been written with spray paint underneath. They read: COME STAY THE NIGHT! and NO SAFER PLACE AROUND!

When we neared the gates, everything fell into place.

Dodge City was an old-world automobile sales lot. Cars filled a massive parking lot—all glittering clean, driven nowhere—and people had affixed curtains to the windows, creating private spaces. The cars were used as hotel rooms now instead of vehicles. People stepped in and out of them, going about their business. Some of the vehicles even had mattresses inside.

And the lights weren't the only amazing feature of the city. Machines operated the gates, kept the place clean, and maintained the guns mounted around the premises.

The fence around Dodge City might've been flimsy, nothing but chain link, but that helped the automated guns target anyone approaching. Sure enough, two machine guns mounted into the concrete ground turned to face us, though nothing fired. They had clearly been added after the war—they were military grade, while the car lot was styled to be as friendly as possible.

Hundreds of people made their homes outside of the fence. Tents, shoddy wood huts, and campfires speckled the surrounding territory.

Bishop drove up to the gate and parked, but he didn't turn off the engine.

"Stay here," he said.

Crouton jerked awake. She blinked a couple times and shot up in her seat, her eyes wide.

Without another word, Bishop hopped out of the vehicle, leaving the door open, and headed toward a group of armed men at the gate. They had Dodge City badges around their neck. No doubt they were enforcers meant to keep the peace.

A man slammed up against the side of the truck, and my heart leapt into my throat.

"Hey there, girlie," he said, his breath odoriferous and his face a waterfall of grease.

I pushed Crouton behind me and glared at the man. What did he want? He wore a few layers of clothes, but that didn't hide his shoulder holster or handgun. And everything on him had a fine layer of dirt or blood.

"Wow, you're mighty fine," he said, offering me the most crooked smile I had ever seen. "How much is Bishop paying you for the night?"

I was on the verge of reaching into the back of the truck and pulling out a grenade when Bishop finally walked back over.

"Get outta here, Thatcher," Bishop snapped. "What the fuck did I say about touchin' my truck?"

"Hey, hey. Me and the lady were havin' us a conversation. Ain't that right, miss?"

Bishop shoved Thatcher away as he stepped back up into the driver's seat. "She doesn't want a disgusting roach in her bed. Beat it."

"I got what every lady wants." Thatcher grabbed his crotch and hefted, chortling like he was the cleverest man alive.

Bishop snorted back a laugh. "Oh, really? Have you seen your teeth? Nine out of ten dentists recommend suicide."

"H-Hey!"

Bishop stepped on the forward pedal and drove us through the gates to Dodge City. Although the situation had been handled, my heart still beat hard in my chest. Men like Thatcher were commonplace, even in Ex Cathedra. I hated the idea of being at the mercy of another.

I reached into the back bed of the truck.

"What're you doing?" Bishop asked.

"I'm getting a bottle of water."

And one of Bishop's gas grenades.

I would keep it on me, just in case. It would be a parting blow should anyone fuck with me—or if Bishop tried anything suspicious. It was petty, but I wanted to know that whoever did me in would at least get their comeuppance.

CHAPTER TEN

Bishop tapped the side of the "hotel room car" with his knuckles. It was a Dodge brand vehicle—large, four doors, a mattress in the back—located in the middle of the Dodge City lot.

"You and Crouton can sleep here," he said.

Other people crowded around their respective "rooms," everyone chatting in casual tones. Although no one acted aggressive, everyone had guns, most of which were on display, like they were rattles on a snake, warning the world of danger should they be messed with. But I preferred that to an atmosphere of quiet worry and terror. At least I knew what the people around me were capable of, and the threat of mutual destruction did keep everyone in line.

"Thank you," I said. "And where will you be sleeping?"

Bishop leaned in closer and smiled. "Are you trying to ask me to stay the night with you?"

I leaned away and crossed my arms over my chest, unable to look him in the eye. "I was just curious."

He stepped back. "Hm. I'll be spending the night with my friend, Joyce."

Bishop motioned to a group of cars separated from the rest. They were rent-by-the-hour and adorned with all sorts of heart-shaped signs.

I lifted an eyebrow. "Your *friend?* Is that what they're called here? We had a different term for them in Ex Cathedra."

Bishop scoffed. "Fine. I'm gonna spend my night with a whore. Happy? Or do you want all the gritty details?"

Crouton tilted her head.

"You don't have to say it in front of her," I said under my breath.

"What? It's not like she's gonna repeat anything I say." Bishop turned away, throwing a hand up in the air. "I was the one who tried to be decent in the first place." A few feet away, he stopped and glanced over his shoulder. "Thanks for helpin' me back there. If you want my doctor friend's info, hit me up. Otherwise, good luck getting to Boulder, or wherever you said you needed to go."

I nodded. "Yeah. Have fun."

It was an awkward way to send him off. I knew it the moment I said the words. Even Bishop stared for a moment before heading out. But I didn't really know what to say to him. A piece of me didn't want him to go too far.

Maybe I just wanted his company.

Pushing the thoughts from my mind, I opened the car and got inside. A single light, powered by an atomic battery welded to the roof, shone above us. Crouton sat up front, adjusting the portal radio tied to the steering wheel. It had two tabs glued to the side, each describing the two radio broadcasts available for the area. One offered music and emergency news, while the other was simply labeled "Family Entertainment."

Crouton switched the radio to the family entertainment channel and smiled as pleasant music played throughout the car.

"You can read?" I asked.

Crouton nodded.

I caught my breath, scolding myself for not asking earlier. "Can you spell your name?"

She held up her empty hands.

"Spell it in the air."

Crouton pantomimed out the letters, writing each large and slow so I could follow along.

C-H-E-L-S-Y

"Chelsy? That's a pretty name."

She shook her head.

"You don't like it?"

Again, she shook her head.

"Would you . . . rather I keep calling you Crouton?"

She nodded.

Odd. I didn't understand her need to avoid her name—I liked the name *Kita*—and although Crouton could spell, I doubted she wanted to have an in-depth discussion one letter at a time.

She jumped from the front and onto the mattress in the back. Multiple blankets padded her fall. She grabbed each and threw them around, creating a soft bed out of our limited materials.

The music cut out, and I tensed, fearing some sort of emergency broadcast.

"And now for story hour," a man spoke nasally over the radio.

The hushed voice of a woman in the background added, "Just read the book this time."

"Okay, okay, I got it." The radioman increased his volume and with a showman's enunciation said, "Tonight's story will be *The Atomic Alert*."

I smiled. Ex Cathedra didn't have radio stations dedicated to such entertainment. The fact anyone would take the time to spread such tales around for the sake of families lifted my spirits. What benefit did the radio stations gain from such an act?

Crouton edged her way to the end of the mattress, her elbows on her knees and her head in both her palms.

"Once upon a time, there was a little boy who lived in a city surrounded on every side by fields with irrigation ditches. He had just left his house to visit his grandmother when he came across a peddler on the side of the road." Each word carried with it an artistic weight, as though the man's calling were melodrama.

The flipping of pages echoed over the radio. "Ugh," the radioman said with a huff. He kept his voice low as he added, "What's with how depressing these are?"

"It's a cautionary tale," the background woman said. "Read the damn book. We talked about this. It's good for kids."

"Everyone dies at the end in horrific detail."

"That's the point of a cautionary tale, *Ruben*. You don't want kids playing in places with radiation."

"Do I really need to read about how the skin sloughs off? Or the bleeding blisters?"

I turned to Crouton and yawned. After I got myself under control, I said, "If anything happens, wake me up, okay? I'll deal with whatever comes our way."

Crouton reached into her jacket and withdrew a three-inch pocket-knife. I flinched away, expecting her to hurt herself somehow, but she twirled it between her fingers and smiled. Then she motioned a few silent stabs and gave me a thumbs-up.

"Violence isn't always the solution," I said, though a little uncertain of the claim. Violence was needed in a great many instances. Those who didn't use violence would be ruled by it—or so my grandfather would say. And I did have a grenade in my pocket. "Where did you get that?"

She spelled out the word *truck*.

"Listen, I don't think you should take things from Bishop without his permission. He seems a little protective of his belongings. Understand?"

She nodded.

"And who taught you how to hold a knife like that?"

Crouton pulled out the three figurines and pointed to the father.

Dallas was a soldier, after all.

"Well, let me try words before you go slicing and dicing, okay?"

Again, she nodded.

The man and woman on the radio continued to argue as I rested back against the mattress. Their words never entered my mind, but the bickering created a pleasant white noise that dulled my overtaxed thoughts. The moment my head hit the blankets, I closed my eyes and breathed evenly. My fears about the future disappeared with my consciousness.

A harsh knock on the side of the car jerked me from the tranquility.

I sat up, my eyes crusty from sleep.

Sleep?

Had I slept? I just went to bed.

I glanced around the car. Crouton slumbered in a burrito of blankets, her long black hair spilling out the top. My three figurines sat on the edge of the mattress, two toppled over, but all three together. The radio buzzed with static inactivity, and the time across the screen told me five hours had passed.

Five hours? I shook my head.

It felt like two seconds.

Another harsh knock drew me back to the present. I scooted to the door and opened it.

A woman stood outside, a backpack on one shoulder and a cigarette between her lips. No, not a cigarette—tobacco had a reddish-brown color, and the inside of her cigarette was black. She smoked a stick of hane, a type of cigarette made from the alien weeds. Easy to grow, easy to dry, easy to roll.

The woman exhaled a line of smoke. "You new here? Just come in?"

I managed to step out of the vehicle without grimacing and offered her a nod.

"Did you see any activity in the north? People around the old government buildings?"

"What's this about?" I asked.

Other people went from car to car, dressed just like the woman, knocking on the doors and asking similar questions. Something to the north. A government building. Seemed strange. I hadn't seen anything suspicious when we drove in. Then again, I had been listening to Bishop nonstop as we traveled.

"People say they saw some of the Iron-Blooded," the woman said. She had a deep scar over her face, one that took a chunk from her nose. "They got into those government buildings somehow. I need to know if you saw anything. I've got some hane if you got info."

"I didn't see anything."

"Eh."

The woman left without even a farewell, straight to another car.

But I didn't care about that. The information she had inadvertently given me sank into my thoughts. The Iron-Blooded got into a building *somehow*—emphasis on the mystery—but I knew. The fission battery. It was how I'd gotten into the military base. The Iron-Blooded used it to power up the facility and get inside.

But why? What did the Iron-Blooded hope to gain in these government buildings? And what kind of buildings were they? *Government building* was a catchall term used for fortified places with lockdown procedures. It could be a military facility, or a lab, or even a records office.

All such buildings housed old-world treasures, however. Everyone wanted inside.

I turned my attention to the scarred woman asking questions. She went from vehicle to vehicle until she reached the end of the lot. Her fellow inquisitors met her and discussed their findings before heading to the gate out of the city.

Junk hunters. Like Bishop.

They searched the wasteland for valuables and traded them in cities. A risky profession, but rewarding. All it took was one good find and most junk hunters could effectively retire. They were the forty-niners of the wasteland—opportunists that went where the salvaging was good.

I rubbed at my face, my thoughts dwelling on the Iron-Blooded.

If these were the same Iron-Blooded that tortured me in the mountains, there couldn't be many left. Not after Judge Gascoigne's attack and Bishop killing a few in the city. I hadn't seen any others, which meant their numbers were ever dwindling.

And they had a fission battery with them. But the junk hunters didn't know that.

My heart rate increased, and my hands shook with nervous anticipation. In theory, I could go to this building and retrieve my battery. In theory.

The car door opened, and Crouton made her way to the edge of the passenger seat. She glanced up at me, her eyes half-lidded.

"Crouton, can you take me to see Bishop?" I asked.

She rubbed her face with the back of her hand and jumped to her feet. With a determined look set on her face, she offered me her shoulder.

The cool evening air swept through Dodge City, whistling between the cars. Although I had slept for five hours, it wasn't morning. The dark clouds hung low in the sky, swollen and close to bursting. Darkness loomed beyond the bright lights of the city limits, obscuring the vast desert.

Rainfall would kill almost any vegetation that wasn't from the aliens due to the nuclear fallout still in the atmosphere and water. It was why people had to use elaborate growing techniques or greenhouses in order to keep Earth crops alive. Though I guessed it didn't matter.

We made our way to the rent-by-the-hour cars, but the moment we got close, a couple men with Dodge City badges—peacekeepers meant to keep the order—stepped in our way.

"We don't allow children to work this area," one guy said.

They both held rifles, but with lax grips.

"We're not here to work," I said. "I need to see a man named Bishop. Do you know him?"

The men exchanged wicked grins.

"Yeah," the guy said. "We know him. What do you want?"

"Can you tell him Kita wants to speak? Or maybe just call me Viper." A piece of me wondered if he actually remembered my real name.

After a short sigh, one of the peacekeepers walked between the love-cars and stopped at one in the middle. He tapped the butt of his gun against the door and waited. A few seconds later, it opened. Bishop leaned his head out, his hair plastered to one side and his eyes still closed.

"What? I still got time."

"Someone's here for you," the peacekeeper said. "A woman and a kid. Said her name was Kita."

Bishop groaned. He shut the door, it shook for a moment, and then he emerged again, his hair still disheveled, but at least he had pants on. I focused on his many tally mark scars as he walked toward us, stretching the entire way.

"What's wrong?" he asked, a slight mocking tone to his voice. "Have a nightmare? Need me to tuck you in?"

A soft odor of booze clung to him. He didn't stagger or lose eye contact, but I did fear he wouldn't be up to the task of leaving town.

I lowered my voice and said, "I need to speak with you about . . . gathering some valuable things."

Maybe it was my cryptic phrasing or quiet tone, but something about my statement intrigued Bishop. He smiled wide enough to flash teeth and then motioned back to the car.

"Oh, yeah? One minute. I'm gonna get my shit and we'll talk about the details in my truck."

It didn't take him long to get his shirt, jacket, and boots. Bishop returned and offered his arm. I half walked with his support, thankful he hadn't picked me up without warning. Then he withdrew a few sandwiches from his bag, each wrapped in brown paper. He handed me one and then another to Crouton.

Flat bread, some sort of meat, and three kinds of vegetables—nothing I had ever eaten together before.

"What is this made out of?" I asked.

"Goat," Bishop said. "And some carrots, beets, and A-grass."

Crouton bit into hers without a second's hesitation. She chewed for a prolonged period of time—no doubt the meat wasn't top quality—but she never stopped or complained.

I examined my sandwich, enjoying the warm feel in my hand. "You paid for this?"

"Yeah. Like I said, thanks for helping me back there."

His truck, parked inside the city at a small lot for junk-hunter vehicles, had a few peacekeepers circling around. Bishop nodded to them, they acknowledged him by name, and we got into the cab of his vehicle without hassle.

"Don't drip the sandwich on the seats," Bishop said, giving Crouton a sidelong glance.

Her fingers, face, and arms looked like a sandwich murder scene. She gobbled down the rest and then stared at her dirty hands. Bishop opened the glove compartment and threw her a small towel.

"Kids," he said with a sigh. Then he turned to me. "Now what're you goin' on about? What stuff should we acquire?"

"Some junk hunters are heading to a government building the Iron-Blooded opened. I think there aren't many Iron-Blooded there, given the numbers that left the mountain and the fact the judge either killed or separated them."

"Uh-huh. And?"

"And if a bunch of junk hunters are there, perhaps we could just sneak in behind them and avoid the Iron-Blooded altogether."

"*We?* You'd weigh me down, Viper. And don't give me any *buts*. You know your leg is messed up."

I'd already known this would become an issue, so I took a deep breath and held up a hand. "Look, I've made it across the wasteland for years on my own. It's because I know how to hack and picklock a lot of these A-tech places."

Bishop stared off into the distance, his gaze unforced. "Okay. And you're sayin' we need to go together because you can get us stuff inside the building? With your skills? And we'll split what we come across, fifty-fifty?"

I liked the concise way he summed up my plan. I nodded, hoping he'd be gung ho, but then he turned back to me with a serious gaze.

"How'd the Iron-Blooded get in?" he asked.

"Most likely my fission battery, but I'm not completely sure."

"That fission battery you lost?"

"Yes. The same one."

"And you want it back?"

I hesitated. Did Bishop want half of the battery? There was no way to split it. Or maybe he would take it for himself?

"I do want it back," I finally said.

He grinned. "Yeah, that's what I was hopin' you'd say. I love cuttin' down Iron-Blooded assholes. You're gonna get some more tally marks, right? Show these lunatics you don't mess with a viper?"

I chuckled. I hadn't planned on revenge, but I had already run over four of them.

There was a lot to hate about Commander Dannik. And the idea of stealing back my fission battery did fill me with more happiness than it probably should have. Perhaps Bishop was right.

"Sure," I said.

I'd need the battery for wherever I ended up at. It could literally sustain me and a small town for the rest of my life, whether or not I made it to the BC Oasis.

Bishop started up the truck. "Let's go raid us some old buildings."

The unrelenting darkness unnerved me a bit. Bishop drove without his headlights for a good portion, just like I had on the mountainside. It was good practice—no one wanted attention out in the middle of nowhere— but the void of night didn't bring with it much visibility.

A lot of animals came out when it was dark, some more aggressive than others. At least, in Ex Cathedra. I assumed it would be the same, considering that the animal population thrived between zones of radiation, free from the vast numbers of humans that once lived there. Some animals could even venture into the radiation without much harm, no doubt having adapted to the terrible environmental hazard after several generations.

Bishop parked, though I had no idea where we were.

"Are we close?" I asked.

He nodded. "We don't wanna drive up, or else everyone will know we're tryin' to cut in on their loot." He pointed at Crouton. "You stay here."

She turned to me, like Bishop's words meant nothing unless I backed them up.

"You should stay here," I said.

Crouton smiled and gave me two thumbs up. She sat back without a fuss, not even a glower, and Bishop seemed pleased with the quick acceptance.

But I knew better. My fourth rule to lying: never ham it up. Most people could spot overacting, even if they couldn't articulate what about the performance seemed off. Crouton was a tad obstinate and never wanted to leave our side. She wasn't planning on listening to us now—she'd sneak out of the truck and follow behind us; I would bet my life on it.

I placed a hand on her shoulder. "It's dangerous. What would Dallas say if you were taken by the Iron-Blooded again? After everything he did to get you free?"

Crouton froze. She stared at me, her blue eyes drilling into mine. Then she turned away and glanced out the passenger window, her faux happiness melting into a melancholy expression. I suspected she would actually stay this time.

Bishop opened the door and jumped out. He grabbed his bag and sniper rifle before he motioned for me to follow. I hopped out, and he took me into his arms immediately. A faster way to travel, but I was starting to hate the mode of transportation. I wanted to walk, but now wasn't the time to satisfy my pride.

"Who's Dallas?" he asked.

"Chelsy's father."

He snorted and laughed. "Who's Chelsy?"

"Oh, uh, that's Crouton's real name."

"Oh, so you *do* know her name. What? You don't trust me? Can't tell me the damn kid's name? What would I even do with the information that you would need to keep it hidden?"

"Sorry," I said as he walked around the truck. "It's not that. Turns out Crouton knows her letters. She spelled her real name out for me in the car."

"And where's Dallas if he's her father? Dead?"

"I . . . don't know. He saved us from the Iron-Blooded." I closed my eyes and forced a smile. "Well, *saved* isn't accurate. He's the one that got me caught in the first place. He traded my life for his daughter's."

"Sounds like a tally mark if I ever heard of one. Any asshole who gets involved with the Iron-Blooded is so inbred they might as well be a fence post."

For a moment, I almost told him it was Dallas I planned to meet in Boulder City, but I thought better of it. I doubted Bishop would want to hear it. Even *I* didn't know how to truly feel about the situation. I couldn't forgive Dallas, even if I understood his motives. But he should have his daughter back.

Bishop's steps shifted with the loose sand and dirt. He held me close as we walked, but he had an odd scent about him. Sex, alcohol, sweat—it wasn't the worst I'd experienced, just distinct. I should've insisted he wash himself before leaving.

"If we're gonna wander around unclaimed territory, we'll need to keep a Geiger counter close," Bishop whispered. "I hate these parts. You never know what kind of bullshit you'll run into."

To my surprise, I spotted lights past a grouping of boulders. Buildings—a couple of them behind a broken wall. Was it a compound?

Bishop set me down near a few knee-high rocks. We crouched together. "Here we are."

I couldn't see a damn thing besides the lights in the distance. Bishop slung his sniper rifle off his back. Before he put the thing together for firing, he flipped a switch on the scope and stared down it.

"More people than I thought there'd be."

"How many?" I asked.

"Maybe ten junk hunters. All millin' about the outside. No sight of the Iron-Blooded."

He passed the butt of the rifle over to me. Although I had some reservations, I took it and glanced down the scope. The night vision green-and-black sight allowed me to see everything that lurked in the darkness. Bishop was correct—ten people wandered around the outside of the compound, some with their hands on their hips, others motioning to the doors.

I turned the scope beyond the compound and glanced around the surrounding territory. Far off, half-hidden by rocks, was an Iron-Blooded jeep.

"They're here," I whispered. "The Iron-Blooded must be inside."

"But they didn't defend the outside? There isn't even a single man positioned as a guard."

Of course not. They didn't have anyone to spare, not if they were going to clean out the inside of a massive compound.

And what could be inside? Something more valuable than a fission battery?

When I returned my attention to the junk hunters, one withdrew a handgun. I recognized the scar over the face—the woman from Dodge City. Before I could grasp much of the situation, she leveled her gun at another and pulled the trigger. The crack of the bullet sent a shiver down my spine.

Nine junk hunters.

"What happened?" Bishop asked.

"One person . . . shot another." I handed him back his rifle. "Why would they do that?"

"Probably couldn't agree on a way to split the findings," Bishop said with a shrug. "People don't like to share. Trust me. Junk hunters do some crazy shit sometimes to gather up as much as possible." He laughed and tapped me on the shoulder with his knuckles. "I thought you were a junk hunter at first, ya know."

Another crack of a handgun.

Eight junk hunters.

Regardless of the distant violence, Bishop continued, still amused, "I thought you must be lyin' to me or tryin' to make off with my stuff after I brought you to civilization. I even paid the guards around Dodge City to stop you from leaving if you tried to sneak off without me. Funny, right? I should've just trusted my gut."

"Good to know," I muttered.

It occurred to me then—why would Bishop trust me? I wasn't willing to give *him* the benefit of the doubt, after all. Of course he thought I was going to do something underhanded. Still, I disliked that he tried to trap me somewhere. I would have to think of contingencies for the future.

"Do you mind if I have the scope back for a second?" I asked.

Bishop handed it over. "If the Iron-Blooded are here, we should wait for our trigger-happy junk hunters to go in first. Maybe the two groups can cull each other and we'll slink in afterward."

I used the scope to examine the outside of the compound. My attention focused on the lettering mounted to the side of the main building. It wasn't English, but Tethlite.

TETH RESEARCH AND DEVELOPMENT
LOCATION #04

A Teth alien research facility. And then I knew why the Iron-Blooded were interested in getting inside—they worshipped those space monsters enough that they'd want to retrieve every relic they could. Or maybe even recover alien DNA.

Or maybe even one of the aliens themselves.

CHAPTER ELEVEN

The clouds overhead rumbled in warning.

We waited for the junk hunters to make their move, but each second that passed filled my thoughts with anxiety. There was a small possibility—infinitesimal—that aliens were inside. But I shook my head. Without power to the compound, they would've died off. No chance any survived.

Absolutely none.

"They're goin' in," Bishop said.

I glanced through the scope and caught the last of the junk hunters entering the compound. From what I saw, there were three entrances, and the junk hunters split up to take each route. No gunshots rang out afterward, which meant the Iron-Blooded weren't lying in wait inside.

Well, unless they used silent weapons, but even then I suspected the junk hunters would manage to react and make some sort of commotion.

Bishop got to his feet and scooped me into his arms. He made his way through the darkness, half stumbling over a cluster of rocks and cursing. We reached our destination in one piece, though.

Rain trickled down all around us as Bishop pressed his back against the wall of the main building. He took in a few deep breaths and then held one. Although the drizzle created a white noise, the echo of footsteps inside could still be heard. Soon they faded into the distance, and Bishop set me down.

"You should have a handgun," he said. "Just in case."

"I can't use it. I just can't."

"And if you get shot?"

"Then I guess I'll end up a tally mark," I intoned.

Bishop glanced away from me. "Suit yourself. But I'll go in first. You search out the rooms I tell you are clear, okay? If we run into trouble, just get behind some furniture."

"I understand."

"And don't go tryin' to hide stuff from me, got it? You said fifty-fifty."

I didn't know how to assure him that I wasn't trying to swindle him out of any items we would salvage—I knew I wouldn't and I had already said I wouldn't, but that didn't ring deep enough. What would?

"You can always search me afterward," I said. "If you're worried."

He glanced over his shoulder, giving me an odd look. "Maybe I will."

"Fine."

Bishop replied with a click of his tongue before slipping inside the building.

I waited, the rain coming down harder with each passing minute. The smell—it had a sour odor that betrayed the chemicals laced in the water.

"It's clear," Bishop called out.

I slipped inside, half wet and shivering. My jacket protected me from the worst of it, but my oversized pants didn't seem to keep the heat in as much as I would have liked.

The lights provided a small bit of comfort. The room around me had several computer stations, each set up neat and compact. Not for aliens— but humans. I glanced around and took in more details. Although the sign outside said this was a Teth research and development facility, this was obviously a human military outpost. I hobbled my way to a computer station, determined to find an explanation.

The archaic systems booted, but only after a long minute of waiting. When I pulled up the map, I found my explanation.

The alien research and development took place in the basement floors— B1 through B4. The ground-floor level was intended for human and alien interactions and press meetings. I didn't stop with the map, however. The more I studied the floor plans, the more I realized the basement floors had always had power, even during and after the Forever Winter.

It made sense. The research done right before the bombs dropped had been top priority. No one would want to risk losing anything over a simple power outage. All the critical floors, therefore, were connected to a backup power generator—a fission reactor.

The top floor, the one deemed not as important, had the same setup as the military base I had searched back in Ex Cathedra, almost like a separate entity altogether.

Bishop jogged back into the room and glanced around. The moment he spotted me, he walked over.

"What have you been doing?" he whispered. "I thought you were following behind me."

"I . . . need to check some stuff."

"With the computers?"

"Yes."

"Does it have an inventory listing of what's here or something?"

"Of course."

I had no idea. And it wasn't what I was curious about. I wanted to know what the Iron-Blooded hoped to gather and whether or not aliens could actually be in the facility.

Bishop stood next to me, his attention focused on the doors, but he never rushed or hurried me along, no matter how much typing I did.

When I brought up a directory of videos, I stopped and thought about the one I had watched at the other military base. It had been a waste of time—I didn't need to know anything about the world of the past—but three videos caught my attention.

TO: Dr. Benjamin Yamasaki, Urgent (*Undelivered*)
TO: Dr. Benjamin Yamasaki, Warning (*Undelivered*)
TO: Dr. Benjamin Yamasaki, Final (*Undelivered*)

Benjamin Yamasaki . . . My grandfather.

Three videos were addressed to him.

Curiosity got the better of me. I opened the first video and sat back to watch it, but the moment the speaker came onto the screen, I gasped.

Bishop whipped around and cocked an eyebrow. "What the fuck is that?"

The video showed us something horrific. Sitting at a computer terminal, much larger than any human, was one of the Teth—a fucking alien. The lights in the video remained low, and I knew why. The Teth didn't care for bright lights, as it dried out their skin. They had no eyes and no need for illumination.

"*Dr. Benjamin Yamasaki, my kin of different blood,*" the alien said, its slur-language singsong when it came from the aliens themselves.

My kin of different blood. A formal honorific reserved for the closest of friends. My grandfather only ever said it to one person when he spoke Tethlite, and that was to his son's wife, my mother. It was a special phrase in Tethlite that caught my attention immediately.

This alien and my grandfather were once close friends.

The alien exhaled a ragged breath.

No matter its connection with my grandfather, it was still disgusting.

Each of the aliens, no matter the caste, had black skin with a matte texture—lusterless and dull. They had four arms: two large, two thin and fine. The large arms contained a mass of muscle and ended in claws. The thin arms and hands had a level of control beyond anything humans could perform. The whole alien species basically had tools for personal combat and tools for master-level craftsmanship all in their limbs.

The alien in the video typed away at the computer terminal with his spindly hands, the fingers twice as long as any human's.

"I told you Miri'Cova would betray us," the alien continued. *"Now the planet will burn. But I got my revenge. As he headed for the space force docks, I sabotaged the flight. He'll drift endlessly in space, his own children his sole source of food until he succumbs to starvation. Or perhaps he'll take the coward's way and end himself. Either way, it wasn't enough. He deserves the fire of a thousand suns, but to dwell on such amusements is folly."*

"Fuck," Bishop whispered. "I've never seen one that can talk. Only the drones."

"This one is an innovator," I said. "They're very intelligent."

The aliens weighed much more than humans. The average innovator carried three hundred pounds of corded muscle. And it showed, even in the video. The desk for the alien was much larger than anything in the front room I sat in.

"Dr. Benjamin Yamasaki, my kin of different blood," it said. *"I fear we've lost. I may never see you again. I whisper safe tidings to the deep that this message finds you before it's too late."*

Then the video cut out. I clicked on the second without a moment's hesitation.

Again, the screen brought up the same alien. I hated the way they spoke. They had no lips, just the massive canines, incisors, and molars. They made all syllables with their tongue, which squirmed around in their mouth—the only sign they were talking if there was no audio.

"*Dr. Benjamin Yamasaki, my kin of different blood,*" it said, a strain to its voice. "*Forgive me, but I could not stop it. In his last effort to spite us, Miri'Cova has tampered with the climate engineering satellites.*"

Held rapt by the message, my mind barely recovered the memories of my grandfather explaining the climate engineering satellites—the CES systems. They were A-tech on a planetary scale, meant to carefully control the weather. No unwanted storms. No adverse effects from greenhouse gases. Perfect weather brought about by a system of flawlessly controlled satellites and lasers that could seed clouds and heat the winds to affect their direction.

My grandfather said they had stopped functioning after the bombs. Humanity's greatest loss.

The alien hissed and then continued, "*Miri'Cova set the satellites to burn Earth's atmosphere.*"

The one statement caught me by surprise. I held my breath, my blood leaving my face.

"*I did all I could from here,*" the alien said. "*But it wasn't enough. I've delayed the attack through the satellite's weather countdown system. I'm sorry, my kin of different blood, but the bombs have already hit. It is now a countdown to extinction—should the atmosphere be destroyed, so will go the last of humanity. I implore you to seek the Meteorological Plexus. If you can reach the plexus, the satellites can be changed from their course. As it stands, they'll do nothing until the appointed time to set the ozone ablaze.*"

A piece of me thought the message was a joke—or perhaps this alien was overreacting. The atmosphere still existed, after all, so whatever he was talking about must have passed. Perhaps my grandfather made it to the Meteorological Plexus and changed the satellites. Though . . . he never mentioned it. Not once. Not even when he told me about the CES systems.

"*Forty-seven years until the satellites activate,*" the alien said, a finality to its tone. "*I hope you see this before then. I have no one else to turn to. The others never responded to my calls. I fear they're dead, just as I will be. Goodbye, my kin of different blood. May we meet again in another void.*"

Then the video switched off.

I waited a few seconds, stunned and unmoving.

How long since the Forever Winter? My heart beat hard against my ribs, to the point each breath came painful and short.

Forty-five and a half years.

No. No.

No.

All of it was coincidence. This was surely some sort of bizarre fever dream or miscommunication. There was no way someone didn't know about this. Someone had to have attempted to fiddle with the CES systems already, and surely they fixed everything. Absolutely no way I was the only one who knew about this impending extinction.

But the two videos now read *delivered* when they had previously been marked as *undelivered*. Which meant I was the first to see these videos since they were created.

No one was here. No one could get inside. My grandfather had been far from here, helping humanity survive during the Forever Winter. And then he died, never to return to this place.

How could I be the only one to know? Even Bishop didn't know, despite the fact he'd watched the video. He didn't speak Tethlite. Literally, I was the only one who knew. The sole person who received a dire message.

All of my problems felt so petty afterward. A fission battery? The BC Oasis? The Iron-Blooded in the building with me? None of it mattered if the atmosphere was due to be destroyed. None of it.

Bishop moved behind me and placed a hand on my shoulder. I flinched, my whole body trembling.

"What's wrong?" he whispered, his eyes fixated on something across the room. "You don't look well."

"Bishop," I said, uncertain of how to word the news. "The world is going to end."

He stifled a laugh. "News flash: the world ended decades ago."

"No . . . it's not like before."

"Look, I don't know why you're freaking out over some home video, but it's just gibberish. If you're looking for a vid to sell, it needs to pass a one-question test. Ask yourself, *can you masturbate to it*? If the answer is *yes*, then it's a good find. If the answer is *no*, then leave it. And trust me, creepy aliens hanging around in a dark room and whispering shit isn't gonna get people excited."

I nodded and exhaled. Of course Bishop would think I was wasting my time. How could something so important just be sitting around?

It couldn't be real. It had to be some problem long since dealt with by somebody else. Certainly it wouldn't fall to *me*, a cripple girl from Ex Cathedra, to deal with such a massive problem.

The creak of floorboards got me tense all over again. Bishop readied his handgun and moved around the desk, his expression intense, but always with a smile.

Crouton emerged from the other side of the door, her blue beanie tight on her head and her jacket wrapped around her body. She froze the moment she spotted Bishop with the gun.

He lowered it and growled out a string of curse words under his breath.

"*What're you doing?*" Bishop hissed. "I told you to wait in the damn truck!"

She offered a few flailed motions with her hands, but ultimately stopped and shrugged. Bishop grabbed the collar of her jacket and jerked her close.

"Listen. You can't be here. Do you understand me? It's dangerous."

Again, she flailed something with her hands, but I didn't know what she was trying to say. Her eyes filled with water, and she stared at the floor, her lip trembling.

Why would she come this way, even after what I said? Was she worried about us? Or perhaps she was afraid of losing someone else. It occurred to me that she didn't have anyone—just two random strangers. No more family. Being left alone might be one of her ultimate fears if she had risked the rainy trek to see us again.

"She can help me walk," I said.

Bishop shot a glare in my direction. I didn't mind.

"Better than sending her back into the darkness," I whispered.

"Fine," Bishop said, curt.

Crouton ran over to me. I patted her back, but I didn't get up from my chair. I clicked on the last video, intent on seeing what else happened.

When the video started up, Crouton grabbed my arm, her eyes wide. Perhaps she had never seen one of the aliens before.

"*Dr. Benjamin Yamasaki, my kin of different blood,*" it said, its voice ragged. "*I fear this will be the last communication I ever make.*"

The alien wore armor—the type all the innovator Teth wore, different than the other alien clans—with skintight sleekness that molded to the muscular frame of the aliens. They stood on two legs, like humans, but they had longer necks that ended in elongated heads. No matter how cordial this alien was, I still thought it was hideous.

"*No word from you,*" it said. "*No word from anyone. My computers tell me the satellites are still set for annihilation. Months now, I've had nothing. The facility maintains itself, but my research will have to come to a close. I thought*

I could . . . improve the last of humanity and Teth kind . . . I thought I should tell you . . . I enjoyed our conversations together . . . and your insight helped with much of my research . . . I must show you something . . . that you helped me create . . ."

Its fading words got under my skin.

Before the alien could finish, it let out a long, ragged breath and walked out of the camera's view.

After a minute of filming the back wall, the video cut out. Nothing else. Determined to get some more useful information, I rewound it and upped the contrast, allowing me to see into the darkness. Where had it been filmed? I saw a sign on the far wall. It read FLOOR 3.

And what had it wanted to say?

It didn't matter. Besides my grandfather, I didn't recognize the name of the other person or understand the situation. Revenge? Vindictive actions? Some sort of betrayal? It was all a soap opera from an era long past. None of those details mattered anymore. All that mattered was what remained.

"What's with you?" Bishop asked. "If you told me you wanted to watch aliens hide around in the dark, I could've taken you someplace nice to see it."

"I'm sorry," I muttered. With Crouton's help, I stood. "We can continue."

"Are you sure? No more detours. Not with the kid in tow, got it?"

"Yes. That's fine."

"Good."

Bishop headed off down the first hall, but my thoughts were on distant possibilities. Could the world be ending soon, and everyone was blissfully unaware?

There was one way to find out. One way to check if the problem had been handled.

I needed to get down a few floors and check the aliens' computer terminal. If I could see the status of the CES system from there, I would know whether someone had dealt with it or not. But . . . even if I knew of Earth's destruction, what did it matter? Knowing I had little over a year to live didn't change much. I could fit as much life as possible in the remaining months, but that would never satisfy me, not when I wanted things to be just right.

I shook the thought from my head.

I could deal with it later. Instead, I resolved to deal with the immediate. I would get my fission battery and check the computer terminal.

And then I would make new plans.

CHAPTER TWELVE

Bishop, this way," I said, pointing to a long hall.

My anxious need to get through the building wouldn't settle. I needed to assuage my dread and find out what had happened with the satellites.

Bishop stopped and made his way back to me, his gaze darting around to each door and entryway. "What's down there?"

"The reserve power room. It's where the Iron-Blooded must have installed the fission battery."

"You're sure?"

"Yes."

Before Bishop could make up his mind, a series of rapid-fire shots rang throughout the building. I held my breath and stared down the hall. The sounds of violence had come from the same direction.

Crouton held my arm tight.

"Seems people found each other," Bishop muttered. "Let's go."

While the building had lights, the overall atmosphere still retained a dark tinge. The windows were open—thanks to whoever removed the lockdown procedures—but the dark rain beyond the panes had all the cheerful warmth of a corpse. The wide-open rooms and hallways echoed with each step of our boots, creating a ghostly afterimage that shadowed our presence.

When Bishop rounded the corner, he flinched and jumped back, a finger over his mouth. Another chorus of gunshots added to the eerie soundtrack of the evening. No shouting between the people fighting, just grunts and wet coughs.

Bishop peered around the corner for half a second.

"One Iron-Blooded," he whispered. "Four junk hunters."

I pieced together the situation in my mind's eye.

A lone Iron-Blooded guarded the battery while his fellows no doubt went deeper into the basement floors. But could the junk hunters handle a single Iron-Blooded? As far as I knew, the Iron-Blooded trained in combat and stealth warfare. They hated their fellow humans and praised the ability to kill others efficiently and effectively. It was sport to them, unless they were converting people to their cause.

Another round of shots. Crouton held me tighter.

Bishop glanced again.

"Two junk hunters."

"What're they doing?" I asked, fearing the battery would get caught in the crossfire. I didn't know what would happen to it if shot repeatedly.

"They're hiding in rooms and using the hallway as a no-man's-land."

When the shooting started a third time, Bishop leaned out and joined the fray. He shot twice and then pulled back. The fighting ended.

"Got 'em," he said with a chuckle. "Fucker didn't even know I was here." He took a deep breath and yelled, "*Who all is out there*? Identify yourself or I'll shoot again!"

"Bishop? That you?"

I recognized the gruff voice, though I couldn't place it in my mind.

Bishop smiled wide. "Thatcher? You weasel. You came out here to steal shit, too, huh?"

Without any hesitation, Bishop rounded the corner and held out his arms. No one shot at him, so I followed as close as I could with Crouton's help. The moment I saw Thatcher, I recognized him—the crude man who wanted me for a night, the one with enough grease on his face for stir-fry.

Thatcher returned Bishop's smile with a crooked one of his own.

"We shoulda gone together," Thatcher said as he patted Bishop on the shoulder in a half hug.

"You know you can't sit in my truck."

"Listen to this. Ya love that hunk of metal so much I wouldn't be surprised to hear ya stick your dick in it."

"Watch your mouth around the kid," Bishop snapped.

Thatcher turned his attention to me and Crouton. He gave us a sidelong glance and then shrugged. "What's this?"

The second junk hunter—the same scarred woman with a chunk out of her nose—walked out from one of the nearby rooms, a handgun with a scope firmly in her grip. She nursed a hane cigarette, the lit nub burning close to her lips.

"Bishop," she said, curt. "I know you like your whores, but you obviously have a problem when you bring them to a place like this."

Bishop waved away the comment. "You got it all wrong, Dezray. I'm movin' up in the world. I'm contracted out now."

"Those two girls are payin' you?"

"That's right. I'm a glorified bodyguard and driver. My mother would finally be proud."

She grinned. "They look too young to have anything useful."

"Didn't you ever learn that appearances can be deceiving?" Bishop asked as he gestured to her gnarled face. "You look like a villain out of one of those old-world movies, but I know you're all right."

Thatcher pointed and laughed, amused to the point I thought he must be drunk. It wasn't even a particularly clever joke.

Dezray sneered as she finished the last of her hane. "Well, if you're here, I'll finally have some competent backup."

Thatcher snorted and stopped laughing. I preferred the outcome, as the man sounded like a dead brain cell, but also because the dark blood of the Iron-Blooded and the two junk hunters pooled in the hallway around my feet.

Anything to speed up the conversation so we could leave.

Crouton stared at the mix of crimson and black, her expression blank but her eyes betraying deep thought.

I motioned to the power reserve room. Crouton took me there, her focus on the blood unwavering. Once I got inside, Thatcher gave me the once-over.

"What're you doin', girlie?"

I didn't answer him. Instead, I dedicated myself to examining the fission battery. Although Bishop had gotten me new tools, they weren't like my old set. My previous equipment had a size and shape for any screw or bolt—all organized, of course. Now I had to keep the tools in my pocket, completely disorganized, most of which would have to do, as they didn't quite fit.

I fussed with the battery's restraints more than I should have. I didn't know why, but the lack of order bothered me more than the copper scent of blood hanging in the stagnant air.

"Is that what I think it is?" Thatcher asked.

The way he worded the question gave me pause. It wasn't interest in his tone, but avarice. I was inches from removing the battery when I heard Thatcher cock his gun.

"Whoa, whoa," Thatcher said. "I think me and Dezray did most of the heavy liftin' gettin' here. If anyone is gettin' that battery, *it's us*."

Dezray lit another hane cigarette and lifted an eyebrow, but she didn't say a word.

"I've got bad news," Bishop said, still amused, but the iciness of his voice couldn't be understated. "We came specifically for that battery. Besides, you'd be dead if it weren't for me. Let's pretend you didn't see this. You'll find other good stuff here, trust me."

"Nah. I don't think so."

Thatcher didn't turn the gun on Bishop—he leveled it at Crouton.

I stood straight, my thoughts grinding to a halt. Crouton's eyes widened, but the rest of her stiffened under the barrel of the pistol.

I swear no one took a breath. Even Dezray kept her cigarette still, never inhaling, the ash flaking to her feet in tiny amounts. Seconds passed in tense silence with only the hum of the distant rain as proof time still continued to flow.

Thatcher smiled and said, "*You* can search around, Bishop. I'll take this, and I won't shoot the girlies. Fair trade, right?"

Bishop fingered his handgun, but Thatcher thrust his pistol closer to Crouton, his grip tight. He narrowed his eyes, as if daring Bishop to test him. No piece of me doubted Thatcher's intent to kill.

With a forced swallow, I flipped the power switch, blanketing everyone in darkness. In the next instant, I dove for Crouton, putting my body between her and the gun. We both slammed to the ground, my body on top of hers. The resulting firefight was short, but it rang in my mind for several seconds. Had I been shot? Adrenaline coated my veins with ice, preventing any feeling.

Dezray whipped out a flashlight and shone it over the room. Bishop was still standing, but Thatcher wasn't as lucky. The disgusting man joined the other corpses on the floor, his body twitching more than most.

"That's two tally marks for the evening," Bishop said with a forced chuckle. He lowered his gun, his hands shaky. "Didn't think I'd have to shoot a guy I knew tonight, but life's weird like that. Ballsy, Viper."

"I knew the moment Thatcher tried to get me involved, it was a bad idea," Dezray said, finally taking a puff on her hane. "Some people are just better off dead."

Crouton helped me stand, and I muttered a thank-you.

"You sure she isn't your daughter?" Bishop asked as he took my arm and straightened my stance. "You fuckin' jumped like it was your flesh and blood in danger."

I ran a hand through my hair, dazed from the encounter, the gunshots still ringing in my ears. "I . . . just didn't want to see her hurt."

She reminded me so much of my sister, Tamura. My body had moved on its own.

If Chelsy died in front of me . . . I didn't think I'd be able to handle it. Not with the terrible memories that lingered at the edge of my thoughts.

Bishop grabbed the fission battery out of the power station and tucked it into his duffel bag. "Welp, that wasn't too hard."

I laughed at the comment. My heart beat fast enough I figured I'd lost a year off my total lifespan from stress alone. Perhaps the battery was a bad luck charm. If such a thing as *luck* existed. I fidgeted with the necklace Bishop had given me, wondering if believing in such forces would calm my convulsing heart.

"Where next?" Bishop asked.

"The third basement floor," I said, my voice unsteady.

"Something specific there?"

"Yes."

Dezray used her flashlight to motion to the hallway. "You weren't jokin' about bein' hired, were you?"

Bishop shook his head.

"We should stick together regardless. There're at least two more Iron-Blooded here, according to what people said in Dodge City. Those alien-lovin' lunatics will shoot at us on the spot, too. Havin' backup will be good for us."

"I know the drill," Bishop said.

"I was lettin' the girls know, so they didn't try talkin' to those lunatics."

"Don't worry about them. That one there is clever and the other's mute."

Two compliments in quick succession got me nervous and unable to find the correct words.

Did Bishop actually think highly of me?

It never surprised me when people assumed I was worthless because of my leg, but I had avoided people so long that true appreciation of my talents was rare. The last person to offer me an earnest compliment was Dallas, and the time before that, my father and sister.

When Bishop flashed me another one of his smiles, it was as if he was saying he acknowledged my many talents beyond the mere physical. I didn't know how to articulate my gratitude, so I nodded and said nothing rather than force something awkward.

With our battery, we headed into the hall. Dezray went first, her flashlight our guiding spirit. She led us straight to the stairs, and my hip ached just looking at them.

Bishop glanced over his shoulder at me. "I can't carry you, not if I'm gonna shoot as well. Can you make it?"

"Yeah," I said.

Nothing would keep me from getting to the aliens' computer terminal.

The whole area around the stairs was more spacious than the rest—even the door stood large enough to take a horse through. The sign next to it read: WEAPONS AND ARMOR DEVELOPMENT.

When Dezray opened the door, a computer system with an artificial voice greeted us in Tethlite. "*Warning. The reactor's coolant systems must be repaired. Radiation levels dangerously high.*"

I caught my breath, my stomach twisting into knots.

"What was that?" Dezray asked.

Bishop turned to me. "You speak gibberish, right? I saw you listenin' to those videos."

"We need to hurry," I whispered. "That's what it's saying."

As a group, we went for the next set of stairs, but that didn't stop me from glancing around.

My grandfather had told me so many tales of the aliens and their living environments, and everything was just as he said. Dark and cold, but intricate with details on every surface. There weren't many lights—Dezray's flashlight was still the brightest thing we had—and I suspected the few bulbs around were for human benefit.

The walls had artistic etchings around every doorway and computer panel. The damn aliens liked to show off their fine motor talents, and apparently valued such skill to a high degree. The etchings depicted Earth, space, the Milky Way, even human cities.

But then I noticed some of the shelves built into the walls were open and empty. No doubt the Iron-Blooded had been here. I hated the idea of them taking A-tech, but I didn't want to risk a confrontation.

Down another set of stairs.

"What's my split?" Dezray asked. "I'm not gonna get into a fight with you, Bishop, but I want to know before more bullets start flyin'."

"You can have my share. Deal?"

"Fine by me. I know you're good on your word."

They tapped their knuckles together in a show of solidarity. I wondered how often Bishop had worked with Dezray. Would that familiarity stop her from shooting him? I doubted it. I saw what she did to the other junk hunters outside. Would she turn on us like Thatcher? I hoped not. Having a second gun around would prove helpful.

When we reached the second basement level, my gaze went straight for the door. It read: MEDICAL RESEARCH AND CRYOSTASIS.

The last word caused my heart to sink.

It was what I had feared—they kept aliens here on ice, safe from the bombs and sleeping until woken to roam the world once again. The Teth were masters of the technique of holding people in a frozen stasis. It was how they managed the long treks through space, the very reason they reached us.

Bishop opened the door, and we entered a labyrinth of rooms and halls. A soft blue glow illuminated the area enough for me to see the mess—like someone had stormed through, flipping every desk and workspace over before smashing the result under their boots. I was on the verge of suggesting we find the sleeping aliens and kill them—they would be in their cryotubes, helpless and unaware—but I didn't want to waste any more time getting to the third basement level.

We walked across broken glass and electronics until I spotted something half-covered by the debris.

I stopped Crouton and crouched to pick up a steel canister—a medical container meant to house nanites. Sure enough, when I read over the Teth-lite instructions, it seemed the canister was ready for injection, complete with a needle and electrical pulse to stimulate the inert nanites.

"What's that?" Bishop whispered.

I tucked the canister into my pants pocket. "A souvenir."

Even if we split our findings fifty-fifty, I didn't have to let him determine what I got. My mind raced with the possibilities of the nanites—the tiny machines helped maintain the health of their host. What if they could fix my hip and restore my ability to walk? Even the slight possibility excited me to the point my chest tightened with anticipation.

I was determined to inject myself with the canister the moment we made it out of his hellish building.

We managed to find the next stairwell and descended without a word between us. Deeper and deeper we went, surrounded on all sides by metal, as if in the gut of the compound.

The third basement floor had a sign that read: ANALYSIS AND REACTOR.

A glowing trefoil sign blinked underneath the Tethlite lettering—the same trefoil sign that denoted radioactive material. Bishop didn't need to read Tethlite to understand. He took me by the upper arm and pulled me back.

"We can't go in here," he said. "We'll need to search somewhere else."

But this was the floor with the computer—the one that could check the climate engineering satellites.

"I have to go in," I said. I needed to know.

"Don't be stupid. You know what happens when you get radiation poisoning, right? It's not worth risking."

It might be.

I took a few shallow breaths. "I'll speak to the computer and ask about the situation." I pulled free of Bishop's grip and placed my hand on the warning terminal. "*What is the situation?*"

I didn't know the exact voice commands, but I knew the A-tech was smart enough to understand, so long as the facility was set up to take voice command.

The computer responded, "*Coolant systems corrupted. Outside maintenance required.*"

"*What's the level of radiation?*"

"*Estimated 1.35Gy of ionizing radiation.*"

I stared at the wall, unseeing.

A standard X-ray in a medical office used .0014Gy of radiation. Nothing too harmful. A human could be exposed for a prolonged period of time without much harm. And while .5Gy of radiation would quickly result in nausea and vomiting, it could be recovered from with proper care and medication.

1Gy of radiation was the point blood cells began to die.

The fact stewed in my thoughts.

But I knew I could still live from such an exposure; it would just be risky. I would need to a see a doctor within a few weeks for treatment, and even then, that wasn't a guarantee. The radiation poison could kill me before then from burns or internal bleeding.

Was the information on the computer worth it? What if the satellites had been dealt with years ago?

The real question was: What if they hadn't been?

"Well?" Bishop asked, jerking me out of my thoughts. "What did it say?"

"It said there's a radiation leak, but it's not bad."

"*Any* radiation leak is bad."

"The level is barely over an X-ray," I muttered. "You said I was clever, right? Well, clever people don't live as long as I do by being reckless."

I didn't want him to stop me—a burning piece of me needed to see the computer at all costs. I'd brave the radiation to find out the future of mankind.

"What's in there?" Bishop asked. "Even if it's a small leak, we can't search for very long."

"We're not searching the floor. I'm going in alone. I need to check one of the computers."

"So this isn't for loot?"

I shook my head.

"Well, then, fuck this place," Bishop said as he threw a hand up in exasperation. "There's no reason to be here."

"I told you. I need to check something."

I motioned Crouton to take me to the door. I wouldn't allow her to accompany me into the irradiated room, but up to the door would be fine. All fission reactors built by the aliens were surrounded with the best material to stop ionizing radiation. I doubted the hallway outside the door would hurt her, especially if I hurried through my search.

I tried to shake my doubts by imagining the ease of my recovery. I had nanites. They were capable of repairing radiation damage over a period of time—they even prevented tumors and most forms of cancer.

This could work.

I could do it.

I had to. For my grandfather. He would've done this if he were still alive.

Before I opened the door, Bishop pulled me back a second time. "How long are you gonna be in there?"

"I'll try to be quick."

"At least take this."

He handed over a small flashlight. I switched it on, but it didn't seem to calm his mood.

Bishop glowered at me, not his usual amused self. Something about the look shook me—I almost decided against my mission—but I turned away and cast the thought from my head.

Everyone backed away before I opened the door.

The computer spoke again. "*Warning. Radiation levels dangerously high near the reactor. All personnel should evacuate the floor.*"

I couldn't stay here long. No matter how much my hip and leg suffered, I pushed my body to the limits.

The dark atmosphere acted as nightmare fuel for my thoughts. Steam wafted across the floor. Hot steam. The kind that carried the radiation from the reactor—the coolant system was definitely in need of repair, but it would never come. No doubt the facility's many machines kept the reactor active, but without the needed coolant, there would eventually be a meltdown.

With a shaky hand, I shone the flashlight around, my head dappled in sweat and my stomach growing queasy. Thankfully, the "Floor 3" in the background of the video had been distinct. I spotted it painted on a wall, and with a few ungraceful hops on my good leg, I reached the alien computer.

Every second inside the room ate at my willpower.

The radiation bombarded my entire body—I couldn't feel it per se, but the knowledge played tricks on my perceptions. My insides churned, but the worst of the problems wouldn't hit until later. That was the terrible reality of radiation poisoning—it was a natural form of torture that took its time until the victim slowly fell apart, bit by bit.

I activated the computer. It took an eternity to boot.

Sluggish computers didn't typically bother me, but in my dire situation, every hesitation on the computer's end tested my patience. I muttered an incessant *c'mon, c'mon, c'mon* as I typed at a ludicrous speed, flying through the menus and screens as fast as the computer could react to my inputs. Where would I find my information? Just searching took time I didn't have.

Something, *anything*, about the climate engineering satellites . . .

Finally, I found it. An analysis section kept track of global A-tech "services." The CES systems were one of them. I clicked for an update and waited.

And waited.

My hands shook.

The results filtered onto the screen, and I somehow tensed further.

CLIMATE ENGINEERING
Set Schedule: 458 Days
Operation: Ignite
Laser Level: Maximum

I rubbed my nose but never blinked, unable to glance away from the screen.

Fuck.

It really was a countdown to extinction.

Hot anger, confusion, and dread mixed in equal parts throughout my body. I trembled and slammed my fist onto the computer terminal. Why was this happening? Why would anyone do this? What could I do about it?

I scrunched my eyes shut, trying to think of a solution—trying to form a goddamn plan—but the shock of the situation wouldn't leave me. The fact that I knew, and no one else, festered in my mind.

Everyone would just . . . die . . . in 458 days.

They wouldn't even know why.

The more I rubbed at my nose, the more I felt a trickle of blood on my upper lip. How long had I been inside the room?

Someone grabbed me by the shoulder and turned me around. I flinched, but Bishop scooped me into his arms before I could do anything else. He jogged back to the door and exited with me, the same hard glower on his face from before.

"What the fuck is your problem?" he snapped. "What were you doin', huh? Just staring at a computer? You wanna get yourself killed? Is that it?"

The doors shut behind him, trapping the radiation in the basement. Crouton and Dezray were nowhere to be seen. I clung to Bishop, desperate to tell someone.

"It was important," I said. "You have to believe me. The world is going to end. Everyone—everything—it's all going to die."

Bishop shook his head. "You're in bad shape. We have the battery. Why don't we leave? You can tell me all about your fever dreams then."

"You don't want anything here?" I thought that was all he cared about.

"We can find other trinkets in safer locations. Right now I feel like we're testin' our luck."

Perhaps he was right, but I didn't get to reply before the computer butted into the conversation.

"*Warning. Cryostasis ended prematurely. Without outside materials, stasis will no longer be possible.*"

The Iron-Blooded were on the floor above us, gathering their aliens.

CHAPTER THIRTEEN

"Where are Dezray and Chelsy?" I whispered.

"Dezray took the kid upstairs to search around."

"Why did you let them go?"

"What?" Bishop carried me to the stairs. "Did you want me to keep them next to the door with all the radiation on the other side? Dezray said she'd keep it to the rooms by the stairs. It's under control."

I gripped his shirt, twisting my fingers into the fabric. "The Iron-Blooded have awoken the aliens here. The ones in cryostasis."

"What makes you think that?"

"The computer sounded off a warning."

"Tsk," Bishop said with a click of his tongue. "You could stand to talk a little more, ya know. Information like that is a big fuckin' deal."

He sprinted up the last of the steps and dashed through the door at the top. My small flashlight barely offered any illumination for our path. And the cold blue glow of the medical floor didn't put me at ease. I kept my fierce grip on Bishop, waiting for the appearance of the aliens. I knew it was a matter of time—and no luck in the world was force enough to save us.

Bishop went to the nearest door and slammed it open. Besides the old medical equipment, it was empty.

He growled something under his breath and went for the next room. Again, dark and empty.

Then a third.

And a fourth.

The vastness of the floor was an obstacle all its own. He didn't call out—not when his voice would echo throughout the empty facility—but the noise he made in his haste was enough to get us caught eventually.

"Quiet," I said, a slight hint of desperation in my tone.

Bishop didn't respond, but he did limit the ruckus. I kept time by the beating of his heart.

Two minutes and it felt like we were walking in circles.

The crash of glass and metal pierced the eerie silence. Bishop's pulse quickened, his heart rate much higher than a moment before. Had Bishop dealt with aliens before? Did he know how dangerous it could be to face off against one of the drones?

Finally, he opened a door and the shine of a flashlight washed over us.

"Bishop," Dezray said. "What's that look for?"

He motioned to the door with a jerk of his head. "We need to go. C'mon. Right now."

Crouton ran to Bishop and clung to his side. But Dezray hesitated. She fidgeted with bottles on the counter—no doubt filled with decades-old medicine—and shoved a few into her bag.

"This place still has plenty to scavenge," she said. "We can avoid the Iron-Blooded if we keep low until they leave."

"If you wanna stay, whatever. I'm leaving."

Dezray clenched her jaw. In one quick motion, she swept her arm over the countertop and funneled the medical bottles into her backpack. I suspected most of the medications would be expired, but that didn't matter. People still purchased them for all sorts of reasons, including getting wasted or simply hoping the contents of the pills would somehow ease their suffering.

She joined us in the hallway, her gaze lingering on the contents of the room.

The harsh breath of something large echoed down the hall.

My whole body iced over.

I didn't even need to look, but Dezray shone her light over it regardless.

At the end of the hall, between us and the route to the stairwell, was one of the aliens.

A Teth drone, to be exact.

It had all the features of the aliens—four arms, large frame, dull unhuman black complexion—but unlike the innovator caste, the drones were skeletal, their skin a paper-thin coat over their muscles and bones.

They didn't speak or even wear clothing, and most conducted themselves no better than animals. The drones were the lowest caste, bred to serve and be controlled through a complex system of pheromones. They could act as guard dogs or workers for intense projects of labor, all while being semi-mindless and free of individuality, serving the whole much like ants or bees.

But that made them scarier.

There was no rationalizing with the alien drones, or appealing to empathy, or even changing their mind after they were tasked. Their sole purpose for existence was to follow the commands of the higher castes, no matter how horrific or brutal they might be.

Bishop set me down and pulled his gun from the holster.

The drone shambled forward, its large clawed hands on both walls of the hallway. It took deep breaths, its system clearly recovering from decades of cryosleep. But as it got closer, its steps increased in speed, like it wanted to run yet couldn't.

Like it was tasked with protecting the facility from interlopers.

"Shoot it," I whispered.

"The Iron-Blooded will figure out we're here," Bishop said.

Dezray lifted her handgun. "It won't matter if that damn thing kills us."

When the monster was within ten feet of us, Bishop shot once. The bullet struck the beast square in the chest. It coughed and stumbled for a second, but then it continued its charge, its large teeth gleaming in the illumination of Dezray's flashlight.

Bishop shot twice more, all bullets hitting the creature somewhere on its body. But it persisted, its breathing more intense, its claws scraping the metal of the walls as it pulled itself forward.

Two feet from us and Bishop unloaded with a round of rapid fire, riddling the drone with everything he had.

Damn drone didn't care.

They were resilient and designed to persevere, even when damaged. They had three hearts and a barely functioning brain and nervous system that didn't need much in the way of resources. And it didn't have a sense of self-preservation, only the drive to complete the task it was given.

Dezray also opened fire, filling the hallway with the sounds of a war zone. When Bishop clicked empty, the beast was within inches, its blood weeping from dozens of bullet holes. Dezray pulled out a second gun and continued to unload, her face screwed up in a look of hard concentration.

Finally, the beast succumbed to the injuries. It fell forward, and Bishop had to back away to avoid the bloody mess. The drone took wet breaths, its long tongue feeling the floor of the hallway as if looking for a way to continue with its mission.

"Three whole fuckin' magazines of bullets," Dezray said, breathless. "This is why no one fucks with those drone nests, I'll tell you."

Bishop exhaled. "I'm gonna have to use a new tally mark system for things like this." He opened his bag and rummaged through the contents. He had a few gas grenades, but otherwise didn't have any other weapons. "Dammit. I didn't bring any extra clips." He ran a shaky hand through his hair. "We really need to get outta here."

My heart wouldn't calm, and my thoughts dwelled on the worst-case scenarios.

We were two floors from the surface, with the Iron-Blooded and their aliens between us. I couldn't walk. We had a child. And one of our gunners had no ammo.

If ever I had wanted luck to exist, it was right now.

"You usin' forty-fives?" Dezray asked.

Bishop nodded.

She reached into the side pocket of her backpack and threw him a loaded clip.

My thoughts went to Crouton, and I turned to face her. Her black hair contrasted harshly with the paleness of her face. I motioned her over and hugged her close.

"It's going to be okay," I said, trying to reassure her, and myself, that we could get through the evening.

Bishop separated us and then scooped me into his arms. He positioned me in such a way that I was pinned to his shoulder, freeing up his right hand for the gun. Crouton stuck close to his side as he jogged down the hallway, Dezray securing our flank.

"There are four other junk hunters upstairs," she said. "If we can reach them, we'll have a better chance of making it out of here. Safety in numbers."

We reached the stairs, and Bishop didn't slow. He took the steps two at a time until we busted through the door, but we were too late. Voices filled the first basement floor, along with the harsh clicks of claws on metal.

Voices that spoke Tethlite.

Human voices.

"What's going on?"

"More junk hunters. Kill them. All of them. They can't be allowed to take any of the A-tech."

"What if it's that fucking judge?"

"Let her come. We have one of our own now."

"Are those the Iron-Blooded?" Bishop asked me between breaths as he stuck close to the walls, slinking through the darkest shadows.

"Yes," I said. "At least two of them."

"Why aren't they getting attacked by the aliens?"

I wrapped my arms around his neck, thankful for his strength. "It's the nanites in their system."

Nanites forced the human body to produce pheromones that registered them as *allies* with the Teth drones. But the nanites didn't give humans the capability to order the drones through pheromones—humans lacked the ability to consciously regulate such a process in their body—which meant there was at least one other alien of higher caste in the facility giving commands to the drones. Perhaps more.

I technically had a canister of nanites, but they wouldn't mark me as an ally right away. It would take hours, perhaps days, to alter my physiology. It wouldn't help us.

Bishop rounded the corner and came to an abrupt halt.

Two drones stood in the hall, the corpses of three mutilated junk hunters at their feet, some even half-eaten. The moment we came in range, the drones turned toward us. They had a keen sense of smell—their nostrils two deep crevasses on their face that looked like long lines—but they also sensed electrical currents, even as minute as the nerve activity in human brains and muscles.

They didn't need eyes to know where we were.

"Run," I whispered.

The drones lunged, their bloody claws outstretched.

Bishop stumbled backward and then ran for another hall, Dezray and Crouton not far behind. The drones didn't move with grace, but they had a single-minded tenacity that kept them pursuing us no matter how many turns Bishop took. And the beasts had longer strides, even if they were uncoordinated after the years of sleep.

"Don't let them cut you," I whispered. "Not with their claws."

The chase, the beat of my heart, the sounds of the alien drones as they took in gulps of air—it all reminded me of the night my father died. Panic strangled my thoughts and windpipe, narrowing my vision to a tunnel.

Or perhaps it was the radiation poisoning.

Blood wept from my nose, spilling onto Bishop's shirt and splashing to the floor.

I was queasy.

A fourth junk hunter stood in front of the door to the ground floor. Bishop lifted his gun as we approached and shot around the man. The ricochet of the bullets frightened the junk hunter. He flinched away and dove behind a computer terminal. It was all Bishop needed to get to the door without trouble. He slammed through, but not before one of the drones leapt over the computer terminal and dug its claws into the side of the junk hunter's head.

Brains and viscera popped from the body like the insides of ruptured fruit. The one drone gobbled down the flesh, excited for the soft bits.

Dezray shot at the second drone, staggering it before it got to the stairs.

But Bishop wasn't as fast as before. He struggled to breathe and took the steps one at a time, sweat causing his clothes to cling to his body. Crouton managed to run ahead. Then Dezray sprinted past.

I tightened my hold around Bishop's neck, my fingernails digging into his skin, my arms shaking. "Please," I practically whispered into his ear. "Please don't get caught."

Bishop leapt over the last few steps and entered the ground floor, but the drone was on his heels, its breath stinking up the air and curling the hairs in my nose. Bishop spun around and fired, striking the alien in the head with more than one shot. The monster slowed and staggered, but it wasn't enough.

The drone swung wide and sliced through Bishop's side, its claws carving through the flesh between ribs. Bishop cried out and hit his knees, dropping me in the process.

Dezray stopped running and opened fire with everything she had. The burst of light from her two handguns created a strobe effect as the drone slashed again, splattering Bishop's blood across the floor.

But the barrage of bullets took its toll. The drone collapsed to the side, broken from the attack and twitching as it died.

Dezray took a few steps back, her eyes glancing between Bishop, me, and Crouton.

"Fuck me," she muttered. "You all are on your own."

Without a second glance back, she took off through the ground floor building, straight for the exit.

The scrabbling of claws echoed in the stairwell. The second drone was on its way. I turned to Crouton, unsure of what to tell her in my last thirty seconds of life. Run? Get to Boulder City? What could I even say?

But then Bishop forced himself to stand. He kept one arm tight over his ribs, covering the terrible injuries. With his other arm, he helped me stand.

"Bishop," I whispered, in a state of disbelief.

He walked over to a nearby room and shoved me in. No words were uttered as he grabbed Crouton by the arm and also pushed her inside. He followed shortly after. Then Bishop shut the door, but without the building's power, we couldn't activate the bolt locks.

After a few deep breaths, Bishop fell back to the floor, his body trembling.

The monster outside ran past the door, no doubt chasing after Dezray's trail—but that also meant it was between us and the exit.

"Are you okay?" I asked. I leaned against the wall to stand, but Bishop couldn't do the same.

He let out a long exhale. "At least the thing that got me paid with its life."

I couldn't say anything.

Bishop glanced down at the gouges through his side. "Why can't I feel the injury?"

My dry mouth almost refused to form words. "It's . . . the drones. Their claws . . . are coated with neurotoxins. They numb and paralyze their victims."

It was why I told him not to get cut. No one ever escapes the drones once they're cut.

Another round of claws on metal got me tense. I listened, frozen in place, as what sounded like several other drones scrambled by. Then there was the clank of something heavy—rhythmic, like footsteps—and it, too, passed the door without stopping.

All our enemies were between us and the exit.

Bishop hit the floor. He managed to prop himself up on one elbow as he dug through his bag. Then he pulled out his KA-BAR knife and slid it across the floor.

"Listen," Bishop said, his voice weak as the neurotoxins gradually stole his ability to function. "Here's what you're gonna do. You're gonna take that knife, and you're gonna cut off one of my hands. You can use it to start my truck, and—"

Crouton slammed her hands over her face, her strangled sobs a sound that ate at my own willpower.

"—and you two are gonna drive straight back to Dodge City." Bishop placed his forehead on the ground and took in a few shallow gulps of air. "It'll be easy. Cut at the wrist. There're two arteries and some nerves you'll need to saw through. With enough time, even the kid could do it."

I stumbled away from the wall until I got to Bishop's side. I went to the floor and placed both my hands on his shoulder, shaking the entire time.

"Don't talk like that," I said. "You'll be okay."

Bishop chuckled and offered me one of his smiles—the best he could, even if his mirth sounded closer to despair than anything I had ever heard from him.

"All flesh is grass," he said. "I was bound to be someone's tally mark."

"Do you have any gauze or Cellucotton? I can—I can bandage this."

"I left it . . . in the truck."

"I'll improvise."

"You're wasting time."

I clenched my jaw, unwilling to let this happen. But then I tasted the blood in my mouth.

My gums bled—a clear sign the radiation was still damaging my body. And here we were, trapped in a tiny room in the middle of a facility swarming with Iron-Blooded and aliens. What was I going to do? How was I going to prevent the inevitable from happening?

"Don't give up," I told Bishop, but in reality, I spoke to myself. "You can do it. You need to hang on."

Bishop closed his eyes, his shirt an odd shade of black and crimson. He held his injuries tight. "Don't make this hard, Kita."

"No, I—"

"You know what you've gotta do."

CHAPTER FOURTEEN

I picked up Bishop's knife.

What did we have to work with? I grabbed his bag and took stock of the situation, needing a shred of order to clear the chaos from my mind.

The gas grenades in his bag caught my eye. Indoors they were useless. I didn't have the equipment to live through the gas, and the stagnant air meant the gas would linger no matter where I threw it, endangering me in the process. But Bishop also had several small adhesive lights—people called them *sticky lights*—meant to be stuck to walls.

I stuck two of them around the room to give me enough illumination to see the corners of the tiny room.

In a moment of clarity, I formed a plan. That fact gave me enough comfort and confidence to dispel my panic.

"Chelsy," I said, using her real name. I hoped it would help her realize how important this was.

She shook her head, her hands still covering her face.

"Chelsy. Come here. I need your help."

No matter what I said, she wouldn't look at me. She backed up into the wall, her head down and her hair spilling in front of her face and hands.

"You have to listen." I turned to face her. "I need you to go out into the hallway and tempt the drones to the room with the corpses of the junk hunters. They'll eat fresh flesh. It shouldn't be difficult."

She took her hands away from her face, her eyes wide and wet with tears. What I asked was horrific, and I could see it reflected in her expression.

"They won't hurt you," I said. "I promise. Remember when your father took you to the Iron-Blooded? When you were sick? They gave you nanites. They put them in your blood. You'll be okay if you go out there."

Chelsy shook her head.

"Once the aliens are inside the power reserve room, you can shut the door. In a confined space, with all that blood, they'll be distracted. Here. Use these sticky lights to jam it shut. Then look for a second way out of the building. There has to be more than one. Any route without the aliens will be fine, but we have to get to Bishop's truck, okay?"

Surely the monsters wouldn't be able to smell things in the hall when in a room with several corpses, and the lights would have an electrical pulse far stronger than human movement. If Chelsy managed to do everything correctly, the drones would be neutralized for a short period of time, at least until they were done eating.

Again, Chelsy shook her head.

I took in a deep breath and then let out a ragged exhale. I couldn't force her to do anything. Could I lie and tell her something that would convince her? Nothing came to mind. Instead, I decided I'd give her the hard truth of the situation.

"Chelsy," I said, my voice low. "You've got two options. You can go out there and attempt to save us, or you can stay here and we'll all die. The choice is yours."

It was probably too much for a child. I knew it before I even said it. But there was no other way. Either she helped me clear a path to get out of the building before I passed out from radiation poisoning, or we were never leaving.

Would a seven-year-old me have been able to handle the situation? I didn't know. Perhaps. Perhaps not. The death of my sister shook me, and I had been thirteen then. It was almost too much to bear, even now, as an adult. Could I really expect someone else to shoulder the weight of life-and-death decisions so early in their life?

Chelsy fidgeted with the hem of her jacket, a stream of steady tears running down her red face. She stared at the floor, her eyes unseeing, mulling over my words. I held my breath as she silently deliberated.

Finally, she pursed her lips, knit her eyebrows, and gave me a curt nod, as though steeling herself to the role of unlikely hero.

I handed Chelsy the flashlight and motioned to the door.

"Don't let the Iron-Blooded see you," I said. "Please hurry."

Chelsy held the flashlight close to her chest as she pushed open the door and slid through the narrow space before closing it again. I waited, unable to hear her footsteps, but hoped she was running.

I didn't know for sure that Chelsy had nanites in her system, and the doubt haunted me for a prolonged moment. But I shook it from my mind and refocused on Bishop. He lay on the floor, his eyes scrunched closed and his wounds still bleeding. With his knife in hand, I cut off his shirt and then sliced it into strips.

I wrapped the fabric around his torso, struggling when it came to getting the strips under his body. Bishop grunted and exhaled, but I knew he wasn't really conscious. The drones did a number on humans, their neurotoxin an effective weapon. And I hated looking at his wounds. The deep gashes through his body that revealed his fleshy insides were almost more than I could handle.

Once I had pressure and fabric over the slashes, I reached for the canister of nanites in my pants pocket.

A piece of me didn't want to use them. There was still a chance Bishop could die, even if I injected him—the trauma to his body too much for the machines to fix—or he could have already lost too much blood, or his body could reject them, as rare as that outcome was. Then the nanites would be wasted. Once injected into an individual, it was next to impossible to get them out without a complete transfusion.

And I wanted to use them for myself.

If I injected Bishop, there was a real possibility I would never find another canister, and then I would be lame for the rest of my life. And the nanites could help cure my radiation poisoning, saving me from days of suffering and potential death.

I *could* leave him to die. Bishop had basically given me his permission to abandon him and saw off his hand to take his truck back to civilization.

But I hated the thought.

Bishop could've dropped me—he could've left me as a distraction for the aliens while he ran for safety, like so many others had in the past. I knew Dezray would have.

Yet Bishop never did. He kept me with him. He risked himself for my safety. How could I live with myself if I deserted him when I still had a chance to save his life?

So, despite my reluctance, I activated the nanites in the canister. Once I removed the cap from the needle, I pulled Bishop's arm straight and found a vein. He stirred for a moment, but he never woke.

"You're going to be okay," I whispered as I injected the nanites into his arm.

The process took longer than I thought. A full sixty seconds for the contents of the canister to drain into Bishop's system. They wouldn't heal him immediately, but it was a good start. They could fight off the toxins and stitch the flesh of his sides back together. All I needed was the Cellucotton from Bishop's truck and I'd hopefully be able to get him back on his feet—so long as he didn't die before then.

Bishop coughed, his own blood and saliva obviously pooling in his mouth.

I grabbed his bag and quickly dragged it over. Then I lifted his head, helped him clear away the liquid, and rested him back down on the softest portion of his bag I could find.

"You're not going to die on me," I said, anger in my tone, my frustrations reaching their limits. "You hear that?" I closed my eyes and balled my hands into fists. "Everyone dies on me, goddammit, but you're not, do you understand?"

My grandfather, my mother, my father, my sister. Even Dallas was likely dead, if I were being honest with myself. Everyone I knew. If I couldn't save even one person—if I couldn't help the people who helped me—why did I even give a damn about the satellites or the fate of the world?

Clearly, I wouldn't be able to prevent jack shit because everything I did was a failure. If I were going to prove myself wrong, I had to make it out of the facility. I had to save Bishop.

I had to.

The door opened. I tensed and whipped around, my heart stuttering on a beat.

Chelsy slipped into the room, her jacket missing and her shimmery pink dress stained with fresh blood. She jogged to my side and motioned for me to stand, her frantic gestures betraying the urgency of the situation.

I grabbed her shoulder and forced myself to my feet, no matter the pain flooding my body. Determination became my fuel and my painkiller. I would make it through the night no matter what.

Together, Chelsy and I hustled through the building. She led me down hallway after hallway, once doubling back and shaking her head, as though she had forgotten the route. I didn't question her, because I didn't want to rattle her further, but one mistake could be our last.

Chelsy pointed to a door at the end of a long hallway, a smile wide on her face. No doubt it was the exit. The knowledge lifted my spirits.

The handle of a nearby door rattled. Chelsy locked up like a startled animal, halting our progress. Before I could urge her to run, Dezray stepped out into the hall, her flashlight off and her pupils growing small when Chelsy shone her light over the woman.

How did she avoid the aliens?

"What're you doing here?" I asked.

Dezray laughed once. "You're not gonna believe this, but there are Ex Cathedra soldiers here. And with a truck. Un-fuckin'-believable. When do those damn grunts ever cross the mountains, huh? Never."

If Ex Cathedra soldiers were here, that meant Judge Gascoigne was as well.

I glanced around, the darkness hiding most details. "The drones went after the soldiers?"

"That's right. And where's Bishop? He's dead, right?"

I didn't answer and allowed her to reach her own conclusion.

Dezray smirked. "That's what he gets for bein' soft. He shoulda ditched you two when he had the chance."

"We're leaving." I urged Chelsy away.

But when we went to walk by, Dezray held up her gun. "No. I'm not soft like Bishop. I'm not gonna die here. Let go of the kid."

"I . . . I need her to walk."

Dezray struck me across the face with the butt of her heavy handgun. The blow momentarily blinded me as blood exploded from my nose and onto my jacket. I hit the floor, dazed and without memory of the last few seconds.

"You're gonna sit right here," Dezray said, pointing the barrel of her firearm down at me. "Slow down any monsters that might come this way. Me and the girl are gonna take off."

"Wait," I said through the agony that was my face. "We can . . . go together. We know of—"

"Fuck that. I saw what happened to Bishop for stickin' by your side. I'm not that kind of junk hunter. I'm the kind that makes it back to civilization."

When Chelsy moved to come to my aid, Dezray pointed the gun at her instead. Chelsy froze, her hands in the air.

"That's not how this's gonna go, kid. You're gonna walk in front of me and open all the doors, just in case. If you're lucky, there won't be any damn aliens. If you're not, I'll get a little forewarning as they chew your face. Understand?"

Chelsy didn't even have a moment to acknowledge her. Dezray grabbed her by the upper arm and shoved her down the hall and toward the exit. I rubbed at my bloody nose, unable to halt the bleeding. Without Chelsy, I'd be moving at a tenth of the speed. But what could I do about it?

I wanted to use my gas grenade on the junk hunter, but I couldn't bear to harm Chelsy in the process. Instead, I watched as Chelsy opened the door to the outside, my heart sinking with every step they got away from me. The cool night air swept into the building, bringing with it the scent of rain and mud. But the rain had stopped some time ago, leaving puddles of foul water around the parking lot.

The fear of being alone in this nightmare facility gripped my thoughts.

"You go first," Dezray whispered as she pushed Chelsy forward.

Chelsy stumbled out into the soaked parking lot. She glanced up, then around the parking lot, and shivered as she rubbed down her arms. When she turned her attention to me, her brow furrowed. I braced myself against the wall and stood, unwilling to let Dezray take Chelsy from me. I moved down the hall, one hobble-step at a time.

"Clear?" Dezray asked.

Chelsy hesitated, and then nodded.

Dezray stepped outside, her gun at the ready.

The next second happened so fast I almost didn't register the facts.

A drone leapt down from the roof, obviously lying in wait for someone to exit. It slammed down on Dezray, crushing her against the cement as its claws sank into her shoulders and throat. With strangled breaths, she tried to aim and fire, but the beast clamped its jaws around her head and crushed her skull with little effort. Then it released, leaving her head mangled, like a piece of half-chewed bubble gum that also wept blood.

The drone turned its head in my direction.

I couldn't breathe. I couldn't act in time.

But Chelsy dashed forward and slammed the door, separating me from her and the monster.

Shaken, and alone in the building, I turned and started back down the hallway, hoping to put as much distance between me and the drone as possible. I had to find a different exit, but without Chelsy, I had no light. Feeling my way through the darkness, I pictured the facility in my mind's eye. I knew how to get out, and I went straight for it.

Once, I tripped over a body, my palms landing in blood when I hit the floor. Didn't matter. I picked myself up and continued anyway.

When I made it to the exit, I knew it could be guarded, just like the last, but there wasn't much to do about it. I could peek out, glance at the roof, and hope to duck back in, but nothing else.

I was reaching for the handle when the door flew open.

Chelsy stood on the other side, her eyes wide. She grabbed my hand and pulled me through, taking me out into the wet parking lot as fast as my lame leg would allow.

The sounds of fighting drew my attention first.

Animalistic screams filled the atmosphere, along with a chorus of ripping flesh and heavy strikes. Despite the darkness, headlights shone across the parking lot from an Ex Cathedra truck, illuminating the cause of the noise.

Judge Gascoigne stood alone in the middle of the parking lot, a swarm of eight drones all around her. She grabbed one, ripped the jaw from its head, and then used the still-warm body to bludgeon another one.

Two drones tried to bite down on her arms, but the steel alloy exoskeleton armor wouldn't be punctured by the likes of bone, no matter how tough the aliens were.

The judge punched another in the face, her knuckles taking with it chunks of flesh. Still, the monsters attacked, attempting to knock her over, their mindless urge to kill their sole motivation.

Judge Gascoigne curled her left hand into a fist, and an eighteen-inch blade extended from the suit's gauntlet. The blades were technically used as tools should a judge ever need to free itself from restraints, but Judge Gascoigne wielded it like an effective weapon, slicing through the drones, spilling their blood all over the parking lot.

"Come on," she taunted. "You pieces of shit are nothing!"

For the second time in my life, I counted Judge Gascoigne as one of my saviors. No doubt she would kill me, but I almost wanted to run up and thank her. Every alien corpse was another point of gratitude.

Chelsy pulled me out of my daze by yanking on my arm. I nodded and held on to her as we jogged across the parking lot and onto the mud of the wasteland. At a few points I slipped, and when the sounds of fighting died down, I decided to fall to my knees behind an outcropping of rocks. Chelsy ducked behind with me, confusion plain on her face.

I glanced back at Judge Gascoigne, who stood only a hundred feet away. Her heavy breathing rang out from her suit, somewhat robotic through the judge armor speakers. All the drones were dead around her, most of them brutally ripped to pieces.

What I wouldn't give for my own suit of JUDGE-X0 exoskeleton armor.

The front door to the facility opened, and two Iron-Blooded walked out. I ducked farther behind the rock, unwilling to chance movement with them close by. They could get to their jeep long before I could make it to Bishop's truck and back. It was better to remain hidden until they left.

Judge Gascoigne rotated her shoulders and shook off some of the excess blood.

"And here we are," she drawled. "I'm going to give you one last chance to hand over my battery. If not, I'll rip you apart like I did these freaks, and then I'll do the same to this building. Do you understand, or should I say it slower?"

"*This one is their leader,*" one of the Iron-Blooded said in Tethlite.

I recognized his voice, even at my distance.

Commander Dannik. The ice of his tone could chill a fire.

He continued, "*She's here to kill you, just as she killed all your brethren. It's as I said—the war carries on.*"

Who was he talking to? Obviously not Judge Gascoigne.

But . . .

Then another creature emerged from the building, this one more massive than anything before. It was one of the Teth aliens—warrior caste—huge and bulking. And it wore its own version of judge armor. The JUDGE-Z12, designed for the aliens and much larger in build than anything humans wore.

When the monster exited the facility, it stood at its full height, at least eleven feet, three feet taller than Gascoigne. Its smaller arms, the ones for fine motor activity, were tucked in the suit with no way to function without taking it off. But the larger arms—the dangerous ones—were just as armored as Gascoigne's, perhaps more.

Judge Gascoigne slowly lifted her gaze to meet the helmet of the alien. A normal person with common sense would've run, but the drivers of the exoskeleton power armor knew no fear by design.

"By the authority vested in me from Ex Cathedra," Gascoigne said, "I order you to stand down. I'm in pursuit of thieves, and this has nothing to do with you."

"*She wears the armor of an ally nation,*" the alien said, its Tethlite language distorted into something creepy through his suit.

Commander Dannik backed up. "*She stole it. The designations on the outside are covered up. She's no ally of yours.*"

"*Then it's as you say. I must speak with an architect at once.*"

"*I will happily take you to ours, but this judge won't let us pass without a fight.*"

Judge Gascoigne snorted. "Speak English or I'll run you through."

I shook my head, stunned by Gascoigne's brazen attitude. Fighting an alien in judge armor? The exoskeleton power suit really *had* removed all sense of fear. Or maybe Gascoigne had a death wish of the highest degree.

"*I see we have little choice,*" the alien said. "*And such weapons shouldn't be in the hands of our enemies. I'll have to pry this one out of her armor.*"

Commander Dannik laughed. "*With the equipment here, we can rip the helmet connectors right from her skull. We always have use for a judge exoskeleton.*"

CHAPTER FIFTEEN

The alien stepped forward, the combined weight of its body and armor cracking the already damaged parking lot. It swung with one of its arms, aiming for Gascoigne's head, but she leaned back, dodging the knuckles.

The speed of reactions the exoskeletons were capable of was determined by the mental acuity of the driver, and although the alien had a better model suit, proven faster, its hangover from the cryostasis no doubt played a factor.

With her knife attachment still extended, Gascoigne lunged forward. She slammed the blade on the side of the alien, but the armor resisted. Sparks flashed. She struck again to the same result. The alien punched down, colliding with her helmet and sending her stumbling.

Although the helmet was firmly attached to the body of the exoskeleton, it was probably the weakest area on the suit. If the screens and computer components inside got damaged, the driver would be at a huge disadvantage—more so than if an arm or attachment were busted. Without heavy weapons to pierce the armor, the alien was attempting to go for the fastest win possible.

Gascoigne jumped back, every action she took shaking the ground and adding the thunderous slam of metal on concrete to the area. Then she dashed around the side of the alien and lunged again. The celerity of her suit's movements shocked me. I had heard stories, but seeing it firsthand was entirely different.

Flecks of the broken parking lot popped into the air with each stomp of her boots.

The two Iron-Blooded backed away until they were against the building, their gazes locked on the conflict. Chelsy tugged at my sleeve, but I shook my head, still unwilling to leave and risk the chance of being spotted.

The corpses of the drones proved to be a mild obstacle for Gascoigne's quick attacks. She pushed the bodies out of her way, taking a few moments between strikes. Each time she landed her blade, another clang rang out, along with a whole new series of sparks.

But the alien wised up to her patterns. When she went in for a sixth strike, it was already prepared. The monster grabbed her arm and pulled her close. With its other fist, it bashed down on her helmet three times in a row, its blows creating just as many metallic sparks as the blade, perhaps more. Why didn't the alien use a blade? Or perhaps it didn't have one.

Held rapt by the violence, I couldn't look away, not even for a moment, not even after Chelsy let go of my sleeve.

Unable to wrench her arm free, Gascoigne continued to strike at the alien's side. At first I thought she had given up and was just slashing without purpose, but then the alien's armor broke at the seam between the plating, exposing the insides.

Gascoigne had intentionally struck the same area over and over, weakening the connector point. If she could manage to slide her blade into the small opening, she could gut the alien inside its own power suit.

The alien must've come to the same conclusion because it let go of Gascoigne and leapt back. It covered the broken section of its abdomen with one arm and waited.

To my surprise—because she didn't even give herself a couple seconds to think—Gascoigne rushed in for another strike. Poised for such an attack, the alien struck with precision. When it slammed her helmet again, a dent formed. Gascoigne fumbled for a moment, clearly disorientated.

The mental image of her skull caving in caused me to cringe.

In my gut, I knew the alien would win, but a tiny piece of me had hoped Gascoigne would've killed all three and then died to some sort of internal injury, ending them all.

The alien grabbed Gascoigne, held her in place, and then smashed his fist down on her damaged helmet. She slumped, her arms going limp. In an impressive display of the exoskeleton's capabilities, the alien lifted Gascoigne off the ground, over its head, and then threw her across the parking lot. She crashed into the Ex Cathedra truck, the impact and smash so loud I covered my ears.

The blow sent the truck sliding back, screeching the entire way and nearly toppling over.

Then the vehicle came to a halt and let off a burst of electricity. Both headlights died.

Silence mixed with the darkness.

Judge Gascoigne didn't get up.

The two Iron-Blooded switched on hand-sized flashlights and hooked them to the front of their shirts. They walked over to the alien and bowed their heads.

"*Impressive,*" Commander Dannik said. "*Clearly superior in every sense of the word.*"

Two people stumbled out of the messed-up truck. Ex Cathedra soldiers—the glint of their dog tags marked them as such—but they weren't in great shape. The entire front of the truck was smashed in from the force of the throw, like a terrible car accident, and the soldiers looked the part. Blood wept from their hair, they didn't walk right, and one vomited a few feet from the vehicle.

Judge Gascoigne, still half-buried in the wreck, didn't move, the dim light of her power cells blinking.

Commander Dannik and the other Iron-Blooded lifted their guns and fired. After a few quick shots, the soldiers were dead, no doubt the last of Ex Cathedra's forces out here in the lawless lands.

The alien walked over to the truck, the broken part of its suit visible, even from where I hid. The hole was larger than I expected. It was a shame Gascoigne hadn't cut it deep before she got herself killed.

The two Iron-Blooded walked over as well. They started the long process of prying Judge Gascoigne's suit from the wreckage, obviously intent on making good with their plan to steal her exoskeleton power suit. I hated the thought of them having it—they were fiends and lunatics, but what could I do?

I caught my breath as my hand slid into my pants pocket.

I had a gas grenade.

The thought caused me to smile sadistically. Outside, I had little fear of getting caught in the gas myself, so long as the wind didn't change direction. And the alien inside the exoskeleton was exposed to the elements, thanks to the hole in the side of its suit.

"Chelsy," I whispered. "I'm going to—"

But when I turned, she was gone. I glanced around, met only with the void of night. Where had she gone? The question sank into my stomach like a rock. Either she went back to Bishop or she went to his truck ahead of me—those were the only two explanations I could think of.

I returned my attention to the Iron-Blooded and their alien. While the men searched around the twisted frame of the truck, the alien judge lifted Gascoigne up.

It was now or never.

With my teeth gritted, I moved closer. Inch by inch, crawling along the mud, I got behind a smaller patch of rocks, right at the edge of the parking lot. Then I pulled the pin on the gas grenade and threw it as hard as I could.

Fortunately, my arms weren't lame like my hip and leg, and the weapon sailed straight into their midst. I ducked down before I could see what happened, hoping beyond hope none of them saw me.

The hiss of gas filled the area. One of the Iron-Blooded screamed, and then all I could hear was the commotion of the alien moving to get away. A second later, the alien judge leapt onto the roof of the building, Commander Dannik on his shoulder. To my delight, Dannik held his bloody arm close to his body, his jaw clenched and visibly red.

But he wasn't dead.

Damn. I really wanted to kill them all.

The A-tech gas clung to flesh and ate away at it, making it a devastating weapon. When I chanced a glance around the rock, I saw the second Iron-Blooded had learned that fact the hard way.

He scrambled to get away but didn't get out of the gas in time to save himself. He screamed and cried, grabbing at his face and arms, tearing his own skin free from his body in a frantic attempt to clear away the thing causing him harm.

I sat back behind the rock, not a fan of gore.

But I did take a small bit of satisfaction from the last of his shouts.

The alien judge and Commander Dannik waited on the roof. Dannik shone his flashlight out around the building. I kept still, behind the rocks, my heart beating hard enough for a heavy run.

The Teth aliens in their suits couldn't rely on their scent or ability to sense electric currents. They relied on their computers to feed them information, which increased the distance they could "see" but limited their bizarre capabilities, resulting in a more human-standard style of vision.

"*The armor's power cells must be recharged,*" the alien said. "*And the landscape is far from what I remember. If there are still enemies nearby, I'm ordering a retreat.*"

Commander Dannik nodded, his body trembling from the damage. "*As you say.*"

Unlike the other Iron-Blooded, Dannik didn't attack his own skin to free himself from the pain. He merely waited—the nanites in his body would work things out so long as he wasn't actively in gas.

The two took off over the rooftop, leaving me to the darkness of the wasteland. The wind blew away from me, taking the gas—a visible reaper on Earth—sailing across the sand and mud. Soon it would dissipate, becoming harmless, but until then I worried it might catch some lone wanderer by surprise.

I took several deep breaths, calming myself as I dwelled on the new reality of the situation. As the minutes passed, the chill set in. I shivered. Would Chelsy return? What would I do if she didn't?

But the mystery ended the moment I spotted her flashlight. She jogged back toward me, shining her light over the rocks, obviously confused when she found nothing.

"Here," I called out.

The light flew over me, and I squinted.

Chelsy ran to me. I hadn't expected the hug that came next. She threw her arms around my neck and squeezed me tight.

"I, uh," I murmured, "I'm glad you're okay, too."

I patted her back, dazed by affection. She held me close for a good thirty seconds and I didn't know what to say, so I just continued to run my hand along her spine.

After Chelsy ended the embrace, she showed me a small medical bag. I glanced through it, disappointed by the small amount of Cellucotton and gauze.

"Is this from Bishop's truck?"

She nodded.

Damn.

Chelsy helped me to my feet, and I turned my attention to the busted Ex Cathedra vehicle. It would have medical supplies. It had to.

I urged her toward it, and we made our way at a slow pace. Although the silence was so thick I sometimes wondered if I was still breathing, the thought of the Iron-Blooded returning filled me with an undying anxiousness. Chelsy must have felt the same way because she clung to my side, her eyes wide.

The Ex Cathedra truck was in ruins. Instead of crawling through it myself—I would never make it out, not with the agony in my body keeping me crippled—I turned to Chelsy.

"Can you search for more bags like this?" I asked.

She didn't need to be asked twice. With a single nod, she hurried over to the truck and scrambled inside.

The metal creaked, and I thought little of it. I doubted her weight would cause the wrecked vehicle to collapse. But then another creak occurred. And then a groan, as though something heavy were being slid across the outside of the vehicle. Chelsy had the flashlight, so all I could do was squint.

"Is everything okay?" I whispered.

My answer came without her offering any sort of reply.

Judge Gascoigne slid off the top of the vehicle, the power cells on her suit flashing a few more times before returning to their solid glowing state. I backed away at a hobble, stunned she had survived such a thrashing.

The people inside the suits were still capable of being hurt through blunt force, even if the suit dampened the impact.

"First there were those damn escapee slaves," Gascoigne said, her voice rough. "Then that traitor who tried to steal from my mining facility."

Judge Gascoigne stood to her full eight-foot height, her suit battered and dented in several spots, including the helmet.

How was she still alive?

"Then a thief took my battery," she continued, her volume increasing with each word. "*Get it all back*, I was told. *Get it or we'll give your suit to someone who can handle these problems.* Fifteen years I served, and this string of fucking problems gets me this treatment."

I continued to back away until I tripped over the broken concrete. I hit my butt, stifled a shout of fleeting pain, and then scooted across the parking lot. Maybe she hadn't seen me—maybe she was too busy venting—but I couldn't allow myself to get caught.

She laughed, hollow and filled with anger. "Then those despicable Iron-Blooded have me chasing them every goddamn inch of the desert. No battery. No truck. No squad. Just this doomed quest."

Judge Gascoigne took a step forward. I tried to angle away, but she turned her broken helmet to match my location. She knew I was here. Of course she did. Of course.

"You threw that grenade?" Gascoigne asked. "I should've guessed. How many types of grenades you carry, huh? One for every situation? Do you have one that'll help you now?"

When I didn't answer, she took a few more steps and closed the distance between us. I stopped moving—what else could I do?—and then she kicked me. A light kick, not as hard as the punch she delivered when we first met, but enough to take the air from my lungs. I tried to stand afterward, but my leg wouldn't cooperate. I collapsed on the ground, struggling to regain my breath.

Judge Gascoigne placed the foot of her exoskeleton on my head and leaned some of her weight on it. My face pressed against the ground, my skull with enough pressure I thought it would burst.

And it would if she applied the rest of her weight.

"D-Don't," I choked out. "Please."

"It's because of you I'm here. Do you even know how much I need this suit? Of course you don't." Again, she laughed, this time more ironic and forced. "You know what? The universe has a sick sense of humor, and I'm usually at the punch line. A cripple girl saved me. She can't even walk. It's like someone upstairs knows what'll eat at my sanity and deliberately throws it in my face."

She applied more weight, my eyeballs on the verge of popping out of their sockets. Rocks dug into my skin, and it was difficult to hear with my ears pressed hard to the sides of my skull.

Judge Gascoigne growled something I couldn't understand, her anger returning in full force. "I'm never going to get that battery back. There's no power here anymore, and those Iron-Blooded freaks are long since gone. I can't even track them now."

I took in a ragged breath. "I don't have it. Please. Let me go."

"Heh. Let you go? Hearing you beg will be the highlight of this whole event. What else am I going to do? I'm not going to lose my suit. Not now. Not ever. That means returning isn't an option."

Would she let me live if I begged? I doubted it.

A tink of metal on metal filled my ear, as if the sound traveled from the suit itself. And then another. And another.

"What's this?" Judge Gascoigne asked, amusement in her tone.

Chelsy came into my view, her small knife in hand. She brandished it like only a child could—earnest and naïve. When she struck at the JUDGE-X0 armor, the blade practically bent. I heard another tink through the armor, shaken that Chelsy would try something so stupid and foolish.

"Chelsy, stop," I shouted. "Get away from her!"

But she didn't listen. She tried pushing the judge away and slashing again—the blade twisted in her weak wrist, and she cut herself in the process. Although she was bleeding and distraught, Chelsy kicked at the suit and growled, the only noise she seemed to consistently make.

"Don't hurt her," I begged.

It wouldn't be hard to kill a child with a battle suit like Gascoigne's. A simple backhand and it would all be over.

No answer.

I thought Judge Gascoigne would kill her, I really did. But the judge never moved. She didn't even say another word after the initial reaction. She just stared down at Chelsy, watching her flail about like a single bee furious at an apiarist and just as ineffective.

For a split second, the metal boot on my head moved, and I figured my time was up. But then Judge Gascoigne removed it and turned away. Chelsy leapt to my side and helped me stand, frantic and breathing heavy.

The judge walked away—in the opposite direction of the Iron-Blooded, away from us and away from anything else.

Where was she heading? I almost asked, but I kept the question to myself. It didn't matter, so long as we never crossed paths again.

Chelsy separated from me, grabbed three medical bags, and then ran back to my side. She'd found two in the truck? The knowledge dispelled most of my fear.

"You did good," I said as I held on to her. "Thank you."

We hurried into the building and straight for the room where I left Bishop.

He sat in the middle of the room, hunched over with his hands on his head. We made our way over, and he acknowledged us with a groggy look, his eyes unfocused.

"Bishop," I said. "Thank goodness you didn't die. Here, lie back. I'll help you."

He did as I asked—a good sign—and I immediately pulled out the Cellucotton.

I continued, "We can wait here until you're strong enough to walk.

Then we'll get back to your truck, okay? Don't worry. We should be safe for the time being. Everything is under control."

Chelsy sat by my side, ready to help.

In one of my few moments in recent history, I felt both relieved and optimistic for the future. We had survived the evening, even if just barely.

My dreams consisted of odd shapes and distant voices. I needed to do something, and I didn't have enough time. Maybe I missed something important.

The anxiety was enough to wake me.

I opened my eyes, confused by my surroundings. Where had I gone to sleep? Where was I now? It wasn't yet morning, but I knew it wasn't long.

It didn't take me long to realize I was still in the cab of Bishop's truck. It was parked behind a rock, unmoving and hidden from most of the world.

Bishop had rearranged the seat so that it leaned back a bit, giving us all something to sleep on. He slept in the middle, Chelsy tucked under one arm and me under the other. His warmth warded off the unforgiving chill that lingered just beyond the windshield.

I stared down at the gauze and Cellucotton I had wrapped around his ribs and chest. Bishop claimed the injury didn't hurt, but I still felt bad for resting against it.

I sat up and rubbed at my eyes.

Every inch of my body hurt, and the moment I was upright, blood spilled from my nose. I looked like nine miles of bad road, bloody, bruised, and beaten. Nothing about me worked right, and I already hated myself for moving out of the comfortable position I had found under Bishop's arm.

"What're you doin'?" Bishop asked, his voice a low rumble and thick with sleep.

"I had nightmares," I whispered.

Bishop reached over and pulled me back onto his warm chest.

I shifted around, trying to avoid his injuries. "I don't want to hurt you and—"

"Shh, shh," he said as he stroked my hair. He never opened his eyes or moved from his spot, like he was half asleep and living through a dream. "I've got you, Viper. Nothin's gonna happen anymore. Close those eyes."

"I can't stop thinking."

Where would we go next? What would I do? Should I continue to Boulder City and potentially meet Dallas? Should I give up on that completely and take Chelsy with me everywhere, claiming her as a relative from here for the rest of my days?

Should I head for the Meteorological Plexus? I didn't even know where it was. But if I didn't . . .

So many possibilities and so little time.

Bishop used his foot to fiddle with his truck's radio. I was impressed—he didn't even need to look at what he was doing; he just felt around with his toes until he hit the right buttons. The station he switched on caught me by surprise.

Pleasant music played. The kind of pleasant music from the old world, with soft violins and wind instruments that blended together like two gusts of wind heading in the same direction. It created a beautiful white noise that helped soothe my troubled thoughts.

"Think about it in the morning," Bishop said as he continued to stroke my hair. "We'll reach Richfield in no time, and everything will be fine."

"Do you . . . really think so?"

"With God's help."

I closed my eyes and enjoyed how the music, without lyrics, matched the steady beat of Bishop's heart.

I would decide in the morning.

CHAPTER SIXTEEN

The nightmares didn't cease, and I couldn't seem to sleep long.

I opened my eyes, unable to see much. My head throbbed—pulsating as though my brain was pressurized and ready to explode. Things happened. Bishop spoke to me. Chelsy tried to show me places of interest out the window. They were fleeting micro-memories drowned out by the pain.

We got near a town. I knew that much. The wall around the community stood tall and sturdy, made of metal sheets, solid posts, and jagged wires, some barbed, others loose and rusty. Two guards were posted outside. They said some things to Bishop, but they didn't register.

Then Bishop shook my shoulder. I turned to him, wondering why he wouldn't stop.

"Remember that doctor I told you about?" he asked.

I think I nodded, but I couldn't tell.

"She lives here."

I closed my eyes and rested back on the seat. If Bishop said a doctor was here, then there was a doctor here. I'd let him handle the details.

"How many colors do you see?"

I rubbed at my nose. Tubes blocked my nostrils, and although I wanted to dislodge them, I let them be. Little by little my thoughts came back to me, allowing me to register the contents of the room. A small space, but comfortable. The open window beckoned the breeze to play with the curtains and dance across my skin.

"How many colors do you see?"

Colors?

I shifted my focus to the paper filled with multicolored dots held up in front of me. "Three," I said, my throat dry.

"Good. And how many dots are there in total?"

"Twenty-seven."

"Very good."

The woman holding the paper gave me a gentle smile. What was her name? She'd said it many times before, but I couldn't piece it together. I must have given her a look of confusion because she set the paper down on a nearby counter and patted my leg.

"It seems you're finally awake, Kita," she said. "I don't know if you were awake enough to remember me, but I'm Dr. Tammy Claire."

I didn't remember her. There were flashes in my mind's eye of her speaking, but otherwise nothing. I nodded along with her words, unconcerned with her specifically and more concerned with my condition.

"Am I going to be okay?" I managed to ask.

"That depends."

Dr. Claire walked around the room and straightened things up.

It was a genuine medical office, not something hastily put together. She had medical equipment, including tools for surgery, an IV stand, needles, and several pairs of gloves. Few places like this existed in Ex Cathedra. They were always busy with patients—people who were dying from cancer, radiation, injuries, or genetic defects. The medicine was never enough, and the doctors often kept security to keep them and their supplies safe.

There wasn't much security in Dr. Claire's office. None at all, in fact.

I ran a clammy hand down my face.

"Depends?" I asked.

"You need to eat more," Dr. Claire said. "Especially foods that will help blood production. Red meat, leafy greens, beans, and egg yolks."

"Okay."

When I ran my hand up into my hair, I hesitated. I pulled my hand back, stunned to find a wad of black locks tangled in my fingers.

"Hair loss is common with radiation poisoning," Dr. Claire said, her voice calm and unchanged. "The loss can be permanent, but most I've treated have regrown their hair afterward. If you want, we can cut your hair short now so that the change isn't drastic."

I didn't want to talk about it. Looking like a sickly blob of weakness was never my goal in life.

I stared at my arm, at the bruising from multiple needle injections, and how my hand shook even when I simply held it up for examination. One of the basic treatments for radiation poisoning was a blood transfusion. Did this clinic have the blood on hand for such a procedure?

"Where are we?" I asked.

"The town of Richfield."

For whatever reason, the name reminded me of something I had nearly forgotten.

"A man named Joel used to live here," I whispered.

Dr. Claire stopped cleaning and turned to me. Her heart-shaped face and golden hair glowed with health, even under the fluorescent lighting. But she knit her eyebrows together, marring her beautiful visage.

"Joel Schultz?" she asked.

"He never said his last name. Just that he was from a town called Richfield."

"Joel was a trapper and a junk hunter. He disappeared a month back."

"The Iron-Blooded," I said. "He found something they were interested in . . . and I saw him before he died. He seemed like a nice guy."

Dr. Claire crossed her arms and stared at the floor. Then she forced a smile. "He was a good man. But please don't spread around such news while you're here. I'll be the one to tell Joel's family."

I didn't want to argue, so I lay back, taking note of the contour of my cot, and closed my eyes. Rest would be good.

Someone picked me up.

When I opened my eyes, I realized it was night. Although the darkness typically unnerved me, especially in unknown places, I recognized the way Bishop held me. Knowing he was nearby dispelled my fears of the shadows and the things hidden within. I clung to his shirt, not even realizing how cold I was until I felt his warmth.

As comfortable and content as I could be, sleep stole my consciousness again.

The resting room inside the clinic was made more for children than it was adults. Toys lined the counters, and old-world pictures of kids playing in wondrous green fields of grass covered the walls. Dr. Claire said I would need to rest for a few weeks before I would be back to normal.

I rubbed at my leg.

Well, as normal as I could get.

She couldn't do anything about the damage that had been done. I figured. It had been too long since the initial injury. And the aggravation brought about by Commander Dannik didn't help.

The only good news came in the diagnostic. Nerve damage. Most of the pain was from nerve damage. It meant, in theory, I could walk—and perhaps one day I would find a way to dull the nerve endings—but for right now, there was little to do about it.

The door opened and in streamed the sound of laughter. Three kids, smiles wide across their faces, ran to a pile of toys on the far counter. Wooden toys, mostly. Little cars, little people, some in the shapes of animals I had only seen in pictures.

Crouton—Chelsy? I couldn't decide what to call her now that the situation was less serious—walked in afterward, also smiling. She held my figurines in her hands and compared them to the toys the others had in their arms.

"We can play with them all together," one girl said, no older than five.

One side of her face drooped low, deformed, and her right hand was nothing more than a stump. No fingers, but she did have a single fingernail growing out of the skin.

Two boys, perhaps six and seven, fought with each other over who would have the largest car.

"You played with it last time," the older one said.

The younger shook his head. "Nuh-uh."

Neither of them had hair. No eyebrows, or eyelashes, or even follicles on their arms.

Without resolving their argument, the older ran from the room, the younger hot on his heels. The girl joined in the chase, laughing the entire time, but Crouton lingered behind. She turned to me and showed off the figurines.

"I made those," I said.

Crouton's eyes widened.

"Do you want me to make more?"

I didn't think she could smile wider, but she did.

"I just need some materials and tools. Let Bishop know. He always finds good stuff."

Crouton gave me a quick hug, careful not to squeeze too tight, and then ran from the room, leaving me alone on the bed. For a moment I wondered if this was the feeling of living a happy life before the bombs. It reminded me of the fantasy I had when I imagined living in the underground greenhouse—the BC Oasis—and how life could be simple and beautiful and without strife or suffering.

It seemed too pleasant to be real.

CHAPTER SEVENTEEN

I rolled to my side as the door opened.

Bishop strolled through and flashed me a smirk. "Oh, good. You're lookin' better."

My bed creaked as I sat up, and while I could feel the springs through the homemade mattress, it was still the best bed I had slept on in several years.

"You just brought me food an hour ago," I said.

"I'm not here for that. I'm here to get you bathed."

I grabbed at the blankets. "I, uh, don't think I can get up."

"That's fine. I'll take you."

Before I could offer any protest, Bishop scooped me, and the blankets, off the bed.

Anywhere I needed to go, he was there to take me. No hint of complaints, no snide remarks at how pathetic I must be.

I wanted to thank him for all that, but I didn't know how without sounding awkward. Those small details didn't much matter, yet here I was, dwelling on them.

"It's taken you a few days, but you got that sparkle back in your eyes, Viper."

"Well, er, thank you."

Bishop walked me through the clinic and out the front door. I clung to him tighter, my face red at the thought of the townspeople seeing us like this. Then again, there weren't many, and everyone had been so nice it was hard to imagine they would mock me.

Richfield had a grand total of one hundred and fifty residents.

The entire town had been built before the bombs, but the repairs were made from the remains of other nearby cities. The patchwork repairs made to the buildings were hidden with paint and pictures, leaving most of the houses looking like something someone plucked right out of a 1950s magazine. Quaint and warm.

Except for the wall around the town.

It was constructed to look as ugly as possible—that was my working theory, anyway. Something to keep the view of the town from random passersby. Most traders were kept from entering, and only those who paid up-front were allowed in to see Dr. Claire. The close-knit group inside the town did almost everything together. Church, farming—all alien produce except for the few things grown indoors—and goat ranching.

"Where are you taking me?" I asked.

"To the hot springs."

I had never visited hot springs before. It didn't surprise me that Richfield had them, either. Their whole town existed solely because of their well—a pipeline to the underground water brought up by their pump. And the smell of sulfur occasionally wafted through the streets, bringing the whole picture together. Underground water and caverns sustained this place and gave it life.

"I don't know if I'm strong enough right now to walk around wet rocks," I said.

"I'll be with you the whole time. Stop fussin'."

I held on to him, my gaze up to focus on his expression. "You seem . . . more accommodating than before."

Bishop laughed.

A citizen of Richfield, wiry from a lifetime of work, glanced up from his porch repair and cocked an eyebrow.

"You saved my life," Bishop said, ignoring the man as he made his way down the main thoroughfare. "And DC told me all about those machines in my blood. That's a pretty big deal. You had those? And then you gave them to me? Who does that?"

"Well . . . I didn't . . ."

I didn't know what to say.

"The least I can do to repay you is help you recover," Bishop said. "And I've done it before when I worked with DC in the past. Helped her with all sorts of people. You're in good hands."

"Wait, wait. Who is DC?"

"The doctor."

Ah. DC. For Dr. Claire.

"We have a lot to talk about," Bishop said, a fair bit of spring in his steps. "I've been waitin' till we could have some time alone, and now seems good."

"What did you want to ask?"

"Well, lots of things, but first, you were blubberin' on and on about everyone dying. I never got those details. Was that some irradiated hallucination, or should I be worried about a zombie outbreak or some shit?"

His statement got me to smile. But it didn't last long. Would he even believe me? While I mulled over the question, I turned my gaze over the town.

To my surprise, Richfield was large for the number of citizens, as though the residents planned for expansion when they constructed their wall. Places like this would cease to exist unless I told everyone who would listen.

"Do you know about the satellites that orbit the planet?" I asked. "The Climate Engineering System?"

"Nope."

"O-Okay . . . Well, they surround the planet, and once upon a time they controlled the weather. Now they're going to destroy the atmosphere."

"And what'll that do?"

"We'll all die. Because there won't be air to breathe, basically."

Again, Bishop laughed. I gritted my teeth, hating the sound of his mirth after such a dire statement.

I gripped his shirt. "You don't believe me?"

"No, no. I believe you."

"Then why are you laughing?"

"What do you want me to do?" he asked, almost incredulous. "Cry? Put a bullet through my head? I've said it before, and I'll say it again—humanity has some bad luck. Almost like the universe hates us. I mean, have you seen how many stupid people there are? And how *rare*, ironically, *common* sense is? It's worth laughing about, trust me. Better than any other response."

I relaxed a bit. "I think the satellites can be altered at a place called the Meteorological Plexus, but I don't know where that is. What do you think I should do about this information, Bishop? I . . . can't seem to make up my mind."

"Make up your mind about what?"

"If I . . . should just ignore it and hope it's all wrong, or maybe I should just enjoy my last year . . ."

"Maybe let that shit slide downhill and someone else deal with it?"

Now it was my turn to laugh. I chuckled into his chest, unable to stifle a smile. "Who would I tell, exactly? There's no authority to bring this to. The ruler of Ex Cathedra? While they're in the middle of a war and campaign of conquest? They'd never listen. Does United California even have a single leader?"

"Yeah, their commander in chief. Some guy whose name I can't remember."

"You think he'll see me and believe a single word I say? Especially if I don't bring any of the evidence with me? And United California is currently fighting Ex Cathedra. Who else is there? Bounty hunters? Will they take a mission with no reward, no details, and no evidence? Especially while people will hire them to deal with marauders and the Iron-Blooded? There's no one else. It's just me. *Me*."

Me.

I could go over the facts a million times in my head, but it wouldn't change anything. Even if I told people, who could I trust to operate computers in the Meteorological Plexus? No one I knew.

"Sounds like you already know the answer," Bishop said with a half smile. "You just don't wanna commit."

I didn't think I could handle it. No, not handle it. I was afraid of failing. What if I got 90 percent of the way and then couldn't make it?

At this point in my life, a simple ladder would be the obstacle that prevented me from seeing my mission through to the end.

Could I live with the stress and haunting realization that I was nothing—a speck in a grand dark universe with no potential for anything? A waste of an existence for having tried and failed?

But I did have a little over a year of life. Should I spend it struggling to save a world that had never helped me or relax and let it all end? Bishop was right. I knew the answer, but resisted it.

Fear whispered dire possibilities into my ear, promising me all sorts of nightmarish situations. Despite that, it was my grandfather who gave me pause. What would he say if he heard me fretting? He'd be disappointed. He had faced a million troubles—brand-new situations—without letting fear dissuade him.

My grandfather was a figure of legend. I wanted to be like him. A person worth remembering. Worth talking about. Worth imitating.

"You made up your mind, then?" Bishop asked.

I nodded. "Yes."

"Yeah, I can tell by the way you hardened your spine that your moxie came back. I take it you don't want to go to Boulder anymore?"

"Well, since I have no idea where to go, and since I'm supposed to bring Crouton to Boulder City, I think we should still go there."

"Maybe we can find someone who knows a thing or two about the old world in Boulder, huh? Sounds like a plan to me."

"So . . . you'll come with me to the Meteorological Plexus?"

Bishop chuckled. "I thought that much was obvious, Viper."

His confidence got me to smile. No hesitation. He would just be there.

"We're still gonna scavenge along the way, right?" he asked. "Guy's gotta pay for food."

"Yes, of course."

Warm steam washed over us, drawing my attention.

The Richfield hot springs wasn't what I had been expecting. Rocks jutted up from the ground, creating pools of water all connected through small tunnels. Curtains and rods were hung between each, creating private spaces, but for extra measure they had hung a sign that read: LEFT FOR MEN, RIGHT FOR WOMEN. Voices echoed from the right, but Bishop ignored all of it and headed for the left.

"What're you doing?" I asked.

"I'm not leaving you alone so you can slip on everything," he said. "I remember you at the ramen cups needin' Crouton to help you out. Don't worry. I've got you this time."

The water in the springs wasn't clear, but a salty white, nearly opaque. The place had a rough scent that irritated my nose. Sulfur never quite smelled right. But after a few minutes, it was all I could smell, basically becoming the white noise of odors.

Bishop picked a pool—about the size of a four-door car—and shut the curtains that surrounded it. The water over the red rocks glistened in the dim sunlight filtered by the overcast skies. Bishop set me down, careful to make sure I had footing, and then pulled his shirt off and started with his belt.

His lack of modesty always took me by surprise. All I had was a simple medical gown and a couple blankets, and while it would be easy to quickly undress, I didn't want to strip in front of him. I was bruised, weak, and my hair was falling out. I didn't want anyone to see me naked—I even avoided mirrors.

Before Bishop pulled off the last of his clothing, I glanced away, heat flooding my face.

Something seemed different between us.

Like Bishop wanted to be here with me.

The slight change in dynamic from when we washed at the ramen cups made me realize he was everything that was the opposite of me—strong, capable, and healthy thanks to the nanites. Part of it was lust, but part of it was jealousy, and I didn't want him to see either emotion.

To dampen such feelings, I imagined the scars on his body. They reduced his overall appearance when visible and reminded me that he might not be entirely stable—mentally. Then again, the scars were shallow, and easily hidden under shirts. Some fit well with the tone of his muscular physique.

Why was I thinking so much about Bishop's body? What was wrong with me? I knew it was inappropriate, but his protectiveness and easy-going charisma made it fun to imagine our trip to the springs going in a much different direction.

"Can I ask you a question?" I asked, keeping my eyes down.

"Whatever you want," Bishop said as he threw his clothes in a pile.

"Have you ever been in love?"

"Hm? Nah. I've never been in a place long enough for a relationship like that."

He avoided so many things. Like the truth.

"Can I ask you another question?" I asked.

Bishop chuckled. "I said, *whatever you want.*"

"Bishop isn't really your middle name, is it?"

For a moment, he didn't move. I refused to turn around and see why not, but from his held breath, I assumed he was simply mulling over my question.

"What makes you think that?" he asked.

"First off, it's so dissimilar to your first and last names."

My fifth rule of lying: never give an impossible, or highly improbable, explanation or answer. I solidified that lesson when I was in the hands of the Iron-Blooded, but it applied here, too. His name was Uriah Geffen. Bishop wasn't a natural part of the name, not even slightly. It was obviously fake from the beginning.

"Secondly," I continued, "you give everyone a nickname. It only makes sense you'd do it to yourself, too."

It occurred to me then: I only knew Dezray's and Thatcher's names because Bishop said them. Those probably weren't their real names at all.

Bishop walked to the edge of the spring, and I had to keep my gaze on my bare feet.

He nudged my shoulder. "Why are you still dressed?"

"I . . . well . . . You need to close your eyes."

"You could fall in, Viper. That's a real concern."

My face burned with each passing second. I couldn't deny his claim, but I couldn't bring myself to move, either.

"Don't worry, I won't be crass or anything," Bishop said. "Trust me. I've seen plenty of naked ladies."

That didn't put me at ease. If anything, it dug under my skin and irritated me more than it should have. The fire in my body shifted from embarrassment to anger in an instant.

"I'll be fine," I said, curt. "Just close your eyes. And turn away."

With a sigh, he turned and stared at the dull gray curtains.

I disrobed in a few simple motions before easing myself into the water, slow and careful. The heat shocked me for a moment—much warmer than I had anticipated—but I understood how such baths could be appealing. After a minute, the heat melted away the aches in my legs.

I slid the rest of the way in, thankful for the swirling opaque water hid most of my features. The smooth rocks made for a comfortable chair.

"You can look now."

Bishop got into the water and exhaled. "I love this place." He sat just a few feet from my location and sank into the water until it was at his collarbones.

"Why do you insist on using nicknames instead of people's real names?" I asked.

"I just like 'em better."

"Will it bother you if I call you Uriah?"

"Yes," he replied faster than I thought. He took a breath and calmed himself a bit. "Okay, look. I don't like callin' people by their names because what's the point of rememberin' them? My nicknames are better anyway. They get the point across."

"They . . . get the point across?"

"Yeah. Easy. Simple. Fun to say. That's how all of life should be, ya know?" Bishop leaned back on the rocks, his arms out to either side.

"Plus, I hate hearin' my own name. My grandma and parents called me Uriah. No one else. After they died, all I can think about is them whenever I hear it."

"Probably not the healthiest way to deal with that," I said.

Bishop shot me a sidelong glance. "Says the woman who can't handle a gun without breakin' down."

The cut stung. It took me a moment to even find my words.

He was right. It was the same damn thing. I was being hypocritical for criticizing him.

I hunched over and kept my face close to the water, my shoulders bunched around my neck. The silence continued, Bishop's annoyance more prevalent than the smell of sulfur. But after a long exhale, he seemed to dispel most of his grievances. Did nothing bother him for very long?

"Do you mind if I asked what happened to them?" I whispered. "Your grandmother and parents?"

Bishop laced his fingers together and placed his hands behind his head. "We lived in this small town in the middle of nowhere. Other town next to us always gave my family grief. Some old-world grudges never die. And then, for reasons I'll never know, a group of punks set fire to my town while most everyone was sleepin'. What kinds of cowards do that?"

"In the middle of the night? No warning?"

"They killed more than just my family. The neighbors and their animals. All of them." Bishop spoke without his usual mirth—without any emotion at all, really, like he was reading from a script.

Bishop tapped the tally marks on his chest. "So now I keep track. Like I said before, anyone that comes to kill me gets to be another tally mark."

The cruelty of mankind knew no bounds, I guessed. But then I remembered the pleasant resting room and the children in the clinic. The warmth of the community sowed a new reality in my mind—perhaps mankind knew great beauty and wonder as well.

"There, now you know the gritty details," Bishop said. "You gonna tell me about your gun problem?"

"I shot my sister," I said without giving my words any thought.

I wanted to tell him, and I knew if I dwelled on it, I never would. Better to just blurt everything out—like ripping off a Band-Aid.

Bishop chuckled. "Oh. I see. Older or younger?"

"Younger," I whispered. "I was thirteen and she was nine."

But then Bishop stopped asking questions.

I closed my eyes, every second of the event as potent as the pain in my body. "It was dark. We were running. And then we got separated but . . . there were aliens and Ex Cathedra soldiers in the area. The aliens had killed my father days prior, and I hadn't eaten or slept much. My sister came up behind me—I didn't realize it was her—I just fired."

The shot echoed in my ears, chilling my blood.

"So, it was an accident," Bishop said.

I clenched my jaw and scrunched my eyes closed harder. "No. It was worse than that." The words scratched my throat as they came out, digging another wound into my body. "I . . . hit her in the side of the chest. Maybe . . . if we weren't out in the wasteland . . . if we were by a doctor . . . it would've been different. "But"—I took in a shaky breath—"I just stood there. She bled out. Staring at me. Unable to breathe because . . . she was drowning in her own . . ."

Bishop leaned forward. "Hey, I get it. I don't need the details."

I could've put her out of her misery and shot her again. I could've thrown down the gun and held her, apologizing a million times over. I could've run for help, even if the attempt would've been futile.

But I didn't do any of those things.

I just stared, unable to look away, as she died.

I never picked up a handgun after that.

"She must have hated me," I said, half crying, half laughing, my tone dark. "I was supposed to be protecting her."

Bishop tried to pull me close. "She didn't hate you."

I jerked away from his touch. "How do you know?" I hissed. He didn't even know the worst of it.

"Sisters never really hate each other in their hearts. I'm sure she's waiting for you, lookin' down from on high, anxious and upset you're so distraught."

"I was the one who killed her."

"She'd still forgive you."

How could she, after what I did? I couldn't even forgive myself. Ever.

The hot water burned at the edge of my limbs. I didn't care. I just sat still, trying to bury the memories back into the deepest depths of my psyche.

Without warning, Bishop kicked his feet up onto the rocks, leaned back, and then pulled me over like I were an old drinking buddy. Pressed up against his side, and under his armpit, I struggled to think of the appropriate response. I shuddered.

Bishop waved his hand through the air. "Did I ever tell you about these two junk hunters I knew?"

"No," I said. "But I don't—"

"They were the human equivalent of wet socks," he continued, ignoring my muttering. "I swear the two of them had enough extra chromosomes to make a third person."

I couldn't help but let out a single laugh.

Bishop smiled. "These two guys were idiots. So when we were exploring some buildings, one of them had the bright idea to swing down into a window two stories below us. He said he saw it in a vid once."

Bishop used his hand to pantomime the entire tale, including using two fingers to signify the walking and jumping.

"The guy got a rope, swung down, and hit the glass so hard he knocked himself out and fell the last four stories to the ground. *Poof.* Dead."

It was a morbid story—a terrible tale of loss—but I still couldn't help but smile. It was a stupid thing to do.

"That's not the best part," Bishop said. "The second guy *did the same damn thing right after.* He said the first guy had weakened the glass. *Double poof.* That guy dies, too. Can you believe it?"

Honestly, the tale didn't surprise me, but the sheer lunacy of the situation did get me laughing again. Bishop joined in, and we both enjoyed the moment together.

I relaxed a bit under his arm, my gaze on a cluster of his tally mark scars. Despite his self-mutilation and masochistic tendencies, Bishop really did have a way of chasing away dark thoughts. I guessed he was an expert, having done it for many years himself.

He grazed his fingers up and down my arm, but I tensed and shook my head. "Please. I don't want—" I held my breath for a moment, searching for the right words.

But what could I say? I hated myself at the moment and couldn't handle such intimacy? Bishop barely touched me, yet I cringed and fretted, focusing in on my own hideous state. It probably wasn't healthy.

"You don't want what?" he asked.

I closed my eyes and crossed my arms tight over my chest. "I . . . I have radiation poisoning."

"It's not a contagious disease."

"But I'm not suitable for . . . this kind of interaction." I took a breath. "I'm not anything like the pretty girls of Dodge City."

Bishop laughed and removed his hand from my arm. "Calm down, Viper. I'm not so hard up for company that I'd pressure a sweet girl, like yourself, to do anything you didn't want. What would my mother say if I did something like that?"

"I'm sick," I said with a huff. "Unless you're into girls who look like half-warm corpses, I doubt I have much to worry about ever."

"You don't give yourself enough credit."

"Dr. Claire wants me to cut my hair. We'll see what you have to say then."

Bishop tapped his chest. "I know about DC's recommendation. I've got my knife with me. Sharpened it and everything. I can help, if you want."

While I didn't want to cut my hair, I knew it would be better than slowly watching it pool on my pillow every morning. I nodded to his suggestion, thankful someone else would help me do it. The prospect of the mirror really did leave me feeling weak.

Bishop pulled his pants over and withdrew his knife. I scooted away from him, my head down, and waited. The moment he touched the blade to my scalp, I closed my eyes and counted the strokes it required. Fortunately, the hair follicles were weak from the radiation, and everything came out easy, no pain.

A hundred and thirty-two strokes later, he ran a hand from the back of my neck to my forehead, the smooth and slightly fuzzy sensation a new experience for me.

"Feel lighter?" he quipped.

I kept my arms crossed tight and bit my lip.

"What's wrong?" he asked.

I didn't want to feel my head. "Nothing."

"Bullshit. C'mon, Viper. You told me all about your sister, but you won't let me know what's happenin' now?"

"Well?" I asked.

"Well, what?"

"What do you think of me now?"

Bishop tucked the knife away. He made the same "tsk" he always did.

I turned my head away from him, all the muscles in my body tense. "See?" I said, my tone strained. "I told you. I'm disgusting."

Much to my surprise, and fear, he laughed. "Women."

"You think I'm overreacting?" I gripped my arms tighter, anger mixing with my shame. "Can you honestly look me in the eyes and tell me I don't look like roadkill?"

"Hey, I know a pretty woman when I see one, right?"

I shot him a glower. "Sure."

"And you trust me not to lie to you?"

"Yes."

"Then stop your pity party, because I think you're good-lookin'." He shrugged. "Sure, you look better with hair, but it'll grow back. Besides, you have qualities that can't be duplicated, ya know? Distinct."

Perhaps I trusted him not to lie to me about something important, but this was obviously not one of those moments. He was lying. Obviously. I knew the truth. But Bishop's attempt to make me feel better did quell the raging emotions warring throughout my body.

Even knowing he wanted to cheer me up was enough to lift my spirits.

The moment ended when an air raid siren ripped through the town. I jerked my attention to the curtain around the pool. Bishop leapt out of the water—without giving me warning—and I quickly turned away, but not in time. I almost yelled at him, but the siren reminded me that now wasn't the time.

"We've got to get back to the clinic," Bishop said, serious. "C'mon. Get out of the water. Right now."

CHAPTER EIGHTEEN

Bishop unceremoniously yanked me out of the hot spring. I ducked down and grabbed my clothing, but by the time I looked back up, he was gone. In a few short moments, I had my hospital gown and blankets back over my body.

The air raid sirens continued.

In my gut, I knew it couldn't be an air strike. I hadn't seen—or heard—of any aircraft since I was young. The fuel costs, and repairs, made such travel impractical. Not to mention the frequent storms and the attention such a vehicle would bring.

But what if someone was using an airplane regardless? My grandfather told me all sorts of stories about impressive aircraft before the war ended, but that didn't help my imagination. What a terrible weapon in the hands of the wrong people.

Bishop returned a few minutes later. He scooped me up and leapt out of the hot springs. A group of women hung by the edge, wrapped in robes, speaking to each other in hushed voices, their brows furrowed.

They weren't panicking or screaming, which told me the siren was probably used for a variety of reasons.

"Where is Crouton?" I asked.

"She's at the clinic."

"What's going on?"

"Marauders."

Ah. A plague of thugs. "The city seems plenty defended."

"Yeah, well, the assholes outside have themselves a mortar."

Even the mere mention stilled my commentary. Mortars were highly effective at breaking defensive walls and lines. They shot small explosive shells in a high arc so that they landed from above.

Ex Cathedra soldiers used them to decimate small outlying towns all the time, anyone who didn't surrender to their authority. Even with a wall—even a well-fortified wall with gunmen posted in turrets—the mortars tore through them every time.

"Why?" was all I could ask.

Why would marauders target Richfield? Imagining the children being ripped to shreds by random indiscriminate fire angered me like only a few things in the world did.

Bishop didn't have a chance to answer me. An explosion hit the town a good fifty feet from us, sending dirt and debris into the air as clouds. The mortar shell left a crater in the road, deep enough to reach my knees, wide enough to lie across. While the blast radius was larger than the crater, it was the shrapnel range that frightened me the most. Fragments of the metal shell could easily tear through flesh and leave insides bleeding.

Fortunately, I didn't see any of the town's denizens besides the guards posted on the wall. They took aim and shot off in the distance, but another explosion rocked the streets and sent more clouds of dirt into the air. Clearly they weren't hitting the enemy.

Bishop got us back to the clinic. He flew through the front door and headed to the back.

Dr. Claire stood next to a metal hatch in the floor, ushering people inside the bunker underneath the building. Bishop and I crowded into the basement space with forty other people, my attention focusing on Crouton the moment I spotted her long black hair. She squirmed her way past the others and stood at Bishop's side.

When Dr. Claire finally came down, she locked the hatch using a touch-screen A-tech system, similar to the one in Bishop's truck.

A single light shone from the ceiling, bright enough to illuminate the corners, but dim enough not to burn my eyes. The far wall of the bunker had the logo "Anonymous Industries" etched into the metal—an old-world corporation that specialized in A-tech products and equipment. Which meant this place was made well before the bombs.

Despite the fact nearly a third of the townspeople were crammed into the same space, they remained cordial and calm, as if dangerous situations were commonplace. Even the children stayed with their parents, as though going through a drill.

Bishop pushed his way to Dr. Claire. "Do you need more gunners? I'm a good shot."

"It'll be over soon," she said.

"Oh, yeah? What's your guarantee?"

"We've had problems with these goons before." She shook her head and tossed back some of her golden hair. "They want a Danegeld, and we refused to pay."

"The fuck's a Danegeld?" Bishop asked.

"Blackmail. Tribute. Racketeering. Whatever you want to call it. These particular marauders are a rail gang. They use the limited railway system to go between a few different towns in the area. They demand money for *protecting us*"—she sneered as she said those two words—"but obviously they're more the problem than anything else."

Bishop mulled over the explanation and took a step back.

The people of Richfield remained quiet through the rumble and shake of the bunker. When I glanced around, I took note of their similarities. Rough skin, blistered hands—some deformed but otherwise healthy, though thin. Simple clothes, no doubt made by someone in town. Everyone shared the collective toll of working in a self-sustaining community.

Everyone but Dr. Claire.

She was different than the others, her youthful appearance as someone in her early twenties a harsh contrast to everyone else, even with people of the same age and gender. Her blemish-free skin was a rarity in the wasteland. Thirty seconds outside and most had scars.

Several minutes after the tremors stopped, Dr. Claire placed her hand on the scanner and allowed everyone out. They thanked her as they went, some half bowing their heads. She smiled and gently touched them on their shoulders as they went by, the reverence on their face plain as day.

When Bishop, Crouton, and I exited the bunker, the lights of the clinic flickered and then died.

The people of Richfield muttered concerns, but Dr. Claire held up her hands.

"Everything will be all right. Find a safety officer and return to your homes. Any electrical problems can be solved."

"Wait here," Bishop said to Crouton.

She offered a tight frown but otherwise didn't protest.

Although we didn't have a home to return to, Bishop and I exited the clinic with the others and glanced around the city, his gaze lingering on the wreckage. To my surprise, very little was damaged. If I had to guess, I would say whoever was aiming the mortar wasn't the greatest shot. Random craters dotted the road, the wall wasn't broken, and most of the houses appeared unscathed. Dust and debris filled the walkways between houses, however, hovering around like a terrible fog that watered the eyes and clogged the lungs.

I coughed a few times until Bishop walked away from the waft of brown and gray.

While he jogged around, surveying the area, I asked, "Why do you seem so concerned?"

"Why wouldn't I be concerned?"

"I threatened to kill you and you laughed. I told you the world was ending, and again, you laughed. Now you seem worried."

But I deduced the answer before Bishop even spoke again. Richfield reminded him of his town when he was a child. I'd bet my life on it.

"I lived here for a few years," Bishop said, his tone terse. "Why do you think they let me in, huh? I don't wanna see them messed with."

We made it to the center of town and found a few of the guards standing around the well. It wasn't a stone circle with a bucket, but a large pump and pump house to keep the generator protected from the elements. To my dismay, the pump house had a smoking hole through the roof like an impromptu chimney. The random mortar fire had struck their primary source of clean water.

"What's going on?" Bishop asked as we approached.

"It's busted," one man said, sweat staining his overalls and shirt. "Damn shell hit it good."

It occurred to me then that the generator for the pump also supplied the town with electricity, which included the clinic.

"We need to go after those marauders," another man said, his rifle close to his chest. "This is their fault, and if we keep doin' nothin', they'll strike again."

"I agree," a woman said.

The man in overalls motioned to the smoke billowing out of the pump house. "First we need our water! If we don't fix this, we'll all be forced to leave, and you know what the marauders will do then."

Bishop backed away from the crowd, shaking his head. "I'm gonna take you back to the clinic. Then I'm gonna help these guys shoot a few assholes."

"Be careful," I said.

He laughed, like he always did. Being careful was a punch line, apparently.

I sat inside the clinic, enjoying the light of two lanterns. The children stayed with me in the resting room, each of them with their toys, all of them disturbingly quiet for their age. Whispers filled the room so infrequently I thought they were the rustling of the wind beyond the window.

While the tense townsfolk hustled around outside, each arguing about the best course of action, I drowned out their words by focusing on the figurines in front of me.

Step by step, I crafted another figurine family, this one with two children and a big strong father. It made me smile to measure everything out—to act like myself before I ran across Dallas—and complete a simple task without much anxiety.

I could understand why people ignored the larger problems of life. Why dwell on the destruction and chaos when focusing in on something simple could bring a small amount of controllable joy?

But I couldn't maintain this. Once I was better—a couple days, at the max—I would need to leave and deal with the big issues.

The moment I finished the figurines, I motioned Crouton over. "Here. Like I promised."

She smiled, but it didn't last long. Her eyes darted to my bald head and back to my face, her disapproval plain as day.

"Would you like another figurine?" I asked, ignoring her. What was I supposed to do about my new situation? All I could do was hope the radiation didn't take my life.

Crouton ran back to her spot and grabbed a piece of paper. When she showed it to me, I glowered.

"You want me to make an alien?"

She nodded.

Not just any alien—one of the mindless drones. Crouton had colored in the skin, drawn its claws and even its teeth. Disgusting.

"Why?" I asked.

I almost laughed. Asking complicated questions felt insulting because we didn't have words to exchange, but Crouton answered by touching her throat and then the throat of the alien in the picture.

The drones were mute. Well, I had never seen them speak. I didn't think they had the capability.

Did Crouton think this made them similar? My imagination filled in the moments I wasn't with her in the research facility. Did she take a liking to the creatures? Pet them? Think they didn't speak because they were also mute?

Crouton pushed the tools and metal bits toward me.

"All right," I said with a sigh. "I'll make you one."

It was a toy. What did it matter?

As I prepared myself to construct a monster out of aluminum, the door opened, revealing a sweaty Bishop.

"Hey," he said, turning his attention straight to me. "You're good with computers, right?"

I kept my gaze on my work. "Is this about the generator?"

"Yeah."

"You know *mechanics* and *computer programming* are two entirely different areas of expertise, right?"

He snorted, laughed, and then walked over to my chair. "If you know why I'm here, why even bother with the questionin' game?"

"I don't know if I can fix a generator. No one here is a repairman or mechanic?"

"Apparently, the guy who took care of the generator died a couple years back, and his apprentice disappeared out in the wasteland a month ago. They said they've got parts—A-tech shit they've collected and kept in storage—but none of them know what's going on."

While I knew the rough basics of machines and how they functioned, it wasn't something I had learned a great deal about. Still, I didn't want to ignore the town when it was in need, especially after everything its people had done.

"I can look at it," I said.

Bishop helped me up. He gave Crouton a quick nod before guiding me to the door and heading through the dark halls of the clinic. The music of insects filled the evening, and once we stepped outside, the songs became crystal clear. I enjoyed the cricket melody while Bishop helped me walk to the generator.

Ten people crowded around, all with flashlights. Lanterns had been hung to give the area even more lighting, but the gloom of the night wasn't so easily dispelled. I still had to stare to see things even twenty feet away.

Dr. Claire stood among the group, a calm presence about her. She quieted everyone down with the wave of one of her hands. "Bishop has returned."

The townsfolk all turned to face us.

I cringed, disliking their scrutiny.

Bishop motioned to the pump house, and we walked in together, the eyes of everyone following along with each slow step. I suspected they didn't trust me. I didn't blame them. Strangers weren't a safe bet out in the wasteland.

The pump house, lit with another half dozen lanterns, sat quiet. The debris and damaged section of the generator had been cleared, leaving ample room to investigate the problem. Fortunately, the townsfolk had also gathered a wide variety of spare parts and stacked them near the wall, as if they wanted to test each but needed to keep them in an order so they didn't double up on the same part.

Bishop helped me to the damaged section.

I had no idea what was missing. I spotted the connectors, and after I stared long enough, I could imagine what the parts looked like, but it wasn't anything I saw on the side of the wall. As a matter of fact, the more I examined the spare parts, the more I realized some weren't even for generators. Most were for vehicles, and I was pretty sure another was for an old-world lawnmower—something for trimming grass because it grew in abundance before the world went to hell.

"Well?" Bishop asked.

Dr. Claire and two other people from town walked into the pump house. They kept quiet, but I knew they expected me to perform a miracle.

Instead, I focused on the side of the generator. Most had connector points for fission batteries, either to act as a backup or to compensate for a faulty generator until it could be repaired.

Although the others waited with bated breath, I turned to Bishop instead. "This could use a fission battery." I didn't say anything afterward. He knew what I was implying.

He gritted his teeth before saying, "Well, *I* don't have a fission battery."

I half smiled, appreciating the fact he considered it mine.

Why did I need it anymore? I didn't, really. I had taken the battery back more out of spite than for a specific purpose. Once, it had been the key to my BC Oasis fantasy, but now that I had bigger problems to deal with, the battery was more of a fifty-pound doorstop.

Then again, it could be used to power up long-forgotten facilities, which could help me and Bishop in the long run. Did I really want to give it to a small town in the middle of nowhere? And it wasn't like this place was safe. They had a marauder problem.

"If we connected a fission battery, I think the whole town would have power again," I said, thinking aloud.

What should I do?

"We have a fission battery," Dr. Claire said. "But we tried connecting it years ago, and it never worked."

I whipped my attention around to the doctor. "*What?* You just have a fission battery sitting around here? An actual fission battery?"

"I believe so."

"Well . . ." I ran my hand over my head, sending a shiver down my spine when I remembered my shaved head. I ripped my hand away and took a deep breath. "That solves your problem. Bring it here and I'll connect it."

Dr. Claire nodded to the man by the door. He dashed away and reappeared only a few minutes later carrying a large blanket.

He walked over to me and slowly unfolded the cloth around the battery.

I silently thanked luck that I wouldn't have to choose between relinquishing my battery or helping the quaint little town. What if the Meteorological Plexus required a fission battery to function? Better safe than sorry.

The man finished unwrapping the battery and held it out to me.

I caught my breath and leapt away, my heart jumping straight into my throat. My mouth dried up and I forced myself to breathe.

Of course they couldn't hook this up to their generator!

It wasn't a fission battery.

"You okay?" Bishop asked.

"It's a bomb," I muttered. "A fission bomb."

Sure, they had the same shape casing, but I knew the difference immediately. The bombs had onboard computers, meant to set detonation parameters, whereas the batteries had nothing of the sort.

This one fifty-pound device was capable of nuking this whole town—wasting it and all the inhabitants to ashes—yet it was in their pile of *used parts?* I almost couldn't stand being so close to it. And to imagine they'd once fucked around, trying to poke it with connectors and attach it to a generator. It was almost enough to make me laugh and cry at the same time.

"It can't be a bomb," Dr. Claire said. "They're much larger than this."

"You're thinking of the firestorm bombs," I said as I scooted away from the man and made my way back to Bishop. "They had to be larger to keep all the . . . well, the stuff that incinerated flesh and harmed the atmosphere. They're much larger. Terrible. But this is definitely a bomb."

I had seen so many informational videos about it. My grandfather watched them over and over again, though I wasn't quite sure why.

"It's really a bomb?" the man asked, turning the thing over on its side. Then he glanced at the doctor. "I don't think she's right in the head yet."

"It's definitely a bomb," I said, curt. "And if you're not careful, you could kill everyone here."

CHAPTER NINETEEN

Bishop and I stepped outside, greeted by the harsh chill of a desert evening.

"You don't think you're overreacting?" he asked.

"Overreacting? They don't even know what they're manhandling. Or, think of it like this, what if a mortar had struck that bomb?"

Of course, being hit by another explosive probably wouldn't result in a full-blown fission reaction, but it could result in a misfire of the bomb, which would still devastate the area. But that was the problem. Even a misfire would likely kill everyone in Richfield.

Perhaps, due to my weakened state, it bothered me more than it should have, but I needed the fresh air and time to think.

Dr. Claire stepped outside with us, her arms crossed tight across her chest.

"I didn't know it was a bomb. Rodriguez said it was a battery when he brought it in, and it doesn't look like any of the bombs I had ever seen before."

An odd statement. How many had she seen?

"I would suggest you get it outside of the town," I said. "Far, far from town."

"What about the generator? What do you suggest for that?"

"Either get a battery or have someone repair it."

"You can't?"

I shook my head. "I don't think I can fix it."

She turned to Bishop. "Then we have little choice. I'll ask you again: Can you bring us someone who can fix the damage? There should be someone in Boulder or Tomato Creek. We can pay them with batteries, guns, and ammunition."

"How long can you all go without the water pump?" Bishop asked.

"We have some water stored, but I can't imagine us lasting more than a few weeks."

"Fine. I'll go in the morning."

I rubbed my hands together and exhaled a stream of warm breath on my palms. "Aren't the marauders out there?"

Bishop shrugged. "Doesn't matter. Someone has to do it."

"Don't go until morning." I grabbed the sleeve of his shirt.

I just needed time to think. What were the chances I would need the fission battery? Did I want to take the risk? No part of me wanted the people of Richfield to suffer, but if they were going to be attacked nonstop by a marauder gang, then what was the purpose of giving them something as important as a powerful energy source?

The two men from the pump house walked out with the fission bomb wrapped snug back in its blankets. One held a shovel and pointed toward the east side of town.

"You can't bury it," I said, on the verge of shouting. I fidgeted with my hands, trying to contain an energetic outburst welling in my chest. If I could've walked properly, I would've stomped over and taken the bomb from them. "Listen. Burying it is a terrible idea."

The onboard computer could become damaged, resulting in an accidental detonation. Or someone could find it. Or, again, a stray mortar could strike the area where it was buried. Allowing random chance to determine the fate of a deadly weapon didn't seem logical or efficient.

"Here, here," Bishop said. "I'll handle it. You head back to the clinic with DC and we'll talk in the morning, all right?"

He would *handle it*? What a statement. My imagination immediately pictured him using it for target practice, but Bishop wasn't that foolish. I hoped.

"All right," I forced myself to say. "I'll be at the clinic."

Dr. Claire offered me her arm. I took it, because I had to get back, but I hated every staggered step. It was irrational—what did it matter if someone else besides Bishop or Crouton helped me?—yet I preferred them in every way over Dr. Claire.

She led me through the streets. The local pub, still lit up with candles and a few lanterns, served drinks to a handful of town guards. They waved to Dr. Claire, and she returned the gesture.

"Do you need anything to eat?" one called out.

"We have plenty of griddle bread," another added.

The doctor shook her head as we passed by the last of the windows.

"Everyone admires you," I said.

"I'm the town's doctor and mayor. I would hope so."

"Hm." It almost bordered on worship.

Dr. Claire lengthened her stride. "I apologize for Bishop. I told him I needed someone to help us with the generator. He never should have bothered a recovering patient."

We reached the clinic, and I worried about Bishop manhandling a fission bomb, but I also couldn't stop thinking about the reverence surrounding Dr. Claire. I wanted to ask her about her origins. Even if she lied, still, I had to try.

Dr. Claire opened the door.

"Are you a Winter Survivor?" I asked.

The Forever Winter had happened nearly fifty years ago, and most who lived through it were either elderly or already dead. But my grandfather had stayed youthful in appearance long after his peers suffered from the touch of entropy. Even when I was a child, people sometimes asked if he were my father or much older sibling.

The aliens brought with them all sorts of tissue-altering science when they arrived in their transports. They had simple ways to stave off the disease of aging, and most of their leaders had long ago altered themselves with implants straight to the brain that forced the body to maintain a certain status quo, rather than falling apart.

I was certain Dr. Claire had one such implant, just like my grandfather. But they were rare before the bombs—for the elite and wealthy. Those lucky enough to get the first and second generation of implants numbered less than a few thousand.

Perhaps I was wrong.

Perhaps Dr. Claire just used old-world terminology because her parents did. Perhaps she had just seen bombs in old vids. Perhaps she learned medicine through the family trade.

Dr. Claire helped me into her clinic, her expression unchanging. "Bishop spoke very highly of you, and I can see why. You possess a great deal of old-world knowledge."

"Then you *are* a Winter Survivor?"

"Yes."

"And you were . . . a doctor before the war?"

She nodded. "I studied medicine before the long winter. After those terrible years, I helped the people of Richfield reestablish themselves. But I don't like such knowledge to get around. People have twisted ideas of the past. I'd rather keep a low profile."

Even my grandfather never wanted anyone to know his real identity.

"How old are you?" I asked.

A gauche question, but my curiosity wouldn't allow me to remain quiet.

"Seventy-three."

Wow. She looked amazing for seventy-three. More than amazing. The sun would be jealous of her radiance. But she conducted herself like someone who had seen much of the world—an old soul in a youthful body.

The next question came to mind so fast I blurted it out.

"Do you know where I can find the Meteorological Plexus?"

She took her time shutting the door as she mulled over my question. The unique chatter of children filled the otherwise dark building with a bit of light and levity. They remained in the resting room, the door cracked open, allowing a sliver of light to shine down the hallway.

"I don't know," Dr. Claire said. "I haven't heard of those in ages."

"Those?"

"Yes. There were several all around the world. They controlled the Climate Engineering System, but that went offline after the bombs." She swept back her golden hair. "I'm of the opinion our terrible weather is a mix of the fallout and the meddling of those satellites. They altered the weather, and now that they aren't doing their job, it has never been able to correct itself."

"You don't know the location of any plexus?"

Dr. Claire shook her head. "I'm sorry. They were conceptually interesting, but they weren't part of my studies or hobbies. Honestly, I think they may all be destroyed. Is there a reason you're asking me this?" She reached out and grazed her fingers along the side of my head, just above the ear. "I looked, but you're not like me. You were only born two decades ago. How is it you have so much information about the past?"

I pushed her hand away, my mind dwelling on the larger problem. "It doesn't matter. Thank you for . . . everything you've done."

What was the point of telling her anything further? And although she came from a time before the bombs, it didn't endear her to me. I would simply find someone else with the information I needed.

* * *

I awoke in silence.

It reminded me of my time back in my cellar. Joel's cellar, really. Every morning I was in silence—alone and without even the company of chirping insects or the cawing of birds.

I sat up, fearful everyone had left. It was illogical; of course the town wouldn't up and vanish in a few short hours, but my groggy thoughts went straight to depressing hypotheticals.

Fortunately, when I got my imagination under control, I realized Bishop was asleep next to my bed. He sat on the floor, his spine against my bedframe, his head tilted back in an awkward position so that his head rested on the mattress.

When I shifted my weight, he jerked to the side.

"Uh," Bishop said with a groan.

I smiled. "Good morning." I really did enjoy the pleasantness of the phrase.

He rubbed at his back as he stretched. "Oh, good. You're awake. Listen. They want me to take off. I'll be back in a couple weeks, tops."

"Looking for a repairman?" I asked.

"Yeah. Don't worry. DC said you and Crouton could stay here."

"I'll be better in a few days."

He stood and pushed his head to the side. The resulting cracks made it sound like he had broken his neck, but he sighed afterward and smiled. "Sure. I'll hurry."

"No, I—" Holding my breath, I steeled myself to the ultimate decision. "I'm just going to give them my battery."

"Oh, yeah?" Bishop cocked an eyebrow. "Just like that?"

"Yes. It's fine."

"All right. I'll go give it to them."

I shook my head. "No. Tell them to start up the generator, even if it doesn't work, before attaching the battery."

The fission battery would easily power a small town like Richfield, and the generator didn't need to be running in order to gain the benefit. But it would serve to hide their source of power.

A fission battery would be easy to take—obviously, because that was how I got mine. If it got out that a small town had one, they would be hounded at the very least by marauders, and at the worst, by soldiers from Ex Cathedra or United California.

But if they pretended the generator still worked, then no one would be the wiser. So long as they didn't discuss it.

"Also," I said, "we should help the town deal with the rail gang."

"*We*, huh?" Bishop took a seat on the edge of my bed. The frame creaked and the mattress strained. "If you want me to go out and gun them down for you, all you have to do is ask nicely."

"No. That'll take too long. I want to leave as soon as possible—a few more days of rest at most. You still have some of those gas grenades? You should bring them to me."

"Why?"

"I'm going to jury-rig something together. Those marauders want a tribute, right? Then we'll give them a tribute. The only one they deserve."

Bishop hit me on the shoulder. I grimaced and massaged at the spot, unsure of why he struck me.

"That's why I like you, Viper," he said with a chuckle. "I agree. We should fuck those guys up."

I rubbed at the back of my neck and smiled. I hadn't thought he would be so enthusiastic, but the more I mulled over the situation, the more I realized I was being foolish. Of course he would be enthusiastic. Of course.

And I guessed hitting me on the shoulder was his way of expressing that enthusiasm. I didn't know why—because why did it matter?—but I liked that he treated me like his junk hunter buddies. I liked thinking I could depend on him. Even though this was a risky plan, even though this would extinguish the last of our stocks that we found in the cache, he was still for it.

"We'll need to stop someplace and let you dig around the rubble some more," Bishop said as he walked to the door, almost like he could read my mind. "Only one atomic battery left."

And no more fission battery or gas grenades.

I nodded. "Yes. We should."

He flashed me one of his smiles before heading out.

CHAPTER TWENTY

You could stay here," Dr. Claire said. "I've asked Bishop to stay for years, but he always denies me. I thought he left because that's what young men do sometimes, but maybe he'll stay if you and Chelsy need someone to watch over you while you get settled."

"Thank you, but I have something to do first."

I stood in her clinic room, admiring the pre-bomb medical instruments.

The thought of living in Richfield enticed me, and if things had been different, I might've taken her up on her offer. Even in my wildest fantasies—the ones where I made it to the BC Oasis and lived a quiet life in an underground greenhouse—I had been alone, thinking the outside world was nothing but blackness and evil. Imagining a community of people striving together to make things bright and wonderful inspired me more than my previous selfish desire to leave everything behind.

"Where is Crouton?" I asked as I picked up an otoscope.

"She's with the Lopez family."

She had been there all day, and it was almost time to go.

Bishop had loaded up his truck with offerings for the rail gang and gone to drop them off at the designated place. Little did the gangsters know, it was rigged to set off the gas grenades when opened. I couldn't be sure it would get them all.

It was a risk—one the citizens of Richfield agreed was worth the chance. If the surviving rail gang became upset, they could try to retaliate against the town. Then again, they could decide the town wasn't worth the effort and move on to easier targets.

My hopes sat squarely in the "wouldn't it be nice if they all died" camp. I set the otoscope down.

"How's the brace?" Dr. Claire asked.

"Fine, thank you."

The brace she had given me, mostly bronze and leather, secured my knee and hip. It made it difficult to move them around, but that kept the random pain to a minimum. Someone from the town had also given me a cane—not a crook cane, like for a shepherd or the elderly—but straight with a knob handle, and something much fancier than I ever imagined owning.

The woman said the cane was made of black onyx and ebony, which worked out as neither glittered like gold or silver, but up close it did have a nice sheen. *It was in my family for years*, she had said when she handed it over. *Even before the Forever Winter.*

They wanted to thank me for the battery, and no matter how many times I said it was unnecessary, the citizens had insisted on giving us supplies and clothing.

"You should take this duster coat," Dr. Claire said.

My old jacket did have more bloodstains than a birthing bed, but I still disliked taking from the town. It was hard to articulate—since I had always imagined living a hermit lifestyle away from everyone—but I wanted the town to thrive. I wanted them to have everything they needed. I wanted the quaint homes of families and craftsmen to outshine the viciousness of the wasteland.

And taking anything from them felt like I was somehow hindering that outcome.

But I allowed her to slip the duster onto my shoulders.

It was made with black leather and clearly designed for a man. Although a duster coat should have fallen to my knees, it went all the way to my ankles. Probably for the best. I didn't want attention, and it hid me well enough. Though I supposed I was looking more and more like a Victorian-era nobleman than someone from the wasteland. All I needed was a frilly collar, a vest, a top hat, and dress pants.

My own imagination got me smiling.

The door opened. I turned to see the newcomer, hoping it was Bishop, but instead Crouton stood in the doorframe. I caught my breath. Her long hair—so beautiful, like the inkiness of night given form—had been cut short, all the way to her jawline. Outrage clawed at my throat as I stifled the urge to demand who had done such a thing to her.

Crouton must have interpreted my reaction as something negative toward her. She touched her short hair and cast her gaze to the floor. Then she pulled her satchel, a small bag given to her by one of the other children, around to the side and she withdrew a pen and notepad. She wrote *ugly?* and then showed it to me.

I slowly shook my head. "But why?"

She walked over, turned around, and then rummaged through her satchel. The clink of metal told me my figurines were no doubt at the bottom. When Crouton faced me again, her arms were behind her back, a smile on her face. Before I could inquire about her game, she presented me with a beanie and wig combo—a simple head cover skillfully crafted from her own locks.

I took the item.

Shock overtook me. I fished for the right words, but nothing came. Nothing felt adequate.

Dr. Claire smiled. "Roger Lopez makes all sorts of clothing. He's quite talented."

Was that what Chelsy had been doing all day? Getting her hair cut and making this?

Chelsy motioned for me to put it on my head, her impatience showing in her repeated gestures, as though I hadn't seen the first or second.

I put it on, fearing it might be hot, but pleasantly surprised to find it wasn't. Then I glanced at myself in the mirror—the first time since arriving.

The person staring back at me was far prettier than I remembered. Although thin, I didn't appear sickly, and the hair fell to my shoulders. When I touched the fine strands, it almost broke my composure.

She had . . . done this for me?

Of course her hair could grow back . . . but still. It felt so personal . . . so much more than anything I deserved.

I rubbed at my eyes, willing myself to stay calm and collected.

Crouton tilted her head from one side to the other. Then she held up the same note, a frown on her face.

I huffed a laugh and then pulled her close. When I embraced her, I tried not to squeeze too tight, but part of me didn't want to let go.

I really didn't deserve someone like Chelsy in my life.

For a moment, it made me think that God and all his infinite forgiveness was giving me a second chance to love and protect my sister, but I didn't want to think such things. Hope was powerful, like alcohol—a little could give you courage, but too much made you a fool. I had known plenty of death in my life. Too much to think everything would be okay from here on out.

Bishop entered the room after a few rapid knocks. "Time to go. Let's—" His eyes widened when he caught sight of me and Crouton, but then he continued with, "—get the last of our shit and hit the road, shall we? I'd hate to keep you two beautiful young ladies from seeing the glorious sunset."

Crouton smiled as she drew something onto her little notepad. She showed off a giant heart, and Bishop chuckled.

"Wouldn't be the first love letter I received."

Dr. Claire, who had been silent and still, almost like she knew she was intruding on a personal moment, took a step forward and bid us farewell with a nod of her head. "You're always welcome back, Bishop. Kita and Chelsy as well."

There wasn't really a sunset, not with the overcast skies. But there were breaks in the clouds and a stream of scarlet, orange, and purple shone sideways through the sky, painting the otherwise dull landscape with color.

When the light hit the tracks of the railroad, it glistened. We drove parallel to it, and it got me on edge. We hadn't seen any of the rail gang, and I wondered if they were gone for good.

The wind picked up. Inside the cab of Bishop's truck, it didn't matter, but the flapping of a tarp in the truck bed did catch my eye. He had his sniper rifle and a duffel bag—standard stuff—but then I caught sight of the last thing I wanted to see.

"Bishop," I said, breathless. "Why do you have the fission bomb?"

"Hm?" he replied, his casual demeanor never waning. "Oh, you said we should take it from town. I told 'em I would."

"Are you insane? I told you it was dangerous to keep around!"

"Hm. Yeah. I get it. We'll dump it in Boulder."

Anger filled me. I motioned to the back and then to him, almost uncertain of what to do with my hands. "You can't! It's a bomb. If you sell it to someone in Boulder, they'll use it. On something."

Bishop gave me a sidelong glance. "Yeah. I've sold guns to plenty of people, Viper. I'm not sure this logic'll hold up."

"But—" I held my breath, my mind on Richfield as I ran through my arguments. "It's not like this could ever be used for self-defense. Its sole purpose is to destroy vast territories. Like towns. Who would even buy this? Soldiers of Ex Cathedra? Or United California?"

"Stop your fussin'," he said. "If you're gonna get that upset, I'll figure out something else."

"It could kill *us*. Why would you keep it in your truck?"

"Where else you want me to carry it?"

It was probably irrational, since it wasn't easy to set off fission bombs, but I couldn't relax. The fact it remained in the truck bed itched at my thoughts and killed my mood.

Bishop continued until we spotted a series of buildings in the distance. They were part of a town—the rubble of the other half sat nearby—and I wondered what had happened.

When the firestorm fission bombs hit, they struck nearly every major city and then some, decimating civilization, but smaller towns remained somewhat intact, though the residents died of radiation and nuclear fallout unless they knew how to keep themselves safe during the Forever Winter.

So what happened out here in the middle of nowhere? A mini war during the winter? Possible. The world went to hell right afterward, or so my grandfather told me.

Bishop parked next to an old bank building. It was two stories, the windows long since busted. He exited the vehicle. Chelsy and I followed suit.

"There's a vault in here," he said. "I've seen it hundreds of times. All the lockers have been cleared out, but the vault has all that A-tech shit on it. I'm hopin' there's some good shit in there."

"You can't leave the bomb in your truck," I said.

Under no circumstances did I want it stolen.

Bishop rolled his eyes. "You want me to lug fifty pounds around?"

"Yes."

No part of me doubted. I hated the thought of it disappearing.

With a groan, Bishop walked around to the back. He grabbed his rifle, slung it over his shoulder, and then stuffed the bomb into his duffel bag. He slung it over his other shoulder before switching on a flashlight and heading for the front door.

I felt guilty ordering him around, especially since he had always been so accommodating. I forced a swallow and crossed my arms. "Uh, thank you. And sorry about this."

He grabbed the handle and held the door open. "Fuck it. I'll carry the damn thing around. It's just like carrying you all over again." After his quip, he smirked.

I didn't know if he was making fun of my weight or my inability to walk, but it put me at ease knowing he was willing to joke about it.

Chelsy yanked the sleeve of my duster. I turned to her and she stared at me, her eyes wide and bright with excitement. She pulled out the alien figurine from her satchel and then pointed to the building.

"No," I said. "There aren't any aliens inside." I glanced to Bishop. "Right?"

He shook his head. "What? No. There aren't any drone nests for miles."

Crestfallen, Chelsy held the figurine close. She stroked the head of the beast, and I again wondered if she somehow bonded with one in the research facility. How could I break the news to her? They didn't make for good pets. She should avoid them at all costs. Well, she had nanites, but that didn't mean something couldn't go wrong.

And they would attack her outright if a Teth of higher caste ordered it directly.

It just wasn't good news.

We walked inside, my stiff leg and cane creating a rhythm of heavy clunks along the wooden floor. The broken roof had obviously allowed rain in, resulting in a paste of grime and pulp that coated every surface.

Bishop jogged across the wide-open room, leapt over the teller counter, and then made his way to a vault mounted into the back wall. He pointed to the computer. When he tapped it, the screen lit up.

"What did I tell ya?" he called out. "C'mon. I really wanna see what's in here."

I made my way over.

Chelsy, on the other hand, immediately went to the flipped-over desks and rummaged through the contents, her gaze fixated on anything with brass or copper.

When I got to the vault computer, I smiled. A simple operating system—the kind my grandfather had taught me on. I typed away, using command codes to bypass the security. Unfortunately, the lock on the vault door had a timer, and I turned to Bishop with a sigh.

"Ten minutes," I said.

"Whatever." He threw down his bag and rifle and leaned against the wall.

I watched the last of the vibrant rays disappear from the sky. The time passed faster than I thought it would. Then the door popped open, and I smiled. What had we found?

Bishop and I walked inside. He shone his light around the five-foot-by-five-foot room.

Nothing.

The place had been cleared out. Everything gone except for the worthless money and paperwork. No batteries, no guns, no ammunition—the vault itself was more useful as a random storage unit than it was a loot box.

I turned to Bishop, fearing he might be angry. "Sorry."

"Eh." He kicked at a small stack of bills. They fluttered around. "I thought this would pay off big-time. It was the first fuckin' place I thought of when you said you could crack these things."

"Do you know of any more?"

"Yeah, but they're—"

An explosion ripped through the bank. I hit the ground, knocked off-balance by the tremor. Bishop held on to the wall, his focus on the front room. He dashed out the second the quaking stopped. I got to my feet and spotted a second explosion outside—the same mortar explosion I witnessed in Richfield.

I pushed myself to get out of the vault.

A mortar had ripped through the roof of the bank, creating a new hole in both the ceiling and floor, exposing a basement level. Bishop knelt next to Chelsy in the middle of the room, the light of his flashlight highlighting the crimson on her clothes.

Unable to take a breath, I hustled over, almost tripping on the overturned chairs and stray fragments of shattered desks. I regained the ability to inhale the moment I realized Chelsy was still moving.

Shrapnel had sliced through her arm, side, and leg. Thin cuts—except for the gouge in her arm—but enough that I knew she must be in pain.

Another explosion, so close to the bank it hurt my ears, sent a wave of dirt and debris wafting into the room. I coughed until I reached Bishop's side.

"Is she okay?" I asked.

Chelsy trembled, her attention focused on the blood. She refused to look anywhere else.

Before Bishop could reply, and before I could truly examine Chelsy, two more mortars hit—one on the corner of the bank while the other hit

Bishop's truck. The building blast left us awash in another wave of debris, and Bishop's vehicle burst into a column of black smoke.

Bishop wheezed, stood upright, and pulled out his handgun.

"Wait," I said between bouts of coughing. My eyes watered. "What're—"

"Get in the vault," he yelled, more anger in his voice than I had ever heard before.

He marched to the front door, no hesitation in his steps.

"Wait, Bishop! Don't leave us. What if—"

But he was already outside. Had he heard me? A thin layer of dust created a brown fog that obscured my vision of him.

I returned my attention to Chelsy. Tears streamed down her face, and she kept her hands far from her injuries, like touching the blood would result in her death. I urged her to stand, but she didn't move.

"You need to get up," I said.

She shook her head, her attention never wandering from her injuries.

The floor creaked and then tilted downward. I turned my attention to the gaping hole in the floor. The desks slowly slid across the floorboards until they came to the edge, applying more pressure to the already weak surface.

Insects scuttled out of the darkness underneath the building—centipedes the size of a human finger, corpse beetles that were black and green, and a whole host of alien arthropods. The kind that resembled millipedes. Several feet long. Thick as paper and the width of a drinking straw. White. Writhing.

What the fuck was under the bank?

"Chelsy," I pleaded. "Please get up."

The floor depressed again, creating a harsher angle only made worse when another set of desks scraped across the floor toward the hole.

I grabbed her arm and yanked, but she continued to cry, her trembling hard to stomach.

What was going on? Our attackers had to be from the rail gang. Perhaps they blamed Bishop, and not the town, for the attack against them. Bishop had been the one to deliver the goods, after all. Were we not successful? Had they all eluded the gas?

Responsibility for our situation ate at me. I knew the risk, but I didn't think they would retaliate so quickly.

But that didn't matter. What mattered was what I would do about it now. The floor continued to sink, and Chelsy refused to move. The floor creaked louder than before, threatening to collapse at any second.

CHAPTER TWENTY-ONE

After a deep inhale, I hacked and wheezed, my throat constricting shut. I grabbed Chelsy by the back of her clothes and dragged her toward the cashier counter despite my lame leg and the unsteady floor. She didn't help, acting like a ragdoll the entire way, but I wasn't in any condition to scold or reprimand her.

Then I slipped.

I hit my injured hip, screamed on impact, and slid down the floorboards along with Bishop's duffel bag, a desk, and two chairs.

I fell into the darkness, gasping until I hit the floor on my back. All air left my lungs in one terrible slam. I rolled to my side and curled into the fetal position as the slam of furniture rang out all around me. Centipedes scurried around in the darkness, and my panicked mind rooted around for all the information I had ever learned about them.

The alien millipedes weren't deadly, but they were known for burying themselves inside the flesh of other living creatures and creating nests between organs. They slowly feasted on the blood and innards, causing the host problems but technically leaving them alive.

If the host had a simple nervous system, the insect could sometimes act as the brain, controlling the creature and forcing it to gorge on food and then puke up the millipede's eggs.

When the hundreds of insect feet scuttled across my skin, I had to hold back another scream. I pushed myself to my feet, my heart smashing against my ribcage. I brushed everything off with unsteady hands, my eyes wide. Then I groped around in the pitch black all around me, searching for Bishop's bag. I grabbed it, switched on a flashlight, and held my breath.

Something was moving in the shadows around me. Not tiny insects. Something larger. Just out of view.

I frantically glanced around, trying to figure out what I would do in my new situation. Smashed desks. Ruined chairs. The most striking objects in the basement were the terrariums around the edge of the room, hundreds of them. Each was smashed open, no doubt from the mortar, and I realized they had been the homes for the insects.

Someone had kept them in here.

To eat.

I knew right away. They were farming the insects. Someone lived here.

The crunch of glass underfoot drew my attention back to the person—or thing—lingering in the darkness. I shone my flashlight around, hoping to get a good look, but the busted furniture cast long shadows.

In a short few seconds, I came to terms with the potential realities before me. In one reality, Bishop had gone outside and died. If that were the case, I didn't have much hope of getting out of town alive.

In the second reality, Bishop was still alive and had dealt with the rail gang—he wouldn't give up until his last breath had been stolen from him, that much I knew—and if that were the case, I needed to stay alive until he came back.

I chose to believe I lived in the second reality.

I limped away from the noise, but the moment a group of insects crawled onto my leg, I gasped and dropped the light. When I picked the light up, I shook away the insects, a chill running down my spine.

Then there was nothing but silence for a few long moments.

I lifted the flashlight and spotted the monster in the basement with me—one of the Teth aliens. It was twenty feet away, at most, creeping closer over the furniture, moving with caution, its mouth open and claws unsheathed.

Bishop's bag and rifle sat in front of me. I didn't have time to assemble a sniper rifle, but I did spot a handgun tucked away in the side pouch of the duffel bag. I *could* pick it up and take advantage of my cover by shooting at the alien. If I didn't, it would attack, and I would be at its mercy.

But when I reached for the handgun, I grew stiff and anxious, already dreading the sensation of it in my hands.

I cursed under my breath between coughs.

Fuck.

I couldn't.

I couldn't will myself to take the damn gun out of the bag and use it. My sister's dying stare plagued my thoughts, haunting me like a waking nightmare, and it drove me to paralysis faster than alien toxin.

So when the alien picked up its pace and leapt over a desk, I lunged as fast as my broken body would allow—away from the gun, my only protection—in the hopes I could think of something to save myself.

When the alien missed, it threw a piece of broken wood, clipping my injured leg. I cried out, lying on the floor, unable to move.

What else was I going to do?

Chelsy threw down a metal container from the story above. It clocked the alien hard on the head, the corner of the box gouging some of its flesh. The creature yelled, and I feared it might leap up for her, but I still couldn't bring myself to reach for the handgun.

"Run," I shouted.

But Chelsy didn't listen. She grabbed another box.

The alien lunged for the darkness of the room, hustling over broken desks. Then it disappeared. No more noise. No more presence. Was there a hallway down here? Another room? How large was this underground facility? It must have been living in the bank for some time.

To my relief, Bishop appeared at the edge of the hole above me, his body a war zone of cuts and blood. He stared down at me, and I breathed several sighs of relief. I couldn't have been happier to see him.

"You okay?" he asked.

"Yes," I murmured. "What happened?"

"Ran out of ammo, so I came back to get some."

It wasn't a joke, but it made me laugh anyway.

"I've gathered tons of tally marks in these parts. And these guys aren't professional in the least bit. Just wanderin' around, willy-nilly. I think they thought they got us with the mortars, then it was all crotch grabs and high fives after that."

"Please help me up," I said. While I enjoyed his stories, I really didn't want to stay in a basement full of bug nests and other potential threats.

Bishop threw down the rope.

I tied it under my armpits and then held on. He pulled me up, though his grip slipped once due to the slick blood over most of his person. Still, he got me up and pulled me close.

To my horror and fascination, the alien millipedes writhed and circled around until they eventually went off the edge and back into the basement. They preferred the darkness.

"DC's brace really helpin' you, huh?" Bishop said as he patted me down. "You're standin' fine."

He spoke like he wasn't even concerned about the creepy alien insects or the destruction all around us. His detachment both impressed and frightened me. He showed more emotion for his truck than any of the dead men.

"Y-Yeah," I said, my nerves returning as my adrenaline waned. I gave him the once-over. "You're hurt."

He shrugged. "You got me those robots, remember? I've seen those Iron-Blooded assholes heal all sorts of weird injuries. Well, until I got to him." He offered an imaginary toast to the dead Iron-Blooded.

"So you're okay?"

Bishop glanced around, frantic. "Where the fuck is my bag?"

I pointed to the basement. Bishop sighed. But before he went down to get it—facing the insects to do so—he scooted Chelsy into his arms and headed for the front door. She clung to him, calmer than before, her gaze still on her injuries. Well, the small ones had already subsided. She stared at the areas regardless, either because of curiosity or dread, I couldn't tell.

"C'mon," Bishop said. "You two wait out here. Once I have my bag, then we'll have to start walkin'."

"I'm sorry about your truck," I said as we walked through the half-ruined town.

"Tsk," Bishop said with a click of his tongue. Then he flashed me a glare. "Don't ever mention that damn truck again. It's fuckin' gone. We don't need to remember it." His tone and voice were terse and his words laced with heat.

He really liked that stupid truck.

I wanted to ask him: *Is this how you deal with everything you don't like? Refuse to talk about it?* But I knew it was more confrontational than I wanted. Bishop killed five rail gang members, which was impressive. He didn't need me harping on him for his deflection coping mechanism.

"But it's a good thing we took that bomb with us," I said.

I couldn't help the I-told-you-so moment.

Bishop glowered at me. "Yeah, yeah. We would've been dead. Whatever."

"It's not *whatever*. I don't think you realize this, Bishop, but we're the only people who know about the satellites. If we had died there, the information would've gone with us."

He rubbed at the collar of his shirt while he mulled over the information. "Okay. Maybe we commission a few fliers or something, huh? Just in case? Fliers with all the info on it."

"Perhaps."

It occurred to me then that saving Crouton might have doomed all humanity. What if they had killed me and Bishop? Even if I saved Crouton then, she would've died to the satellites later. But I didn't think I would've changed my actions.

Crouton . . . Chelsy . . . I switched between her names, even in my head, depending on the situation.

Bishop held Crouton in his arms, her eyelids hanging heavy. We bandaged her arm, but the other areas she had been hit with shrapnel didn't require much attention. The nanites would speed up the process of recovery, which meant she would need a lot to eat in the coming days.

My mind wandered, absorbing the myriad of problems before me.

Maybe I should have fliers made in the hopes someone would take them seriously and also move to prevent the disaster.

Bishop pointed to a building, and we turned in that direction.

"Oh, I got an idea," he said. "We can use the bomb to blow up that plexus place. Good, right? Get rid of two problems at once."

"No," I said, curt. "I don't think you understand. I need to *use* the equipment in the plexus to stop the satellites. If you blow it up, I can't use it. Get it? Blowing up the plexus is the exact opposite of what I want to happen."

I still feared the place was already destroyed, though.

Bishop nodded along with my words. "All right. I gotcha. We need the place intact. Then I still don't know what you want me to do with this explosive."

I didn't know what to do, either.

The sounds of movement in the ghost town caused us to stop. Crouton opened her eyes as we turned around. The gloom hindered my sight, but the unmistakable scratch of claws on asphalt sent goose bumps across my skin.

"I thought you said there weren't aliens here," I whispered.

Bishop shook his head. "There aren't."

He was wrong. I would know those sounds anywhere.

Bishop set Crouton down and unslung the rifle on his shoulder. With his eyes glued to the road, he assembled his weapon. Another round of claw noises and he froze. The alien wasn't far. A hundred feet away. Maybe fifty.

Bishop switched the night vision on for his scope. He moved next to a fire hydrant and rested his rifle on top of it before aiming.

"Stand back," he murmured.

I dragged Crouton to the far sidewalk. She grabbed at my arm and showed me the alien figurine.

"Yeah," I said. "Shh."

She showed me the figurine again. I pushed it down, unable to look away from the shadows.

An odd thought struck me. Was this the thing living under the bank? Was it the one farming the insects? If so, it wasn't a drone. It was something else—a different caste of alien.

The creature moved closer to us.

Bishop fired.

It screeched and hit the road as the shell from Bishop's rifle clinked onto the street. Bishop remained focused. He kept his gun aimed and his finger on the trigger.

"*Wait*," the beast said from the darkness, its Tethlite strained. Then, to my surprise, it spoke in English. "Wait."

I hated the way the aliens spoke English. They had no lips, so all they did was keep their mouth open while their tongue made all the noises for them. They had a wet sound to their voice—the added noises of the tongue in saliva as they spoke—that came straight from the horrors of a scary movie. At least their own language had a lyrical chime to it.

Bishop paused and then turned to me, his eyes wide.

"It can speak?" he whispered.

"Just shoot it," I said.

Crouton held her figurine close, her eyes just as wide as Bishop's.

Bishop hesitated. "You're not gonna say anything in gibberish?"

I really didn't want to. I wanted the damn thing to stop existing. But I gritted my teeth and asked, "*Why are you stalking us?*" I didn't want to hear it speak English. Not ever.

It didn't answer.

I exhaled. "Shoot it before it does something."

Bishop stared down the scope and then said, "It's keepin' its head pressed to the ground. Just . . . lyin' there."

Aliens conducted themselves differently than humans. They had a strict hierarchy due to their caste system. It wasn't like any human caste system—where one was simply the caste of their parents regardless of talent or skill. The aliens based theirs on genetic makeup.

Aliens were designed for a role from birth. Warriors with more muscle and aggression. Innovators with more cognitive abilities and the capacity for near-perfect memory. They took their roles seriously, and when one was lesser than another, they followed the commands of higher-ups.

The Teth hierarchy, as compared to the other alien groups, required the lessers to genuflect to superiors, more a show of submission than anything else. Was this alien trying to submit to us? The mere thought disgusted me.

"*What caste are you?*" I asked.

"*Outrider.*"

They were pawns to the warrior caste, just above drones. They were some of the least intelligent of the aliens. Why was this one here? Perhaps it was impressed with Bishop's fighting. Maybe it wanted protection—the Teth aliens often made large social circles and packs. That was why my grandfather made an alliance with them over the Vay and the Frest—the other two alien groups weren't nearly as cooperative.

"*Leave us alone,*" I said.

After a few seconds, the creature stirred. Bishop readied his rifle, unaware of my command.

"It's fine," I said in English. "It's leaving."

The alien shuffled between the broken buildings, half limping, the scrape of its claws growing fainter and fainter. Crouton stared at the point where its shadowy figure had disappeared, a frown on her face.

Bishop stood and rotated his arm. "I avoided aliens for years. Now look at this. Since meeting you, I've almost been killed by them twice. And now I've seen 'em speak. Crazy."

"I wish we would avoid them."

He laughed. "Why do you speak gibberish then? Seems like you should be doin' more with these things. You could be like that asshole in Boulder."

I didn't know what he was talking about. My mind remained preoccupied with haunting visions of the past. My grandfather loved the aliens, but they killed so much of my family it was hard to grapple with the conflicting realities.

Why couldn't I just avoid them? That's all I wanted. But fate kept pulling them into my path. Especially with the Iron-Blooded.

"Let's go," I said. "The sooner we get to Boulder City, the better."

CHAPTER TWENTY-TWO

The broken building, once a two-story high school, offered little in the way of comfort. A strong breeze swept past us, the howl of the wind shaking loose doors and rattling debris against the walls. Bishop motioned me to go inside.

I stared at the front door, my eyebrows knitted.

"I think there's about a thirty percent chance we survive the night if we stay here," I said.

Bishop snorted and laughed. Then he hit me on the shoulder with the back of his hand. I rubbed at my arm, surprised by his strength and wondering if I would bruise. Or perhaps it was the soreness from the fall in the bank. I couldn't tell.

"That's the first joke I've heard out of you," he said.

"I've joked before."

"Uh-huh. You've joshed around about as often as you've held a gun. Jokes kill your brother or something?"

The sting of his verbal jab cut deep. I knew he was trying to make light of my situation, and maybe even help me move past it, but all it did was still the blood in my veins. Awash in the cold sensation of grief, I barely noticed as he opened the door and allowed Crouton inside.

"Hey," he said. "Look, I'm sorry. I knew it was callous the moment I said it, but it just slipped."

I shook my head. "No. It's fine."

I didn't want to hold on to the past. I didn't want it to control me like it did. Perhaps his jokes would help me move past it all.

My grandfather told me everyone had inner doubts, fears, and prob-lems. He said everyone dealt with adversity in one form or another, but the people worth a damn—the ones worth knowing and imitating—never defined themselves by that. I hadn't thought much about his wisdom when he first said it, but I realized then that I needed to take his words to heart and live them.

We walked through the silent halls of the high school, the harsh shad-ows moving with the sway of Bishop's flashlight. Every locker was open, revealing their empty shelves or moldy contents. The place retained a hint of teenage sweat, and I wondered what it would have been like to attend school before the bombs.

With knowledge came great power.

My grandfather had said people took the limitless databases of infor-mation for granted. People ditched school. Remained ignorant on impor-tant issues. Never bothered to learn history or study the ramifications of politics.

Maybe the Joel from my cellar had been right. Maybe good times did create weak men.

I shook my head.

My grandfather came from the same time frame, and he knew so much about the world . . . I didn't know who was right, but looking to cast blame on something wasn't helping. I pushed the thoughts from my head.

"In here," Bishop said.

We walked into a classroom with a hole in the ceiling. Fresh air wafted down; no doubt a window was open upstairs.

To my surprise, the place was clean and arranged to look like a lounge. Chairs and couches—old, but still with cushions—all faced the far wall.

Bishop plugged a wire into an atomic battery slot, and a projector flick-ered to life, though it strained and buzzed, like an animal taking in the last gasps of life. The projector shone across the wall, creating a large faux television. When he clicked through the projector files, he brought up several options for films. Most of them were labeled "scholastic" but a few had been renamed with several Xs.

Bishop stopped on *The Teth Are Our Friends*.

The resulting cartoon immediately captivated Crouton's attention. The cute versions of the aliens—four arms, no eyes, long faces with visible teeth—almost made them seem pleasant.

Crouton hopped onto a chair and watched, rapt, with the alien figurine in her hands. She zoned out completely, even without sound from the projector, and barely blinked.

Bishop scratched at his soiled clothes. "Listen. You two wait here. I've hidden stuff around this area a few times, just in case of an emergency."

I grabbed his arm. "No. You should stay."

"It'll be fine. This place is rarely touched. Been cleaned out for decades. Junk hunters don't come here."

"There's an alien outside. What if it comes back?"

He didn't have an argument for that.

"All right," Bishop finally said with a huff. "We'll stick together."

Content we would have at least one person with a gun, I walked over to a nearby couch. Before I sat down, Bishop grabbed my elbow and yanked me away. I swayed on my good foot and cocked an eyebrow.

"Not that one," he said. "Sit . . . over here." He motioned to another couch on the side.

"Is this an instance where I would be disgusted if I had a UV light?" I asked as I took a seat on a clean cushion.

Bishop snapped his fingers and then pointed at me. "Hey. There's a kid nearby."

"UV lights can also pick up traces of urine and blood. What did you think I was referring to?"

He tried to stifle a laugh and failed. "That's joke number two. If you make any more, I'll have to assume you're a different person wearin' the skin of Viper and masqueradin' around like one of those damn alien insects."

I chuckled.

Crouton clapped her hands together. Bishop and I snapped our attention to her, my heart rate increasing. She pointed to the screen, and I took a calming breath.

A cartoony version of adolescent aliens played together with a group of human children. I was certain the video was meant to make them all seem friendly and pleasant, but aliens of different castes weren't all sunshine and rainbows.

Sure, the innovators and domestic castes were, but the others tended to be violent and rough, even at a young age. And human children weren't allowed near the drones, no matter the situation.

Whatever propaganda this was, it would give Crouton the wrong impression.

"Turn this off," I said.

Crouton shook her head and leapt from the chair. She held her hands together, her fingers laced, and pleaded with her eyes.

"Just let her have fun," Bishop said. "It's cute."

I exhaled. "Fine."

Crouton golf-clapped. Then she rummaged through her bag and drew up a couple notes. She handed me a heart and then handed Bishop a picture of his truck.

He narrowed his eyes into a glare. "Dammit, kid. What did I say about my truck? We don't bring it up anymore."

To my surprise, she held her hand over her mouth, covering a wide smile. Was she actually fucking with Bishop? Had she drawn his truck just to agitate him? It amused me, and I couldn't help but join in the smiling.

"You, too?" He shot me a glare. "This isn't funny. You two realize we're walkin' all the way to the next stop, right? Then we'll be ridin' a dune buggy, and I doubt you two will be laughin' then."

"You have a dune buggy?" I asked.

"I left it with a pair of my old buddies after I got my truck. It's a piece of shit, and the seats have no cushions. You'll see. It'll be a long drive to Boulder."

Crouton dramatically rolled her eyes and returned to her seat.

A second later, she sat up straight, a look of shock across her face. The cartoon showed the aliens stepping on thorns—no blood because it was a children's show, not because they had no vital fluid—and moments afterward they recovered from the minor injuries.

Crouton clapped again, and once she was sure she had our attention, she pulled off her bandages and pointed to her mostly healed arm.

Perfect. One more thing she had in common with the aliens. I almost didn't want to acknowledge it.

"We're all Iron-Blooded," Bishop said as he took a seat on the couch with me. He threw down his bag and rifle before pulling out a knife. He gave me a quick glance. "Well, you're not."

"Thank you," I drawled. "I had almost forgotten."

"That reminds me. I've been meanin' to try something."

Bishop busted out a lighter and heated the edge of his blade. Then, like before, he rolled up his sleeve and cut himself a whole new cluster of five tally marks. He held his breath while he worked, his masochism enough to draw Crouton's attention away from the cartoon.

"Think this'll stay?" Bishop asked. "Now that I have machines in my blood, I mean."

I nodded. "You may have to do it a few times for the scar to really stay, but the nanites aren't perfect, they just make sure you function. Those are some pretty superficial scars and cauterizing them will lend to them staying."

"Good."

Crouton held up another sign. It had the word *NO* written across it in fat handwriting. Then she pursed her lips and glared.

Bishop kicked a foot up onto the armrest of the couch. "What? You don't like it?"

She shook her head.

"I'm fine. Barely felt a thing."

She made a gagging motion.

While I probably could've sat around and enjoyed their company all night, my gaze fell to the floor. Papers and pamphlets covered the surface, all fused together through time and gunk. Some of the images remained, and the word *Boulder* immediately got my attention.

It was a brochure for a Nevada university. The very fact sparked my imagination.

Universities had vast stores of information. I lived in one for a few years with my grandfather. If one still existed in Boulder City, perhaps I could simply look up where all the Meteorological Plexuses were located. No need to rely on the flawed memory of a random person, and I wouldn't have to ask around, either—all I would need was directions to the university.

I tried to lift the brochure up, but it was nothing but pulp after I ripped it from the floor.

Didn't matter. Knowing I had a plan—even if just a plan for the next step to my mission—eased my doubt.

"Don't do this to me," Bishop said with a huff. He placed his hands on his hips and shook his head.

"It's your own damn fault," the man said. Bishop had called him *Carjack*, but the other people had called him Mateo. I preferred the name Mateo.

I stood with Crouton a few feet away from the chain-link fence that surrounded the garage and refueling station.

Wood boards had been woven with the chain link for privacy purposes, but we were close enough to see through the cracks. Mateo and his whole family lived in the sizable building, obviously sustaining themselves as junk hunters and small-time farmers. Their isolated life reminded me of my time in the cellar. They clearly didn't want company. The mother and her three children stood in the convenience store portion of the refueling station, staring out from the window and glaring.

Mateo and his brother, Diego, had met Bishop at the gate, but they never invited us inside. They were both in their late thirties, maybe older, but their thinning hair and shaky hands told me they probably both had been exposed to bad radiation repeatedly over their lives.

I wondered how long they had before they just started to lose pieces of themselves.

Mateo shook his head. "I told you I wasn't gonna help you if you became a bounty hunter."

"I'm not," Bishop said. "I haven't taken any bounties."

"Everyone knows what you did for Richfield. All those other rail gangs will be on the lookout for you. You know there are more. There's always more. We don't want none of your trouble."

"At least give me back my buggy."

Diego stepped forward. Of the two brothers, he was the leaner and taller one, built much like Bishop—large and capable. "You've left it here for a while. I think it's only fair we keep it."

Bishop clicked his tongue in disgust. I worried the encounter would devolve into a fight, but Bishop never reached for any of his weapons.

"We also helped you move all those things you stole from the Iron-Blooded," Mateo stated. "We've done a lot for you, Bishop. Now look what you've done. Agitating all those thugs. They'll come here, you'll see. That's what you brought on my family. You've endangered my kids."

"Really?" Bishop snapped. "You wanted me to just sit back and let Richfield get wiped off the map?"

"They coulda paid like everyone else. The gangs weren't askin' for much."

"Fuck those guys. They shouldn't get what they want because they're willing to forsake decency. What if they threatened Blink or Toast?"

"You leave my kids out of this," Mateo said, his face growing redder and redder as the conversation continued.

"Would you just pay them then? Huh?"

I took a step forward. "Bishop. Enough."

He gave me a cross glance before exhaling.

"Please," I said to Mateo. "We just want to get to Boulder City. We have an injured girl with us. We're taking her back to her father."

I motioned to Crouton. Her bloody bandages were still on her arm, even though the injury had long since healed.

I saw the look in Mateo's eyes when Bishop brought up his kids—it was the same look when I said we were reuniting Crouton with her father. He understood. He would empathize. He would give us the buggy—but then he would never want to see us again.

Everyone remained silent for a prolonged moment.

Then Mateo rubbed at his thinning goatee, his gaze set to his feet.

Diego shook his head. "That kid isn't our concern."

"Give him the buggy," Mateo muttered. "I don't want a dead kid on my doorstep." He pointed to Bishop. "But you're not welcome here anymore. You stay away from us."

"I won't be back," Bishop said, his words more a promise than a statement.

While Mateo stood guard at the gate, Diego jogged back to the garage. It took him a few minutes, but he returned driving a small dune buggy—a vehicle with no real sides or top, just a skeleton frame, an engine, and two seats. The dents and faded paint told a story of hardship and suffering. I wondered how old it was, and how much longer it would last.

It ran quiet, though. No combustion.

Diego stepped out of it and motioned to the seat with a quick wave of his arm. Bishop took the driver's seat. Crouton and I shared the passenger's seat. The rifle and bag went between us.

Without even so much as a goodbye, Bishop punched the forward pedal, and we left.

Bishop was right. The seats had all the support and comfort of a broken piece of plywood. Two hours into our trek and I might've chosen to lose the ability to walk so long as all feeling left me from the waist down.

Fortunately, Bishop drove with confidence, weaving through the twisted corpses of trees and following smaller trails away from the main road. It felt like we were making faster progress by taking a "back path," but I really had nothing to base such a feeling on. I just trusted Bishop would get us there fast.

"Are we going to stop?" I asked.

"No."

"I thought you knew places I could open? For scavenging?"

"I do. But we're trailing trouble. I'd rather get to Boulder and lie low for a bit before running around the wastes. After that, we'll get some goods. All right?"

I nodded. "Okay."

His rush to get to Boulder City didn't panic me. I wanted to get there as fast as possible as well, not only because of the trouble that plagued my every step, but because the delay caused me ever-building anxiety.

We passed an air force base. I recognized the aircraft boneyard—a place for retired aircraft so that the parts could be removed and sold. It would have been interesting to explore, had it not been for the drones that made the place home. The aliens skulked around the territory, like a swarm of bees around a hive. Their thin bodies, four arms, and wiry legs made them look like spiders from a distance.

Bishop and Crouton could explore the inside, in theory, thanks to their nanites, but the risk was too great. What if there were Iron-Blooded? There was no reason to tempt fate further.

Crouton stared at it as we went by, however.

"They're dangerous," I said.

She made no effort to respond.

Bishop switched on the radio. The music played with a white static, but gradually became clearer the longer we went. At one point a warning played over the speakers.

"Three Ex Cathedra judges have appeared on the eastern side of the Colorado River, looking to recruit nationless young men into the Ex Cathedra army," the DJ said. "My listeners should know already, but interactions with judges are risky for everyone involved. Those interested should approach with caution, and to everyone else, stay clear of the area until the judges have vacated."

Although the music returned, it didn't help my troubled mind.

No one from Ex Cathedra would help me in my quest.

Crouton fell asleep against me, despite the bumps and jostling of the vehicle. Bishop, although normally chatty, kept his jaw clenched, no doubt also suffering from the discomfort of the vehicle. I patted him on the shoulder once, to try to cheer him up. He gave me an odd look, like he had no idea what I was trying to say.

At least I tried.

The long day faded, giving way to the void of night.

Then it appeared. Right at the edge of twilight and at the end of my patience.

Boulder City.

The lights pierced the darkness, reaching high into the clouds and creating a fake sunrise with their radiance. So many—spotlights, floodlights, lights from electronic billboards, lights from buildings, lights from cars, personal flashlights.

Every direction there was a new source of illumination. White. Blue, Green. Red. Every color. Every intensity.

And the city was huge. Larger than anything I had imagined. Thousands of people had to live there. Maybe a hundred thousand, maybe more. I really had no idea. It was just . . . packed with people. Traders, junk hunters, soldiers, farmers, craftsmen. The only thing that connected them was the grime and dirt that stained everyone's clothes in equal amounts.

Bishop drove by groups of people walking toward the city, most with large packs on their back. They regarded us with suspicious stares, and Bishop kept his gun out in the open for everyone to see.

Never had I imagined something so grand and gritty all at the same time. The wall that surrounded the city—a city with towering buildings, some thirty stories tall—had enough soldiers on top for an entire company, maybe even a small battalion.

"Wow," I said in breathless awe as we drew closer. Despite the excitement in my pulse, Crouton never woke.

Bishop snorted. "Flashy? Yes. Safe? No. You should stay close to me the entire time we're here, got it?"

"Yeah. I will."

CHAPTER TWENTY-THREE

Graffiti marked the sheet metal and concrete that made the outer wall. A million advertisements mingled with odd phrases and gang insignias. The colors alone captivated my attention, and I took in the words, one by one, as Bishop waited in a line behind other vehicles wanting to get into the city.

SONS OF SILENCE

BEST WOMEN AT THE NEON CARDHOUSE

JASPER'S GUNS AND PAWN

When we got to the gates, two men with gas masks walked up to either side of the dune buggy. They were simple air-filter masks, black and covering the face, with straps that wrapped around the back of the head, exposing their ears and hair. The glass over their eyes was a two-way mirror. I saw my reflection, but I couldn't see them.

They motioned with rifles, pointing to each of us. Crouton woke then, groggy and confused. She flinched at the sight of the guards and clung to me, but I patted her back and whispered calming nothings. She relaxed and breathed easy, her eyes panning over the surroundings.

When one guard spoke, it reminded me of the judges, their voices filtered with a mechanical tint.

"Standing policy in Boulder is to neutralize violence," the man said, his disinterest thick. "Use of firearms won't be tolerated. You've been warned."

Bishop huffed. "I've been here before."

The men motioned us forward.

Bishop drove into the city, onto the roads lined with trash, and continued deeper into the urban jungle. The increase in temperature and the thick odor of human stink gave the whole place the feel of a locker room. Still, despite the grit, I liked to imagine a world filled with cities of equal size, maybe larger. Human ingenuity on display, so great and so fantastic the buildings stood tall in defiance of gravity—technological castles in a world of ruin.

Even Crouton admired the sights. She drew the surroundings as best she could on a few pages of her notepad, trying hard to capture details, her fine motor skills quite keen for someone her age. And in a moving vehicle to boot.

We couldn't go fast, not with the number of people who walked in front of vehicles. Businesses operated out of most windows and open buildings. There were pubs, tailors, and even gun repair shops. The most shocking aspect was people paying with coins.

"They have money?" I asked as I grabbed Bishop's arm. Bartering was the primary "currency" everywhere I had been.

"That's from U-Cali. Most venders here take it, but some won't."

"Why use United California money?"

"Boulder does a shit ton of trade with them."

Bishop motioned to a street of buildings. No, not buildings—factories. They pumped out ammunition, guns, car parts, and other useful items. The trains in the distance made sense. Raw supplies came in, crafted and specialized goods went out. The sheer industry of the place got my hopes up. If cities like Boulder existed, there were probably others.

Perhaps it wouldn't be long before the world would enter a genuine phase of recovery.

As long as the atmosphere wasn't destroyed.

Crouton grabbed my arm and shook me.

She pointed to a pixelated sign of topless women, advertising something, but I didn't bother staring long enough to find out. I turned her attention away from the crude imagery, my face hot, and I pointed out a bright white cat statue in front of a shop. Crouton pulled out her notepad and wrote down three exclamation points.

"It's pretty exciting," I said. "Bishop, do you know any sights suitable for a little girl?"

His half-lidded gaze betrayed his fatigue. He ran a hand through his hair and shrugged. "I dunno. They've got circuses or something."

We had been awake an equal amount of time, so I didn't understand his exhaustion, but I also didn't think it necessary to question it. Perhaps he hadn't slept well the night before.

City guards walked down the street in pairs, their rifles up and their gas masks unmistakable. Though their equipment did make me wonder how often gas attacks took place. Or perhaps it was to protect them from stray particles and the off chance someone tried to use gas. The masks wouldn't protect them from A-tech gas—the kind that ate flesh—but the standard tear gas wouldn't amount to much.

Bishop parked in front of a place with an electric sign that read: QUEEN'S PAWN. He exited the vehicle, took everything out, including the keys, and then motioned to the door.

His hard-set expression didn't match his typical demeanor, but again, I didn't inquire.

Before we walked inside, he asked, "You sure we can't just unload this bomb? It'll be easy, and we could get a lot for it. Tons. A nice pickup truck, like the thing I had last."

"No," I said. "We can't." No matter how easy it would make our trek. I didn't want to part with it.

"Tsk. Fine. Let's go."

We walked inside.

The whole building was one giant room, basically, but most of it was fenced off with large bars. A man sat behind a desk—behind the safety of the bars—with a shotgun next to him. He nursed a hane cigarette, the smoke hanging thick in the air. The most distinguishing feature about the man was the terrible blond wig, so yellow it might as well have been made of macaroni, long enough to pass his shoulders.

Everything else he wore fit in with the surroundings. A stained shirt, well-worn jeans, and a large jacket with plenty of pockets.

The vast room behind him stored an array of useful objects. Guns lined a shelf on the wall, boxes piled in the corners had cases and cases of loaded magazines, and every part imaginable for common machines littered the middle. Pawn shops were common in Ex Cathedra, but I hadn't ever seen any quite as large as Queen's Pawn.

The man with the wig glanced up and then rubbed at his thick stubble. "Bishop. You dog. Still alive, I see."

He had the gravelly voice of someone who'd smoked since the womb.

Bishop sauntered over to the bars. "Pawn. Still fat and ugly, I see."

"What did I tell you about callin' me that? It's Egan, jackass."

"Yeah, yeah."

Egan stood and walked around the desk. His left leg—if it could even be called that anymore—was nothing more than a mechanical peg leg. It braced him fine, but he waddled because of it . . . well, he waddled because of that and his weight. Bishop hadn't been exaggerating. Egan probably weighed close to three hundred pounds, and he wasn't even six feet tall.

The stubble beard, glaringly hideous wig, and spherical body made for an interesting combination. Crouton must have agreed because she hadn't stopped staring since the man stood.

"What do you have for me this time?" Egan asked as he blew a stream of smoke out his nostrils. "Anything worth a damn?"

"A buggy."

"Oh, yeah? Nice. What're you looking for in return?"

"Ammunition. Maybe some batteries. Some fresh clothes. And a rent ticket, if you have one around."

Egan removed his stick of hane from his mouth and then whistled. A young boy, perhaps nineteen, walked out of a door on the far wall. He jogged past the boxes of ammunition and then to Egan's desk, his eyebrows up.

"Jenson, go outside with Bishop and examine his buggy," Egan said. "If it works, drive it around to the back. No dickin' around. If anything's wrong, you come tell me."

The boy nodded. "Right." Then he walked over to a door built into the bars and let himself into the front room. He and Bishop walked out the front door, leaving me and Crouton with the bloated pawn shop owner.

I must have been staring a bit too long because Egan offered me a kissy face, his large lips shiny with saliva.

For a moment, I didn't know how to respond.

On the one hand, I supposed this meant I wasn't hideous, but on the other hand, Egan had a face and body that looked like something I drew with my left hand. And insulting him with a look of disgust didn't seem like a prudent option—it was also rude. What if he wouldn't trade with Bishop because I offended him?

Crouton wasn't conflicted in her response. She held up the same *NO* page she'd made for Bishop. Then she shook her head, gave him a glare, and stuck out her tongue.

I pulled her close and forced a smile. "Never mind us."

"You should teach the brat some manners," Egan stated.

When I glanced down, I spotted Crouton furiously drawing a fat man being stabbed. I held her tighter against my body and continued with my false cheer.

I forced a smile. "Can I ask you a few questions?"

Egan waddled back around behind his desk, puffing his hane like an old-fashioned train as he went. "You can ask whatever you want. Doesn't mean I'll have the answers."

"Do you know where I can go to find someone in the city?"

"The guard stations—those precinct buildings. They try to keep track of people. Or keep them locked up till they pay off debts. Either-or."

Crouton squirmed under my grip, trying hard to show her picture. I gave her a curt shake of my head. She calmed a bit, but kept her tight frown.

I continued, "Do you know where I can find a university? I heard there used to be a few in town."

"Those old buildings are on the east side," Egan said with a grunt as he took a seat. "Not open to the public, though. You'll hafta pay." Then he squinted. "What're you and Bishop doin' here in Boulder? He said he was keepin' away after all that shady business."

Shady business? But I shook my head. "We're just looking for people and places. Hence why I asked."

He cocked an eyebrow and exhaled a long line of smoke, finishing his hane. Then he pulled out a tin box and lit up another one.

Didn't surprise me. While there weren't many harmful ingredients inside the roll of the hane cigarettes, they did tend to be highly addictive. After the first few sticks, studies showed individuals increased perception and alertness due to the unique proteins found in the alien vegetation. These proteins also improved the ability to retain information. But after a few weeks of use, non-use resulted in a drastic drop of perception, essentially requiring the user to maintain a steady intake of hane or suffer withdrawals.

I had been tempted to pick up the vice given I was physically limited. I had put all my stock in cognitive abilities. Any slight improvement fascinated me, like imagining my body as a machine capable of being upgraded. Before the bombs, humanity had obviously been working on a concept. Anti-aging implants, nanites that improved recovery, a constant influx of the hane's unique proteins—every tiny bit improved an individual to pinnacle heights.

Egan noticed me staring again and held out the tin, offering me a stick. I shook my head. "No, thank you."

Despite his looks, Egan didn't seem entirely unpleasant. And when I gave his pawn shop a second glance, I noticed how organized it really was. The items seemed to be categorized by type, then by size, and then lastly in alphabetical order. It impressed me, likely because I had such low expectations given his appearance.

Then I noticed a piece of body armor—a bulletproof vest—marked with a human skull and an alien skull.

"You do business with the Iron-Blooded?" I asked.

Egan glanced over his shoulder, giving the armor a quick stare. "Hm? Maybe. You can't really tell if someone is Iron-Blooded unless they bleed or announce it. I think I got that from a guy who claimed to kill one, though."

"Are there many around here?"

"Lots."

His declaration got under my skin. "Where are they?"

"On the other side of the dam. They infest that government facility."

A dam. I took note, wondering if it were the source of Boulder City's amazing electrical power.

Bishop reentered the pawn shop, his haggard appearance more prominent than before. Egan gathered up the items Bishop requested and then passed them between the bars without any discussions, like this was a standard transaction. Bishop stuffed his new haul into the duffel bag, straining the seams.

"This is for the apartments near the pits," Egan said as he handed over a small strip of paper. "It's good for thirty days."

"Thanks, Pawn."

Egan shook his head and glared, but he didn't say anything else.

"The end is coming. A new darkness is upon us!"

When I first heard the shouts, I thought other people knew about the disaster awaiting humanity.

A man dressed in a trench coat motioned for people to step into a building labeled "church" in an ominous red paint. The windows were covered, and the inside had half the lights needed to see one's way through. There weren't discernible symbols of old-world practices, like crosses or stars or a lotus.

"Sixty percent," Bishop said as he pushed us along.

I gave him an odd look.

He forced a smile. "The likelihood we'll be murdered if we go inside."

I laughed, but Bishop quieted himself after a few short seconds. Even Crouton frowned at the uncharacteristic lack of mirth. Hesitant and curious, I placed my hand on his shoulder.

"Are you okay?"

He let out a long exhale. "I just need to rest."

We walked the long streets of Boulder City. Despite the midnight hour, crowds of people pushed and shoved, some talking loud enough to be considered shouting. Music played from nearby shops and buildings, mixing together into a mind-numbing cacophony.

But I pushed that from my thoughts and urged Bishop to stop. "You seem pale."

"It happens."

"Are you ill? Or maybe—"

I caught my breath when a terrible idea came into my mind. Bishop waited with his eyes closed, swaying on his feet.

"I got us an apartment," he said. "It's just a few more blocks. We can lie down."

I lifted his shirt and exposed his sides. He flinched, but didn't stop me. Sure enough, between some of his tally mark scars were the red circle wounds of the alien millipedes. At least two of them. I grazed my thumb over the injuries, and he grimaced.

"Why didn't you say anything?" I asked.

"Say what?"

"That those insects got on you?"

Bishop shrugged. "I thought I brushed them away."

Crouton grabbed my arm. She jumped with boundless energy, her eyes alight. Then she showed me the alien figurine. I grabbed her shoulder and held her down.

"Not now."

She pointed, but I turned away.

How would I deal with Bishop's insect problem? The nanites in his blood helped him recover, and I assumed they would kill the millipedes, but that would result in their three-foot-long bodies still inside his body. Could I cut them out? Would we need to visit a doctor? Surely Boulder City had some sort of clinic.

Bishop pushed his shirt back down. "Let's get to our place. Then we can deal with the fuckin' problem." Even his voice sounded ill.

He continued forward with a portion of the crowd, but when I turned to hold on to Crouton, I couldn't find her. I glanced around, certain she was close two seconds ago, but I didn't see her. Panic wrapped an icy hand around my throat, limiting my breathing and chilling my thoughts.

Where was she?

The sea of people pushed past me, some obviously irritated I wasn't moving. A few muttered curses, and others pointed to the side, as though I should get out of their way. But I paid them little attention.

"Chelsy?" I called out, hoping the use of her real name would tell her this situation was serious.

No sign of her.

I walked back the way we came, glancing down alleyways and staring at each child as they walked by. Nothing. No sign of Chelsy. Panic quickly bloomed into dread. What had Bishop said? The city wasn't safe? Of course it wasn't. What if, in the ten seconds I wasn't watching her, something had happened? Someone could've taken her, and I had no idea where.

What was so important that I didn't pay attention to her?

"Chelsy!"

Even yelling, my voice quickly died when confronted with the millions of other sounds and voices.

Perhaps Bishop would be better suited for searching.

But when I turned back to find him, he was also gone. He was ill, however, and barely paying attention to anything even when we were walking. Of course he wouldn't have realized I wasn't with him. He might have even already made it all the way to his apartment.

It wouldn't be hard to find the apartments. They weren't going anywhere. But Chelsy wasn't the same. I opted to continue my pursuit of her.

I continued back down the road, my eyes wide and taking in every sight. The copious amounts of light helped my search, though it yielded nothing.

Then I saw something odd.

The crowd parted, leaving a wide berth around the door to one of the multistory buildings. It didn't take me long to figure out why. Two drone aliens knelt on either side of the front door, their heads low and their larger hands pressed down on the sidewalk.

Obviously people avoided them—the drones could kill dozens of people in the crowded streets of Boulder City before the guards would be able to stop them. But the aliens weren't alone. City guards stood on either side of them, like they were a squad meant to protect the entrance to the building.

Chelsy stood in front of one of the aliens. The guards didn't push her back or tell her to leave. They allowed her to get closer and closer, until she was inches from the monster's jaws.

"Chelsy!"

She snapped her attention to me.

I pushed myself to walk as fast as I could until I was at the edge of the crowd. I didn't want to get any closer, either, so I motioned her to return. Chelsy turned away, like she hadn't seen my gestures, and instead petted the alien on its "face."

"Leave it alone," I said, more desperate than I wanted to sound, but I couldn't help it.

A few onlookers chuckled. They made no move to change the situation and instead watched with mild interest.

Chelsy stroked the alien's arm. The beast made no move. It took in even breaths, the force of its exhales enough to ruffle her short hair. She smiled and then hugged the creature, wrapping her arms around its forearm.

With my teeth gritted, I marched across the no-man's-land between the crowd and the aliens. Chelsy frowned when I approached and kept her arms tight around the alien.

"Get away from it," I said, curt. "It's dangerous."

The men of the city guard chortled. I turned to one and motioned to the alien.

"What's this even doing here? Aren't you afraid it'll attack someone?"

"It's just keepin' watch," the man said. "As long as your girl doesn't try to enter the building, it won't hurt her."

"You can't know that for sure." No human could.

"Look, take your kid and leave, all right? We've got work to do."

But Chelsy refused to move. She showed the alien the figurine—even though the alien had no eyes and it was completely meaningless—but she did it anyway.

I grabbed her shoulder and jerked her away. "Stop. We need to go."

The front door to the building opened, and an electric tension ran through everyone in the nearby area. The guards stood at attention, the aliens straightened their posture, and those in the crowded street took a step back. I held Chelsy, but I only made it two steps before I saw who exited.

A man in an old-world business suit stepped out.

He wore a sleek combat vest over his button-up shirt, and a pair of black skintight gloves, but he didn't stand out as much as the person wearing a JUDGE-X0 exoskeleton. No. Not just *any person.* Although the suit had a different paint job, and the word DEFECTOR had been spray-painted across the front, I knew from the dent in the helmet that it was Judge Gascoigne.

Shock overtook me for a second.

I'd thought I'd never see her again. I'd *hoped* I would never see her again.

The same thing must have struck her, because after she ducked under the doorframe and stepped out onto the street, she froze up, her helmet turned in my direction.

"What's this?" the man in the bizarre combination of suit and combat vest said. "Did someone come to see my gargoyles up close? Don't worry. They won't bite unless I tell them to. Come on over and see them." He gave me and Chelsy a smile, almost like he was hoping we'd get close—like a Venus flytrap or an anglerfish hoped things got close.

"Come on," I whispered to Chelsy. "We should go."

Judge Gascoigne placed a hand down on the man's shoulder. He gave her a quick glance over his shoulder. "Yes?"

"That woman is a thief," Gascoigne said, her voice just as off-putting as it was before. "She's stolen quite a bit from me."

"And you want me to do something about it?"

"Arrest her. She should pay for what she's done."

I took a hobbled step backward. I thought—irrationally, but still—that because Gascoigne had let me go when last we met, she wouldn't try to harm me now.

The man snapped his fingers. The city guards and drones turned their attention to me, guns up and claws outstretched.

CHAPTER TWENTY-FOUR

I just didn't want to get cut by the claws of the aliens. Anything but that. So I stepped closer to the city guards and allowed them to apprehend me. I couldn't outrun a sandwich, so there was little point in making a fool of myself by trying to escape.

They manhandled me at first, torquing my arms behind my back, but after little resistance, they secured my hands with cuffs and eased up.

When the guards grabbed Chelsy, however, I struggled against their hold. "Hey. She's not part of this."

"Yes, she is," Gascoigne said. "They're a duo of criminals. The girl is her accomplice."

Chelsy turned to me, her blue eyes searching mine. I shook my head, hoping she would just cooperate. I didn't know anything about Boulder City, or what would happen to people apprehended for theft, but I did know what a bunch of rifles and alien drones were capable of.

In Ex Cathedra, people served their time in forced servitude, or if their crimes were egregious, they faced the firing squad.

The men at the front gates of Boulder warned us before entering that crimes wouldn't be tolerated. How would they deal with thieves? A part of me wanted to protest the accusation, since what I had stolen was from Ex Cathedra and not Judge Gascoigne, but on the other hand, I didn't want to admit to thieving of any kind, lest they take that as indicative of character.

The man in charge of the guards gave a dismissive wave. "Search them."

Again, the rough hands were better than the aliens, but the monsters did circle close, breathing deep. A crowd of people remained to watch, but others continued on their way, avoiding eye contact.

The guards took Chelsy's bag and dumped it out, spilling the simple collection of writing tools and toys across the cracked street. Chelsy glared at the men, but she couldn't maintain her anger after glancing down at her meager belongings. Her lower lip quavered.

The guards took my cane, and all my tools, but otherwise I had nothing.

"Thieves, huh?" the odd man in the suit asked Gascoigne. "Are you sure you're not paranoid? First Luce and now these random girls?"

Judge Gascoigne stared at me, her lack of response disconcerting. Finally she said, "You said you'd assist me, Theon. Arresting this woman will help."

"What belongings are yours? The cane, perhaps?"

Without warning, Gascoigne grabbed the man—Theon—by his upper arm and yanked him close. She held him up, on the tips of his feet, as her exoskeleton hand gripped hard around his bicep. The drones screeched and leapt at Gascoigne, their claws up.

"Calm down, calm down," Theon said loudly enough to be heard by everyone involved, not just his beasts. He chortled afterward, and the aliens settled back into predatory circling. "No need to be upset. You want the girl arrested? She's arrested. I'm making good on my word, aren't I? I'm helping you out."

Gascoigne released him. He tumbled back, but maintained his calm demeanor.

The city guards motioned to me and Chelsy.

"Put them in holding cells," Theon said as he brushed off his sleeve. "I'll deal with it all later."

"I want to be part of it," Gascoigne drawled.

"If that's what you want, of course. I'm on your side, after all."

Life seemed tenaciously determined to fuck with me at every turn.

I stared at the wall of the holding cell, dwelling on the cold seat and stagnant air. What was I doing here? And how could I get back on path?

After my grandfather had passed away, my goals in life became infinitely more confusing. He always had a plan and a purpose. Leading people. Spreading knowledge. Teaching morals. I had tried to emulate him at every step—always planning, using logic—but my objectives always slipped through my fingers like water. No. Water might be easier to hold.

And now that I had an objective bigger than myself, bigger than anything I had ever had to deal with, I didn't know how to solve it or even prepare for it. The frustration ran deep.

My grandfather had once said it was the lack of willpower that kept the average man from succeeding. They gave up too quick, he said. Either because of excuses or lack of drive—they blamed their troubles on everyone else but themselves, and thus, drowned in them.

"I won't drown," I murmured to myself. Anything to keep my spirits up—anything to stave off the foreboding sense that I might never find the Meteorological Plexus.

Damn. At the rate I was going, I'd be dead before I got out of Boulder City. The thought caused me to chuckle, if only because of how often I told myself I needed to keep going no matter what.

"What was that?"

I glanced through the bars of my holding cell door. A city guard, his mask still up and his voice mechanical, stared in at me.

I shook my head. "Sorry. Nothing."

He returned his attention to the card game in front of him. His tiny seat and coffee table "desk" were amusing, but it was clear the surrounding holding cells were hardly used. No doubt the building had been a police station before the bombs, but it had become more of a storage room afterward. Twice people were brought in, waited for an hour or two, and then were taken away. I was the only one held as though I would have to be here for some time.

"Where's Chelsy?" I asked. "The little girl who came in with me?"

"She's in a different ward," the man said as he set down another card.

"Can I see her?"

"Orders are to keep you here."

"Then can you bring her to see me?"

The man glanced over at me with a grumble. But it didn't last long. The cards kept him preoccupied, and he went back to focusing on the game. "I'm not your liaison."

His left hand didn't move while he played the game. It stayed in the same clawlike position, resting on his knee. Even when other guards came in—he'd jump up to greet them, they'd have a pleasant chat—he never used the hand.

If I had to guess, he was injured a while back and now only suitable for stationary work. His buddies took pity on him, visiting when they didn't have to. He seemed eager for those moments the most, always turning his attention to the door at the slightest of noises.

I stared for an inordinate amount of time, and then he turned to me. "What is it?"

"This is a precinct, right?" I asked.

"Yeah."

"And records are kept here? Of people?"

The man ticked another card on the pile. "Yeah."

"Can I ask you about somebody living in the city?"

"What the hell did I just say about being your liaison?" the man snapped. Then he shuffled his chair so that it faced away from the door of my holding cell. With some effort, he moved the table as well, but not by much. "Just stay quiet until you're summoned, got it? I don't wanna have to make you, but I can."

I remained seated in my cell.

Two days locked up.

How many days did I have left to stop the Climate Engineering System? Would it be enough?

And not seeing Bishop and Chelsy the entire time got under my skin. Were they okay? How would I even know? What if Bishop collapsed and the millipedes in his body harmed him beyond nanite repair? And what if Chelsy was being harmed? A little girl, away from anyone who cared about her—I'd hate to imagine what would happen.

I refocused my attention on the immediate.

"You shouldn't clear a spot unless you have a king ready," I said.

My guard, Julius, cursed under his breath as he rearranged his cards. Solitaire wasn't a game I ever played much—the thought of wasting time on nothing made my grandfather angry—but since I had nothing but time . . .

As Julius prepared for a new game, I asked, "Ever been to Ex Cathedra?"

He shook his head.

"Everyone wants to join the military there. That's why I signed up."

Julius huffed. "Only career path there, right? You're all war hawks."

There it was, my first rule to lying—tell them what they already believe first, then everything that came after seemed more plausible. Sure,

Ex Cathedra was on the war path, but most Ex Cathedra citizens didn't want conflict in their lives. They wanted stability and prosperity. Those who pushed for war were the leaders in the capital. But people in Boulder obviously believed everyone in Ex Cathedra was bred from the same war-obsessed ilk.

"Well, did I ever tell you about my injured hip?"

He stopped shuffling his deck and turned to me. "No."

"I was a courier for the Ex Cathedra army when I was hit by grenade shrapnel. Sliced right through me. Couldn't walk right afterward, and then I was dishonorably discharged."

Rules two and three—give a simple explanation with confidence and with no facts that could be easily verified. It wasn't like he could check my history, and people got injured on the front lines all the time.

"Rough," he said.

"Yeah. Worst part was leaving my squad. They were like family."

Julius went silent and resumed placing his cards. His pensive demeanor slowed his game. The way the city guard operated was much like the brotherhood companies I saw in Ex Cathedra. Anything to relate us was what I wanted. Similarities could be used to prey on empathy.

"One of my squad left Ex Cathedra and went to Boulder City," I said. "He told me I should meet him here, but I don't know where to start. I mean, once all this gets cleared, I'll need a place to go."

Julius set his cards in rows.

"His name is Dallas," I continued. I never did get his last name. Could he be found with a first name alone? I hoped so. Actually, all I hoped was that he was actually in the city.

After staring at his cards for a long moment, Julius let out half a laugh. "Fine. I'll see what I can look up."

He knew I was manipulating him. Of course. I wasn't entirely subtle about it.

"Thank you," I said.

"Don't go mentionin' this to anyone, though. I'm not supposed to be doing anythin' with you. Got specific orders. No talkin'. No touchin'. Someone singled you out specifically."

"The judge," I muttered.

"She your old commander or something?" Julius asked. "I've seen her fight in the pits. Brutal."

"Fight?"

"Yeah. They bring in aliens and shit, and then the judge lays waste to them for the crowds. Pretty entertaining. Lots of betting how long it'll take or whether she'll make it."

"Of course she'll make it. She's in an exoskeleton power armor suit."

"Yeah, but if she doesn't win in a certain period of time, her suit powers down and then she's at the mercy of the aliens. Good fun, really."

Power down, huh?

When the exoskeleton suits drained their power cells, they did unlock so that the drivers didn't become stuck inside, but why would anyone participate in an event where they would be surrounded by hostiles when their power cells were low? It would make for good entertainment, but I doubted Gascoigne was actually in any danger. Surely such stunts were rehearsed—nothing but a show for the audience, like a lion tamer with a toothless cat.

Fuck. Five days incarcerated. Two without food.

I bit down on my pointer finger, staring at the shadows in the room. Were they treating Chelsy the same way? What if I died here? What an obituary that would make. *Broken girl thinks she can solve problems, save the world, and live a happy life. Dies in a holding cell, forgotten, without ever having reached her destination.*

Truly epic. I could already hear the songs they'd sing.

The door to the main room opened and Julius stepped in after chatting with the switching guard. I perked up, hoping he would have more than water with him. He didn't. But he did walk to the bars and tap on one with his clawlike hand.

I turned to him.

"Found your squad mate," he said. "He works with the guard. He's currently posted at the docks."

Hearing about Dallas made me happier than I thought it would. He'd betrayed me, but the trek to get here, spending time with his daughter, and the anticipation of finding him had built an expectation I hadn't been aware of.

"Wait, did you say docks?" I asked. "Isn't this city landlocked?"

"That's just what they call the train stations. He's there at night. So . . . whenever you get released . . . you can hit him up."

"Thank you."

But I didn't have the strength for much more conversation.

*　*　*

In the middle of the night, while I tried to sleep against the wall, someone walked into the holding cell area. They switched on the lights, hurting my eyes, but I scooted to the edge of my bench, hoping they brought food. My stomach complained and growled, threatening to consume itself in its need to sustain me.

Three guards walked to my cell, opened my door, and yanked me out. I didn't protest, but they continued to manhandle me all the way out of the precinct. They secured my arms behind my back and kept a hand on my shoulder. Outside, waiting near the curb, was a small transport van. Groups of children stood around the steps of the precinct, a few turning their gaze to me as we walked by.

The guards put me in the back of the vehicle and locked me to a bar mounted to the frame. The seat was uncomfortable, and my leg ached, but not as much as my guts. Everything was relative, I supposed.

Fatigue ate at me. I kept my eats closed. No. I meant eyes. I kept my *eyes* closed. But it was difficult to think of anything other than eating.

Then we came to a stop and the men hauled me out of the vehicle, their hands blistered and their voices gruff. Part of me wished I had told Julius goodbye. He had a wife and two kids, and he enjoyed whittling when at home. All around a pleasant guy. I needed more people like him in my life.

I caught my breath.

Whatever street we were on was brighter than the rest. It was what I imagined standing in sunlight would feel like, aglow in illumination that chased away every shadow. Spotlights lit up most of the sidewalk and signs advertised all sorts of places to gamble or see live women. The city guards brought me to a building—once a palatial mansion—surrounded by a fence so charged with electricity it snapped and popped. They led me through the gate and all the way to wide double doors in the front.

I wanted to ask what the fuck we were doing, but I just let them lead the way. Anything was better than starving to death in a holding cell.

The inside of the mansion had been stripped away of the fanciest of materials and replaced with pragmatic components, like steel and sheet metal. And it operated more like a hotel, with lots of people living in the rooms while servants bustled back and forth. Some sort of show house or place for VIP gamblers, perhaps.

The city guards stopped when they came to another double-wide door. Only one led me inside.

Judge Gascoigne waited within.

She stood at the far end of a room with vaulted ceilings, a table of food, lounging pillows, and three scantily clad women. The spacious accommodations allowed her exoskeleton to move about without trouble, and it was sleek enough to fit through the large doors, but I imagined it still caused grief. Most soldiers before the bombs would take their suits off before entering buildings, and I thought most judges still did that in Ex Cathedra.

The guard unlocked my cuffs.

"Here's the girl," he said.

Judge Gascoigne turned to us. "Good. Now get out. All of you. Except the thief."

The man turned and left. The women waved to Gascoigne as they went, each offering a cheery farewell, much to my surprise, almost like they were sad to go.

Once alone in the vast room—perhaps it was once a ballroom?—Gascoigne walked over to me, the stomp of her suit shaking the floor. I didn't move from my spot, because movement would be difficult, and instead waited until she was inches from me.

"Hungry?" Gascoigne drawled.

I didn't say anything. If she asked, then she knew about my treatment in the precinct. Was she trying to rile me? She seemed like the type that reveled in power and flaunted it whenever she could. I didn't want to give her the satisfaction.

Gascoigne huffed. "Think your daughter is hungry?"

The one question broke my willpower.

"What do you want?" I asked, resigned to whatever fate she named.

"Heh. Watch your tone."

Judge Gascoigne struck me on the shoulder with the back of her hand—nothing hard enough to break bone, but with sufficient force to bruise my flesh and send me tumbling to the ground. I bit back my cries and remained down. Not only did she enjoy her power, she seemed to enjoy hurting people as well. Just my luck.

"Get up," Gascoigne commanded.

I did as best I could with the aid of the wall, but it obviously wasn't fast enough for her. Gascoigne grabbed the back of my duster, hauled me to my feet, and then tossed me into a nearby table. She barely used her suit's strength, but I hit the edge of the furniture hard, spilling the food to the floor. The harsh angle of wood dug straight into my kidney. If there wasn't blood in my urine tomorrow, I'd be surprised.

With my body trembling, I hit the floor on my knees and then collapsed forward, my arms around my side. When Gascoigne got close, I held my breath and scrunched my eyes shut.

Damn. If she wanted to kill me, she should've done it when she had her boot to my head. Why let me go? Was it just to do it all over again? I wanted to ask, but the words didn't come.

"I can't believe you followed me," Gascoigne said as she grabbed the back of my duster for a second time. "Or were you trying to steal something from me again? Is that it?"

Vomit threatened to spill out of me at any second. I held it back and shook my head.

She released me, and I crumpled in front of her feet, my face against the rough carpet of the floor, my insides rebelling against me.

"I'm glad you did follow me, though," Gascoigne said with a chuckle. "Because you're going to steal shit for me."

I didn't move.

"That, or I'll have your kid killed."

I snapped my eyes open at the statement. I tried to stand, I really did, but I couldn't get past my hands and knees.

Gascoigne laughed. Then she grabbed my arm and lifted me straight up. "You're pathetic. I hate the sight of you. But here you are. Time and time again."

"Please leave Chelsy out of this," I said.

I almost added, *she's not even my daughter*, but I decided against it. The information wouldn't change anything, and I doubt Gascoigne cared. All she knew was that I'd steal to keep Chelsy safe, regardless of our relationship.

"Maybe you should've thought twice before fucking with me," Gascoigne said. "Now everyone associated with you is fair game as far as I'm concerned."

"Will you at least feed her while I . . . do whatever it is you want?"

"I'll consider it."

The callous statement agitated me more than anything else she had said or demanded. But I couldn't argue.

"What do you want me to steal?"

I wanted to tell her it was foolish to have me do anything. I didn't know Boulder City—I had no idea where I was, I didn't have any of my tools, and without sleep and food I was more corpse-like than ever before. She wanted me to perform a job for her? Not the best conditions to see me succeed. Or maybe this was all some elaborate torture meant to prey on my darkest fears. Ingenious if it was, but I doubted Gascoigne was a mastermind of horror.

Gascoigne pushed me away. I stumbled until my lower back hit the edge of the table. Bracing myself against it, the judge walked over and grabbed me by the neck. She forced me to look up at her, her grip so tight I could feel my pulse against the metal mesh that made up the palm of the suit's gauntlet.

"What's your name?" she asked, taking me by surprise.

"Kita," I replied, though I almost included my last name, just in case my first alone would anger her. One slip of her grip and she could end me.

"Kita. I want you to steal a set of power cells for the JUDGE-X0 suit. My suit. I know the asshole who has them, and he keeps them protected with all his other A-tech bullshit. I saw what you did to the systems in the silver mine. You get me these power cells, and I won't rip apart your little girl. Understand?"

CHAPTER TWENTY-FIVE

I understand."

Judge Gascoigne released me.

As I took in deep breaths, she turned away and walked back to the far wall, the harsh contrast of her high-tech suit clashing with the old-world woods and sculpted architecture. Then again, everything looked out of place. Radios had been bolted into the walls, power outlets were locked down for specific appliances, and bars over the windows jutted from the walls, obviously added long after the building's construction, creating a Frankenstein version of a house.

"His name is Sun Luce," Gascoigne hissed. "The man who has my power cells."

"O-Okay," I said through a cough.

"He's one of the three individuals running this dumpster fire they call a city—the finance guy. He keeps my batteries in his penthouse, along with all the other A-tech junk he has." She clenched and unclenched her fists and then waved to the door. "Do I need to articulate what will happen to the kid if you mention this to anyone or you get caught? Or can you figure that out for yourself?"

I rubbed at my neck. "What if I just got you *other* power cells?"

Surely there had to be something, *somewhere*, easier than stealing from one of the individuals running all of Boulder City.

"I don't care where you get them," Gascoigne growled, "but I've already been looking. I think that asshole purchased any spare cells up, just to spite me. He said mine were broken—that he needs to fix them—but you don't *fix* power cells. And he refuses to return them, effectively trapping me here."

"How is your suit still operating without power cells?"

"I have one."

The JUDGE-X0 suits used ten power cells, and without the others, I suspected the suit could only run for a few days at most before needing to be recharged.

"Trapping you?" I asked as I moved toward the door. I was curious, but I also wanted to be as far away from Gascoigne as possible. "You could just get out of the suit and leave. You might be able to find power cells elsewhere in the wastes."

Laughing, Gascoigne turned and rotated her shoulders. Before I reached the door, the locks on the front portion of her suit clicked and hissed.

Her suit unfastened and allowed the front to unfold open, each metal plate of the armor woven over the other, requiring them to unfold one at a time. Once complete, the thing resembled some sort of high-tech iron maiden, the insides exposed for the world to see.

I froze, stunned to finally catch a glimpse of Gascoigne herself.

She wore nothing but a sports bra and long pair of tight jersey shorts, exposing her damaged body and modifications. Her right leg and knee looked far worse than anything that had happened to me. Her kneecap was missing, along with half her calf, and the scars twisted along her body all the way to her ankle. Two tubes ran from her side into the suit itself—the types of tubes required for blood dialysis.

Gascoigne couldn't live without the suit. It literally sustained her life.

I caught my breath, remembering the first time I encountered Gascoigne. I had used an EMP grenade, disabling her suit completely. No wonder she harbored a strong hatred for me. I had almost inadvertently killed her.

The exoskeleton suit hissed a second time and slowly folded downward until it became a throne-like chair. Gascoigne sat within, taking deep breaths. Despite her damage, she was muscular and tall, like most drivers of the suits. Her hair was cut short, and I noticed an injury on her scalp.

Her fight with the alien warrior had resulted in her dented helmet—and the gouge to her head was noticeable. Was she okay? It seemed "scabbed" over, but the long, deep line of red looked as though it cracked the skull, perhaps worse.

And some of the helmet connectors—the attachments embedded in her scalp at a few places—appeared tilted or out of line. The wires remained connected to the helmet, no doubt so it could keep track of her health, but it still disgusted and intrigued me.

She ran a hand over her face. Her expression, so hard-set and angular, pierced straight to my core.

"Any other bright ideas?" Gascoigne asked, her voice softer outside of the suit, but still gruff and laced with a certain amount of aggression that was impossible to fake. Then she reached out of the suit to a nearby table and took a drink of water.

When I didn't answer, she said, "Get my damn power cells."

I left without any further discussion.

Boulder City shook occasionally with the rumble of music.

The excitement and entertainment waned the closer I got to the docks. Closer to Dallas. While Bishop had never betrayed my trust, the docks were closer than the apartments. I wanted to see them both—and ask both to help me in my struggle—and I knew Dallas would do anything for Chelsy.

I would see him first and then go to Bishop.

The loading stations for the trains bustled with hundreds of people. I leaned against the wall of a warehouse, my arms crossed tight over my chest, my attention focused on a nearby garbage can. Could there be food inside? Probably. Did I want to subject myself to the leftovers of others? No. Not yet. I wasn't that desperate. I was running on a second wind, as though my stomach had eaten one of my kidneys to sustain me for another few hours.

Standing around wouldn't help me, however. I had to walk, no matter how painful, until I managed to find—

"Kita?"

His voice, muffled by the metallic gas mask, almost didn't register with my memory. I turned to the side, my eyes wide, and stared at the city guard standing next to me.

"Dallas?" I asked.

He stepped closer, his brown crew cut what I remembered. "It's me. Did you . . . bring Chelsy?"

"She's here in the city." I didn't know how to explain the rest, so I stopped myself from speaking while I gathered my thoughts.

Before I could say anything else, Dallas embraced me, his grip tight and his appreciation pouring off him in waves. "Thank you," he said, breathless. "I thought . . . I imagined . . . I just couldn't sleep at night."

Speechless, I wrapped my arms around him and returned the gesture. He didn't let go. If anything, he squeezed me harder, his fingers twisting into my duster. He smelled of alcohol and grime, but so did most people on the docks.

When Dallas broke away, he kept me at arm's length, both his hands on my biceps. "Kita. Listen. I've got most of what I owe you, but I also did something else."

"What?" I remembered him saying he would pay me back for everything he took, but I knew there was no way he ever could. It's not like he'd ever find a spare fission battery lying around.

"I secured tickets to U-Cali, all the way to the ports."

I lifted both eyebrows but couldn't manage to find the words.

"That's what you wanted, isn't it?" he asked. "To leave this place and find a boat to take you up the coast? That's what this will do."

"I . . . can't do that anymore."

"Why not?" Dallas asked.

"I have other things I need to do before I head for the BC Oasis."

Dallas took a long breath before pulling me back into a tight embrace. I didn't know why, but he was harsher this time around, holding me as though he wouldn't let go, not ever.

"I can't thank you enough for bringing my daughter back to me," he said, his voice strained. "Thank you. I was beginning to think I had lost her forever."

Again, I returned his embrace, thankful for his warmth. The chill of the evening winds wouldn't relent, and my lack of food didn't help much, either.

"I left messages in graffiti on walls for you," Dallas continued. "I sent couriers to other towns, hoping someone might've heard something, but I got nothing. Over and over. I don't know how you got here, but thank you so much."

"Dallas," I muttered. "Chelsy is technically being held by the city guard."

He eased up and took a step back. "Why?"

"I was arrested for theft. Accused by the same judge who we saw in

Ex Cathedra. She's here, and she gave me instructions on how I could go about getting Chelsy back. I'm sorry. I brought her here, but I didn't keep her entirely safe."

Dallas didn't say anything. And with his mask, it was impossible to tell what he was thinking. No expression, no eyes to see into. I expected him to be upset, not pensive.

"You're shaking," he said.

I rubbed at my arms, both cold and on the last bit of my strength. "I haven't eaten in some time."

He took my elbow and led me away from the station. "Let me get you something. You can tell me everything then."

I hung on to his arm and nodded.

"—and then that's when she demanded the power cells," I said between gulps of warm soup. The broth could have been from an old drainage ditch and I wouldn't have noticed. I barely noticed when it was finished.

"I saw a judge in the pits," Dallas said. "I had no idea it was the same one you fucked with."

"Hm. Yeah. She's been following me since Ex Cathedra. Now she thinks I'm following her." I took a gulp of my water and then leaned back on the bench.

Wind swept through the "park" at a swift rate. Although the city labeled our surroundings as a natural trail, I knew better. The trees were nothing but plastic, and the grass was some sort of artificial material meant for old-world sports games. If it wasn't alien—since most alien vegetation grew despite radiation and lack of sunlight—real plants tended to stay on the shriveled side.

At least the tall trees offered a canopy. It made me wonder what standing in a real forest would be like.

But the prolonged silence didn't help calm my nerves. I wanted levity—some sort of joke. No doubt having Bishop around had tainted my view on what a normal conversation should look like.

"Ever have a nightmare where you can't seem to escape something chasing you?" I asked, grasping for anything. "Seeing the judge on every corner is like that. Only in real life."

Dallas stared at me, and I stared back, looking at my own reflection.

"You're talkative," he said. "Different than before."

I held my breath.

When I had first met Dallas, I hadn't spoken to anyone in a long time. Now it felt much different, like I couldn't imagine a life without talking.

"Is that bad?" I asked.

"No. I prefer this."

I rubbed at my neck and nodded, happier than I expected to hear such a statement.

"Do you think, as a member of the city guard, you could just get Chelsy out of incarceration?" I asked.

"I doubt it, but I'll try. I haven't worked on the guard long, and the precinct you were at isn't in my wheelhouse."

"So we should plan on needing Gascoigne's approval for her release."

"What're we waiting for then?" Dallas got to his feet. Then he offered me his arm. "I know the man Gascoigne is talking about. Sun Luce doesn't try to keep himself hidden. He's always in the gambling halls. And he likes to make examples of people who can't pay. The man lives a hedonistic lifestyle that makes most of the guards around town jealous."

The pieces to the puzzle were starting to make sense in my mind.

Judge Gascoigne probably came to Boulder City looking for a place to recharge her power cells on a regular basis. Given the word "DEFECTOR" painted on her suit, I suspected she gave up all ties with Ex Cathedra, especially since they threatened to take her suit if she came back empty-handed.

This Sun Luce guy probably said he could charge her power cells in exchange for some gambling entertainment. But then he took most of her cells, preventing her from going very far. And now she had to perform—the threat of not recharging the only cell no doubt held over her head.

I didn't care for Judge Gascoigne, but Sun Luce wasn't endearing himself to me, that was for sure.

Dallas led me through the artificial park, past the tents of people living in the area, and out to the streets. I pointed to the apartment buildings a few blocks down, the ones near the pits and where Bishop said he had procured a room.

"There," I said. "The man I told you about. Bishop. That's where he should be."

"And this is the one who wants to help you get to the Meteorological Plexus?"

I nodded, but I held my tongue at the same time. I hadn't told Dallas exactly why I wanted to go there—just that I had to go for scavenging reasons. Part of me worried that telling the world about the disaster would lead to extremists who *wanted* the disaster. It was probably irrational, but the more I thought about it, the more I really did worry.

Some people were insane. And there wasn't much I could do to change that.

We walked the few blocks and came to the first of the apartment buildings. Hundreds of people gathered around the outside, eating and drinking out on the streets or from open windows and small porches.

Boulder City had a suffocating aura, and it was the most prevalent in the cramped housing and busy businesses. Junk hunters were hauling in all sorts of goods while city trucks brought in alien vegetation from the farms that grew near the dam. At all points during the day, there was activity and noise.

"Hey," someone barked.

I barely had time to turn around before I caught sight of Bishop. He grabbed me by the shoulder and shoved Dallas away, separating us.

"If you've got a problem with the girl, then you have a problem with me," Bishop said.

"Wait, Bishop," I began. "It's not like that. He's not a random member of the city guard. This is Dallas. Do you remember me telling you about him?"

The tension between them persisted. They stared for a long moment, and then Bishop forced a chuckle. "So, he's alive, huh?"

Dallas kept his hand on the strap of his rifle. "That's right. I'm alive."

"Let me remember this correctly . . . You're the one who betrayed a woman and left her in the hands of lunatics? And then you abandoned your daughter, in the care of a stranger, only to gallivant your way through the desert and see if they could make it to you? You're *that* guy, right?"

Again, I couldn't see Dallas's expression, but the mounting silence conveyed his mood just fine.

"We don't need to be confrontational," I said, my hands up. "I sought Dallas out, and it's his daughter held in the precinct."

Bishop answered with a click of his tongue. "Tsk. He's no Father of the Year, that's for sure. Guy doesn't even deserve a participation trophy as far as I'm concerned. We can rescue Crouton without his help. It'll be safer that way. No backstabbing."

"Aren't you just a hired gun?" Dallas asked, terse. "You have no stakes in this."

"I lost quite a bit gettin' Crouton and Viper here. Including *my truck*. And I told Viper I'd see her through to the damn plexus, and that's what I'm gonna do. Tell him, Viper. Tell him I've never gone back on my word."

I hobbled between them, but neither seemed to notice much. "Please," I said. "We don't have time for this. Bishop, Dallas—I think both of you are honestly concerned for Chelsy. Let's put aside any arguments for the time being until she's safe. All right?"

They both took a step back, but neither of them relaxed. Before anything else could happen, Bishop scooped me up into his arms and headed for the main road. Dallas jogged to his side, but neither acknowledged the other.

"You just tell me where we need to go," Bishop said. "We'll get Crouton back."

CHAPTER TWENTY-SIX

I gripped Bishop's shirt. "Where's your bag?"

"In my apartment."

"You left it there?"

I knew he knew what I was talking about—the fission bomb. It was the third thing on my mind, right after Chelsy and the damn satellites. And now I felt that if I weren't micromanaging all three problems, they would never be solved.

"I can't drag it around everywhere," Bishop said. "This is better. Trust me."

Unlike Richfield, where the population numbered less than two hundred, a fission bomb in Boulder City would kill thousands, perhaps hundreds of thousands. And what if it was stolen? The dread settled into my being, so permanent it became a second shadow.

Dallas said nothing, but he glanced between me and Bishop, obviously aware we were talking about something far more important than a simple bag.

Bishop held me close, smiling. "So, what the fuck happened to you? Up and disappeared? I heard you and Crouton got arrested, but why? And how'd you get out?"

I almost laughed.

Bishop didn't know what was going on, but he backed me up when I said we needed to rescue Chelsy, so I guessed I didn't need to explain everything before he was gung ho. A reckless attitude—I could never employ it—but I did appreciate having his support at the drop of a hat.

"We should discuss this while we head to the precinct," Dallas said. "I don't want to waste time."

Bishop shot him a sidelong glance. "We're talkin' while we walk. We don't need ongoing commentary."

As if God himself wanted to end the animosity, a strong breeze whipped through the streets, laced with sand from beyond the walls and scratching exposed skin. I had to close my eyes, and so did Bishop, but Dallas's mask kept him protected. Bishop opened his jacket and half tucked me inside, shielding my face.

Sandstorms appearing with any regularity would justify the need for the city guard to have gas masks. The fact put me at ease—at least the reason didn't involve a frequent chemical attack on the city.

The walk through the city became infinitely easier. Most crowds dispersed because of the storm, and those who didn't kept to the sides of the road, sheltered by the buildings. I explained the situation to Bishop as we went, but the winds made it a tedious process. He kept his eyes closed the majority of the trek, only risking opening them when in the protection of an alley.

When we arrived, Dallas jogged up the stairs and into the building. The children I saw from earlier remained around, huddled together behind bags of trash and fake trees.

"Why are those children here?" I asked Bishop.

He moved behind a dumpster on the corner of the street and huffed. "Parents are locked up, most likely. They don't care for the kids in those situations, so they just have to wait."

The sand and dirt—and hazardous particles—twisted round the area, coating everything in a fine layer of dust. The howl and intensity of the wind picked up, dragging with it plastic leaves from the fake trees, yellowed paper, and a whole stream of filth, anything from soiled clothes to scraps of moldy food.

Dallas exited the precinct and walked back to us. We ducked into a nearby soup kitchen, the smell of poorly made borscht thick in the air. While most got in line to get a bowl of the reddish gruel, we made our way to the back corner and took a seat at a tiny table.

"She's not in the precinct," Dallas said as he repositioned his seat closer to me. "They moved her."

Bishop huffed but didn't reply.

"I'll get the power cells then," I said as I brushed myself off.

Dallas withdrew a second gas mask from his jacket. He glanced around the crowded area before passing it to Bishop under the table. "Put this on. You'll look like the standard goon they hire for guard work, but don't say anything if anyone approaches you. If you don't have a badge, you can get gunned down. Standing orders are to kill those impersonating city guards. Let me do all the talking."

"No, thanks," Bishop said, pushing the mask away.

"Listen. It makes for a plausible story if we're both guards, and this is a thief we apprehended. It doesn't make sense if you two are hanging around me. That's not how the guards operate. They walk in pairs. I'm already taking a risk by skipping out on my post. We don't want unnecessary attention."

"I'm not puttin' the damn mask on. Maybe you can wander around as the city's dog, and we'll handle the rest."

"Certain areas are restricted except to those who pay or to the guards. The city has rules you obviously aren't aware of. We should take advantage of this circumstance."

Bishop clicked his tongue. "Tsk. If you have a plan, why don't you explain it to us?" His tone—sarcastic to the last syllable—didn't help the situation.

Dallas gritted his teeth. "I can *explain* it to you, but I can't *understand* it for you."

"*What was that?*" Bishop growled.

"Why don't you let me and Kita handle the specifics? We'll call you when we need something shot."

Bishop leaned forward in his chair, but I placed my hand on his chest and shook my head. "You should put the mask on," I said. "If anything, it'll help if more winds pick up."

After a few long moments, Bishop sat back in his chair and took the mask. He slipped it over his head, transforming into someone that was almost unrecognizable with the single piece of equipment. He adjusted it into place and then turned to me.

"Happy?" he asked, his voice disturbing, more so than the others. He had a sort of mirth to his tone that didn't translate well when made mechanical—almost like he was deranged.

"Uh," I began. "It's good. Try not to speak, though."

Dallas chortled.

"Shaddup," Bishop growled. He sounded more like a guard then.

"As amusing as this all is," Dallas drawled, "I want to see my little girl. Sun Luce lives above the Desert Diamond. It's a gambling hall, the largest in the city. There are thousands of people there at any given moment, and a fourth of the guard is always posted. They're there mostly to guard the lower floors while Sun Luce is up in a penthouse, but still."

The crowded soup kitchen probably wasn't the best place to discuss a theft, but on the other hand, the place had a white noise of conversation that drowned out words once they got a few feet away.

"Let's not get into specifics," I said. "But I need to know more about the layout of the building before I can say what we should do. Why don't we head there? It's okay to walk around inside, right? And if you two look like guards, maybe you can search the places I can't."

In theory, all I needed to do was get to the A-tech safe that held the power cells. The safe itself didn't worry me, but getting there felt like an insurmountable task when I envisioned it in my mind's eye.

"We should wait for the storm to die down a bit," Dallas said. "Then we should head out straight away."

"All right."

I leaned back in my chair, wondering if Chelsy had enough to eat. Then I glanced over at Bishop and knitted my eyebrows together.

"Are you okay?" I asked.

Bishop tilted his head to the side. "Why wouldn't I be?"

"The insects. Last I saw, you weren't feeling too well." He looked fine, but I had to know.

Bishop pushed aside his jacket and lifted his shirt, exposing his side for me to see. He once had red and pink circle wounds, but they had completely healed over, leaving no trace of their existence.

"I went and saw a doctor," he said. "Well, he called himself a doctor, but he conducted himself more like a snake oil salesman."

"He got them out?"

I grazed my fingers over his skin, happy he didn't flinch or grimace. And everything felt taut, as it should.

"Those bugs were deep inside me." Bishop chortled. "Apparently, they're not so good for you when they're three-foot-long centipedes just chillin' between organs. The guy got them out, and now I'm good to go. Healed right up."

"Hm."

When I glanced back to Dallas, I was surprised to see him leaning on the table, his hands laced tightly together as he watched our exchange.

Again, I really had no idea what his facial expression was, but it wasn't like he left his dislike for Bishop unclear. Though the constant tension between them threatened to wear down what little willpower I had left. A small part of me just wanted them to fight it out so we wouldn't have to deal with it again, but I knew that wasn't a good idea.

Bishop liked his tally marks, after all.

Goddamn.

The Desert Diamond stood peerless among half a dozen other buildings. It was a place where electricity went to die—lights shone off every surface, capturing everyone's attention. All thirty floors shone like a beacon, and my palms grew sweaty just looking at it.

I had only seen skyscrapers in movies before.

My sister and I had loved one movie in particular where the bad guy was thrown from the top story to his death, but I had always categorized them as mere fantasy.

Seeing one in full operation excited me in a way few things ever had.

Bishop, Dallas, and I stood outside on the sidewalk across the street. I kept my head tilted back, my eyes on the many floors.

"Sun Luce lives on the twentieth floor," Dallas said.

I counted the windows until I found the correct one. "How is the view from there?"

"Interesting."

"I can imagine."

Bishop hit my shoulder with his knuckles and then pointed to a small group of women outside the front door. They wore little, but everything on their body—from the thongs to the feathery bras—shimmered in the light, demanding attention, even within the already flashy environment.

"I know a few of them," Bishop said. "I'll be right back. Maybe they have some useful information."

"All right." I wondered if he really wanted to ask questions about Sun Luce or if he simply wanted to flirt. Either way, it didn't matter much, and perhaps he could find something out.

Men with push brooms cleared the street of sand, and the moment Bishop managed to dance around them and get to the other side, Dallas took me by the upper arm and led me a few feet down the road to a corner.

"Kita," Dallas said, his voice low.

"Yes?"

"I know I haven't done right by you. I don't expect you'll ever forgive me—and you shouldn't—but I need you to know that you've done me a great favor."

"Chelsy is in danger," I said. "I didn't really bring her back to you."

"Yet here you are, helping me get her back."

"Well, I feel responsible for what happened. And I don't want to see her harmed."

Dallas shook his head. "The other guards at the precinct said she was well cared for while she was there."

"Did Julius say that?"

Dallas paused for a minute and then nodded. "He said her . . . mother . . . was very concerned, so he kept a close eye on Chelsy whenever he could. Listen. Even if she's not with me right now, she never would've made it here if it hadn't been for your efforts. And your continued efforts, to be honest. If you had left town after the judge set you free, my daughter would be dead, and I never would've been the wiser."

"I couldn't let Chelsy wander off on her own. And I can't leave her with Gascoigne. She's an intelligent little girl, and it would be a shame if the world lost her, especially after everything else it has lost."

Dallas let out a ragged exhale and nodded. I really wanted to see his facial expression, to know what he truly felt about the situation, but all I got were the tiny signs of emotion that weren't filtered out by the mask. He took in another few breaths before he said, "What I'm trying to say is that there are few people I trust in this life. One of them was already taken from me, and when she died, I . . ."

Another round of steadying breaths.

"I trust you," he finally said. "I know you shouldn't trust me, but despite that, you returned my daughter. I need to thank you."

"You've said it enough," I replied, my face growing hot.

Guilt coursed through my veins. A part of me had protected Chelsy for selfish reasons. She reminded me of my sister, and I couldn't stand the thought of losing her a second time. Did I deserve praise for easing my own guilt? And I couldn't even admit it. I wanted to—I wanted to tell him that my motives weren't entirely selfless—but I didn't. I liked his praise and the raw emotion of the moment.

So I said nothing.

"How are you paying *him*?" Dallas asked with a jerk of his head toward Bishop's location.

"Well, I told him that he could have half of the things we scavenged. That I would break into secure locations and then we'd split the findings."

"Nothing else?"

I shook my head.

"He hasn't touched you, has he? Or demanded your body for his gun or protection?"

The question caught me by surprise. I continued to shake my head. "No. Nothing like that." He had his prostitutes, after all.

Dallas exhaled. "Good. I figured a man like him wouldn't have bothered with self-control. I mean, the way he just *picks you up*. I don't like it."

"Well, Bishop did carry me a good portion of the trip here."

It pained me to utter the words, like I was a burden everyone else needed to care for, but I knew Bishop didn't think that, not after I sacrificed the nanites to save his life. He really had treated me different since that day—like he, too, couldn't thank me enough.

"As far as I'm concerned, we don't need him," Dallas said, curt. "I know he helped you get to Boulder City, and he's quick to point out his own trustworthiness, but men like him operate for themselves. I'm sure he's killed hundreds."

"He has killed a lot of people," I said. "But he's a good guy."

Dallas kept his hand on my upper arm and pulled me closer until we were mere inches apart. "After you're done scavenging the Meteorological Plexus, let me escort you to U-Cali. I'll take you to the ports and the boat—all the way to your damn underground greenhouse. As long as Chelsy is with us, I'll make my way to anywhere you think would be a safe place to start over."

I didn't know what to say. I mulled over the statements, wondering if the BC Oasis was even a viable option. Perhaps I should've told him the importance of my trip to the plexus, but the option was stolen from me when Bishop stepped up onto the sidewalk corner.

"What're we talkin' about?" Bishop asked.

Dallas shook his head. "It's of no concern."

"Heh. Right. Well, Kitten told me all about the ins and outs of the gambling hall."

"*Kitten*? Is that her name?"

"Yeah. Her last name. Wait till you hear her first." Bishop laughed, but I had no idea why. Obviously, I had missed the punch line.

Dallas just stared at him.

After a few moments, Bishop quieted himself with a huff. "Really? Nothing?"

"This isn't the time," Dallas stated. "Why don't you keep focused and tell us anything relevant you might have discovered? If you've got nothing, you can return to the whores."

"Sure your name's not Richard?" Bishop asked, smiling. "I'd love to call you by an appropriate nickname."

That time, I got the joke. I laughed once, Dallas snapped his attention to me, and I coughed to stifle the rest. "Bishop, did Ms. Kitten say anything worthwhile?"

"Only that Sun Luce is a man that doesn't keep a strict schedule. He comes through all the time, but nobody knows when."

"And the whores knew this?" Dallas asked. "Is it even reliable information?"

"He apparently likes himself some whores. The ladies said he usually gets a few or buys slaves from those dealers before throwin' them out on the streets. So I'd say it's good info."

"I'd like to walk around inside," I said. "Maybe see how accessible the twentieth floor is."

Dallas offered me his arm before Bishop.

I didn't take it.

Instead, I waited for Bishop's assistance. Once I had Bishop's arm, we crossed the street. Bishop had never let me down. Never betrayed me. Dallas needed to know I trusted him.

The front door to the gambling hall swung open when we neared. The musky scent of human sweat stung my nose, but only for a few seconds as we crossed the threshold. Once inside, an odd fragrance of chemical cleaner and air fresheners mixed together into something unpleasant but tolerable.

"We shouldn't be walking together," Dallas said. "I'll stay with Bishop, and we'll look around the stairs and elevator. Can you make it on your own? There shouldn't be any trouble in here."

I rubbed at my leg and hip. "Yeah, I can make it."

No matter what he asked, I would've said I could handle it. I really didn't like admitting that perhaps I shouldn't be walking around, but since we weren't under the pressure of a tight time constraint, a slow walk wouldn't kill me.

Bishop let go of my arm. Then he and Dallas took off toward the gambling room floor. A man in a tight tux walked up to stop them, but Dallas flashed his badge and then chatted for a moment before continuing on.

I hadn't even realized I had been holding my breath until they made it inside, past a point I could no longer see them. What if the doorman had discovered Bishop's identity? The Desert Diamond had a ton of people inside, including a whole host of guards, each armed with a heavy rifle.

It wouldn't take them long to gun somebody down.

When I attempted to walk onto the gambling room floor, the same man in the tux approached me with a smile.

"Hello," he said. "Welcome to the Desert Diamond. Do you have any guns or knives on you?"

"No," I said.

He waved over one of the idle guards. "I'm sorry, but we'll need to check you first."

"Guns and knives aren't allowed inside?"

"We have lockers if you need them, but the establishment prefers to have a monopoly on violence."

The guard rummaged through my pockets, handsy to the point of irritation, but I kept my mouth shut. I didn't want to start any trouble, and I doubted my complaining would result in the man being punished.

Once satisfied I had nothing, the guard let me pass.

"Enjoy your stay," the man in the tux said.

I gave him a curt nod and then hobbled inside. I kept to the wall, leaning against it despite the odd looks it garnered me. A few times I spotted sloppy drunks doing the same, so it didn't seem too out of place, but still. I wanted my cane back.

The gambling room floor had many pillars and plastic plants. No windows. No clocks. It was hard to really know where I was going, especially with the thick layer of smoke that hovered around the ceiling. I rubbed at my watery eyes as I walked around. Making a mental map of the ground floor was my top priority. Then I would find a method to ascend, and then I needed to find a method of leaving without being stopped.

The people around me snapped their attention to the door. In an instant, I saw the shift in their demeanor from jovial to concerned. They backed away, becoming quiet, and when I turned around, I could see why.

Theon—the man with the alien drones—walked into the building, the same drones flanking him on either side. He combed his fingers through his blond hair as he strode in, a slight smile on his face.

But then he spotted me and stopped, recognition clear on his face.

I forced myself to swallow and tried to move away, but I knew it was pointless.

"If it isn't the thief," Theon said as he walked over to me.

Not even thirty steps in and already I had been caught. Perhaps it was time to remove "master thief" from my mental résumé.

He placed a hand on my shoulder and gripped me tight. "Why don't you come with me? Wouldn't want you doing anything questionable, now would we?"

CHAPTER TWENTY-SEVEN

Theon brought me to a side room off the gambling floor.

While smoke dominated the air outside, his room appeared unsullied. Pristine, organized, and wide open enough to allow his drones to walk around.

He had two of those disgusting aliens in the room. Bodyguards, obviously.

Theon sauntered over to a wooden desk and took a seat, leaving me to fend for myself on the other side. I took a moment to glance around the windowless walls. Bookshelves, piled high with books and old-world tablets, made up most of the decoration.

Were they from the old university? Some appeared to be advanced math books and texts on history.

"I knew that judge was foolish," Theon said as he swiveled his chair around to face me directly. "But I never suspected she would think sending a random thief after her belongings was a worthwhile plan."

He already knew what I was here for? But I couldn't admit to it.

"I'm not sure what you're talking about," I said.

Theon lifted a perfect eyebrow. "Hm. Well, maybe we got off on the wrong foot. Let me introduce myself. I'm Architect Theon Sellers. Anything the judge has promised you isn't worth getting caught over. Especially when you would be stealing from one of the most powerful individuals here in the wastes."

"Architect?" I asked. "As in, the caste of aliens? Or you build buildings?"

The drones circled close, and Theon smiled. "I think you know which."

I stifled a laugh, but I couldn't keep the smile from my face.

"You think it's funny?" he asked.

"I think it's audacious."

Architect was the highest caste of alien, better than the rest in every regard, and their default leader in any situation. They were the architects of society, not just buildings, and they were so rare and powerful among their own kind that, of the eight million aliens who originally arrived on Earth, only three of them were of the architect caste.

"It's like declaring yourself the supreme emperor," I continued, still smiling. "It borders on the childish."

One drone walked around behind the desk and stood at Theon's side. Theon stroked the beast's arm as he said, "I have a long history with the Teth. Different. Unusual. Let's just say there aren't many options for titles among them."

"They . . . listen to your command?" I motioned to the drones.

It was impossible. No way a human could control them. There had to be a reason—a logical reason—they kept so close and protected him. Some other caste must have ordered it. But I didn't see an alien of a different caste, not a single one since I arrived in the city. Humans lacked the ability to produce the pheromones necessary to command the mindless drones. It was just impossible. Impossible.

"They listen," Theon said.

"Why?"

He shrugged. "I'm psychic."

Again, I had to stifle a laugh, but I couldn't keep it all in.

"Amused?" he asked.

"You might as well have said you were a wizard, that's how close to reality your explanation was."

"So, you don't believe me."

"Of course not. I don't know why they follow you, but I know that's not the reason."

I crossed my arms over my chest, disgusted with the aliens' heavy breathing, and focused on keeping myself calm. I didn't know what Theon wanted—or why he would tell such tall tales—but I couldn't jeopardize my mission by getting arrested a second time. Even if he wasn't an alien architect, he did seem to have authority over the guards.

Theon chortled as he leaned back in his chair. "And here I thought the judge had made a huge mistake, but I can see now why she thought you could retrieve her belongings. You know a good deal about the Teth. More than your average wasteland denizen, I'd wager."

"I was just looking around. That's not a crime."

"I'm curious, why don't you tell me where you learned so much about the aliens?"

With a shrug, I said, "I've seen some old-world informational videos."

A plausible explanation. Not too far-fetched, not extreme. I knew a few people in Ex Cathedra who had become educated on the aliens from old PSAs. It fit my second rule of lying—a simple statement without too many details.

But Theon narrowed his eyes as he stared at me. His drones settled into comfortable positions during the few moments of silence.

"You're lying," Theon finally said. "Interesting. That means the real explanation is probably more fascinating. Hm."

"I have places I need to be," I said, edging toward the door one half step at a time. It worried me he could see through my subterfuge when I offered him so little. "It was nice meeting you, Mr. Sellers."

I refused to call him *architect*.

"I don't think you understand," Theon continued. "I know why you're here. The judge wants you to get her power cells back."

I didn't reply.

"Since you're obviously more educated than the dullards I typically interact with, I'll cut to the chase. What is it she's offering you to do this? Giving you back your daughter?"

I tensed.

Should I answer him? Affirming with a nod would be tantamount to admitting I came here to steal. On the other hand, he seemed sure of my purpose. But if he already knew everything, why ask me? What did he gain from having me answer the questions? A small part of me—a tiny part— started to wonder if he actually *was* psychic.

I knew he wasn't. I knew. Because that was impossible. But I did wonder.

"I can have your daughter released from the city guard's custody," Theon said with a smile, taking my long silence as some sort of admission to his earlier question. "You'd like that, wouldn't you?"

"You'd give her to me without any requirements?" I asked. "No strings attached?"

"Not quite. You see, I'm also interested in those power cells."

The statement caught me by surprise. But I could piece together the conversation. "You want me to bring you the power cells instead," I drawled.

He smiled wider. "That's right."

"But Judge Gascoigne will—"

"Be upset? Probably. But I can still get your daughter out of custody."

Judge Gascoigne wasn't a stable individual. Hell, she was bordering on sadistic, and I didn't want to jeopardize Chelsy's safety by angering her. All I wanted was to get her out of Gascoigne's clutches as fast as possible.

"What else do you want?" Theon asked. "More than your daughter. Money? A-tech? Security?"

The questioning got me nervous. I rubbed at my arms as I panned my gaze over the bookshelves, my mind immediately focusing on the myriad of problems that lay before me. But the old textbooks demanded my attention.

"I want to know more about the Meteorological Plexus," I said.

Both Theon's eyebrows shot to his hairline. "The Meteorological Plexus? Interesting."

"You know of it?" I asked, so fast I almost tripped over my words.

"I know of several. I'm surprised someone like you would want—" He caught his breath and stared at the desk for a moment before resuming with, "That doesn't matter. Here's what I'm going to offer you. I'll get your daughter, and I'll get you all the information on the three closest plexuses I have at my disposal. All you have to do is bring *me* the power cells instead."

That did sound good.

But I still hesitated.

I didn't know anything about Theon, other than he was a liar. His title was a lie, his explanations were lies, and it almost felt too good to be true that he would have information on the Meteorological Plexus. But he did recognize the name of the place. He was the first person to react when I said it, like he knew the significance.

And giving him the power cells would anger Judge Gascoigne. If she ever learned of my treachery, I supposed.

"I'll think about it," I said.

Theon stood. The two alien drones stirred, moving to flank him. He opened one of his desk drawers and withdrew a plastic keycard. Then he walked to my side and placed the card in the front pocket of my duster.

"This'll allow you to get up the elevator without any hassle," he said. "But it'll only work for the next twenty-four hours. If you succeed within that time frame, meet me at the Frenton Building. The place I arrested you. Do we have a deal?"

"I said I would think about it."

"Good."

Theon guided me to the door, his alien friends close behind us.

"I'll be waiting to hear from you," he said as he opened the door, allowing me out. "Hopefully you're as talented as you are educated. I'd hate to hear of a wannabe thief thrown into the pits. People like you don't last long."

"Do either of you know anything about the man who calls himself Architect Theon Sellers?" I asked.

Bishop and Dallas had spread out napkins and paperwork across the tiny table. They had drawn floor plans and written notes on each of them. Most of it was scribbles, and difficult to read, but they had gathered quite a bit of information.

"He's one of the men in charge of the city," Dallas said. "He works with Sun Luce. Everyone knows about Theon—he's famous even beyond the walls, all the way to U-Cali."

"Because he's psychic?"

Dallas snorted and forced a laugh. "That's what he says, but anyone with half a day's worth of education knows that's bullshit. Unfortunately, most people in the city think it's true simply because he has aliens at his beck and call. If ignorance were currency, we'd be living in a land of milk and honey."

I mulled over the statements.

Although Dallas and Bishop wore similar outfits, with masks fitted over their faces, it was easy to distinguish them. Bishop was taller and larger, whereas Dallas stood with a stiffness to his posture and a readiness to his stance, his combat training evident for anyone who knew soldiers. I stared at the two of them across the table while I thought over the situation. How could I use them to the best of my ability in planning?

Bishop ripped off his gas mask as he arranged his information. He kept his gaze down and his lips tight together.

The cramped confines of Dallas's apartment made it difficult to spread out or get fresh air. The place had two rooms: a kitchen and bedroom combo, and a bathroom. The end. Well, there was a novel's worth of rust, scratches, and dents in the wall, like an entire circus had lived in the apartment before Dallas. I tried not to think about it, not when I had more pressing issues at hand.

"Do you know anything about Theon?" I asked Bishop. He seemed quiet.

"Yeah. I know him. I did a few jobs for him in the past."

"Like what?"

We were alone in the apartment, but the walls were thin enough to hear a plant breathing in the next room over. Fortunately—or unfortunately—music played from an apartment three down, creating a low hum that shook the floors and caused the single overhead light to sway gently back and forth.

"So," Bishop began, "the city used to be run by four people. Theon hired me to kill one of the others. He paid me with an A-tech truck and some supplies for Richfield and Tomato Creek."

"You're an assassin?" Dallas asked.

Bishop chuckled. "For the right amount, I'm whatever people want me to be."

"So you're a glorified whore with a gun?"

Bishop gave Dallas a sidelong glance. "Something like that. I've gotta pay the bills, after all."

"And if someone paid you enough, you'd turn us in?"

"Tsk. You're a wet blanket of the highest order. I wouldn't betray Viper. She's saved my life multiple times now."

"Theon wants Judge Gascoigne's power cells," I interjected. Bishop and Dallas's constant tension could erode a saint's patience, but I didn't have the energy to fuss over it. "He told me he could get Chelsy out and give me information on the Meteorological Plexus if I did."

Bishop whistled. "Yeah. I can see that."

"What do you mean?"

"Well, when I worked for him, Theon was really afraid of the others tryin' to kill him. They hate his aliens, I guess. Not entirely sure. Anyway, he never went anywhere without protection. Maybe Theon wants to force the judge to be his guard."

"Or he wants the judge to kill Sun Luce," Dallas muttered.

I turned to Dallas, an eyebrow up. "You think so?"

"He already has aliens and men with rifles to protect him. Adding a random judge—one he would be blackmailing, mind you—probably wouldn't be the best plan to keep him safe."

Bishop shrugged. "Okay. So what do you think he wants?"

"Given what I've learned just now, I'm leaning more toward another assassination."

"Oh, yeah?"

"Think about it for two seconds. Sun Luce and the judge already have a shaky relationship. If the judge snapped and killed the guy, most people wouldn't be surprised. No one would suspect Theon. And then the city would have two people who ran the show."

"Sounds about right," Bishop said.

Did I care about the power struggle in Boulder City?

Not when I had a million other things with higher priority.

Then again, why was I saving humanity if I was just going to let it fall back into the dregs? Supporting political coups wasn't really something I wanted to do. On the other hand, if Theon had the information I needed, he was my best option. The information was paramount.

But maybe I could still get it elsewhere.

The options weighed heavy on my mind, practically blackening my vision.

"What would the two of you do?" I asked.

Dallas huffed. "All I care about is Chelsy's safety."

"Go with Theon," Bishop said. "He makes good on his deals. And then we can head out to the plexus right afterward."

"You don't care that he's likely going to force the judge to kill people?" I asked.

"Do you really care about that judge or anyone she would kill? Seems like an appropriate fate for her. Those judges are nothing more than tools anyway."

"I'm not a fan of wanton violence."

Bishop shrugged. "Fair enough. But if you give the cells to the judge, she might not follow through with her word. You're not worried about that?"

I had always worried about that. There would be nothing stopping the judge from killing me after I gave her the power cells. And there was no reason for her to release Chelsy afterward, either. I had to trust her—rely on her word and honor—and I had no idea if I could.

Even when she let me live, I didn't really understand why. What motivated her besides power and control? I wasn't sure.

"Why don't we talk about this while we get some fresh air?" Bishop asked as he motioned to the door. "I need to get my bag anyway. We can go together."

I did want to keep the bomb close.

Dallas shook his head. "Why don't you get the bag yourself and let Kita rest? I can watch her."

"Viper's a grown-ass woman. She can decide for herself where she wants to go."

They both turned to me.

"I'd like to accompany you to retrieve the bag," I said. "But we should return quickly."

Both Dallas and Bishop relaxed a bit, but it was clear neither were entirely happy with my statement. I appreciated their concern, because it had been a long time since anyone fretted over my health and safety, and I found myself smiling sometimes when they asked if I was okay.

Bishop opened the door for me, and I made my way out into the hall. He stepped out and closed it behind us, smiling the whole time.

"This'll be easy," he said. "If we plan it right, we can leave the city right after you drop off the cells."

"Nothing has been easy this entire trek," I quipped.

"You got radiation poisoning pretty easy."

I opened my mouth to retort but instead ended up chuckling. "Touché."

Bishop scooped me up into his arms. I tensed and shook my head.

"Put me down. I'd rather walk."

"You're always in pain then," he said, his voice low. "I don't like that."

"I'd still rather walk."

Bishop set me down and frowned. "Why? Don't want D-Bag gettin' jealous?"

It was a terrible nickname, but it was better than the first two he had used.

"It's embarrassing," I said as I made my way for the stairs.

"You've never been like this before."

"We weren't around so many other people before. It's . . . different. I don't like the feel of their eyes."

I didn't like feeling pathetic. But I couldn't say the word. I hated the ring of it in my ears, reminding me of the lost potential. I just wanted to ignore it. Even if it hurt, even if every step sent agony through me, I'd rather people didn't assume I was halfway in the grave and nothing but a burden.

After three steps down, Bishop walked in front of me and stopped. He met my gaze—he was lower on the steps, about my height—and for a second my pulse increased. Bishop didn't usually conduct himself with such a serious expression.

"You don't have to pretend in front of me," he said. "I know you better than anyone."

"That's not true," I said on reflex, before giving it any thought.

"Isn't it? Who else knows about your sister?"

My throat tightened. There was a reason I rarely spoke about it—I didn't want anyone to know. I couldn't bring myself to answer him.

"You don't have any other family," Bishop continued. "You've been tight-lipped about your reason for going to the plexus, but you told me at least thirty times. C'mon, Viper. If you need help, just ask me. For fuck's sake, I watched you recover from the brink of death. I've seen you at your worst, and I'm still here."

"It isn't *you*," I snapped. "It's everyone else. I don't want them seeing me . . . I don't want to appear . . ."

"Weak?"

"I just want to walk, all right? I don't want anyone to think I can't."

Bishop stepped aside as I continued down the stairs. Two floors down and he remained silent, traveling at my slow pace. I didn't want any pain between us, so I exhaled and asked, "What do you think the likelihood is we'll live through all this, Bishop?"

"What's *all this* mean?"

"Getting to the plexus."

"I'd say it's a good ninety percent."

"That high?"

He shrugged. "We've gotten through worse. How bad could the plexus really be, right? You'll walk in, do what you need to do, and we'll be humanity's quiet saviors. Wham-bam-thank-you-ma'am."

I smiled. Would it be that simple? Part of me knew Bishop had jinxed us somehow. Then again, bad luck was just as irrational as good luck. Perhaps it would be that easy.

"If we live, would you go with me to United California?" I asked.

"Sure. Why not? I've run these roads long enough."

His flippant attitude grated at my already thin patience.

"Dallas has tickets for a train," I said. "He wants to go with me. He wants to take Chelsy away from all this strife."

"Feh." Bishop shrugged. "It's great you get along with him, but I still don't trust the guy."

"He's . . . Well, I know what's important to him, and it's easier to understand and connect then. He loves his daughter." He loved his wife.

"Yeah, but like I said, you don't share everythin' with the man. Do you really trust him that much?"

I had known Dallas for less time, but already I felt I knew him better—not because I knew everything in his past, but because I had a good grasp on who Dallas was as a person.

"At least he calls me by my name," I said, my voice low. I stopped walking and turned my gaze to Bishop's.

He answered with a dismissive wave of his hand. "I give everyone a nickname."

"I'd rather you call me Kita."

Bishop had only said my real name once. When he thought he was about to die. I didn't know why, but the moment stuck in my memory. Since then, I never liked it when he used his nickname for me. It felt wrong, somehow. Off.

"Does it really matter?" Bishop asked. He slid his hands into his pockets and narrowed his eyes. "Why don't we just enjoy what life we have while we have it? You want serious? Jackass back there will give you all the stern looks and frigid conversation you can handle."

"That's not what I'm saying."

"Then why're you ridin' me for this? You got something else you want to say? Say it."

But it was difficult to articulate what I really wanted.

I didn't like thinking that Bishop kept a wall between him and everything else. I didn't like thinking he would easily forget about me because he couldn't even be bothered to remember my real name. I loved his easygoing nature, the way he made me laugh when I thought I had become incapable of such emotions, but . . .

It was like he didn't really want to invest or care in anything.

"Bishop," I said.

He waited.

"I don't want to argue. I'll just stay here."

Bishop turned away. "If that's what you want."

"You'll bring the bag back?"

"Yeah."

Without another word, Bishop took off down the rest of the stairs. I turned back around and headed up, wondering if I should've said what

I did. Then again, Bishop brushed off the whole conversation like he brushed off everything—like it didn't fucking matter.

Of course, *did* it matter? Probably not. It was foolish to make a big deal of my name, and even before I reached the top of the creaky stairway, I knew I would apologize to him. Even if he didn't care, even if he considered apologies pointless, I didn't want anything between us.

Bishop was a bright light in my life. That fact swirled in my thoughts.

My hip throbbed by the time I made it to Dallas's apartment. To my surprise, the door stood ajar. I pushed it in and ambled inside, leaning heavy on the doorframe.

Dallas sat at the table, categorizing the information into neat piles.

When a couple of teenagers wandered down the stairway, their conversation echoed in the stairwell and easily drifted into the apartment through the open door.

"What's that supposed to mean?" one teen barked.

The other growled a word of frustration before saying, "It's an easy job. I can't believe you won't do it, just for the night."

I shut the door.

Dallas had been listening to me and Bishop.

When I turned to him, Dallas removed his gas mask, revealing his scarred face. He had the mark of the Iron-Blooded on one side, but the nanites prevented it from becoming gnarly. The lines of the two skulls were faint—like a white tattoo—but still visible against the hue of his tanned skin.

"You going to tell me about this plexus?" he asked. "It's obvious it's no scavenging job."

I took a seat at the table, thankful to take the weight off my leg. "Yeah. It's important."

Dallas moved from his chair to one that was closer. "Then please, tell me."

I told him, but it didn't ease the stress or dread.

The problem had yet to be solved, and I couldn't relax until it was.

CHAPTER TWENTY-EIGHT

Plans gave me confidence.

I focused on that thought as I made my way to the elevator with Bishop and Dallas. A million things could go wrong, but confidence acted as both a sword and shield in uncertain situations. Could I maintain it? Yes. I wasn't going to question myself. I wouldn't fail.

"You look good," Bishop said, his mask-voice laced with something more than amusement.

My outfit blended in with our surroundings, but it also reminded me I had a plethora of social anxieties.

My outfit wasn't anything like the women out in front—with their feathers and sequins—but it did expose more skin than anything I had worn before. Well, outside of my birthday suit, I suppose.

I wore a black bikini top with a pair of jean shorts. Bishop had suggested I cover the scars on my hip, so an ink marking—a faux tattoo—covered that portion of my side.

"Would you keep your eyes forward?" Dallas snapped. "Remember, you're a city guard."

"Tsk. It might be more suspicious if I weren't looking."

"Just stay quiet. We're almost there."

We reached the elevator on the ground floor of the Desert Diamond. After stepping inside, my attention went straight to the card reader. Sure enough, the higher floors were restricted. We had Theon's card, but I hesitated for a moment as Dallas slid it through the reader.

Old buildings like this kept record of who used keycards and when. By using it, we were basically announcing our presence to anyone paying attention.

Would Theon be watching?

My hands grew shaky and my pulse quick. Bishop said we could trust him, but there wasn't anything stopping him from fucking with us, either. And it made me nervous thinking he was keeping an eye on our criminal activities.

The elevator went upward at a slow pace.

I ran a hand through my short hair.

When I caught sight of myself in the reflection of the polished metal in the elevator, however, I was surprised by the punkish-looking pixie girl staring back.

The worst part of my disguise was the perfume of alcohol. I didn't drink, because half a sip was enough to do me in, and the harsh tang of rum irritated my stomach.

"Not much longer now," Dallas said.

Bishop leaned against the wall. "You sure you're gonna be able to get Kita out of the area without trouble?"

"We'll make it out," Dallas stated with confidence.

"You're not gonna ditch her and take the power cells to the judge yourself, are you?"

"Enough, Bishop," I said. "You should just focus on getting us a vehicle."

"Don't worry. I'm sure Pawn will have something."

"Did you ever find anything worth trading him?" Dallas asked.

"I have a sniper rifle he's always wanted."

The elevator stopped, killing the conversation between us.

I rubbed my palms across my skintight shorts, wondering what sort of situation we would walk into. The penthouse was the one aspect of the plan where I couldn't think through every contingency. I didn't know of everything inside the penthouse. Well, I knew the layout, and there was an A-tech safe and power cells, but not much else. Dallas figured out Sun Luce lived alone, no family, and that guards took turns keeping the front room safe, but even that was too vague for my comfort.

The elevator door opened.

Bishop and Dallas carried me out of the elevator by my arms. I went mostly limp, my head hung, my heart pounding loud enough to hinder my hearing, but I managed to push down my anxiety enough to keep focus.

Two guards stood watch in the penthouse front room. They both stepped forward when we approached, but neither hefted their rifles. One motioned to me and half laughed.

"What's this?" he asked.

"Sun Luce told us to bring this one to his room," Dallas said.

The two guards exchanged glances, their masks preventing me from knowing what they felt about the situation. If they denied us entry, the plan was to subdue them. I really didn't want to have to resort to violence so soon into the operation—the moment we did, it would start a count-down to much bigger problems.

After a few moments of silence, both Dallas and Bishop tensed.

Finally, one guard pulled out a two-way radio transceiver. He clicked it on and asked, "Hey, is the boss around?"

My heart stopped. I hadn't thought they would call in our presence. It was obvious from the way Dallas tightened his grip on my arm he hadn't considered such a situation, either. Dallas didn't have a radio transceiver, after all. But I guess the guards in charge of Sun Luce's safety were just better equipped.

Someone on the other end of the radio responded, "No. Why?"

"Eh. Just wanted to check somethin'. Never mind." The guard clicked off the device and shrugged. "The boss already has a girl for the evening, but I guess if he wants two, he wants two."

The other guard opened the door. "Let the girl go. She can go in by herself."

Dallas shook his head. "She's drunk." Then he and Bishop released my arms. It wasn't a charade when I hit the floor, but I did have to conceal my grimace. Dallas lifted me straight into his arms. "I'll take her in."

"She have anything on her?"

"No. But you can check if you want."

The guards glanced me over, but it didn't take long. I wasn't wearing much. Which was the point. Nothing to incriminate. Nothing out of the ordinary.

Satisfied, the guards stepped aside. We walked in, leaving Bishop in the front room.

A lifestyle I thought died with the old world greeted us the instant we entered the main hallway.

Art adorned the wall, fluffy carpets covered the floor, and a gentle breeze wafted down from the climate-controlled vents. The luxury even extended to the sweet aroma of incense, so drastic a contrast from the air outside I could detect it through the stench of alcohol.

Dallas carried me through the penthouse, glancing into each room we passed. I clung to him, no longer feigning drunkenness, ready to find what I needed so we could leave.

"I'll be out on the street," Dallas whispered. "You sure you can do this?"

"Yes."

"What about the other woman?"

I hadn't planned on that, either. But still, I couldn't turn back. "I'll take care of it."

"All right."

Dallas opened the door to the bedroom and froze. Sitting on the edge of the bed was a young woman—sixteen at most, but possibly as young as fourteen—her long red hair a stream of liquid fire. She glanced up, her eyes wide, her tiny body stiff.

The wide-open space, and large bed, reminded me of the homes I used to fantasize about when I read old-world magazines. It wasn't really the time to gawk and admire, but what brief glances I got, I enjoyed.

With slow steps, Dallas took me to the bed and set me down on the soft comforter. He said nothing to the girl, and she said nothing to him. Before he stepped away, he withdrew a small plastic bag from his pants pocket and passed it to me, taking careful precautions not to alert the girl. I took the bag of tools and kept them close.

Then Dallas left, much faster than he entered.

Once the door snapped shut, I took a moment to glance over at the girl. She stared back at me.

I sat up on the bed and rubbed at my arms, trying to clear my mind and alter my plans on the fly. I knew the layout of the penthouse. I knew where I would find the safe. But how would I get there without the girl knowing? And what if she went straight to the guards the moment I started doing anything suspicious?

"Are you okay?" she asked, her voice lyrical.

"I . . . drank too much."

She pointed to the far door. "There's a restroom."

"I need something to calm my stomach."

"There's a kitchen."

Her helpful attitude caught me a bit off guard. "Thank you."

While I went to stand, the girl said, "My name is Carlee."

"I'm . . . Tamura."

Would it really matter if she had my real name? Probably not. But I couldn't take the risk.

She fidgeted with the hem of her simple shirt-dress, the light aqua color complementing her smooth alabaster skin.

"I'll be right back," I said.

I got to my feet, wobbled around, and then ambled my way toward the door.

Carlee watched me go the entire way, but never got off the bed or said anything else. Once out of the room, I shut the door and hustled as fast as I could, leaning on the wall as I went despite the decorations that attempted to impede my travel. I didn't care if I knocked around old oil paintings or framed news articles. And although I avoided toppling over any stands or potted plants, I did push them aside to accommodate my travel.

The kitchen was close, but I passed the door and headed into the study.

To no one's surprise, the door was locked.

I knelt down, gritting my teeth as I positioned myself on one knee, and used the tools Dallas had given me to unlock the obstacle. Once open, I stepped inside, turned around, and then locked the door again, preventing Carlee from stumbling upon me while I worked.

A glass door led out to the terrace, creating a breathtaking view, even for a standard room with a couple bookshelves and a desk. But the entrance to the vault was on the opposite wall, not hidden in any way, no doubt because of the secure defenses. It looked like many other vaults made before the bombs, including the one I first opened when Bishop found me. They were all constructed by one of two companies—the only ones with mass A-tech products at the time the world ended.

I shuffled over and went straight for the computer.

To my surprise, and panic, it didn't look quite like the ones I had fiddled with before. I started up the operating system and cursed under my breath. It wasn't as old as some of the others, and after I managed to get into the command console, I realized some of my old tricks didn't work.

With a huff, I tapped the back of my hand to my forehead.

It wasn't impossible, but it would take me far longer than I expected.

Minutes added up. A piece of me wondered if Sun Luce would actually arrive before I completed my task. What would I even say to him? There was nothing to say. No lie that could possibly explain my actions. Throwing myself from the terrace would be a possible option at that point.

While I typed, I glanced to my left and right. The heavy presence of eyes weighed on me, but I didn't see anyone or anything. Then a terrible thought struck me.

What if there were cameras?

I forced an exhale and worked as fast as I could, trying to remember every obscure Tethlite coding lesson I had ever learned.

Then I finally got it. I reset the passwords, half laughing to myself. Once the vault door opened, I went inside and froze.

Damn.

The entire vault room was filled with A-tech weaponry, gadgets, and parts.

I shuffled in at a slow pace, my attention jumping from one thing to the next. And it was a large room. Large enough that Sun Luce kept his own JUDGE-X0 exoskeleton in the corner.

Although I had planned on taking stock of the vault and grabbing anything I deemed helpful, I hadn't imagined there would be a warehouse's worth of inventory. I went back to the study, opened the glass door to the terrace, and stepped out. The wind whipped around me, sending shivers and goose bumps across my skin, but I ignored that in favor of grabbing a few pillows off the luxury seating.

I used a pocketknife and cut them open to remove the insides, creating impromptu sacks. Then I made my way back to the vault.

Sun Luce really did have a nice collection—so nice I didn't actually recognize some of the items.

Even though they could've been valuable, I kept my attention on what I could use. A few EMP grenades, atomic batteries, powerful plastic explosives, some the size of a pill container, and a couple computer tablets. While satellites still circled Earth and could connect electronics to one another, many of the major systems had failed, resulting in only short-range connectivity to other devices or hardwired cables.

I didn't know many places that still had connections to one another, but I still liked the idea of tinkering with portable computers. Perhaps I could store information on them or use them like old-world cell phones for a limited range.

Once I had two pillows almost full, I refocused and searched through the treasure trove for the reason of my visit—Judge Gascoigne's power cells. To my ever-increasing worry, I didn't see them. I pushed aside object after object, including an implant—one of the implants that practically halted aging.

I grazed my fingertips over it, wondering if it would be worth taking, but I knew it wasn't something I could immediately use. Still . . .

Maybe he had a canister of nanites?

Then I shook my head.

I needed to find those damn power cells. Nothing else mattered at the moment.

I laughed when I spotted them: right next to the exoskeleton power suit. I hobbled over, grabbed all nine, each the size of three fingers, and then shoved them in the pillow. Fortunately, most of what I had taken was light.

I tied the two pillows together and returned to the terrace.

In my original plan—the one where I was alone in the penthouse—I would've used the bedsheets to fashion a net. But I didn't have those. Instead, I sliced open the last of the pillows, emptied them out, and then ripped them into long ribbons of fabric. Then I tied them to my sacks of goodies with lots of loops, creating a net.

Over the edge of the terrace, and a few stories down, was a group of artificial trees. I held the bags over the railing, and once my arms began to burn, I released. The odd amalgamation of pillow casing landed in the branches. My makeshift net snagged, causing the sacks to swing back and forth, dangling over the ground below.

If Dallas upheld his end of the plan, he was near the tree, waiting for me to drop off the goods. He would get the items off the branch, and we would have everything we needed to get Chelsy back.

With a sigh of relief, I ambled off the terrace, back through the study, and then opened the door to the hall.

I caught my breath.

Carlee stood in the hallway, staring at me as I exited the secure room. For a moment, neither of us spoke, but her wide eyes darted from the door handle to me, and I knew she was aware of the precarious situation.

Then she took a step back.

CHAPTER TWENTY-NINE

"Wait," I said.

Carlee hesitated. She lingered in the hallway, glancing over her shoulder. I really couldn't handle a situation in which she called for the guards. My only solace would be that the power cells were already in Dallas's possession. At least he would be able to reunite with his daughter if I were caught.

I leaned against the wall, trying to take a nonaggressive stance. "Carlee. Just wait a moment."

"You're not supposed to be in there," she murmured.

"Why are you here, Carlee?"

She took in a breath and then said, "What do you mean?"

"Are you here because you're being forced?"

"No."

"Then why? Is he offering you money? Did he say you'd get a job?"

"Money. But . . . he won't give me anything if he thinks we broke all his rules and messed with his stuff."

"Don't do this," I said. I didn't move or attempt to approach her, and I kept a calm, even voice. "If you help me leave, you'll make more than ten times whatever he was going to pay you."

She lifted both eyebrows. "Ten times?"

"That's right." Well, at least I was guessing ten times. I doubted he would pay an exorbitant amount for a prostitute, but I never really knew. I also didn't have time to crunch the numbers. "Come here. I'll show you."

Carlee once again hesitated.

Before she could decide, I opened the study door. "There's enough A-tech in here to drown in. Imagine all the stuff you could pawn for that."

I only knew one thing about her—she wanted money—and I was going to milk that hard.

After a painstakingly long decision-making period, Carlee walked into the study. I pointed to the vault across the room and waited. Although she had been tepid in the hallway, the moment she laid eyes on the vault, she jogged over.

"You opened this?" she asked. "Amazing." Then she entered, not even bothering to wait for my credentials or explanation.

A thought hit me.

I could lock her in.

It would solve the problem of dealing with her, but it would also result in her punishment for my crime. Did I want that? Was that something my grandfather would condone? I was the only one who knew about the fate of the world, after all—better my safety than hers.

Who was I kidding? Just remembering her concerned tone and empathetic looks stilled my actions. I'd hate myself for trapping her for my own safety, even if it were the logical choice, given the stakes.

Carlee returned half a minute later. She hadn't taken much. Six thin computer chips, each circular and pristine. I didn't know what they were, but she seemed excited for them.

"Let's go," she said.

"That's all you want?"

She nodded. "This is way more than he promised me. And I don't think I could sneak anything else out. It's all too big."

I was about to tell her my solution with the tree, but I opted to remain silent. Time was of the essence. Carlee tucked the computer chips into the seam of her dress—almost like she had smuggled things in and out of places before—and then tilted her head from side to side.

"What're you going to do?" she asked.

"Vomit."

Carlee frowned.

That had been my plan in the beginning, and it could still work. I grabbed her arm, pointed to the front door, and we headed off. The hair all over my body stood on end, energized by my anxiety. The pressure to make it out of the building narrowed my thoughts into a tunnel until I could think of nothing else.

Once at the front door, Carlee stopped.

I leaned forward, rammed my fingers down my throat, and completed my planned charade. The acidic burn irritated my nose and mouth as I vomited. There wasn't much in terms of substance, but Carlee grimaced and held her hands over her mouth.

"You thought this through," she muttered.

Before I could give her a proper response, she jumped to the front door and opened it.

Both guards turned around, their rifles up. But then they spotted me and my mess across the carpet.

"What happened?" one barked.

Carlee gently took my arm and helped me forward. "She's sick. I don't think—"

"Get her out of here! There's nothin' the boss hates more than his shit gettin' dirty." One guard yanked me out and half threw me toward the elevator. I stumbled and landed on my knees.

"I'll take her down," Carlee said. She walked out and helped me to my feet.

"The boss isn't gonna like it if you aren't here."

"I'll be back," she said a little too quickly.

"You won't get paid if you disappear."

"I understand."

One of the guards walked with us to the elevator, got inside, and then slid his keycard. He turned to Carlee and shook his head. "You take her to the restroom and then come right back to the elevator, got it?"

Carlee forced a smile.

I hung on to her arm, swaying on my feet to appear buzzed, and I kept my gaze down. Either to be kind, or because she wanted to help me with my act, Carlee ran a hand up and down my back. Her tender touch probably would've helped me if I were actually intoxicated. I almost wanted to thank her.

Once at the bottom, Carlee and I exited the elevator. She headed for the front door, no doubt eager to flee, but I motioned to the restroom.

"You really want to go there?" she asked. "We need to leave as quickly as possible."

"My friend is meeting me there. You can go, though."

She helped me the short distance across the main gambling room and then gave me a curt wave. "Thank you." She dashed away, heading for the front door without glancing back.

I entered the restroom and went for the back stall. A pungent odor of urine, seemingly caked into the floor, hung thick enough I had to gag, but I pushed past it to make my rendezvous. Although the stall was small, and the floor wet, I slid inside to find Dallas waiting for me.

He handed over my duster and wig, effectively transforming me into a new person. He had his mask off, and his gaze ran over me with a hint of concern.

"Are you okay?" he whispered.

"Yeah," I said. "I'm good."

Dallas kept a hand on my shoulder while I zipped up the floor-length jacket, as though to make sure I knew he was here to steady me.

I patted his wrist, grateful for his presence.

The scar on his face—the brand, really—no doubt would've attracted attention, so he kept it covered with a few strips of adhesive bandages. Edges of the white brand poked out, but it was nothing discernible.

I cracked half a smile. "You're a brave man to put up with this meetup location."

"Whatever it takes to see Chelsy again."

His conviction inspired me. I responded with a nod, dedicated to seeing Chelsy returned to our care.

He exited the stall. I waited a few moments, listening to the drunken people of the Desert Diamond go through their washing motions, before I headed out as well. I met Dallas again outside, and we went straight toward the front door. Along the way, however, my attention fell to the room Theon had taken me when he cornered me for our talk.

"Did you ever see Theon enter the Desert Diamond?" I whispered.

Dallas shook his head. "He's definitely not in the building."

Everyone would know. He couldn't sneak around with his drone guards, and everyone acted differently in his presence.

I pulled on Dallas's arm and got him to stop.

Although I hadn't told Bishop or Dallas my decision in regard to the power cells, I already knew what I wanted to do.

I wanted to return them to Judge Gascoigne.

Not because she was virtuous and Theon wasn't, but because if I gave her the power cells, her actions from then on out wouldn't be on my conscience. If I gave her cells to anyone else, and they did force her to do their bidding, I knew I would also carry some sort of guilt for the action.

That didn't mean I wanted to leave without Theon's information, however. It was for the good of humanity that I figure out where a Meteorological

Plexus was, so I grabbed Dallas's arm and motioned him toward Theon's door.

"We need to get in there."

Dallas walked me over. When I grabbed the handle, I realized it was locked. With my tools, I gained entry within a matter of seconds. Dallas kept himself between me and the patrons of the gambling hall, but once I had the door open, we both stepped inside.

The quiet study looked exactly as I remembered it from a few hours earlier. I urged Dallas to hurry over to the computer. He motioned as if to pick me up, and I nodded. He carried me over to the desk and muttered an apology.

"You can read, right?" I asked.

"Yes."

"Check the books on the bookshelves. Anything about maps, or weather, or advanced A-tech engineering. I need the location of a Meteorological Plexus."

Dallas ran to the first set of books and read the spines.

While he checked the physical records, I typed away at the computer. It wasn't password protected or even locked, much to my surprise. Then again, it seemed as though the computer wasn't attached to anything crucial. It had information—lots of records from the old Nevada University—but nothing about the Desert Diamond or current order for Boulder City.

Didn't matter. I needed old information anyway.

I caught my breath the moment I found a file regarding the plexuses.

Then my heart dropped into my stomach, my body reacting to the news faster than my brain could properly process it all.

METEOROLOGICAL PLEXUS #08 – Chanute Space Force Base Champaign County, Illinois

I didn't even need to read anything else about the place.

It was located in Ex Cathedra.

Well, north of Ex Cathedra, not yet incorporated into the expanding nation, but still far from my current location. My hands shook as I processed the information.

Would I go back to get to the plexus? Yes. Of course. Would it kill me to cross the lawless lands, the mountains, and the war-torn fields of Ex

Cathedra? Without a doubt. I had struggled so long to escape. My sanity would take the biggest toll.

But a glimmer of hope stopped my dread fast in its tracks.

There were other plexuses listed. Theon really had gathered everything he said he would.

Were there any closer? I immediately homed in on the location listings. Anything with the "Nevada" tag would do, or anything closer to my location than Ex Cathedra, really. Would there be one? I hoped beyond reason.

Then my prayers were answered. I practically giggled aloud with joy.

METEOROLOGICAL PLEXUS #05 – Thompson Space Force Base
Mohave County, Arizona

"Are you okay?" Dallas whispered.

I nodded. "Y-Yeah. Of course."

"You made a weird sound."

"That's just the half gasp I make when I've discovered information I've been pining over for the last few months."

He let out a single laugh. "You do that so often you recognize the sound, huh?"

"I'm a little weird like that." I couldn't hold back the chuckles at that point. My happiness over the information, coupled with Dallas's quip, made the tense situation melt away, leaving me aglow in hope and optimism.

The Thompson Space Force Base wasn't far. It was on the other side of the river from Boulder City and within easy travel range if we had a vehicle. Soon I wouldn't have to worry. I'd be there, examining the controls and figuring out a way to stop it all.

I was so close!

Part of me wanted to keep laughing, actually. I was way closer than I thought thirty minutes ago.

Dallas walked around behind me and watched as I continued to investigate. Had Theon procured maps of the space force base? To my disappointment, I found none, but I did find something a bit more interesting. The space force base had several underground entrances, all of which led off the hyperloop located underneath the facility.

The hyperloop transportation system was a high-tech subway, basically. A sealed tube with a pod that ran underground, free of air resistance or friction, allowing for ridiculous speeds. My grandfather had said they ran throughout the continent, allowing people to easily get from one coast to the other.

Ex Cathedra had plans to restart the hyperloop tunnels in the areas they had conquered, but the maintenance of the tubes and pods were beyond anything they were capable of. It was another reason they stressed conquest—to have the resources necessary to reestablish old-world wonders.

A hyperloop tunnel existed under Boulder City and led straight to the space force base. But without a running pod, it would likely be far slower than driving across land and over the dam.

Still, the information fascinated me. If we struggled to find an entrance above ground, it was good to know we would have a second chance underground.

Oh, shit.

I hadn't noticed due to my excitement, but the computer flashed in the corner portion of the screen, indicating remote access.

Someone was watching the computer the entire time I had been on it.

Actively watching.

The knowledge got me pensive. If Theon were monitoring the computer, he would know I broke in to steal the information he promised me, which would tip him off to the fact I wasn't planning on giving him the power cells.

I backed away from the desk. "We need to leave."

Dallas picked me up and headed for the door.

"Someone knows we're here," I said. "We have to get to Chelsy as soon as possible."

"You don't have to tell me twice."

We exited into the smoke-filled gambling room. My attention snapped to the front door, and my chest tightened. A dozen masked guards stood around the entrance, Carlee among them. She shook her head and pointed, her panic apparent even if I couldn't hear her words. She seemed to be explaining something, and I knew it couldn't be good for me.

Fuck. She must have gotten caught somehow.

I should've learned my lesson in the silver mine! I couldn't allow people to run off who knew what I was doing. All Carlee would have to tell them was that I had a limp and no disguise would hide me from their investigation.

"We need a different exit," I whispered.

"There are a few entrances for guards only," Dallas said. "But it'll be suspicious if I'm by myself."

Without Bishop, it would be a risk.

The guards at the front door spread out and questioned the gambling patrons.

"Let's go," I said.

Dallas turned around and headed for the back. He allowed me to get to my feet, but basically carried me by the upper arm the entire time, helping me not visibly limp as we went. When he had his back turned to the crowds, he pulled his mask out of his jacket and yanked it over his head. Then he continued to the back hallway.

"Where's your rifle?" I asked.

"I left it. Citizens can't have guns inside the Desert Diamond. That's how I entered when I came to get you."

Dammit. Without weapons, our escape seemed even farther away.

We passed several rooms, most of which were marked Desert Diamond personnel, but they were either unguarded or had off-duty men milling about in front of them with hane between their lips. An exit sat at the end of the hallway, beckoning us like a siren. Two guards stood on either side, both obviously on duty. We hustled to them, and I held my breath, unsure of what Dallas had planned.

One guard held up a hand. "Hold it. No one's supposed to leave."

"Why not?" Dallas asked. "This one got rowdy and drunk. I'm kicking her out."

"Look, we got orders to keep people inside."

"Well, what do you want me to do with her?"

The guard snorted and shrugged. "Lock her to one of the heavy desks in a back room. I don't give a shit."

Dallas let out a long sigh. The guards both took a step back and shook their heads, like they wanted to help, but couldn't. When Dallas set me down, I didn't know what he wanted, so I awkwardly leaned back into the wall.

"What're you doing?" one guard asked.

Dallas grabbed the man's knife from his hip and then stabbed upward in one powerful motion, lodging the blade straight through the chin and into the head. The second guard slung his rifle off his shoulder. Dallas grabbed his hand and the barrel of the gun, preventing any fire, but it didn't stop the man from yelling.

"We have a situation! Shoot this guy!"

The Boulder City guards weren't as trained as Ex Cathedra soldiers, that much became evident.

Dallas used the same trick he did on the first guy—pulling the knife and stabbing into a vulnerable area under the chin, a place the mask didn't seem to protect. The gush of blood coated the hallway floor, but I remained still. A flurry of movement happened a few dozen feet from me as off-duty guards scrambled back into rooms in order to grab their equipment.

Dallas slammed open the exit and yanked me outside in his mad dash to flee the building.

I hadn't taken a breath. I couldn't, not with my constricted throat.

Running at full tilt, and with me in his arms, Dallas made it across the street. He turned down the first narrow alleyway and kept his pace. Before we disappeared from view, I caught a glimpse of the Desert Diamond. City guards rushed around, gathering in teams, yelling orders like an agitated nest of wasps ready to focus their aggression.

I gritted my teeth. "We have to get to the judge before they realize what I've taken. Or else Chelsy—"

"I'm aware," Dallas growled.

CHAPTER THIRTY

Dallas ripped off his mask and took in deep breaths as he ran.

"Go on without me," I said.

It didn't make sense to carry me. I slowed him down. He could run twice as fast if he didn't have my extra weight. Would Gascoigne care if someone else delivered the power cells? I didn't know, but at this point, it was worth the risk.

But Dallas didn't stop. He continued running, even after we exited the alleyway and made it back to the street. Passersby ducked away, and some even yelled curses, but no one tried to stop us. I struggled a bit, trying to force Dallas to give in and set me down. He shot me a glare and tightened his grip, never slowing.

"Think about Chelsy," I said.

He hesitated for a single stride, his focus wavering. "We're almost there," he said. Then he continued, taking in ragged breaths through his teeth.

We weren't anywhere close to Gascoigne, but I did recognize the street we turned onto. And Queen's Pawn stood out like a beacon. If Bishop had procured a vehicle, it would drastically reduce the time to our destination.

Dallas made it to the front door before he set me down. Sweat soaked his shirt and jacket. Before he could go inside, Bishop stepped out, my makeshift sacks of stolen goods slung over his shoulder. He must've stayed with Dallas until they had it, which meant he hadn't been in the pawn shop long.

Bishop tensed at the sight of us, his gaze darting back and forth.

"Done?" he asked. "Damn."

"You got us something?" Dallas asked between heavy pants.

Bishop shook his head. "No. Pawn doesn't have anything."

"What?"

"He does a lot of trading. We'll have to—"

Dallas grabbed him by the jacket and shook. "You didn't get us a vehicle?"

"Watch your tone, asshole."

"You had one fucking job!" Dallas didn't let go. If anything, he tightened his grip and shook harder. "We don't have time for your incompetence."

With one powerful shove, Bishop broke Dallas's hold. Then he stepped up to the other man, quiet and cold, like the encounter would devolve into an honest-to-god brawl in the middle of the street.

Dallas grabbed the sacks off Bishop's shoulder and then dashed around him. Bishop tried to snatch them back, but Dallas leaned away and ran down the street, weaving between the denizens of Boulder City with little trouble.

"He's askin' for a beatin'," Bishop said.

I shook my head. "Stop. We need a vehicle right now. I don't care if we have to steal one."

"What's goin' on? Were you caught?"

I nodded.

"Fuck," Bishop drawled. Then he ran a hand through his hair and cursed another string of profanities. "You could've told me when you rolled up."

"Bishop, we don't have time for this. A vehicle. Where can we get one?"

"I wasn't lyin'. Pawn doesn't have anything he's willing to trade."

I hobbled around him and slammed through the door of the pawn shop. With a single-minded intensity, I made my way to the bars and leaned heavily against them, barely aware of Bishop entering and following me over.

"Pawn," I said. Then I shook my head. "Sorry. I mean *Egan*."

He glanced up from his work at the desk, an eyebrow lifted. "Humph. What's your problem?"

"Do you have a personal vehicle? Something you use for yourself?"

"I already told Bishop I don't got nothin' for you. And I'm definitely not trading my personal transport."

"That's fine," I said, squeezing the bars. "Please just give us a ride. That's all we need."

"A ride?"

"We'll pay."

Bishop pulled me away from the bars and cocked half a smile. "Calm down. You're actin' hysterical."

"It's to save the little girl I had with me," I continued, ignoring Bishop. "My little girl."

Egan didn't know the difference. And maybe it would strike a chord. I didn't care. Whatever it took. The mounting pressure to see Chelsy safe and sound stirred all the terrible memories of my dying sister. I couldn't fail Chelsy. I couldn't.

Egan stood.

He rubbed at the thick stubble on his face while he made his way over to the wall and grabbed a large metal key ring. "All right. I'll drive you. But only because you remembered my name."

"Thank you," I said.

"It's around back. I'll take it to the front. Wait on the curb."

With his heavy step and peg leg, I heard him the entire way to the back door. When he finally got outside, I turned to Bishop. He stared down at me, a neutral expression, and narrowed his eyes.

"Dallas ran off with the goods."

"We'll take the most direct route and pick him up," I said. "Come on. Let's go."

He scooped me up, and we exited the pawn shop. The chaos from the Desert Diamond must've spread because those on the streets no longer ambled or engaged in quiet conversation. Many were in groups, whispering to each other and pointing to the main road. There was no doubt in my mind the city guard would be spreading the word in the hopes of catching me.

I'd taken a lot of stuff. And Sun Luce was one of the individuals in charge of the city. What if he ordered the gates closed? I could see it happening. It would be the first step I took in order to catch a runaway thief.

Damn.

My options narrowed with each passing second.

My mind conjured up terrible scenarios, only making the situation worse. What if Gascoigne refused to give us Chelsy? What would we do then? We couldn't leave. Dallas would never allow that.

A van pulled around the building, pulling me from the quicksand of dread my thoughts had become. Egan stopped in front of us and motioned to the back doors.

It was a storage van with side doors and no windows. Bishop opened it up and set me inside, though there weren't any seats, just empty boxes and ropes. Bishop ran around to the passenger seat and got in. He told Egan the directions and then tapped on the vehicle's dashboard.

"Time isn't our ally," Bishop said.

Egan nodded. "I got ya, but if the guard gets involved, I'm throwin' you out of this vehicle, got it?"

"That's fair."

The van jerked into high gear. I tumbled around the back, but I didn't complain. Instead, I kept tense and ready, like a coiled snake, prepared to leap out and deal with the situation when we arrived at the converted mansion to face Gascoigne.

We jerked to a stop, and I fell against the front seat. The side door opened and Dallas leapt in, sweatier and breathing harder than before. He gave me a quick glance before slamming the door shut.

"Let's go."

Again, the vehicle lurched forward. Dallas caught me mid-fall and maintained a tight grip on my shoulder. He took the moment to steady his breath, but it was obvious he couldn't relax either. While we waited to reach our destination, he unslung the sacks off his shoulder and pushed them toward me.

I withdrew the power cells and nodded.

"I'll go in and give these to her," I said.

"Bishop and I will be guards. I want to be close by, just in case."

"We don't know where Chelsy is. Maybe she's at a different precinct?"

Or maybe Theon had her.

The thought ate at me.

I hadn't considered it until just then. What would I do if that were the case? I hated being at the whim and mercy of other people, especially since everyone had so many goals and agendas that didn't align with mine, but what could I do? I only had a few precious minutes to think of something.

And they disappeared in an instant.

Egan parked his van. "Lots of guards in this area," he murmured.

I found it difficult to breathe.

Dallas grabbed Bishop's shoulder. "Put your damn mask on. We're going inside."

They both donned their gas masks. Egan glanced between them, squinting and sneering at the same time.

"Get out," he snapped. "What did I tell you about trouble? Impersonating one of the—"

Dallas had already thrown open the side door and pulled me out to accompany him. Bishop tapped the dashboard a second time before getting out on his side.

"Thanks, Pawn. Might want to get out of the area, though."

"Goddammit, Bishop."

Bishop laughed and slammed the door. Egan didn't offer any other commentary as Dallas gathered our stolen goods and shut his side of the van. The instant he could, Egan hit the gas and sped away.

Guards really did infest the area, but the more I looked around, the more I realized it appeared as it did the first time I saw Gascoigne. The city guard was just posted to this area, no doubt to protect the mansion property from the filth and crime of the lower end districts of the city. None of the men with rifles seemed to be on an active lookout or stopping individuals from entering or exiting the building.

It was only a matter of time, however.

Bishop and Dallas took me past the electric fence, the steady hum a reminder of the power coursing through it. I didn't know why, but my thoughts jumped from one possible scenario to the next, always thinking up the least favorable conditions. What if we got stuck with our backs to the fence? It would be a terrible way to die.

We entered the building, and the guards within regarded us with quick glances.

"That way," I whispered to Dallas. "That's the room."

They awkwardly brought me along, confused by the interior layout of a fancy mansion turned high-end hotel. When we reached Gascoigne's door, I had to remind myself to take in air.

Bishop opened it up.

Gascoigne waited inside, but my attention snapped to Chelsy.

There she was! Just sitting by the back wall, writing something down in her notebook. She glanced up and her eyes went wide. I wanted to go to her, and I could tell Dallas did, too, but Gascoigne stepped between us, chilling the mood in the room to an icy silence.

"What's this?" Gascoigne finally asked, motioning to me. "I didn't summon her."

"She wanted to see you," Dallas said.

"Is that right? Then leave her. I don't need you two."

A long second went by where Bishop and Dallas didn't move.

I knew what Dallas was thinking. He didn't want to leave without Chelsy. He briefly turned her way, his grip tight on my upper arm. But if he went to her now, Gascoigne would stop him. And she was just unstable enough that risking her anger wasn't worth it.

"I'll handle this," I murmured.

Bishop and Dallas exchanged glances before nodding and backing out the door. Once it snapped shut, I hobbled forward, the power cells in my duster pockets.

"You have them already?" Judge Gascoigne asked. "I'm impressed. I had money on you leaving town to find some substitute somewhere."

I withdrew the power cells and showed them to her. "Here. Like you wanted. Now give me back Chelsy."

"Come here."

The command took me by surprise. What could she possibly want? But I didn't argue. I ambled over, as straight and as tall as I could for someone with a limp, and then I held out one of the cells. Gascoigne knelt down on one knee. The front of her suit unlocked, allowing the whole thing to peel outward, revealing the inner workings. Once free of the restraints, Gascoigne tilted her head from one side to the other.

"You see those slots?" she asked as she pointed to the power cell compartments located in the shoulders of the suit. "Reinsert the cells."

From her angle inside the suit, I saw how she'd have a hard time doing it herself. Drivers typically got out to do their maintenance work on their exoskeletons, but part of me wondered if Gascoigne ever left her suit. Ever. Obviously, she had to at some points—the exoskeletons had some management for bodily functions, but they were temporary at best.

I glanced over at Chelsy.

She caught her breath when our eyes locked. Then she offered me a small smile and showed me a quick drawing of a heart. But she didn't get up, almost as if she were ordered to remain seated or else.

She did seem fine, however. No bruises. No broken bones.

"What're you waiting for?" Gascoigne snapped.

"S-Sorry. One second."

With an unsteady hand, I inserted one of the power cells, taking note that the suit required it to be inserted carefully, most likely to prevent damage. There was already a power cell in—glowing green to indicate its functionality—but the one I inserted did nothing. It remained cold and empty, not helping the suit in the slightest.

I worried Gascoigne would complain or blame me for the problem, but she said nothing.

When I inserted another one, it flashed a few times before maintaining a solid orange color, indicating it was at the halfway mark for power reserves. Were they actually broken? Or had Sun Luce not charged them?

Gascoigne stared at me, almost unblinking, her hard gaze so focused it bordered on psychopathic. I tried to ignore it, but her hazel eyes studied every inch of my face while I lifted the third cell to plug it into place.

"You're rather pretty when you're not covered in blood and under the steel of my boot," she said.

I almost laughed—a dull, ironic laugh, but still. I wasn't sure how to take the odd compliment. "Thank you," I stated.

Chelsy slid to the edge of her seat, inching close. Gascoigne shot her a glare, and Chelsy returned to her original position within half a second.

"You . . . didn't hurt her, did you?" I asked as I placed the fourth cell into its slot.

"No." Gascoigne huffed. "She never did anything that warranted correction."

"Thank you. For not harming her unnecessarily."

"Heh."

With the suit open, and so close to Gascoigne, it was easy to see the old damage on her body. Whatever had happened to her—several years ago, if I had to guess—really did a number. It seemed she had no kidneys. Well, no functioning kidneys. And her lower gut had a few twisted scars I imagined would have shredded her intestines, maybe even more.

The two tubes running from her to the suit had insert slots mounted to her body, like someone had prepared her body ahead of time. Typically the tubes were for emergencies—to keep a driver alive during desperate situations—and the tubes could be inserted directly into the veins; the A-tech would then take over to handle the rest. But the intent wasn't for it to last forever. It was a quick and easy measure meant to treat a driver until they made it to a hospital.

The last four slots for the power cells were on the other side of the suit. I stepped to the other side, and Gascoigne glowered.

"That worried?" she asked. "You haven't stopped shaking since you got here."

I fitted in the fifth power cell. "You've almost killed me on several occasions. I don't think this is an irrational reaction to your company."

Gascoigne forced a single laugh. "You shouldn't have been following me, then."

"I never followed you."

"Don't give me that. What're you trying to steal this time?"

"Nothing. I want to get out of the city as soon as possible."

"Heh." She turned to Chelsy and whistled. "Kid. Get me some water and bread."

Chelsy jumped from her seat and fetched a glass and plate from the far table. When she got close, she smiled up at me. I continued inserting the power cells, but returned the gesture as best I could.

Gascoigne had an unsettling mien. She ate her bread like she was punishing it for disappointing her, and she continued to stare at me with the same intensity as before.

A knock on the door startled me.

Gascoigne barely reacted, however. She handed Chelsy back the plate and glass and then let out a long exhale before shouting, "What?"

One of the city guards walked in. For the brief moment the door was open, I spotted Bishop and Dallas right outside, like they were assigned to watch Gascoigne's quarters.

The guard held a radio transceiver in his hand. "Judge Gascoigne, Sun Luce wishes to speak with you."

The news stilled my trembling and my heart. I already knew what he was going to say. My mouth went dry as I inserted the sixth cell. Three more and I could leave.

"Tell him I'm busy," Gascoigne said.

"Now is not the time for difficulty, Judge," the radio crackled. Sun Luce had a sophistication and education to his voice unlike most I had heard in the area.

"What do you want, then?" she asked.

"I have been given some disturbing news, and I need to check in with you. Perhaps you could meet me for a talk? If you would kindly exit your suit, I will meet you outside."

Gascoigne rotated her shoulders and tensed her muscles. "I'm not getting out of my suit. How many fucking times do I have to tell you?"

The guard holding the transceiver just stood in the middle of the room, the device held up, no doubt an awkward expression under his mask. Still, it didn't stop the conversation.

"Those suits were not designed to be lived in," Sun Luce said. "You are doing damage to your brain by keeping those helmet connectors in place. Alternate solutions can be arranged."

"I can handle it. I'm not getting out of the suit."

"Very well. I will have to trust Theon's assessment when he says you are unstable then."

"Why would Theon ever say that?" Gascoigne growled. She gripped the edge of the exoskeleton, her jaw clenched. "He wouldn't—"

"He claims you sent a thief into my quarters. And he has proof. So either you come outside, without your suit, and we can discuss this, or I will be forced to take your actions as an act of violence against the city."

I finished the seventh power cell and froze. Gascoigne returned her gaze to mine.

"So you were caught."

CHAPTER THIRTY-ONE

Theon turned me in to Sun Luce? Why? What if I revealed to Sun Luce Theon's treachery? Or was this Theon's way of preemptively covering his own tracks? If I exposed Theon's plans now, it would look more like a lie to save myself from punishment. And if Theon got us killed, we wouldn't be able to provide any evidence or details.

Judge Gascoigne's suit flared to life. I staggered back as the front of it laced together and sealed, returning it to its mobile state.

"They're *my* power cells," Gascoigne said as she stood. "I'm not going to apologize for taking them back. And it's a complete exaggeration to call it violence against the city."

The guard took a step back, but kept the transceiver up.

Sun Luce said, "Your thief took a lot more than the power cells."

I caught my breath, ready for Gascoigne's outrage. Instead, she laughed— genuinely—and said, "Serves you right. I should've told her to light your whole damn place on fire."

Her statements weren't helping to prove the "unstable" claim false.

"Theon told me all about your private conversations," Sun Luce continued. "Did you think you could get away with attacking members of this city?"

"You believe everything that bastard says?"

"I believe the recordings he has supplied me."

Gascoigne's long bout of silence almost made me laugh.

Theon sold her out, too. He acted as her confidant and the moment he needed to throw her out as cover, he did. I could imagine him talking to

Gascoigne about attacking Sun Luce, only to supply half the conversation later to make it look like she was a power-hungry lunatic. Theon was prepared to use her either way—either as an agent of murder or a meatshield for his own activities.

Maybe I should've just given him the power cells and allowed the city to die from its own gangrenous authority. It would've been easier for me.

Dammit.

"So what're you trying to say?" Gascoigne asked with a chuckle. "You going to come in and force me out of my suit?"

"If that is what it comes down to."

With the conversation obviously over, the guard with the transceiver took a step backward. Gascoigne backhanded him. He flew a few feet and hit the edge of the room, where the floor met the wall, and then crumpled into a limp pile, his leg twitching. I wondered if he would live through the simple attack, but before I could do anything else, Gascoigne rounded on me and Chelsy.

"You've made this difficult," she said.

I pushed Chelsy behind me and pressed us both up against the wall. "If you were planning on attacking Sun Luce, it was only a matter of time before this happened."

"Heh. Enough excuses. I'll take care of you two, and then I'll take care of the guards on my way out of town."

Lights shone from underneath the heavy curtains over the windows. Gascoigne turned her attention to the commotion. She walked over and glanced out. I took the moment to look as well, peeking out into the artificial daylight of the neon city.

I didn't know Theon or Sun Luce or any of the players in Boulder City, but it was becoming apparent they weren't individuals to mess with.

A couple dozen of the city guard waited outside, some inside the electric fence, some outside. But that wasn't what I focused on. I spotted several throwing down tesla mines—shock weaponry used to kill infantry with powerful bursts of electricity. Unlike explosives, the tesla mines could be activated multiple times before they were spent. Dying of cardiac arrest wasn't high on my list of ways to go, however.

The city guards also drove a truck to the front gate. Mounted on the back, with a man swiveling the barrel, was a tank-buster gun. The armor-piercing rounds, .57 caliber, could blow a hole clean through a Mark III JUDGE-X0 suit.

"Oh, they want a fight," Judge Gascoigne said. "They'll regret ever crossing my path."

"They're going to kill you," I said, my heart beating hard against my chest with every word I hastily spoke. "They have tesla mines and—"

"I learned my lesson," Gascoigne snapped. "This suit isn't like the last. I won't be immobilized by EMPs or shocks or anything else. Those gun bunnies outside are filled with a sense of false confidence. Easy targets."

"The mines they have will slow you down. And then they'll shoot you with the tank-buster when you can't evade. That's all it'll take. Look outside again. You'll see. They have a plan."

Gascoigne hesitated for a moment. "A plan? Of course he has a plan. That asshole has always wanted my suit. Since the moment I walked into town."

"If you're not careful, he'll get it."

She became silent.

Was I convincing her? I could only hope. Not because Gascoigne and I were best-friends-forever, but because she was one of the few people who stood a decent chance of getting out of the city, even in this terrible predicament.

A predicament *she caused*, but still. Now that I was part of it, I had to somehow weasel my way out and get across the river.

Maybe Gascoigne could help me.

Or, better yet, we could help each other.

"They're going to try and taunt you outside," I said.

"Taunt me?"

"Yes. Sun Luce might be right when he said you're not thinking properly. The connectors in your suit's helmet use overriding electric signals to stimulate certain parts of the brain. Since you've been in your suit so long, it may be messing with your ability to reason. He's going to try to exploit it."

The voice of a man over a loudspeaker cut through the walls, interrupting our conversation with shrill words. "Judge Gascoigne, you're under arrest. Exit your exoskeleton or we'll be forced to take you down by any means necessary." He ended his declaration with a slight chuckle.

There it was. Their taunt. Daring her to come outside or else they would deal with her.

Gascoigne must have realized it. She went still and didn't say anything.

"Don't you want to get out of the city alive?" I asked.

Gascoigne huffed. "I want Sun Luce to suffer."

"Even if that's your goal, he's not outside. You should think of another way to get to him."

"What makes you think he won't be outside?"

"Just think about it," I said. "He won't fight you. Not when you're in an exoskeleton. He's sent some expendable guards to handle you while he sits back in safety. He's wearing you down."

Gascoigne didn't respond. She waited, unmoving, while she mulled over my comments.

In the moment of quiet, Chelsy pointed at the door. I placed a hand on her head. My breath came out in short bursts. I didn't want to endanger her. The guards were after me and Gascoigne—no one else. And Bishop and Dallas were right outside. But how to get her out without angering the judge?

When I glanced back at Gascoigne, her hand was up and grazing the chest of her exoskeleton. The glowing lights—the indicators of her power cells—had changed from green to orange.

All her power cells were low. Either that or the broken ones were messing with the suit's functionality. Both were real possibilities, but it meant Gascoigne wouldn't be functioning for much longer.

"Gascoigne," I said.

She turned to me but said nothing.

"You need to recharge the cells."

"I came to Boulder City to do just that," she said. "And look what it's gotten me."

I held my breath. Boulder City had an abundance of power—there had to be *someplace* within the city to recharge them—but I didn't know where. "The dam," I said. "It's the source of power for all of Boulder City. I'm sure there's something there, or nearby, that could help you."

"The dam, huh? I wouldn't know the first thing about finding access to power for the cells. I always had someone else do the maintenance of my suit, and I thought I could get that here, but . . ."

"I know a great deal about the JUDGE-X0 suits," I said as I pushed away from the wall. "I'll help you recharge the power cells if you let Chelsy go. Please. She isn't involved in this."

The lights shone through slivers in the curtains a second time, heightening the tension.

Gascoigne chortled. "Fine. You come with me. The girl can go."

She walked over and grabbed my forearm with enough force that I swore she cut off circulation to my hand in an instant. I bit back my shout and gritted my teeth.

"We'll have a fun run to the wall, but I can't guarantee you'll make it in one piece," Gascoigne said, a smile on her voice. "What's the fastest way out of town?"

I didn't know. I barely knew Boulder City. But I did know going anywhere on the streets would result in facing the tank-buster gun. It was mounted to a truck, after all. Highly mobile. It would follow us with ease, and as long as they had the ammunition, they would eventually get Gascoigne. Or me.

But a solution struck me.

One I should've mentioned to begin with.

"There's a subway system," I said through clenched teeth. "And a hyper-loop. Underground. We should go there."

"The subway?" Gascoigne repeated, her voice distant.

Gascoigne turned, her grip still tight on my arm, and walked toward the door. Chelsy tried to pull me back, but it was a naïve effort that only resulted in her stumbling after me.

"It's okay," I said to her. "Just tell your father where we're heading."

The mere mention of her father got Chelsy's eyes wide.

Gascoigne opened the door.

Bishop and Dallas both turned to face us, their gas masks still on.

I waved them away before Gascoigne got close. "Get back!"

They leapt out of Gascoigne's path, and she ignored them as she made her way to the open front room.

Dallas immediately grabbed Chelsy and pulled her into his arms. She fought against him until he removed his mask. Then she caught her breath and wrapped her arms tight around his neck, her expression something I had never seen from her before. She cried onto his shoulder.

The servants and other residents of the mansion cleared out of our way, some locking themselves in rooms, even though that was futile. A JUDGE-X0 exoskeleton could smash into any room here so long as it wasn't reinforced with steel bars.

"This'll be a rough ride," Gascoigne said. "For you." She laughed at her comment as she turned toward the back door—away from the trap waiting for her outside.

Then she slammed open the door, crouched low to avoid some of the ceilings, and continued down the hallway to the back. She dragged me the entire way, my arm hurting as much as my damaged hip, and it took all my willpower to prevent myself from crying out.

Gascoigne exited the building into the back and headed straight for the fence. There weren't many guards around the back side—probably because they banked on Gascoigne charging out the front—but a few did open fire.

I threw my other arm over my face, unable to look. I would get shot for sure. It was just a matter of one poorly aimed bullet.

I didn't know if it was to protect me, or if it was because I was nothing but a burden, but Gascoigne threw me down and rushed the first man in her way. I hit the ground and remained down, praying no one turned their attention to me.

The bullets did nothing to Gascoigne, ricocheting off her impressive armor. And when she made it to the man, she extended the blade on her suit and stabbed it through his chest in one powerful thrust, practically punching a hole through his body, not just slicing one.

The shock and awe of the brutal attack shook the other guards.

The two remaining actually stopped attacking and took off around the side of the building. Once they made it to the front, they would undoubtedly inform the rest of the force of Gascoigne's uncharacteristic retreat.

Gascoigne didn't stop with the guard.

She continued to the electric fence and kicked down a portion, the smash ringing out all around us. The electricity wouldn't affect her suit, and crushing the fence created a path off the property. Then she returned to me.

My arm was bruised from her earlier aggression, and I hid away from her grasp. Gascoigne growled as she grabbed the back of my duster and hauled me all the way to the edge of the property.

"Please," I said. "You'll kill me faster than the bullets. Be gentle."

She slowed for a moment and then picked me up. Unlike Bishop and Dallas, who were both careful—both warm and protective—Gascoigne's cold steel-alloy exoskeleton power suit didn't make for a comfortable ride. And she trapped me against the frame, her arm half crushing the air out of my lungs.

Where were Dallas and Bishop?

I stared at the mansion, hoping one of them would emerge, but neither did. They should've been right on our tail. Would Dallas leave now that he had Chelsy? He might. He'd made it clear from the beginning she was all that mattered to him.

And Bishop . . .

He tended not to get too attached to anything. Perhaps he figured chasing me was too much of a hassle. Or perhaps our slight argument bothered him more than he let on.

Would they both really leave me?

Gascoigne took off running down the street, passing trucks, citizens, and street after street in her haste.

Twice I heard the sound of gunfire over the stomp of Gascoigne's suit, but I didn't catch where it came from. Everyone turned to us as we passed, some pointing, others shouting.

We'd be followed, and once underground, there wouldn't be anywhere to hide. And it would be a straight line right to us.

Perhaps it wasn't such a good idea.

"Gascoigne," I said, breathless. "Wait. I changed my mind. We shouldn't go to the subway. We should get a van, something with a cover to hide you and—"

"No," she said, cutting me off. "You're right. The subway is the quickest route. We'll head directly to the dam. Nothing in between."

She slowed near a subway entrance and jumped over the railing, straight to the stairs that led underground.

People flew out of her way, some screaming and others calling for the guards. Gascoigne pushed anyone in her way aside, including a few punks that pulled handguns. With little regard for anything, she stomped down into the musty subway station, the stench of human waste practically built into the bricks of the walls and embedded in the supportive pillars.

People lived in the old subway. No trains ran, and no pods were inside the hyperloop, not since the bombs hit. The place had all the warmth and happiness of an open coffin, and the people living in the semi-darkness were basically corpses. Their thin frames and sickly complexions spoke volumes. Twice I nearly gagged as Gascoigne continued deeper into the black hole that was the train tunnel.

Shouting from the city guard echoed all around us. They were coming down, and soon the place would be swarming with them. What if they swept the place with a blanket of bullets? Or threw a myriad of explosives into the tunnel?

A tremor shook the area. Dirt and broken cement rained down from the ceiling and a rush of wind whipped past us. An explosion. No doubt in my mind. Were they planning on burying us? The thought plunged my mind to a dark place.

Crushed to death. Not the best way to go.

Gascoigne stopped walking and turned. Then she put me down and rotated her shoulders. A wave of debris and trash rushed by us, carried by the aftershock of the underground explosion. I shielded my eyes and leaned against the wall of the subway, shivering until the wind ended. Only then did I cough and attempt to get a good look at who was heading our way.

"Dammit!" someone shouted, their voice ringing all around us.

The yell stilled my breathing.

"The subway doesn't go anywhere!" they continued. "It's a dead end! You've trapped us here with that stunt. Why didn't you listen?"

A dead end? I hadn't even considered a problem with the tunnels themselves. Was every tunnel blocked off? Or just the ones in the city? I didn't know.

But who was coming for us now? I couldn't make out the voices due to the echo and the slight rumbling that persisted after the explosion.

After a few moments, however, silence came over the area. The subway settled, the dirt wafted to the ground, and all that was left was the distant murmuring of the subway people and the flicker of the occasional dim lightbulb from the ceiling of the tunnel.

Gascoigne turned back to me. "We should be on our way. Those peons aren't going to rush in after me, not unless they have a death wish."

"Didn't you hear? There's a dead end."

"I'll get through it."

She walked over to me, picked me back up, and continued on as if nothing had changed.

"What if they use more explosives?" I asked. "We could be buried here."

"If they want even a part of my suit, they're not going to wreck the tunnels. I'm more worried about them cutting us off."

Damn.

Where were Dallas and Bishop when I needed them? They were all I could think about. Well, that and Chelsy's safety. Even if they left me, I wanted to know they were all safe. It would give my troubled mind at least one piece of solace.

CHAPTER THIRTY-TWO

A fork in the subway tunnel led to another station in Boulder City and a route straight to the dam. Before Judge Gascoigne turned toward the dam, I spotted the Boulder City reinforcements preparing down the tracks. Their flashlights danced in the tunnel, betraying their haste to set everything up.

They couldn't bring the tank-buster down into the subway, so what were they hoping to do? Perhaps they had something else. Gascoigne's lack of consideration for her safety would make the encounter a clusterfuck.

"What're you going to do?" I asked when she came to a stop at the crossroad.

"Not sure yet. But you're going to wait here."

She set me down and pushed me toward the route to the dam. I hit the ground on my forearms, the dirt and filth of the neglected subway caked onto every surface, even the rails. I brushed myself off as I got up onto my good foot.

Gascoigne didn't wait around. She headed straight for the Boulder City guards, despite her low power cells and damaged suit. What was she hoping to do? Stall them? Or perhaps this was a form of intimidation. They would be less likely to charge after us if she left a graveyard's worth of corpses in her wake.

"They'll have a weapon," I shouted to her as she left. "Watch out for something that'll pierce armor."

Gunshots echoed down the tunnel. I covered my ears, the sounds building and building, as if trapped underground with nowhere to go but my eardrums. I gritted my teeth and wondered how long the encounter could last.

To my dismay, lights shone down the subway—from the direction Gascoigne and I had come—stilling my breathing. People followed us? We would be flanked and caught within a pincer attack. No way Gascoigne would win then, so long as they had even one way to break her suit. But I didn't have a weapon, or a way to warn her.

And what if they attacked me?

I turned and hobbled down the subway toward the dam. Were there places to hide? No. Not really. There were small ledges for maintenance work, and the occasional electrical box, but there wasn't much in the way of places to hide out.

The gunshots didn't cease.

I continued toward the dam regardless of my doubts. The lights in the tunnel were hit or miss. Some shone bright—like spotlights—while others were out, creating a long stretch of black between visible portions of the subway. Fortunately, the ground was flat and easy to travel over, even with a bad leg.

Another tremor.

I kept one hand on the wall at all times.

Thankfully, I made it far from the fighting without falling. Hope welled in my thoughts, resulting in a smile. Maybe I would get away. But could I make it to the plexus on my own? No supplies? No weapons? I would try, dammit. That's all I could do.

My gaze landed on graffiti tattooed to the wall.

DEAD END

I continued to shuffle past it, my dread returning in full force. Was the path to the dam blocked off? Of course. That was what those people were screaming about. A dead end. But I had to check. I had to see.

The fighting drifted away in the distance. Either I was too far away or it had finally ended; I didn't know which. And then, sure enough, the last light in the tunnel revealed a makeshift wall made out of sheet metal and debris. It, too, had graffiti.

DRONES AHEAD

TURN BACK

My scattered thoughts came together like a jigsaw puzzle.

Egan had told me about Iron-Blooded in the area. He had said they were across the river. Lots of them. That was where the plexus was. Across the river. And the dam was between me and the plexus, apparently blocked off from the city because of an infestation of alien drones.

I exhaled.

I couldn't take the subway or hyperloop tunnels to my destination.

And I couldn't turn around because of the fighting.

"What am I going to do?" I muttered.

I slid down the subway wall until I landed in a sitting position. My destination felt so close, yet every obstacle threatened to break me. Why? Why was my determination being tested? How much more did I need to go through before I reached the plexus?

Lights flashed in the tunnel behind me. I glanced over my shoulder, certain it wasn't Gascoigne.

"Kita? Kita! Are you here?"

I caught my breath, my heart beating fast.

"Dallas?" I asked.

The heavy stomp of boots on cement rang out as Dallas ran to me. I smiled when he approached and wrapped my arms around him when he stooped down to grab me. His warm touch dispelled the doubt I had moments earlier.

"Are you okay?" he asked between pants. When he tried to lift me, he half stumbled forward, his balance off and his breathing deep.

"I'm fine. Are *you* okay?"

"Yes. Yes . . . I just need . . . a moment to rest."

More footsteps traveled down the subway tunnel. Bishop and Chelsy appeared under the lights, their attention on something behind them.

"What're you all doing here?" I asked.

Dallas shook his head. "We came for you. C'mon. We need to go."

"All of you? But it's dangerous here. Chelsy shouldn't—"

"I'm not letting her out of my sight again. The guards are busy with the judge. Now is the time for us to go."

Bishop stopped and hefted his sniper rifle. He switched the scope on and aimed while standing.

Dallas stood and kept his gun up, but his breathing remained labored. While they prepared for whoever was coming, Chelsy ran to me, beaming. I pulled her close and murmured my thanks to good luck she was safe.

Bishop fired three times, the powerful shots reverberating off the walls. The butt of his rifle dug into his shoulder, and he took a step back, cursing under his breath. Dallas joined in on the firefight, but it didn't help my hearing. Even Chelsy held her hands tight over her ears, water welling in the corners of her eyes.

"I'm gonna do it," Bishop yelled.

"No," Dallas snapped. "Think of this place's structural integrity. You could kill us!"

"Those explosives are the only thing that saved us last time. We would've been caught if I hadn't blocked the tunnel. I'm gonna use them."

"You can't."

"I just did."

"Wait," I tried to interject, but it was too late.

A quake rocked the subway tunnel and another blast of dirt, cement dust, and garbage rushed by, collecting at the dead end and wafting toward us again from the backdraft.

I breathed in once and regretted it, my lungs filling with a burning sensation and my eyes clouding from debris. I coughed and wheezed, but I kept Chelsy close, trying to shield her from the smoke.

Damn.

Did Bishop not see the dead end? What was he thinking? Even if he had explosives to blow down the makeshift wall, there were drones on the other side! We couldn't go this way!

For a few short minutes, nothing else happened. The dust swirled around us in clouds, but most of it had settled to the ground. Then a few of Boulder City's guards opened fire. Dallas and Bishop slammed their backs to the walls and waited, but I didn't hear any bullets streak past us.

Three of the gas mask guards ran up closer, their rifles up. They weren't pointing them at Dallas or Bishop, however. They were firing backward, into the shadows.

Gascoigne emerged from the darkness, her bloodstained exoskeleton a thing of nightmares. And the dust swirled into the fresh blood, creating a gory mud.

She easily dispatched one of the guards, her blade cutting through the man's torso—through his sternum and lungs—leaving him with a gaping hole.

Bishop and Dallas shot the other two guards before anything else could happen.

Gascoigne stumbled. She got down to one knee, her suit damaged even beyond what it was before. A few of the front metal plates were missing, and her broken helmet now had a wide fissure. Not enough to see inside, but enough to see the vital circuitry.

Dallas and Bishop opened fire, both aiming for the cracked portions of the suit, including her helmet.

She remained down, and sparks flew off her suit where the bullets hit exposed inner workings. The JUDGE-X0 Mark III was built with several redundant systems, so I doubted anything would be taken offline by a single lucky bullet, but perhaps they would get to her flesh underneath.

She was physically broken, after all.

"Wait," I shouted.

They stopped firing.

Gascoigne never moved. She remained kneeling, one hand gripping her knee.

"Is she dead?" Bishop asked.

I shook my head. "No. Her suit would've opened."

"We're just wasting ammo," Dallas muttered. He slung his rifle back over his shoulder. "We need to focus on getting out of here."

"I was helping her," I said. "She wants to recharge the power cells of her suit."

"Why would we help her? I remember working under her at the silver mines. She can be unstable. And now that she's down, I don't think we should go out of our way to pick her back up."

Dallas made a logical point. Why was she kneeling? I suspected she had been hurt internally somehow. Was she bleeding out? Perhaps. Should we care for a semi-enemy when we were so close to our destination?

Bishop lowered his weapon, but he didn't put it away. "What're we supposed to do now?"

"How did you explode the tunnel?" I asked.

Bishop dropped his duffel bag to the ground. When he opened it up, I spotted all the things I stole from Sun Luce, along with the fission bomb and a few extra things, no doubt from Queen's Pawn. Bishop removed some A-tech plastic explosives and flashed me a smile.

"This shit works wonders," he said. "It's moldable. Sticks to anything. Remote detonation with this here trigger. I slapped some of it around the tunnels while we ran by."

The plastic explosives had blasting caps inside, each set off by a remote detonation device, no doubt synced long in advance.

I stared down the subway tunnel. "You two followed me?"

Bishop nodded. "Yeah. The judge was way faster, but it wasn't hard following her wake through town."

Chelsy ran to Dallas. They embraced, and Dallas took a seat on the subway rails, his skin dappled with sweat. Chelsy sat next to him and wrapped her arms around one of his. He offered her a weak smile.

Bishop took a few steps toward the dead end, though he never turned his back to Judge Gascoigne. He took some of the plastic explosives and patted it against one of the sheets of metal in the center of the barricade.

"What're you doing?" I asked.

Dallas snapped his attention to the wall. "What did I tell you? This is a dead end for a reason. There are aliens beyond this point."

"Yeah, but there has to be access to the surface," Bishop said. "We need to get out of this death pit, and we're not going out the way we came. Don't worry. I used a small amount."

"I can't go with you," I said. "Even if the drones don't see you as a threat, they'll home in on me."

"Then we'll shoot them. Or we'll think of something else. But we can't stay here."

"You're reckless," Dallas hissed.

"But I acted, didn't I?" Bishop shrugged. "You're the one who slowed us down when you didn't have any answers. When it's crunch time, I get shit done."

"We should stay here for a bit," I said.

Dallas was obviously on the edge of fatigue, fighting exhaustion with little in the way of aid. He hadn't slept in some time, and after running several blocks through town, fighting dozens of men, and traversing the subway system, I was surprised he hadn't collapsed. Nanites helped with oxygen dispersal throughout the body, sure, but they didn't replace the need to rest.

Bishop motioned to the collapsed part of the subway system. "You don't think they'll find a way through?"

Cracks in the ceiling leaked streams of dusted cement. Dallas had been right. The subways were old. Parts of the tunnels broke to the explosives with ease, and if we continued to set them off, we could kill ourselves. I bet the Boulder City guards knew that, too.

"Listen," I said. "I don't hear them toiling away trying to get in here. They know it's a dead end. There's literally no reason for them to rush when they have us trapped. Or maybe they even think we're already dead. Either way, they can excavate without destroying any more of the city."

Bishop clicked his tongue. "Tsk."

"The plexus can be reached through the hyperloop tunnels," I said.

Both Dallas and Bishop focused their attention on me.

"It's on the other side of the river," I continued. "So I think it's a good idea if we continue this way, even if it wasn't the best choice originally."

"How long will it take to get there by foot?" Dallas asked.

I ran a hand over my sweaty face, clearing away the dust and grime. "If I had to guess . . . fourteen hours."

We hadn't brought much food or water, and there were aliens between us and the destination. But I didn't care. We were so close. Fourteen hours was nothing compared to the distance I had already traveled. All that mattered was getting there in one piece.

Dallas moved over to the wall and rested against it. Chelsy followed him each step, practically tripping over him, until she was situated next to him once again. Dallas held her close and then closed his eyes. It didn't take him long to exhale and relax even in the tense situation we found ourselves.

"What should we do with her?" Bishop asked as he gestured to Judge Gascoigne.

"I told her I would help her with the power cells," I said. "But I never said I would be her doctor and drag her to the dam. If she manages to stand, we should help each other. But if she can't . . ."

"All right. But I'm not gonna sleep if she's still around." Bishop glared at her. "Just in case. She's dangerous."

"Probably a good idea."

We couldn't risk staying too long, but I didn't want to bother Dallas while he rested. Although sleep pulled at my eyelids, promising me relief, I couldn't let go of my thoughts long enough to drift away.

Bishop paced a small portion of the tunnel, restless, though I didn't know why.

Chelsy slept next to her father.

And Gascoigne never moved. It worried me more than anything else. She wasn't dead—her suit would have opened—but she hadn't said anything, either. Was she suffering? Or conserving power? I hadn't really tried to engage her in conversation, either.

But the longer I stared, the more I realized something was wrong. The glowing lights for her power cells were dim and yellow. Why were her cells draining so fast? It didn't make any sense. However, if the old ones were broken, it could be messing with her system.

I shoved my hand into my pocket and withdrew the last two power cells I had yet to insert. With a deep breath, and using the wall, I got up.

Bishop glanced over. I shook my head, confident I could move around. "It'll be okay," I said.

I hobbled closer to Gascoigne to get a better look. Sure enough, her suit was running low on power. Perhaps the damage was causing the system to drain the cells faster than normal. I wasn't sure, but I knew I could probably troubleshoot if Gascoigne weren't in the way.

Bishop walked up behind me and placed a hand on my shoulder. I gripped his fingers and kept him next to me.

He really was a light in the darkness. I felt safer with Bishop around.

"Waiting to kill me?" Gascoigne asked, her cold metallic voice complementing her sardonic tone.

"We don't have to wait," Bishop said, smiling. "You could step out and we could end it all right now."

"How considerate of you."

"We're not going to kill you," I said. "Can you stand?"

She didn't answer me.

Bishop gave me a sidelong glance. "So, do you know how to pilot one of these?"

I shook my head. "No. Well, that's not true. I've seen instructional videos, but that's not the point. The connectors embedded in the skull are required to drive them. I don't have those."

"Damn. I would've loved one."

Bishop walked closer to the exoskeleton power suit—more brazen than I ever would've been—and examined it from multiple angles. "So, you judges trained from birth or something? I heard rumors."

Gascoigne chuckled. "No."

"Do they give many to women? I hadn't heard of a female judge before."

"I'm one of the lucky ones," Gascoigne said, her tone sardonic.

"Your daddy a military general? Is that what happened?"

"My *daddy*"—she drawled the word with a hint of disgust—"was killed by a judge when the Ex Cathedra army came to take our town."

"Yikes," Bishop quipped. "I heard they executed captured men who didn't immediately fall in line. Was he a troublemaker?"

"Bishop," I snapped.

Why would he be so callous? He was talking about her murdered father.

But Gascoigne only chuckled again, like the morbid topic was something normal or casual. Her prolonged time in the suit must have contributed to her desensitization.

"He fought the judge," Gascoigne said, her voice more distant than before. "But he lost. And the judge killed him. Crushed his head underfoot."

"They made you watch?" Bishop asked, both his eyebrows lifted.

"They didn't know I was there." She laughed once. "Then I ran out and fought the judge myself. I got a rock. Hit the bastard a couple times in the leg."

The words of her story struck me with an unexpected intensity. It colored our past encounter with something darker than I ever expected. Gascoigne had once been Chelsy, struggling to fight against forces beyond her might and comprehension.

Bishop shrugged. "I take it you didn't save your father?"

"Of course I didn't, you buffoon," Gascoigne snapped. "*I started this by telling you he died.* No, my attack was futile. I suppose it saved me in the end, however. The soldiers took me back to the capital—they thought I was amusing."

"How old were you?"

"Five."

Bishop got within inches of her, his gaze locked on the reinforced shoulder plating. "Damn. They brainwashed you after that? Fed you propaganda or some bullshit until you became a soldier?"

Gascoigne huffed. "There was no need. I learned my lesson. In life there are two kinds of people: sheep and wolves. Sheep may have it easier finding peace, but wolves never become victims. I *wanted* to become a judge."

Before Bishop could say anything else, Gascoigne stood—faster than I expected, faster than Bishop could properly react.

He lifted his rifle, but Gascoigne grabbed it and rammed it back into his chest. The crunch and half gasp afterward sent goose bumps over my skin. Bishop hit the ground and curled in around himself.

Gascoigne stood, Bishop's rifle still in her hand.

"Wait, there's no need to fight," I said.

She turned to face me.

I held up the two power cells, trying to remain calm and collected. "I think I figured out why your suit is malfunctioning."

"Good," Gascoigne said.

"But you can't hurt them." I motioned to the others. "If you do, you'll never make it out of here. There's no way you have enough power in your busted suit to escape the subway or hyperloop without getting caught, and I won't fix anything if one of them dies."

"Is that right?"

"We already had a deal," I said. "We can still help each other get to the dam. We should cooperate."

And an exoskeleton would deal with our alien problem. It was a win-win so long as she didn't turn on us.

Bishop rolled to his side and coughed up a mouthful of blood.

The groans and hacking woke Dallas and Chelsy. They both jumped to their feet, their eyes wide and locked on Gascoigne.

No one said anything. I held my breath. It wasn't such a bad idea, but it did feel unstable. Something I didn't have control over. But then again, could it last fourteen hours? That was all I needed.

Fourteen hours of cooperation.

CHAPTER THIRTY-THREE

I fidgeted with the last two power cells I never managed to insert. "You should allow me to look at your other power cells."

Gascoigne turned her attention to the writhing Bishop and then to Dallas and Chelsy. Her gaze lingered on them for a moment, obviously ignoring me. "Heh. The Ex Cathedra traitor who attempted to steal from the mines. So you're a band of thieves. I should've known."

"I think some of your power cells may be damaged," I continued, trying to convince her. "If you let me switch a few out, maybe I can keep your suit going a little longer."

Gascoigne dropped the sniper rifle. The clank against the rails echoed throughout the stuffy tunnel. She touched the chest piece of her exoskeleton, her fingers lingering over the lights of the power cell indicators.

"I will continue like this," she said, a hint of finality to her tone.

There wasn't much I could say. If Gascoigne didn't want to let me switch out the cells, it wasn't like I could force her. And eventually the issue would become moot. So I shrugged and took half a step back.

"All right."

Bishop got to his knees. He kept a hand over his chest and shook his head.

"Are you okay?" I asked.

"Yeah," he said, breathless. "Fine." After a few deep inhales he added, with a smile, "I've been through worse." Then he forced himself to stand.

No one spoke after that.

Bishop gathered up his rifle and returned to pacing. Dallas kept Chelsy close, his gaze locked on Judge Gascoigne. The judge didn't move around much. She remained still, her helmet removing all possibility of deciphering her expression. But we couldn't wait. If Dallas was rested, it was time.

"We should blast our way past the wall," I said.

Bishop continued to rub at his chest. "Oh, yeah? Ready?"

"Yes. We need to go."

"Stand back then."

Again, the tunnel went silent. No one said anything as they moved far from the graffiti wall that warned about the drones.

Gascoigne moved only a few feet, no doubt unconcerned with the small blast. Once everyone was away, Bishop used his trigger detonator to set off the plastic explosive. The resulting tremor and blast of debris was much less than the ones previously, but I still had to cover my face to prevent dust and cement from getting into my eyes.

The hole created could accommodate a small child, but not much else.

Gascoigne walked to the wall and grabbed the edge of the opening. She pried the metal sheets aside, exposing junk, cement, and trash. Bishop jogged to her side, set another round of explosives—the same small size as before—and then backed away.

After the second blast, there was enough space for the judge to make it through.

I coughed a few times as Bishop picked me up. I held on to him, surprised he would be the one to carry me.

Bishop seemed so distant lately, it was hard to really know what he thought. But I appreciated his strength and assistance. I relaxed in Bishop's grip.

Dallas waited for the judge to go first. He kept a hand on Chelsy at all times, like she would be whisked away from him if he loosened his grip for even a second. She didn't seem to mind. If anything, she held on to his arm with the same fervent intensity.

Judge Gascoigne stepped across the threshold and continued down the blocked-off tunnel. Bishop and I went after, followed by Dallas and Chelsy. The new tunnel had the same patchy lighting situation, with small illuminated areas surrounded by a sea of darkness. To my surprise, I didn't see any drones. That didn't mean they weren't farther down the tunnel, however.

We walked in close proximity to each other, but it was obvious that neither Bishop nor Dallas wanted to get close to Gascoigne. They kept at opposite sides of the tunnel while Gascoigne walked down the middle, the stomp of her exoskeleton boots ringing with each step.

The trek went on in silence for longer than thirty minutes, the scenery unchanging. I was almost afraid to glance behind us—like the entire subway was an illusion and we were secretly walking in place, never going anywhere. That was insane, of course. But I still thought it.

Dallas accidentally kicked a piece of trash, resulting in a quiet clack against the tracks. I tensed, already on edge, and Bishop stared down at me with a lifted eyebrow.

"Sorry," I murmured.

Bishop tightened his hold on me for a second. Then he cleared his throat. Everyone gave him a quick glance.

"So," Bishop began. "Judge. What's your name?"

"Judge Gascoigne," she stated.

"What's your first name?"

"As far as you're concerned, it's *Judge*."

"Oh. I see. You're one of *those* types of people. A part-time comedian. The life of the party."

She said nothing.

Bishop smiled. "What's your favorite color?"

Dallas snapped his attention to Bishop, a sneer on his face, as if struck with disapproving disbelief. He didn't comment, though.

"My favorite color?" Gascoigne drawled, perhaps also in a state of disbelief.

Their reactions got me smiling. I didn't know what it was about Bishop, but he did always seem to lighten my mood. Even in the darkest of tunnels.

Chelsy whipped out her notepad and wrote something down. She handed it to her father. Dallas read it over and said, "Your favorite color is black?"

She nodded.

"I thought it was pink."

She shook her head and frowned. Then she pointed to her short hair.

Dallas held her close. "I'll keep it in mind when we get you new clothes."

"Well?" Bishop asked. "Judge? Color?"

"I don't care about colors," she said.

"I should've guessed. Okay, how about this—you have a lover? Married? Pining after someone? Unrequited love?"

Gascoigne turned to stare at him for a moment while she walked. Then she returned her gaze to the tunnel. "No."

"We're really rounding you out as a person, aren't we? So many interests. So many hobbies."

His sarcasm was so thick I was surprised he didn't choke on it.

"Heh," Gascoigne said. "You don't become a judge by focusing on *colors* and *unrequited love*."

Bishop snapped his fingers and pointed at her. "What about kids? You have any kids?"

"I'm sterile."

I cringed. I wasn't sure why—because she hadn't said she became sterile through violent means—but I had seen the scars on her body. I was willing to guess something had happened to her. And now she wasn't whole.

Bishop replied with a nervous chuckle. "Yikes. Hey, Father of the Year, help me out here. Make some conversation."

"A closed mouth gathers no foot," Dallas quipped.

"That's it? You're no help at all."

"We have a long way to go. Maybe you should conserve your energy and stop talking."

"Nah, I've got plenty of stamina. Just ask any number of my lady friends."

Dallas didn't dignify the statement with a response. Gascoigne, on the other hand, chuckled.

"You like that?" Bishop asked, smiling. "At least you're not dead inside. Unlike a certain someone."

"From my experience," Dallas interjected, "men who continually claim they've been with countless women are greatly exaggerating."

Bishop stared down at me. "You can vouch for me, right?"

The way he asked it, I knew he meant to vouch for his many nights with women—but it did sound as though he was asking me to confirm our own many trysts. Hot in the face, I took note of Dallas's glower and straightened posture. He waited, breath bated, as though he needed to know my response.

"Will the lot of you keep it down?" Gascoigne snapped. "There are drones up ahead."

The jovial atmosphere shattered in an instant.

Dallas set Chelsy down and hefted his rifle. Bishop did the same with me, but he never stopped smiling. If anything, he seemed pleased with how the conversation ended and even gave me an odd look before readying his sniper rifle.

Bishop peered down his scope. "Ten of them. Heading our way at a steady clip."

In the distance, the nightmarish shapes of alien drones appeared under the spotlight and then disappeared into the darkness. Again and again, becoming closer and larger with each subsequent light they passed.

I motioned Chelsy to me. She jumped over the rails and ran straight into my arms. Before the fighting began, I placed her hands over her ears and ducked close to the wall, knowing the echo would be just as intense as before.

Gascoigne dashed down the tunnel, her exoskeleton almost as loud as the damn guns.

Dallas and Bishop opened fire moments later, filling the tunnel not only with noise, but strobe-lighting as well. Fortunately, the drones didn't have the capacity for complex strategy. They ran straight for the JUDGE-X0 suit, biting and clawing at it with all their might. The bullets slowed them, sure, but they ignored such injuries in favor of killing the first thing in their path.

But they weren't a match for Gascoigne. She cut into them, fighting one after another, even with a drone hanging from her suit's arm, its teeth stuck on the metal panels.

Gascoigne punched and sliced, carving up the aliens while Dallas and Bishop provided support. But the lights on her suit kept my attention. She needed power.

The last drone—if it had a mind—should've learned from the mistakes of the others and fled. But instead, it clawed at Gascoigne's helmet, snagging the fissure and wrenching off more of the metal plating. Gascoigne crushed its throat with her gauntlet, squeezing out flesh and muscle from between her fingers, but the damage had been done.

Perhaps the suit was wasting power through the damaged sections.

After a moment where nobody moved, Gascoigne turned back around to face us.

"Do you see any more?" she asked.

Bishop used his scope and then shook his head. "The tunnel curves up ahead. There aren't any drones until then."

"Keep me informed."

Bishop replied with a sarcastic salute.

Quiet descended over the tunnel.

Bishop returned to my side. Without a word, he scooped me into his arms and continued forward, no hesitation in his step. But when we drew closer to the corpses of the aliens, I gripped his shirt.

"Wait," I said.

"What is it?" he asked as he came to a halt.

"Let me look at them."

He set me down and I examined the torn bodies of the alien drones. One corpse—its innards splattered across the subway rails—had been carrying eggs. The dying drone babies sat in a pool of gore, no movement among them.

"What is this?" Bishop asked.

"Children."

"Alien children?"

"Yes."

Dallas, Chelsy, and Gascoigne examined the bodies with a critical eye after they spotted the egg sacs. The Teth carried leathery soft-shelled eggs in their bodies until a few days before they were to hatch.

"There are a lot of drones nowadays," Dallas intoned. "More than there were a few years ago."

"It only takes them a few months to gestate," Gascoigne said.

The two statements blanketed the group in a cold stillness. There were more and more drones, but their numbers were typically kept in check by the lack of food. Drone nests near insect-heavy areas or drones close enough to civilization to get the occasional family could grow larger, but the other groups eventually turned on themselves and became cannibalistic.

Chelsy fidgeted with the hem of her shirt as she stared at the unmoving corpses.

"You know what I've always wondered?" Bishop asked, breaking the melancholy between us. "How can you tell if they're male or female?"

"They're hermaphrodites," I said.

Dallas scoffed. "Really, Bishop? That was the first question you had? In a situation like this?"

"Oh, I'm sorry," Bishop said. "I should've asked, *when do you think these things will out-produce humanity? When do you think every city will be overrun with monsters hell-bent on ripping everyone apart?* Is that what you wanted? Because we can get real serious, real fast."

Chelsy's bottom lip quavered.

"Enough," Dallas snapped. He ran a hand over his head. "I was out of line. We shouldn't discuss this."

As though Gascoigne hadn't heard a single word of their argument, she turned to me and asked, "They're hermaphrodites?"

I nodded. "Yes. All of the aliens are. But their reproduction is a lot more complicated than that. If two aliens of mismatching caste reproduce, they create drones. Aliens of the same caste create more of themselves, but only when close to a member of the architect caste. Otherwise, their union results in more drones."

"You're sure of this?"

"Yes."

"Why do you know so much about aliens?" Gascoigne asked.

It took me a moment to realize no one knew. I'd told the Iron-Blooded about my grandfather, but not Dallas or Bishop.

"My grandfather dedicated himself to alien research and cooperation," I said.

Bishop chortled. "He must be spinning in his grave."

"He is probably doing a goddamn barrel roll at this point."

While we spoke, Chelsy drew flowers on pages of her notepad and placed them on top of the alien corpses. Her father grabbed her after the last one and carried her in his arms.

"We should keep going," Dallas said. "I don't want to linger here any longer than necessary."

Two hours in and we reached a portion of the tunnel with no lights.

Even though Dallas and Bishop had flashlights, and portions of Gascoigne's suit blinked and glowed orange, nothing about the passageway felt welcoming.

The poorly lit tunnel made finding darkness easy, and the low moans of ventilated air, coupled with the occasional stillness, made for a gloomy atmosphere. A chill permeated the area as well, like the entire tunnel had never known warmth. I rubbed at my arms when Bishop set me down.

The others stopped as well, though it was clear they didn't understand why.

"I got something from Pawn while I was in town," Bishop said. "It's for you, Crouton."

Chelsy perked up.

Bishop pulled a small velvet bag from his pocket. He walked over to Chelsy and offered her a carefree smile. Then he took Dallas's flashlight and affixed something to the end—something from the bag. It was a piece of stained glass that changed the flashlight into a kaleidoscope of shapes and colors. He twisted it around in his hand for a moment, showcasing the movement, and then handed the flashlight to Chelsy.

"You like it?" he asked.

She nodded as a smile grew across her face. She offered Bishop a piece of paper with a heart drawn on it in return.

"No need to thank me, Crouton," he said.

Dallas stared at Bishop for a moment before he muttered, "I should be the one thanking you."

"The fuck did you just call her?" Gascoigne asked, startling everyone with her gruff voice. "Did you seriously name a little girl *Crouton*? I can see the lot of you are eccentric wastelanders, but this takes it to a whole new level."

"Her name is Chelsy," Dallas snapped.

"Then why call her *Crouton*?"

Bishop threw a hand up in the air as he walked back to me. "C'mon, you guys. Haven't you heard the old-world commercials?"

No one said anything.

"It's because you're all from Ex Cathedra," Bishop said with a huff. "But over here, on the other side of the mountains, we like to listen to old-world recordings for our entertainment. Including commercials. They have jingles."

I thought back to our time in the other school. He had wanted to watch a bunch of prerecorded videos.

Bishop snapped his fingers in time with a living beat that only he could hear. Then he sang, "*Salads better watch their croutons, especially when they climb on rocks. Salads better watch their croutons, even when they have chicken pox.*"

While Chelsy clapped in time with the odd beat, Dallas frowned.

"Stop," he said. "We don't need to hear you sing."

"Is that what he was doing?" Gascoigne asked. "You must have a loose definition of the word *sing*."

I folded my arms over my chest, baffled by the lyrics. "What was that even a commercial for?"

"A car," Bishop said with a shrug. "The salads were adults, and the croutons were kids, and the commercial talked about seat belts or some shit. I just liked the jingle."

Before we could discuss anything else, Gascoigne turned on her heel and stomped down the tunnel. "We don't have time for this. We have places to be."

CHAPTER THIRTY-FOUR

My mind wandered as we traveled, but the conversation eventually broke through my haze.

"Do you think U-Cali will fall?" Dallas asked, keeping his voice low.

I didn't know if it was the anxiety of nearing the dam or if the echoes bothered everyone, but speech was kept to whispers.

Judge Gascoigne walked ahead, her footsteps a steady rhythm, like the heartbeat of the subway. "U-Cali will eventually capitulate. It's inevitable."

"But they have land cannons and soldiers."

"They're nothing but a collection of city-states. A single city has access to land cannons, and the rest aren't capable of fighting Ex Cathedra soldiers. Their defensive positions weaken every day, and their numbers dwindle. Their battle fatigue is already showing."

"Ever think that's all just propaganda?" Bishop asked. He kept me in his arms like before, but we never talked about, or addressed, anything between us. That was how Bishop operated with everything, though.

"Do you even know what the word *propaganda* means?" Gascoigne asked. "You seem to use it for anything relating to warfare. Propaganda is false information used to sway citizens or enemy soldiers. Ex Cathedra isn't hiding its agenda. It has been quite clear. Unite humanity from sea to shining sea so that it can face the darkness together."

"What if people don't want to unite?"

"Sometimes sheep don't realize they're weak. They need to be taught a lesson."

Bishop chuckled. "Are you saying all independent towns are weak?"

"That's right. Do you hear of marauders in Ex Cathedra? Of course you don't. We have soldiers and infrastructure to deal with such problems. Podunk towns have none of that. They think they can sit around, peaceful, and not be bothered, but such a mentality invites predators. If all remaining civilization joined with us, they could be protected. We could finally rebuild humanity. Save the world from destruction."

Gascoigne's voice—for the first time ever—swelled with conviction. She believed what she said without hesitation. Without doubt.

I supposed there weren't marauders attacking Ex Cathedra cities like the rail gang attacked Richfield, but that didn't mean Ex Cathedra was without problems.

"We're saving humanity," Bishop said. "Right now. That's our mission."

I almost wanted to tell him to keep quiet, but I held my breath and listened instead.

"Heh," Gascoigne said. "Merely existing isn't helping humanity. It requires change. And dedication. An understanding of things larger than one's self." She gripped her hands and shook her head. "That's the problem with simpletons. They focus on the immediate, not the large scale. Their personal relationships and struggles are more important than mankind's health or success. They need to be guided."

The conversation died down, snuffed out by Gascoigne's zeal.

That was fine. We were close to the dam—halfway through our trek—and then we could continue to the Meteorological Plexus.

The tunnel opened up into a subway station, with a stairway up to the dam, and a tunnel that led to the hyperloop. If we took the hyperloop tunnel, we would reach the plexus. But first we had to stop at the dam.

Gascoigne headed up the stairs, stepping awkwardly on the steps designed for smaller individuals. Dallas and Chelsy went up after, Chelsy's silent yawn a perfect punctuation for how most of us felt. The long walk, coupled with the lack of food, really took its toll.

Bishop carried me up last, moving slower than normal.

"Are you okay?" I asked.

"Yeah," Bishop said. "Well, except for the bruise on my chest from the judge. That hurts like a bitch."

Not a hint of discontentment or anger.

"You can talk to me," I said.

"News flash: I'm doin' that right now."

"I meant, about what's bothering you."

A slam of metal on metal ended our conversation.

Bishop dashed up the rest of the steps until we entered a building. It was a reception area for visitors to the dam. Signs for a gift shop adorned the walls, the colors faded but still visible. One large sign, positioned above a reception desk, read: WELCOME TO THE NEW AND IMPROVED HOOVER DAM! TOURS AVAILABLE EVERY WEEKDAY!

A cartoonish picture of an alien and human sat on either side of the letters.

Gascoigne stood at the door to the dam—a heavy steel door half busted from a sturdy kick. She gripped the side and pulled the door the rest of the way, the metal screeching in protest. Chelsy, now fully awake, covered her ears with her hands. Finally, Gascoigne opened it wide enough to crouch through.

"Damn, she's loud," Bishop said.

I nodded. "I wonder if there are any drones nearby."

"I guess we'll find out."

As a group, Dallas, Chelsy, Bishop, and I entered the dam; the muffled sound of water, coupled with the hum of machines and electricity, created a powerful white noise. Gascoigne waited on the other side of the door, unmoving. At first I thought she wanted me to be close, but then the flashlights illuminated the area, giving me perspective.

Dozens of drones were in the dam. But they didn't turn and attack, like the others we had run across.

These drones wandered between the machines, keeping the equipment clean and the floor clear of dirt and dust. Their four arms worked at once, making the task simple, and their skeletal bodies, while tall and lanky, didn't take up much space. They ignored us completely, no doubt because the commands they were issued had nothing to do with interlopers.

But I hated the way they "glanced" over whenever the flashlight was shone on them—they could feel the light, even if they couldn't see it—knowing we were here but returning to their task. If I didn't know they were basically mindless, I would assume they were lulling us into a false sense of security.

"Are they cleaning?" Bishop balked.

I nodded. "Yes. You shouldn't be so surprised. Drones are also capable of construction and other menial tasks." It was their primary function back before fighting became so common.

"*Shouldn't be surprised*? I'm sorry, these assholes tried to kill me, remember? And now they're monstrous janitors. It's gonna take me a moment to wrap my head around the situation."

He held me tighter than before, either because he was concerned for my safety or because he couldn't relax, I didn't know.

Dallas set Chelsy down and kept his handgun out at all times, his eyes shifting from one alien to the next. "They won't turn on us?" he whispered.

"They will if you attack one," I said. "But otherwise they'll continue to do as they've been instructed."

Judge Gascoigne walked over to one of the drones, inches from it, and reached out with her gauntleted hand.

"Don't hurt it," I said.

She tapped the creature's head, petting it. The creature moved away from her and continued working.

"Interesting," Gascoigne drawled. "They're like Theon's dogs."

Theon.

I still didn't know how he commanded his aliens. Other alien castes could give instructions to the drones, but the other castes were rarer and rarer, it seemed.

Chelsy ran to the closest alien the moment her father glanced away for even a second. The beast took little notice of her, but Chelsy crouched down and wiped the floor with her hand, imitating what the beast was doing with a specialized washcloth. Like she was helping it.

Why did she insist on obsessing over the creatures? Couldn't she see it was pointless? They were lesser than dogs and ten times as deadly. A terrible combination.

Dallas walked over and pulled her away, not saying a word as though he could accidentally disturb the monsters. Chelsy frowned, but listened to her father.

The white noise made it difficult to hear the aliens breathe, and for that I was grateful. We continued into the dam, my gaze finally falling to the rest of the facility. The ceiling rose up for a good forty feet to accommodate some of the machines. Massive cylinders and pistons worked nonstop, supplying the surrounding area with electricity even though the demand greatly dropped after the bombs. It had once been a purely hydroelectric power supply, but after the upgrade, and introduction of A-tech, the dam also created energy through solar power and hydrolysis, more than doubling its output through purely renewable means.

And it would run forever, much like the silver mine, kept alive by its own power and machines, so long as the equipment didn't fall apart.

As we walked, my mind then returned to the drones.

Who was telling them to keep the place in operational order? Could it be Theon? No. That would be silly. I knew it wasn't him. I knew.

"Wait," I said when the light hit a nearby wall. "Over there. Look."

Everyone stared in the direction I pointed.

Mounted on the wall, between two large storage containers, was a map. Bishop brought me over, and I stared for a moment, shocked at what I found.

The dam was also a source of research and development for the old-world government. Power tests, and A-tech integration, were key staples to the expanded dam. But while that was interesting, it didn't actually help me. Instead, I looked for a recharging station—there were some near the employees' quarters—and I sighed in relief when I found one.

Most A-tech batteries, so long as they were rechargeable, could be connected to an A-tech charging station. The interconnectivity of the technology was one of its many strong points.

"We need to go this way," I said, motioning to a far corner of the massive industrial room.

No one protested. They complied with my instructions, quiet and pensive. Were they as tense as I was? An uneasy feeling filled the air. I found it difficult to breathe. Each inhale came shorter than the last.

Bishop cradled me close, half smiling. "Don't worry," he whispered. "I've got you."

It reminded me of the night we escaped from the underground reactor. He had comforted me the same way. It helped me a little. But just a little.

We entered the employees' area—more like a gift shop, complete with windows that looked out into the machine floor—another large room with plenty of space. No aliens, which eased my anxiety, but not by much. Bishop set me down, and I ambled over to the charging station in the back. It was standard design—like a tanning bed or electronic coffin—meant to charge batteries and power cells placed within.

I turned to Gascoigne. "I need the other power cells."

Dallas and Bishop turned to her.

Would she open her suit in our presence? Before I could ask, she knelt and allowed the suit to peel open, revealing her physical being within. Although I had seen her a few times, she looked different than before— wan and sickly. She hadn't slept or rested the entire trek.

Dallas stared for a moment and then looked away. "I remember seeing you like this. A few times you gave speeches to the new soldiers in the mines."

Gascoigne rotated her shoulders once they were free of the suit. "That's right. Those neonates all shook and balked at my work schedules, but it made them stronger."

"You weren't popular. Most soldiers didn't want to work twelve hours every day."

I reached in and withdrew the power cells one at a time. Sure enough, when I unplugged one, the others lit back up, as though it were messing with the power distribution. It irritated me that Gascoigne wouldn't let me solve the problem, but since she lived in the damn suit, I supposed it wasn't unreasonable that she'd be irritated with people poking around it.

Bishop walked over and leaned against her open exoskeleton as if relaxing against a wall. Then he motioned to Gascoigne's forehead. "Your eyebrows are cute. How long have they been together?"

She shot him a sidelong glance. Was he trying to get her angry? It wasn't even like she had a unibrow—there was dried blood between her eyebrows from an injury on her head. The dent in her helmet dug at the old wound on her scalp, preventing it from healing right.

"I'm just joshin' with you," Bishop said as he tapped on the suit. "But on a serious note, given all the wires in your side and the way you refuse to step out of the suit, you're trapped in it, is that right?"

"Do you have something to say?" Gascoigne asked.

"How long have you required a power suit to live?"

"Four years," she said, much to my curiosity. I thought she wouldn't answer such personal questions.

"And you never leave? Ever?"

"I have to for very specific reasons. But otherwise, no."

"Well, now everything makes sense," Bishop said with a laugh.

Gascoigne narrowed her eyes. "And what's that?"

"Your bad attitude. Your terse speech. Your lack of hobbies. If I went four years without getting laid, I'd be the same way."

"*Bishop*," Dallas hissed. "What is your problem?"

Bishop clicked his tongue and pushed away from the exoskeleton. Although Dallas was upset with the crude comment, Gascoigne seemed mildly amused. One side of her mouth twitched upward in half a smile, making it the second time Bishop had managed to amuse her. And he was the only one—he really did have a talent.

Or maybe I just didn't understand Gascoigne. I figured such comments would bother her, but my predictions never came true.

When I got to the last power cell, I stopped. If I took them all out, her suit wouldn't be able to function.

"What's wrong?" she asked.

"I'll just charge the others."

"You can remove the last one."

"Don't you need, uh, the blood dialysis?"

"I can survive a week or so without it."

I didn't know how long a human could survive without kidneys, but I figured Gascoigne would be acutely aware so I had to take her word. Although hesitant, I reached up and grabbed the last power cell. When it was removed from the suit, a harsh beeping sounded twice, and most of the suit's inner lights faded.

Gascoigne rubbed at her side, right where the tubes were buried in her flesh. "How long will this take?"

"It'll take—"

A hundred bullets ripped through the glass of the gift shop windows, heralded by the harsh echo and ring of rifle fire.

I hit the floor, searing pain flooding my thoughts—my imagination filling in the story, picturing my chest riddled with holes. The flashlights didn't provide me with enough light, and I was left panicked.

There were five, maybe six, people outside of the employee area, hiding behind machines in the main industrial room, firing at us with spray-n-pray tactics. Another round of bullets blanketed the room, the harsh buzz as they sailed by a terrible sound I'd never forget.

I grabbed my chest.

No holes.

But I knew I couldn't stand, lest I get shot. Adrenaline flooded my body, icing my veins and giving me the focus to move.

"Fuck," Gascoigne hissed.

She was alive? If she were going to move, she needed one of her power cells. The moment there was a short lapse in fire, I stood and felt my way to the power cell slots.

But a hot, sticky substance coated most surfaces of the exoskeleton. It made it hard to concentrate until I heard another round of clicking from outside the gift shop. I plugged in one power cell and the suit flared to life.

Gascoigne had been shot. Or at least grazed with a bullet; it was hard to tell in the commotion. No doubt the suit had shielded her somewhat from the barrage, even when open, but blood ran the length of her body.

The suit closed before I could do anything about it, and she turned to the windows. A third wave of bullets hit the gift shop, but they didn't slow the judge from moving toward them.

Someone grabbed me. I gasped, but I recognized Bishop straight away.

"We have to go," he shouted.

Then Bishop ran out of the shop and took a hard turn. Through the white noise of the machines and water, I heard the drones scramble to move around. Their claws created a harsh click I'd know anywhere.

"How many times were you shot?" Bishop asked as he ran.

I was shot? I grabbed at my body, but it was hard to feel anything.

"I don't know," I whispered.

Then the lights came on. Illumination flooded the area—blinding, almost—and I blinked a few times to regain my sight. Bishop ducked behind a grouping of machines, sweat coating his skin.

The rifle fire didn't stop, and I had no idea where Dallas and Chelsy were. Had they been shot? Were they okay? I needed to know.

Standing at a far door, however, was the last thing I wanted to see. It was the alien from the research facility, the one wearing the JUDGE-Z12 alien armor. The damaged suit, still broken from the fight outside the research facility, shone under the harsh fluorescent lighting. The monster turned its attention to Gascoigne.

CHAPTER THIRTY-FIVE

Bishop and I stayed behind cover. He set me down and unslung his sniper rifle and duffel bag. We had lots of options, but two people versus an alien in an exoskeleton wasn't good odds. And then I spotted the men who fired on us—Iron-Blooded soldiers taking cover throughout the room. They must have snuck up on us in the dark. How long had they been watching?

Gascoigne lunged at a group and attacked. Two unlucky bastards weren't fast enough to escape.

Even with nanites, she crushed the life out of them in a matter of seconds.

The drones waited to the side, as though commanded to stand down.

The alien judge rushed forward. It met Gascoigne in the middle of the industrial room, its heavy footsteps mixing with the ambient noise to create a cacophony.

Gascoigne turned to face it, but what resulted was anything but "a fight."

I didn't know if it was because Gascoigne was tired, or if it was because she wasn't well, but her movements were sluggish when compared to the alien's.

It grabbed her by the helmet and slammed her to the floor, cracking the cement.

Gascoigne's suit hissed and beeped, the power indicators flashing red.

That was it. Time's up.

And the alien knew it, too. It stepped away as the suit peeled open, allowing the driver to escape. I held my breath as her fragile body was exposed. Blood continued to weep from her injuries. She had been pale before, but the eggshell white of her skin was an all-new complexion. It betrayed her suffering.

The alien judge grabbed Gascoigne and yanked her from the suit, ripping the tubes from her side and holding her by a shoulder. Neither Bishop nor I moved. I don't even think either of us took a breath.

"Bravo, my friend," a man said, his voice echoing between machines.

The Iron-Blooded soldiers—the ones still alive—stepped out from cover and nodded. Theon Sellers walked into the room, his odd suit and combat vest easily distinguishable, even from our distance. He was Iron-Blooded. I should've guessed. I should've known. I hadn't even thought to question him when we met, but it made sense now.

Theon walked up to the alien judge and patted its side.

"But this isn't the one I warned you about. We need to find the girl. She's small, and nonthreatening, but obviously the ringleader."

The alien set Gascoigne on the floor. She didn't struggle or complain, or even cry out, despite her many injuries, and I wondered if she would even remain conscious for much longer.

"*Is she here?*" the alien asked, its Tethlite lyrical.

"Yes," Theon answered. "She ran when the fighting started. But she's definitely here."

The alien turned to the nearest drones, the ones waiting on the sidelines. "*Find the interlopers. Bring them to me.*"

My mouth filled with cotton, and I couldn't take in air. Bishop continued to watch the scene, blissfully unaware of the command.

Where were Chelsy and Dallas?

"Bishop, we . . . we need to go. Right now."

But it was too late. The drones around us already knew where we were. They could smell us and sense the movements of our muscles, and they lunged before I had a chance to formulate a complete plan.

Bishop turned to me and hefted his rifle, but an alien leapt from around a machine and cut him from the shoulder to the elbow in one vicious slash.

Then a second one hit him from the side, cutting into his ribs and up to his shoulder blade. He cried out as he hit his knees. Although the nanites in his blood would minimize the impact of the neurotoxin, it wouldn't prevent the effect.

Then one cut me from behind, gouging out a chunk of my flesh along the side of my spine. For a moment, my vision went white.

I hit the floor, my breath ragged.

It was only then that I noticed my arm had a bullet hole in the bicep. It throbbed. And I was bleeding. Too much bleeding.

The information burned more than the injuries. Actually, the pain of the injuries faded away as the neurotoxin took full effect over my body.

My nightmares had become a reality. The drones picked me and Bishop up and hurried to the alien judge, just as they were instructed. We left a trail of crimson dots all the way to Theon and his monster buddy.

"There she is," Theon said with a smile. "I can't believe she made it this far. I knew when she asked about the plexus something must be amiss, but I never figured she'd make it out of the city like she did."

The drones dropped us at the feet of the alien from the warrior caste, next to Gascoigne, and then backed away. I still couldn't feel the physical pain, but each second that ticked by added another layer of panic to my thoughts.

They were going to kill us. And the plexus was so close . . .

Barely able to move, I closed my eyes and said, "You're all in danger. The . . . Meteorological Plexus . . . you don't understand. It's going to destroy everything."

The Iron-Blooded soldiers gathered around and pointed their rifles down at us. My heart beat hard enough that I felt it against the concrete, despite the toxin.

Theon said nothing.

He wouldn't listen.

I had to convince one of them. Just one.

"*The climate engineering satellites,*" I said in Tethlite. "*They're set to destroy the atmosphere. We're not here to hurt you. I'm just here to alter their function.*"

Theon lifted his hand, and the Iron-Blooded aimed with their rifles.

The alien judge belayed the order with a quick flick of his wrist. All the Iron-Blooded immediately stood down and took a step back.

I knew Theon couldn't possibly be an architect. If he were, none of them would've questioned his orders.

"*You know about the climate engineering satellites?*" the alien asked.

My vision blurred, and it was hard to feel anything, even my own breathing. "*Yes . . . I came to stop it . . .*"

"*She speaks Tethlite,*" the alien said to Theon. "*And you said she had a connection to the Teth. We must present her to the architect.*"

"The architect shouldn't be bothered with wasteland scum like this," Theon said, his Tethlite perfect. *"I have everything under control, and we don't need any more humans."*

"The architect made it clear. All qualified humans were to be brought into the fold."

"But in this case—"

"You aren't capable of making decisions for the architect," the alien growled.

All the Iron-Blooded, including Theon, grimaced and took another step back. Theon recovered faster and offered a quick bow of his head. *"As you say, Warrior Fera'Cova."*

A pack of drones walked up to the group, Dallas and Chelsy in their many claws.

"Leave her alone," Dallas shouted. He twisted in their grasp, despite the many injuries, but each second he grew weaker and shorter on breath.

Chelsy didn't move. The drone held her like a soiled toy, dangling her by an arm and leg. She wasn't conscious, and blood stained her clothes and ran in rivulets down her arms and face. The drones had cut her. I closed my eyes to avoid the sight.

"She's just a little girl! Please. Don't do this."

Dallas's pleading only added to the horror of the situation.

"We don't need the others," Theon drawled. *"They don't speak Tethlite. They're nothing but fodder."*

The Iron-Blooded soldiers readied their rifles again, and I opened my eyes to see a couple step forward.

"Look at them," the alien—Fera'Cova—said. *"Their blood is laced with nanites. Their origin and purpose is hazy enough that the architect should be the one to decide. Such humans could provide good breeding stock in the future."*

Dallas, Bishop, and Chelsy's blood all ran darker than normal. When I closed my eyes again, it was to offer a silent thanks to the universe that I wouldn't have to watch and listen to their deaths while I was incapable of moving.

"You heard Warrior Fera'Cova," Theon said, snapping his fingers. *"Take these four and confine them. We will take the girl to the architect. Do nothing until you hear a command from us."*

The Iron-Blooded soldiers bowed their heads in unison.

So, Theon had some sort of authority. But it was hard to deduce what that was when reality swirled in front of my eyes.

Then Fera'Cova picked up my limp body, and I lost consciousness.

* * *

"The medicine should wake her."

My eyes fluttered open only to be greeted by a harsh contrast of light and darkness. I was still underground, that much I knew, and the lights were from the ceiling corners, too bright to be normal lights.

"I can smell it in her blood. She is a descendant of Dr. Benjamin Yamasaki."

"Then she has found her way home."

I rolled to my side, my strength coming back in waves. Each breath cleared my thoughts of fog, crystalizing into coherent musings within a matter of seconds. But I couldn't stand. Instead, I sat up and held my injured arm close. I had bandages and medicine—A-tech anti-inflammatory and painkillers—but I wasn't whole.

Then I saw everything. The others in the room.

The architect.

It stood in front of the lights, its body half-silhouetted but still distinct.

All architects—real alien architects—had features none of the other aliens possessed. They had manes and crests made of spines. The spines started at their head and ran down between their shoulder blades, some three feet in length, some shorter. And they weren't just for show.

While other aliens had neurotoxins in their claws, the architects could create a gas that wafted from their mane, deadly to anything but the architect itself.

Architects controlled which of the castes could breed. Back in Teth history, before they were space travelers, before they came to Earth, they lived in tribes, the architect their leader. If the architect wanted more warriors, it stimulated the warriors to procreate. If the architect wanted more innovators, it would do the same with them. Each architect built a society based around their perceived needs, building complex social structures exactly as they deemed necessary.

"I am Teth Architect Riven," the architect said, a calm tone to its powerful voice. *"You will state your name."*

I glanced around the room. The judge alien stood off to the side, half in shadows. Theon was also here. Along with Commander Dannik—his presence unmistakable. And there was another alien. An innovator.

Was this some sort of hearing?

"I am—" I shook my head and replied in Tethlite, *"—I am Kita Yamasaki."*

The innovator moved around, more excitement in its motions than the others. Everyone else shifted their weight, nervousness on display.

"*You are kin of different blood,*" Architect Riven said. "*You needn't be afraid. I knew Benjamin well.*"

"*You met my grandfather?*"

"*He was one of the first to welcome my kind. His intelligence, compassion, and innovation are unrivaled among your species.*"

I caught my breath.

All architects in a line took the same name—whenever Architect Riven reproduced, it would name its child Riven—so the knowledge that this was the same architect who interacted with my grandfather came as a surprise. That meant Architect Riven was a Winter Survivor. No, much older than that. One of the first Teth to arrive on Earth.

After absorbing the information, I relaxed a bit.

Although the situation was foreign, and I had no idea where I was, or where anyone else was, I had hope. Perhaps the architect would listen to me. Perhaps it would even help me. Of course! This could be it. I could finally put an end to my insane quest.

"*Architect Riven,*" I said. I swallowed and took in a gulp of air. "*I've brought dire news. Please, listen to me. I know it's the truth. The climate engineering satellites have been tampered with. They're set to ignite the atmosphere. It'll destroy all life on Earth as we know it.*" I held a hand to my chest, taking in more air. "*But we still have time. If we make it to the Meteorological Plexus, we can alter the parameters.*"

For a long moment, no one said anything.

Did they hear me? I wondered. Even when I glanced around, no one moved. Should I repeat myself?

"*Is that why you've come here?*" Architect Riven asked.

"*Yes,*" I said. "*I discovered the problem elsewhere. It was a message addressed to my grandfather. To Benjamin. But I took it upon myself to correct the problem in his stead.*"

"*There is no need to fret, child. There is no problem.*"

It took me a moment.

Had the architect already changed the satellites?

No. I saw the readout at the research facility. Unless the architect had made changes within the last few months, it was still set for destruction.

"*But,*" I began, "*I've seen the data. I know what the satellites are capable of.*"

"*Yes. Listen closely and I will tell you everything you need to know.*"

I held my breath, ready for the good news—ready to stop worrying.

"I am aware the CES satellites are set for destruction, and I have chosen to keep them that way."

"What?" I blurted out.

"You will remain quiet while the architect explains," Fera'Cova growled.

Architect Riven continued, *"Again, there is no need to fret. As we speak, the transport ship that brought the Teth to Earth is in orbit around Mars, collecting data through automated systems. The ship has no pilot I can contact, but it does have a fail-safe. If the destination planet, Earth, is to be wiped out, the transport will return before the destruction date to collect any Teth who wish to return home."*

My heart stopped for a second. I already knew the punch line.

"But," I whispered, *"the transport ship can't descend into the atmosphere. Even if it returns to Earth, it'll remain in orbit. How will you reach it?"*

"I have spent the last four decades repairing a Teth spaceship docked here at the Thompson Space Force Base," Architect Riven said, still serene, despite the horrid decision being discussed. *"Once the transport ship is within orbit, the Teth ship will take us up past the atmosphere and straight into the transport's docking bay."*

I exhaled. *"But . . . there are so many humans on Earth. If you do this, you'll kill them all."*

"I have spent the last four decades collecting humans." Architect Riven gestured to Theon and Dannik. Then the architect motioned to me. *"I'm so glad you returned home, kin of different blood. I thought I had lost all traces of Benjamin when the bombs hit, but now I will be able to save his legacy. You, along with my human coterie, will join us on the journey. You and your species will rebuild on my homeworld."*

The reality set in hard.

Architect Riven was planning on leaving Earth. I could barely believe it. Hot anger and icy dread mixed in my blood in equal amounts.

"So many lives will end if you do this," I said, trying to play on some sort of empathy, trying to stay civil despite the urge to yell. *"Teth and human alike. You can't rebuild here? Or find another way to summon the transport?"*

"I've spent over forty-six years trying to summon the transport. This was my last option, if all others failed." Architect Riven shook its head. *"When we arrived, we allowed humans to guide our actions, as it was their planet. I can see now that was a mistake. We aren't equals. I must make the decisions lest we have a repeat of what happened before."*

"But, to let all of humanity die . . . to let all the Teth die . . ."

Even if parts of the world were ruined and wasting, there was still hope. Right? To sentence them all to death was unreasonable. Insane. Wasn't it?

Architect Riven stepped forward, the lighting still creating harsh lines and shadows. "*Every year we stay here, more Teth die off. Not the drones—they can maintain forever—but the real Teth die from disease, humans, and circumstance. The ratio of mindless drones to fully functioning Teth grows wider and wider. Don't you see?*" The architect wasn't as calm as before. Its voice rose, and its conviction practically shook the walls. "*Every day my kind grows stupid and directionless. Despite my efforts, I have collected very little of the other castes. I will watch the world burn before I allow any more of them to perish under my watch.*"

I rubbed at my face, a headache building. A sense of hopelessness set in. The architect had the same passion Gascoigne did—the same determination. What the fuck was I going to do? Fight them all? Of course not. *Of course not.*

The architect took a breath before continuing, "*Kin of different blood, you needn't worry. You will live, just not here. Humanity's long night of suffering has come to an end. Unfortunately, there will be no dawn. Not on Earth.*"

"*What about the others?*" I asked, grasping for anything I could latch on to. Anything positive. "*The ones who came with me? Two men, a child, and a woman.*"

"*Although I don't want to take those who don't understand Tethlite, I will allow them to accompany us. Consider it a gift. Hopefully, their presence will calm you.*"

The innovator stepped forward, its dull black skin muted under the harsh lights, its jumpsuit one designed for space travel. "*Architect Riven, allow me to care for this one. Benjamin was one of my closest confidants.*"

"*So be it.*"

"*Thank you, Architect. Your wisdom will save us all.*"

CHAPTER THIRTY-SIX

The Iron-Blooded used the hyperloop tunnels as their personal roadways. It didn't take us long to reach the Thompson Space Force Base, especially when my mind buzzed, blocking out my perceptions and drowning me in murky thoughts. The vehicle, a troop transport, moved at a steady clip until we reached the station at the surface.

"I am Teth Innovator Gale'Naris," the innovator said in English—damn near perfect pronunciation.

But I didn't want to speak in English. "*You knew my grandfather?*" I asked in Tethlite.

"Yes. I was born here on Earth, and he gave me my name."

Before I could ask anything else, my attention was caught by the massive spire building at the edge of the base. It twisted high into the air, several beams of metal lacing together to become one, a work of art and old-world architecture. It was a spire for communication into space, and I knew immediately, without the need to ask, that it was the Meteorological Plexus.

Right there.

"Kita," Gale'Naris said. "Would you like to go inside?"

I nodded, my thoughts fixated on the structure.

Our driver was Iron-Blooded—a man with a rifle—but Gale'Naris had a drone at its beck and call at all times.

Once the vehicle stopped, the innovator motioned to the drone, and it lifted me from my seat and carried me along. I hated the claws, but at the same time, it was familiar. My grandfather once had many alien allies.

Gale'Naris walked into the plexus, its servant drone following behind, and we went straight to the command console, only a few rooms in. The control room, obviously rebuilt after much damage, had several computer terminals, each displaying a readout of the satellite's status. Without hesitation, the innovator motioned to the main controls.

It impressed me how much work Architect Riven had gone through to save its kind. No obstacle stopped the architect, not even a broken plexus.

"Please," Gale'Naris said. "Do what you must."

The drone set me down. I hobbled to the computer, expecting a trick or an attack, but none came. I typed at the console, wondering what would happen if I just changed the satellites without asking.

The moment of truth.

I couldn't.

I knew it the instant I tried to access the main code. It wasn't anything I was familiar with. Whatever operating system the plexus ran, it wasn't one of the systems my grandfather taught me. And unlike the old systems, which weren't secure, the system for the plexus seemed to have a million safeguards, and that was just the surface of my short investigation.

I didn't know how to get around any of it.

"*You wanted me to see it was impossible,*" I intoned.

Gale'Naris placed one of its smaller hands—a crafting hand—on my shoulder. "I apologize. But you needed to understand. Architect Riven personally designed the security. There will be no changing the will of the architect. Accept our hospitality and allow us to care for you."

"*Is it like this with every plexus?*"

"They are connected through the satellite system. All have been changed to avoid anyone interfering with the architect's plans."

I didn't answer.

Gale'Naris motioned to the drone again, and I was taken out of the plexus, barely seeing my surroundings, numb to the change in location in almost every regard.

How could I alter any of it? My drive drained from me with each passing second. It was as if I were drowning and I couldn't see the surface anymore. Why should I fight against it? There was an entire army's worth of people and aliens here, all dedicated to the destruction of the planet.

I was just one person.

A weak little girl.

Unable to accomplish a single thing I had set out to do.

Had I reached the BC Oasis? Had I altered the satellites? All that struggle and hardship and suffering.

All for nothing.

Reality hit hard. Worse than a sucker punch to the gut.

Gale'Naris led me into the base's hanger. And there it was. The spacecraft capable of escaping the atmosphere. It reached six hundred feet in
length, large enough to house three thousand crew members, maybe more
if they crammed the thing, and its exterior shone with a white luster.

"This is our ship," Gale'Naris said. "You'll appreciate everything once
you've seen our progress."

We entered up a ramp, into the dimly lit interior. Some lights were
around, not for the aliens, but for the humans. Not enough to see the corners of the rooms, or even very far, but enough to navigate. I suspected it
was the reason most of the Iron-Blooded guarded the outside, rather than
walking around the inside of the ship.

As a matter of fact, the ship was damn near empty. I spotted a handful
of drones tending to the equipment, but otherwise nothing.

Wall panels remained open, exposing the inner workings of the ship.
They were still repairing some systems, but from what I could tell, most of
the work was completed and awaiting a final inspection.

"I'm excited to have humans travel with us," Gale'Naris continued,
even without my participation in the conversation. "Architect Riven has
designed a system of hierarchy for all those that serve. The architect wishes
for humans to integrate without much cultural shock once we reach
our homeworld, which is why we've been breeding individuals for two
generations."

"Breeding?" I asked, finally switching to English.

"Yes. We raise the humans here, teach them Tethlite, and give them
a role. I must admit, some humans are a tad unruly, especially those we
didn't raise. Human females sometimes protest the schedule of impregna-
tion, and the human males tend to be violent or rebellious when faced with
absolute authority. Benjamin had a much easier temperament."

It half amused me, half frightened me, that the aliens didn't understand
human individuality.

They thought they could train humans to fit the mold of a caste? I supposed it made sense to them. The aliens wanted harsh order, like their own
society, and they thought humans only needed a slight adjustment to fall
into line.

And although the aliens had been on Earth for some time, they had lived through nothing but moments of high stress or turmoil—not the best circumstances to grasp humanity's true nature.

"And Theon?" I asked. "He's your chosen human architect?"

"Yes. An experiment. He has been tasked with gathering individuals from Boulder City. Slowly he has taken more and more control of the governing body, and before we leave, hopefully he will have reaped those with the most potential to live among our new society."

We walked the halls of the spaceship, the ceilings high but the corridors narrow. I didn't pay much attention to the directions, only to the fact that we continued deeper and deeper.

"Here is the crèche," Gale'Naris said as he motioned to a door.

The drone brought me into a circular room, one complete with medical stations and canisters of liquid.

A *crèche* was a sacred place for aliens, even outside of spaceships. A crèche housed unhatched eggs and also functioned as a nursery for the youngest aliens until they could move on their own.

I glanced around the room, my eyes lingering on the canisters. They were filled with leather eggs. Teth eggs. Frozen in time thanks to the cryostasis gel that held them in place.

Once I was set down, I made my way over to the first station, unable to look away from the unborn creatures.

Gale'Naris placed a hand on a canister—one the length and thickness of my forearm. The glass window on the side displayed the egg inside. The writing at the top, done with a texture font, read: ARCHITECT.

I reached out to touch it, but Gale'Naris grabbed my arm and held it away. After a tense moment, the innovator relaxed. "I apologize. These are so rare."

I knew.

The architects only ever produced two eggs—like cloning themselves—a process separate from the mating habits of other aliens. The eggs were rare and special, and something told me this might have been Architect Riven's last architect egg. After this, the architect would never reproduce.

"Look here," Gale'Naris said. "Children from several other castes. We have stored them in case something goes wrong. These medical casings act as both incubation and cryosleep. We can keep the children suspended in time until we need them."

"Why show me this?"

"Don't you understand? We have contingencies."

Again, I didn't answer.

Even if Architect Riven died, they would simply raise up the other architect and continue with their plot. The other alien children were likely preventive measures, just in case something went terribly wrong, so they wouldn't lose a caste outright.

The drone lifted me, and we continued our depressing tour of humanity's end.

Gale'Naris stopped at another room—the infirmary—and led me to a small surgery tank. The tanks, only six inches high, were filled with a highly oxygenated medical gel. The gel prevented bleeding during surgery and filled the lungs of the person in the tank, keeping them tranquilized and pain free during the process. Such advancements in medicine had been lost after the bombs, but the Teth ship still had power and resources.

The innovator hesitated for a moment before reaching out and stroking my hair. I froze, disliking the touch but uncertain of what to do about it. Surely it would stop soon.

The drone set me down and backed up to the door, blocking the path out.

"Your scent," Gale'Naris said. "It's so similar to Benjamin's. I never thought I'd experience such familiarity again."

Without asking, or even giving me warning, Gale'Naris slid my duster off and peeled away the last of my clothes. Its hands on my skin grated at my patience—I hated the feel of fingers grazing parts that people rarely ever saw—and after a few seconds, I jerked away and hit the wall. It wasn't sexual. At least, I didn't think it was. But still. I hated it.

The alien appearance, its four arms and exposed teeth, made the entire situation unnerving.

Gale'Naris shook its head. "You're imperfect. I will make you whole."

The innovator grabbed my arm and dragged me to the surgery tank. Without much effort, Gale'Naris lifted me up and set me inside, sitting up, so that only my hips and legs were submerged. Some of the displaced gel slid down the outside into a tray to catch excess, but the tank was built for aliens and large because of it. I didn't displace much.

"Benjamin provided much advice for me over my lifetime," the innovator said. Gale'Naris inserted earbuds into my ears. "He advocated we work together. Think of him while I modify you for your new life. He would have joined us without complaint."

Some part of me wanted to struggle, but apathy took hold.

Did it really matter what happened?

What was I going to do about it?

Then Gale'Naris pressed me back into the tank. I closed my eyes and shivered once the last of the gel washed over my face. The chill and firmer-than-water texture combined to make an eerie experience, especially across my naked body.

For whatever reason, it made me think of newborns and the birthing process.

The first breath I took while submerged—the one where the gel went straight into my lungs—paralyzed me in place as my body gave in to the sedatives. All feeling disappeared. Panic gripped my thoughts, but then the earbuds played soothing notes of pleasant music. Teth music. Things I hadn't heard in years.

Surgery would soon begin. I tried not to think about it.

Gale'Naris lifted me from the surgery tank.

Limp and unfeeling, I didn't move when the innovator set me on a table and wiped away the gel. After a few minutes—once the goo in my lungs had lost all the oxygenation—my chest burned, and I coughed up the slimy substance.

For hours, I had been in surgery. My mouth tasted like a mix of laundry soap and plastic.

But it hadn't felt like much time passed, not when I was imprisoned in my own thoughts.

"Given Benjamin's successes, you will be granted the role of innovator," Gale'Naris said as it stroked my matted hair.

I remained quiet.

"I've laced your blood with nanites and mended the nerve damage in your body. You will live much longer than any of your race. You're whole now—and I've even added connectors to your skull so you can wear various types of power armor. I will keep you close, my kin of different blood. A promise to make up for our failure to keep Benjamin safe."

The way it treated me was very alien.

Gale'Naris thought my grandfather and I were almost interchangeable because we came from the same line—the same human caste.

"Walk," Gale'Naris commanded.

Apathy almost prevented me from moving. I swung my legs over the side, surprised at the lack of pain, and then eased myself into the standing position. No agony. No stress. I took a few steps forward, my mind grappling with the new reality as I stumbled, but walking came back to me within half a second, much like the famous saying about riding bicycles.

I had feared being seen as pathetic for my physical shortcomings, but in a case of dark irony, I didn't feel any less pathetic now that I could walk.

I crossed my arms over my bare chest and shivered.

"Are you . . . not happy?" Gale'Naris asked. "I thought such a recovery would please you."

It didn't matter how miraculous my recovery was. It barely registered in my thoughts.

"I will assign some of our human men to watch over you."

"No," I said, curt. Anything but the Iron-Blooded. "I don't want that. I'd rather see the people who came with me."

"They're being treated." Gale'Naris shook its head. "The woman, child, and one of the men are worthless to our program. Architect Riven almost expelled them, but given they came with you, we've decided to keep them."

"Worthless?"

"The woman cannot reproduce. The child and man have several genetic defects that will be inherited by offspring."

"When can I see them?" I asked.

"I will arrange a meeting once they have been processed. Until then, please recover. Your distress doesn't suit the situation. You should be elated. Soon you will be away from the hardships of this world and in the care of superior beings."

The spaceship housed the medical technologies and equipment meant to be taken with them once they left the planet.

Four days I stayed on the ship with Gale'Naris. I went where it wanted me to, I did as it instructed, and I rarely spoke. Few comforts eased my doubt, but walking was one of them. I ran a few places, just because. When blood beat through my system, I didn't feel winded for long. My body, improved beyond what I thought capable, lifted my spirits.

Even still—dread cannibalized all other emotions.

"You brought many things with you," Gale'Naris said as it took me to a locker storage area on the ship. "Many weapons and junk, but some crude drawings and figurines as well." The innovator opened one of the lockers and displayed everything Bishop had been dragging around in his duffel bag. Even his sniper rifle was stored in the giant car-sized steel alloy container.

"Why did you keep all this?" I asked, my gaze lingering on the grenades and fission bomb. Why hadn't it given such weaponry to the Iron-Blooded?

Gale'Naris shook its head. "I wanted them to be kept separate. While our human warriors have been given free rein to scour the lands for humans worth bringing into the fold, I know of their dark methods. Benjamin wouldn't approve. Architect Riven gave them permission under the reasoning that we didn't have time to fret about such concerns, but the architect never said I had to aid our human warriors. So I kept these weapons from them."

The innovator didn't want needless people to die. It was a slightly comforting thought.

"Where is Gascoigne's suit?" I asked.

"They took it to the base's armory. The female driver may not live through her operation."

I found nothing that would comfort me in the locker. Even Chelsy's drawings did little.

Gale'Naris led me away, taking me, finally, to see the others. Well, Bishop and Gascoigne. Dallas and Chelsy still "needed longer." Gale'Naris didn't elaborate, and my imagination threatened to send me into a bout of depression, but I didn't allow it. They wouldn't kill them. Gale'Naris had assured me.

The innovator guided me out of the ship—its name the *Salvation*, which I hated—and brought me back to the Thompson Space Force Base. While the Iron-Blooded gave me odd glances, I didn't pay them much attention.

We entered a massive room with barred cells. Perhaps they'd once kept animals or research drones here, since the base had engaged in more than military tactics before the bombs. Now it housed humans, like a creepy zoo.

The cages were small, maybe the size of two closets, and each human inside had been stripped of all clothing.

Gale'Naris had given me old-world military fatigues, monochrome with gray and in a disruptive pattern. They weren't fashion-forward, but they did fit, and they were reasonably comfortable. At no point did they restrict my movement.

There weren't many humans in the zoo, perhaps twenty, and some were doubled up in cells, for whatever reason.

Were the aliens breeding people here? Or just indoctrinating them? A few women were pregnant, and a few of the men didn't look like they'd survive the night, not with the terrible gouges and burns across their body.

We stopped at the end of the room, at the back, away from most of the others in captivity.

Bishop leaned against the far cement wall, his tally mark scars a dead giveaway to his identity, even if his gaze was on the ceiling. Gascoigne sat in the corner, wrapped tightly into a ball, her knees against her chest and her arms around her legs. She was still damaged, but not actively bleeding. Pale and shivering.

"You didn't help her?" I asked. They had the ability. My hip was a testament to that fact.

Gale'Naris shook its head. "Like I said, she's considered worthless. No further resources are to be spared on her."

Bishop turned his attention to me, and his eyes widened. "You came back."

His voice—for a moment, I felt like my old self. I leaned against the bars. "Bishop. I need to speak to you." But first I turned to Gale'Naris. "If Gascoigne isn't helped soon, she'll die."

"I'm aware," Gale'Naris replied. "She's missing crucial internal organs. Fortunately, growing new ones is a possibility, and I will advocate we do so, but it will take up equipment we could be using for others."

"I would appreciate it if you at least didn't allow her to die."

Gale'Naris bowed his head. "I will see what I can do."

Bishop walked over, his arms crossed, and gazed down at me. Our eyes met, and he searched mine as though he'd understand everything if only he stared long enough. Then he turned slightly, keeping himself at an angle, one leg slightly up, no doubt for modesty purposes. He hadn't ever been one ashamed of his nudity, and in my apathy I didn't much care, but I wondered why he would alter his behaviors at this point.

"Bishop," I whispered.

He glanced at me, and then to the other cells, only to return his gaze to me afterward. "I thought the worst, you know. Fill me in. What's happening? What's gonna happen to us?"

"I'll leave you two be," Gale'Naris said as it turned and walked away.

CHAPTER THIRTY-SEVEN

’ll tell you everything," I said. "But . . . I don't think you'll like it."

"Nobody speaks English around here," Bishop said the second Gale’Naris left our close proximity. "All of them speak gibberish. It's frustrating. Any news is good news at this point."

I looked him over, pleased to see he wasn't injured.

"Are you okay?" I asked. "Did they hurt you?"

"My pride, maybe. They bring us food, but they don't treat us like people. More like animals."

"Is Gascoigne . . . okay?"

We both turned our attention to her. She kept her head down, buried in her arms, and didn't move, even though I knew she was awake.

Bishop leaned his weight against the bars and cocked half a smile. "I don't understand her specific psychological holdups, but I do admire her commitment to them."

"What do you mean?"

"I mean, on a scale of one to ten in terms of mental health, she's aiming to get a disorder named after her."

"Bishop," I said with an exhale. I placed one of my hands on his arm and pressed my forehead onto one of the bars. "No jokes. Please. Will she be all right?"

He clicked his tongue. "Tsk. She doesn't want anyone to touch her. It's a hassle to get her to eat. I think she wishes she died back at the dam, but I keep tellin’ her it'll be all right. Unfortunately, she doesn't like me very much. Actually, I don't think she likes anyone with a penis, to be frank."

Even though we spoke about Gascoigne loud enough for her to hear, she made no move or indication.

Bishop and I stared at her for a moment, but she remained seated, her head down. I remained still for a long period of time, wondering if she would ever explain. But it didn't matter. None of it mattered, really. Not if we were all abandoning Earth to be pets of aliens.

So I pushed it from my mind. Some problems just had to wait.

"Bishop," I said. "I met with an alien architect."

The words obviously meant little to him. Bishop listened as though the information were almost meaningless. Still, he had to know the rest.

"They're planning on using the CES satellites to summon a transport ship. They're going to destroy Earth and take everyone here as their . . . allies, for lack of a better term, to their homeworld."

"Us?" Bishop balked.

"Yes."

Again, he glanced around the room, but this time it was as if he truly saw it for what it was. A facility for breeding and creating humans. A cruel corner in a dying empire of aliens meant as an experiment.

Bishop said nothing as his gaze lingered on the imprisoned men and women.

At first he tensed, his hands gripping tight on his arms. Then he stared at the floor, and after a few deep inhales, his stress visibly faded.

"Bishop," I said, terse. "I came here to ask for your advice, but I already know what you're going to say."

"Oh, yeah?"

"That's right. Because it's always the same."

"I doubt that."

"When I met you, back near the mountains, you were a man just waiting to die. Admit it. Everything you did. All the fights you got yourself in. You didn't care. You still don't care. Your advice is to walk the path of *not giving a shit*."

He held his breath. I opened my eyes and glared at him. For a moment, silence came between us. There were others in the room—whispers and movements—but it all disappeared into the background.

Bishop glowered. "Well, I *didn't* give a shit. Until I met you. Now I have a lot to care about."

His simple response surprised me. I hadn't been expecting that.

"Then I need your advice," I whispered as I leaned against the bars of his zoo cage. "This situation we're in . . . I don't know what to do. Fight the aliens? Just go along with everything?"

Calm and gentle, Bishop said, "You're like this, you know. You half-ass things."

I shook my head. "Please. *Please*. No jokes."

"I'm not joking, *Kita*. I see the way you debate everything in your head. Always doubting. Always fretting. That's the worst of all worlds. You either have to commit to not givin' a shit, or you need to give the situation everything you have, so there can be no regrets. Do you understand?"

"That's not true," I said, curt. "I'm not like that."

"Look at the way you avoid guns. If you didn't care about your past, it wouldn't be a problem. If you cared about something more than yourself, and you had to use the gun to defend it, again, it wouldn't be a problem. But here you are, stuck in the middle, wallowing. Anything is better than wallowing."

Bishop leaned onto the other side of the bars and rubbed my shoulder, comforting me, even though I'd started this off by yelling at him. I grabbed his hand and massaged his knuckles.

"You're a light in the darkness," I murmured.

"Hardly."

"I don't want to wallow anymore."

Bishop nodded. "So you have to make a choice. It's easy living when you care about nothing. I know. That was me. Life is really hard when you give a damn. And it hurts. It'll hurt like a bitch if you lose the people and things you care about the most."

"What if I . . . told you I wanted to fight for everyone here? That saving humanity, and Earth, was what I really cared about?"

I feared Bishop would tell me to give it up. I worried he would convince me to take the path of least resistance.

"You want to fight everyone here?" Bishop motioned to the room. Then he made a bigger circle with his hand, as though including the whole military base. "That's what you want to do?"

"Yes."

"Then do it. Just don't half-ass it."

"Would you help me if I asked you to?" I asked.

I would go it alone if I had to, but I really didn't want that path. I *wanted* other people in my life.

"Kita."

The way Bishop said my name stunned me for a moment.

"Listen," he said. "I've met lots of folks around the wasteland. Most of them I forget—genuinely—but you're different. I think a lot about you. I wanted to help you reach this crazy objective since the moment you decided on it."

I chuckled. My eyes hurt with tears. I rubbed them away. "Truly?"

Bishop tapped the bars. "I'm a lot of things, but a liar ain't one of them."

I didn't know why, but in that moment, most of my doubts faded. Optimism was a drug. I wished I could get high on it all the time.

"You know what's weird?" he asked as he smacked my shoulder. "Every time I've been naked in front of you, you've been bawlin' your eyes out. Probably not a good sign."

I couldn't help but laugh. My face grew hotter with each chuckle. Technically, I had been talking to him the entire time without focusing on his flesh—because I had more pressing matters to deal with—but now it became awkward. I turned my back to the cell and rested against it.

"I'm not naked this time," I murmured as I recalled our stay in Richfield.

"Much to my disappointment."

Despite the grim situation, despite the reality of not knowing how anything could be saved, Bishop still made me smile.

"You're looking healthy, too," Bishop continued. "I take it the aliens fixed you up?"

I rubbed at my hip and nodded. No pain. None whatsoever.

Bishop admired me. "They're amazing and nightmarish all at the same time. Maybe you should teach me gibberish."

"Maybe." The conversation of medical advances drew me back to the present. I pushed away from the bars. "Gascoigne," I said. "I asked the aliens to help you. I think they will. So you shouldn't focus on dying."

She tightened her grip on her legs, but otherwise said nothing.

"I'll make sure she's okay," Bishop said. "But don't take long to get back to us."

"I won't. I just need time to think. I'll . . . I'll find a way to make this right. I swear it. I'm not going to half-ass anything."

It was his turn to laugh. He grabbed my hand and kissed my knuckles. "I'll be here."

The gentle act surprised me. I didn't know how to feel, so I replied in kind, pressing my lips to his hand. The look he gave me—something intimate, more than I had ever experienced with another—took the breath from my lungs and left me lightheaded.

Bishop. No one made me feel the same way he did. We were similar, yet different. Like the moon and the stars. Complementary.

Our exchange redoubled my determination to make things right.

I would save Earth, and the last of humanity, or I would die trying. There would be no middle ground.

CHAPTER THIRTY-EIGHT

I want to leave," I said.

Gale'Naris continued to inspect the inner workings of the spacecraft. It felt the wires and lingered around the circuit boards. Although the aliens had no eyes, their ability to sense electrical currents couldn't be understated—electroception, they called it.

"If you stay on Earth, you'll die," Gale'Naris said.

"You say you knew my grandfather."

Gale'Naris stopped working and waited.

"If you really knew him, you'd understand why I would want to stay."

Perhaps the statement struck a chord, because Gale'Naris remained silent for several seconds. Then the innovator reached out and touched my hair, its longer crafter fingers weaving through the short black locks.

At first, the touching bothered me, but I remembered why the aliens did it. They showed affection through touch and intimacy, no doubt due to their lack of purely visual stimuli. I'd seen it a few times with the alien allies that surrounded my grandfather, and many more times in the last few days I had spent aboard the spaceship.

They put a lot of stock into their sense of touch. Everything the Teth made had a texture. The walls. The countertops. The clothes. And they associated certain textures with specific feelings and emotions.

I reached up and touched Gale'Naris's wrist to return the affection. It was what the innovator wanted.

"It would be a shame to lose you," Gale'Naris said. "At least let me breed you before you go. So that we may take your legacy with us."

I knew Gale'Naris didn't mean to breed me personally; the innovator wanted me with one of the Iron-Blooded studs, but the way it was stated . . . I shuddered.

The Teth saw intimacy and child-bearing differently than most humans. The Teth community cared for each other, because each member of the caste had a different role to play in the community. Domestic castes—the legacy watchers and the pedagogues—would raise all children born of any castes, like one big loving family.

I shook my head. "No. None of my line would be happy abandoning Earth."

"I could keep the child in the crèche until after our journey."

"While I understand that's an honor"—keeping a human child with the Teth architect was unheard-of—"I still have to decline."

Gale'Naris exhaled and withdrew its hand. Without a human face, it was difficult to judge an alien's mood, but I knew from the breathing, and the way the smaller crafting hands fidgeted, how most felt in any given situation.

"Please," I said. "Let me and my friends go. Give us back our things. We want to stay here for our final days."

Gale'Naris shook its head. "You were distraught when you learned of Architect Riven's plans. I don't want to see you do anything rash. While Architect Riven had deep respect for Benjamin, punishment will be severe to those who interfere with our migration from Earth."

"You know I would never harm the Teth. You're kin of different blood, after all."

"Yes," the innovator muttered. "That is true. Still, I will grieve a second time if you were to leave."

"There will be no need to grieve. This time I will have chosen my fate."

Gale'Naris pulled me close and grazed my neck and face. "I will honor your wishes."

"Thank you."

Ten years ago, when I was thirteen, I stopped carrying guns. But no one wandered the wasteland alone without a weapon. So I developed the skills of lying. I learned them in the same fashion my grandfather taught me other things. By rules, memorization, and application.

However, one rule of lying—the ultimate rule, with no number— was *the liar must possess a certain degree of intelligence and strategy*. Lying required understanding one's self and understanding the person being lied to. It was much like Sun Tzu's rules of warfare. He wrote: "If you know both yourself and your enemy, you can win a hundred battles without jeopardy." Sun Tzu was a brilliant man and no doubt a competent manipulator if he wanted to be.

It sometimes pained me to lie to people. Good people. People that didn't deserve a teenage girl stealing from them back when I had nothing. But I did it anyway to survive.

Gale'Naris obviously cared about me. Well, not *me*, but my grandfather, and for that, I hated lying.

But it had to be done. And with my newfound conviction, I knew I would have no regrets.

I waited for the innovator in the spaceship's infirmary. Gale'Naris walked in with Bishop's duffel bag clutched in its clawed hand. The innovator handed over a few weapons—the EMP and shock grenades, two handguns, a few atomic batteries, and a whole bag of medical supplies I hadn't brought with me—but nothing else.

"The sniper rifle, fission bomb, and plastic explosives stay here," Gale'Naris said. "Such weaponry will worry the architect unless it remains within Teth hands."

"I understand," I said as I took the bag. I rummaged through the contents and examined each piece, one by one. "Thank you for the supplies. I was hoping to take a few more for the woman. The sick one."

"She should live now, even if her quality of life isn't much. We fixed her insides."

"Thank you."

"You can have whatever you want from the infirmary. I'll take responsibility and justify the losses."

I forced a smile. "Again, thank you." I exhaled. "Where can I find my companions?"

"They're waiting for you by the hyperloop. I'll guide you to the vehicle, and you will be deposited in Boulder City."

"You've thought of everything."

I stared at Gale'Naris, the matted black skin a disgusting feature, but I rarely noticed it anymore. Only when I focused. The innovator had been kind to me over the last week.

So when I walked to the door, guilt coursed through me as I withdrew one of the shock grenades, armed it, and threw it back into the room. I ducked into the hall before it triggered, shielding myself with the bulkhead of the ship to avoid the high-powered voltage and amperage.

Shock grenades didn't kill—they weren't tesla mines—but they did burn and incapacitate even the aliens. Gale'Naris half shouted, but the electricity seized the alien's muscles. The innovator collapsed to the floor with a heavy thud, twitching and grunting. I reentered moments afterward, my hands shaking, my thoughts cycling through a few key components of my plan over and over again, as if I'd forget them unless I chanted them in my mind.

Get the syringe. Get the syringe.

Before Gale'Naris had entered the room, I'd filled one of the alien syringes—the large ones—with the medical gel from the surgery tank. The substance was thicker, too thick to go into a vein, but when injected into muscle tissue, it still paralyzed the victim. I stabbed Gale'Naris in the back, once in the alien equivalent to the trapezius muscle, and once in the latissimus dorsi—both large muscle groups.

It must've been painful. I knew. The gel wasn't meant to be used in such a fashion. But I didn't want Gale'Naris moving around, and killing it seemed unnecessary. Gale'Naris could still die if I left, I knew, though there wasn't much I could do about it. Perhaps it would escape. It was a risk I had to take.

I could do what I needed to in a few minutes.

Get to the lockers. Get to the lockers.

I still understood how to undo locks, after all, and the security in the spaceship wasn't much. The outside, however, would be a different story. But first I needed things from the ship. Then . . . then I could leave.

Go faster. Go faster.

I walked off the *Salvation*, trying to remain calm and casual, but my mind made every slight twitch of my gait into something huge and noticeable. Did they know? Were they watching? The drones didn't attack me, and the Iron-Blooded continued their rounds without much more than a second glance.

Even though Gale'Naris wasn't with me, most knew of my status among them. All the leaders of the Teth—the architect and its close confidants— lived at the dam, making me one of the higher-ranked individuals at the space force base, though that didn't mean much.

I just had to avoid the grunts until I reached the hyperloop.

Slow down, act normal.

My heart beat like it was trying to escape my chest, so I held my breath, hoping to suffocate it into submission.

The instant I spotted Dallas, Chelsy, and Bishop, I wanted to run, but despite my anxious energy, I restrained myself. Instead, I smiled. Dallas and Bishop had been given old-world military fatigues, while Chelsy wore a strange outfit—like a military drummer or formal wear—but it was sized for her.

Her eyes went wide at the sight of me, and she pointed to my leg, casting a silent accusation.

"They helped me get better," I said as I walked up to the group.

To my surprise, though I was too stressed to truly appreciate the gesture, Dallas embraced me. It was quick, over in the next moment, but the way he looked at me—like seeing me in a whole new light—stuck in my mind.

"I'm glad you're okay," he said.

I nodded, but my nerves remained. Then I turned to Bishop. "Where is our vehicle?"

Bishop crossed his arms and jerked his head to the side, motioning to a small truck. "The vehicle is right there. But . . . did you do everything you needed to do? None of the Iron-Blooded will tell us what's going on. Has everything changed with the satellites?"

"We can talk about it later," I said, curt. "Wait. Where's Gascoigne?"

Bishop shook his head. "She refused to go. Was insanely difficult about everything, too. I'm tellin' you. She hasn't been herself since she lost her suit."

"No. *No*. We need to get her. Right now."

Maybe I sounded manic, because all three of them stared at me with questioning expressions.

"We can leave her," Bishop said. "If she wants to stay in this hellhole, what's it matter to us?"

No. Gascoigne heard everything when I spoke to Bishop. I didn't have a plan then, but I had made it very clear I wanted to fight against the architect's decision. What if she told the Iron-Blooded once we left? It would be like the girls in the mine again. Or like Carlee in Boulder City. I couldn't leave people that would mess up my plans.

She had to come with us.

"We need to take her," I said. "And we need to get her fast."

Dallas lifted an eyebrow but otherwise said nothing.

I grabbed Bishop by the arm. He nodded and pointed to the cells. "Okay. We'll get her."

"Have the truck running," I said to Dallas. "We'll be right back."

He didn't protest. He simply grabbed his daughter and headed for the truck as though my word had been a command.

I handed Bishop the heavy duffel bag. He slung it over his shoulder and hefted the weight like it was a piece of him that he had been missing.

"Make sure you keep it safe," I said.

He smirked and whispered, "I've carried this bomb around for a long time now. I think I know how to handle it."

I walked as fast as I could without running. Visiting the human zoo hadn't been part of my plan. Nothing ever went exactly as I wanted it, but this one detour had the potential to end everything. Every minute wasted was another minute we drew closer to destruction.

Sweat dappled my skin.

Bishop said nothing. Perhaps he knew how stressed I was. Or maybe he could sense the dire urgency in my movements. Either way. It wouldn't be long before everything was over—but I was the only one who truly understood.

The only one who knew of the countdown.

I barely saw the other people in their cages. I wanted to help them, I really did, but sometimes fighting the bonfire was more important than snuffing out the embers on individual straws of hay.

We reached Gascoigne. She waited, clothed, in the corner of the cell, still in the same position I saw her last. While Bishop claimed she was unstable, I hadn't seen any evidence of it. She just sat still.

An Iron-Blooded man walked over to us and motioned to the cell. "*What're you doing here?*" he asked in Tethlite.

Bishop shook his head. "Gibberish."

"*She's with me,*" I said. "*Release her.*"

"*She said she didn't want to go.*"

"*I'm taking her anyway. Open the cell door.*"

The man hesitated, likely disagreeing with my tone, but he didn't comment. Instead, he used his keys to open the cell door.

I pointed to Gascoigne. "Pick her up," I commanded Bishop.

He chuckled. "Yes, ma'am."

"Don't you fucking touch me," Gascoigne hissed, startling me and the Iron-Blooded soldier. She tensed in the corner, glaring at us and gritting her teeth, conducting herself no better than a feral animal. "I want nothing to do with you. I know what's happening. I'll stay here."

"No, you won't," Bishop said as he crossed the cell and stood next to her. "C'mon."

"I swear to God—"

Bishop didn't care. He stooped down and picked her up, but that might've been a mistake. She thrashed in his arms and then bit down on his bicep.

Even through the military fatigues, crimson stained the sleeve of Bishop's outfit. She had pierced his skin with her teeth.

Bishop hissed but kept her close to his chest regardless, trapping her against him. "Joke's on you," he said. "I cut myself all the time. I can handle it."

Half of Gascoigne's body didn't function like it should. One leg kicked weakly, and the pain on her face when she twisted her torso was plain to see.

She was a lot like me—or how I used to be. Only worse. But still. I didn't care. All that mattered was escaping.

"Let's go," I said. "Quickly."

Gascoigne struggled again, this time attempting to slam her palm up into Bishop's nose. He dropped her momentarily when she cocked herself for the attack, throwing her off-balance. Then he grabbed her arms and pinned her to the ground, attempting to keep her from hurting him any further.

"*I said let me go,*" Gascoigne hissed.

"Calm down," Bishop barked. "I'm not going to hurt you. Unless you make me."

"Fuck you." She spat on him, hitting his chin and neck. Bishop's anger and disgust weren't hard to see. If anything, I thought he might attack her, but he held back.

"Listen," he said. "I was true to my word, wasn't I? I didn't fuck with you the entire time we shared this cell. Trust me."

I jogged into the cell and knelt next to her and Bishop. They both stared in mild surprise, though I ignored the looks to focus on the heart of the issue.

"Everything will be okay," I said. I placed my hand on her side. Her pulse beat steady under my touch. "Let us help you."

"There's nothing to help," Gascoigne drawled, an edge of anger to her voice. "I don't care about whatever you're doing. Leave. Me."

"It's not what you think. We can still get through this."

"Maybe you can, but I'm done with this. I've got nothing left, and I sure as hell won't be a pathetic half corpse dragged all over the wasteland to be used."

So much venom—I could practically taste it.

Bishop tightened his grip, forcing her to stare back up at him.

"I'm tellin' you right now," he said. "If you keep it together until we're out of here, I'll happily shoot you once we're back out on the wastes, if that's what you really want. Got it? You won't have to suffer for much longer."

Shoot her? Was that what she really wanted?

For whatever reason, the declaration calmed her.

Bishop scooped her up in his arms and held her close, his bicep still bleeding, though not much. We exited the cell, my panic still as high as before, but now with the extra burden of wasted time. Everything would be thrown off, but I didn't have much choice.

"What's the plan?" Bishop asked.

It wasn't fair, but I didn't have the sanity to explain it all to him. "Trust me," I said. "We need to leave here. No matter what. It's important beyond words. Okay? You said you'd help me, and that's what I need help with."

We ran out of the human zoo and back to the vehicles near the hyperloop.

Dallas and Chelsy waited on the back of the truck bed, both with nervous glances and confused expressions. They stiffened once Bishop, Gascoigne, and I ran up to the truck bed. I motioned for Bishop to set Gascoigne down and go to the passenger seat in the cab. I hopped onto the back, wishing we could accelerate all our basic movements to save time.

The Iron-Blooded driver started up the electric engine and headed for the hyperloop tunnel.

But it was too late.

An explosion rocked the spaceship. Drones and Iron-Blooded soldiers rushed to the ramp and were met with a burst of air and debris. The truck driver slammed on the brakes and glanced out the window.

Bishop didn't miss a beat. He pulled out a handgun and shot the Iron-Blooded driver through the temple before pushing him out of the driver's seat and taking it for himself.

I silently thanked his dedication. I hadn't given him much, but he still trusted I would do him right.

Dallas gripped Chelsy as the truck sped into the hyperloop tunnel. "What is going on?" he demanded.

"I destroyed the Teth's crèche," I said. I hadn't thought the explosives would go off while we were still around the spaceship, but keeping Gascoigne had turned our escape into a straight run.

"Why?" Dallas asked, his arm protectively in front of his daughter. "Why would you ever do that? They'll come for us now. They won't stop. They were letting us go until you attacked them!"

Gascoigne gripped the edge of the truck, her skin pale and sweat soaking her fatigues. "Fuck. A crèche? Those aliens won't let that go."

Chelsy stared at me, confusion in her large eyes. Was she waiting for me to explain?

I tapped the cab window. "We need the other gun."

Dallas passed back the only other .45 handgun we had. I took it, a slight hesitation in my grip, but less than before, and I handed it to Dallas. "We're heading for the dam, but we're not going inside. We need to make it there fast. Please. Trust me."

He spun the handgun around in his hands. "Are you . . . planning for us to live through the escape?"

I nodded.

I planned on escaping. I planned on saving Earth from the satellites. And I planned on helping humanity escape its darkest night by running to the dawn as fast as I could.

"The aliens were going to destroy Earth, and I couldn't let them," I said. "I'm sorry, Dallas. I almost left you and Chelsy, just in case I failed, so that the two of you could live a life away from this planet, but—"

"You didn't change the satellites?" Dallas asked.

"No. The architect has seen to it that no one else will be able to alter the atmosphere ignition."

"Then what can we possibly do?"

I met his gaze with hard determination. "Force the architect to change the satellites."

Dallas stared at me in confusion, no doubt questioning the first few steps to my plan, but that was okay. I didn't have time to explain it all, but once we were safe, I would reveal everything.

The vehicle sped along, covering a massive amount of distance in a short time. The radio buzzed in the cab, no doubt explaining the explosion in the crèche to the rest of the Iron-Blooded in the dam. The Teth would be upset. Of course they would. Soldiers would be sent after us. Forces would be waiting at the other end of the tunnel.

This was it. If we could make it out of the tunnels, away from the Thompson Space Force Base and the Hoover Dam, I knew we would succeed. But the dark hyperloop tunnel didn't offer much in the way of assurances.

CHAPTER THIRTY-NINE

It didn't take us long to reach an opening in the hyperloop tunnel. The subway and the hyperloop were never meant to be connected, but a hole had been constructed, linking the two. I suspected the Iron-Blooded were responsible, since it allowed them access to both systems with ease.

The subway stop would have a route to the surface. From there, we could escape.

But the moment Bishop turned the truck toward the hole linking both tunnels, bullets blazed through the front windshield and riddled the vehicle's outside with a dozen dents. Everyone ducked, protected by the military-grade frame of the truck.

Six Iron-Blooded soldiers stood between us and the exit. They had been waiting, guarding this route, just in case.

We had to hurry. We had to hurry.

"Bishop," I shouted. "The bag! I brought as much as I could."

He rummaged through the container—I hoped to God he did it gently—and then threw a shock grenade at the cluster of Iron-Blooded. Unfortunately, the enemy soldiers threw a grenade of their own. It landed on the other side of the truck with a heavy clink, but everyone knew what it was the instant it sailed over our heads.

Dallas shielded Chelsy with his body. I slammed myself on the truck bed along with Gascoigne. In the next instant the explosive went off, rocking the vehicle and sending shrapnel flying through the hyperloop tunnel in all directions.

It left a ringing in my ear.

The shock grenade lit up the tunnels with bursts of white and blue electricity. The charged air left my hair standing on end, but the burst never reached the truck.

Bishop threw another grenade—an EMP grenade—and my heart stopped. The electromagnetic pulse would harm the nanites in the Iron-Blooded's blood, causing them to malfunction and clot. It would kill them. But everyone in the truck, except for perhaps Gascoigne, had nanites in their system as well.

I took deep breaths and reminded myself of the limited range of the EMP. Only fifty feet. If he threw it far enough, we wouldn't be affected.

Dallas rolled to the side, his left arm shredded to the bone from the shrapnel of the enemy's grenade. Chelsy clung to him, her eyes wet, but her attention snapped to the back of the truck when an enemy Iron-Blooded ran over, obviously hoping to take advantage of our disorientated state.

The man spotted us in the back of the vehicle. I reached for Dallas's handgun, lying on the truck bed next to him, my reflexes much faster than anything I had before Gale'Naris fixed me.

The man hefted his rifle.

I lifted my handgun.

In that instant, I could have sworn we both fired, but the man's neck exploded in the next half second, a rain of dark blood hitting the tunnel floor as my .45 bullet sliced through his throat. He fell to his back, his body convulsing as it went into shock.

Then I pushed Chelsy against the truck cab, my hand shaking. "Stay down."

Dallas gritted his teeth as he ripped the shreds of his fatigue's sleeves into strips. With the haste of a professional, he fashioned a quick binding for his arm, tying it off with the use of his mouth. It was hard to hear due to the ringing in my ear, but the gunshots didn't stop. Bishop continued firing, though the return fire became less and less. His use of grenades helped him to overpower the larger numbers.

The enemies never threw another grenade, but the stomp and rumble told me more trouble was on its way.

Then Dallas turned to me. He held out his hand for the handgun and I relinquished it, not wanting to chance a regression back into mental paralysis.

"Kita," Dallas said. "Thank you. Please, stay back. I'll keep you both safe."

"The judge," Gascoigne intoned. "It's here."

I glanced over the edge of the truck bed, my adrenaline-soaked mind taking in every detail and focusing on it with obsession. Two Iron-Blooded soldiers remained behind cover in the subway station. The alien judge—warrior caste, Fera'Cova—stepped down the stairs onto the platform. It was the sound of the judge's boots that caused the rumble I heard.

Bishop shot one of the remaining Iron-Blooded, his aim tested and true after hundreds of shootouts. But it didn't matter for the alien judge. The monster wrapped in exoskeleton protection walked across the subway station, down into the subway furrow, and then up again on our side.

Dallas yanked me and Chelsy from the truck bed and hopped into the hyperloop tunnel. Bishop threw himself from the cab, the duffel bag hung on one shoulder. Gascoigne, unable to flee, was the only one on the truck when the judge slammed into it. She tumbled around the back and then hit the floor of the hyperloop tunnel hard, her body bruising in a matter of moments.

But the alien judge didn't stop at just hitting the vehicle.

Fera'Cova struck the engine with a gauntleted fist, denting in the hood and wrecking the frame. He wanted to prevent us from leaving. I knew it in my gut.

Bishop dashed over and grabbed my arm. "Up, c'mon!"

Before I could say anything, he tossed another shock grenade, as far as he could, to the other side of the judge. The resulting burst of electricity homed in on the electric engine of the busted vehicle and arced across the JUDGE-Z12 armor. The damaged part of the armor—the part Gascoigne had cut open with her own suit's blade—allowed the effects of the burst to affect the driver.

Fera'Cova fell to one knee as the crackle of charged energy flared around the suit.

I stood. Bishop ran over and yanked Gascoigne up into his arms, his strength on display, but his fatigue already visible.

My mind snapped to the last Iron-Blooded still alive in the subway and I whipped my head around. The man writhed on the floor, one hand clutched over his chest. No doubt in the throes of a heart attack brought about by the inactive nanites clumping in his blood. Any second I suspected he would also suffer from a stroke.

"Hurry," Gascoigne yelled. "Use another one! The judge suit is about to recover!"

Bishop dropped Gascoigne, reached into the duffel bag, and withdrew the last shock grenade. He threw it like the last, far enough down the hyperloop that it wouldn't also shock us, but the crackle in the air threatened to send the electricity farther than before.

The alien had only been down for ten seconds before Gascoigne said it would recover. That wasn't long enough to escape, not without a vehicle. And without another shock grenade, we wouldn't have any way of slowing it.

Bishop ripped open side pockets on the duffel bag and dropped some ammunition, plastic explosives, and medical supplies all over the floor of the hyperloop. He searched with frantic glances, obviously trying to determine the best course of action.

Without a second's hesitation, Dallas leapt over, grabbed the plastic explosive, and ran toward the alien judge. He slammed the moldable plastic into the fissure of the suit, stuffing it deep.

"Get away from it," Gascoigne snapped. "You're not—"

The alien judge stood. Dallas tried to back away, but he was no match for the speed of the exoskeleton. Fera'Cova grabbed Dallas by the arm and yanked him off his feet.

I took Chelsy by the hand and ran for the stairs. Whatever was about to happen, we couldn't be near—and, frankly, I didn't want Chelsy to see it.

While Bishop scooped up Gascoigne and the explosive triggers, the alien judge ripped off Dallas's right arm with enough force to take the armpit and a whole layer of skin down his side, exposing the red grain of muscle of the ribs. Dallas screamed, the intensity and agony enough to chill blood. Every shred of fiber on Dallas's shirt went with his mangled arm, leaving the mess of his body visible.

If Chelsy could have yelled, she would have. The expression on her face alone seared every one of my senses. I clung to her and held her tight, burying her face in my body as I dove behind one of the subway's many concrete pillars. Bishop tumbled into the subway furrow, he and Gascoigne hitting the tracks and rolling between them.

The judge discarded Dallas with a flick of its wrist, sending him sliding in a pool of his blood.

Bishop set off the plastic explosive. The blast shook the subway, breaking apart concrete and damaging the walls. Debris whipped around the area, mixing with dust and stinging my eyes. I coughed and hacked, making sure to keep Chelsy close.

Again, my ears rang, but it didn't last long. Soon everything was a dull white noise.

Once the dust settled, I glanced around the pillar. The JUDGE-Z12 suit looked as though something had burst out of it. The metal panels were peeled outward, and chunks of gory flesh from Fera'Cova's mangled body dripped out in piles.

Lights inside the hyperloop tunnel drew my attention. More trucks were coming, which meant more Iron-Blooded soldiers and certainly a whole host of drones.

Bishop climbed out of the subway furrow, Gascoigne hanging on his back. I ran to him, my attention on the duffel bag until I saw it was safe. During my moment of distraction, however, Chelsy darted away from me. She ran straight to her father's body. Dust clung to his blood, creating a paste that covered most of his skin.

I dashed to her, grabbed her elbow, and tried to pull her away. She shook her head, fighting against me with all her might. She clung to Dallas. She wouldn't leave without him.

Dallas trembled.

Was he dead? No. He wasn't. But . . .

Bishop was already by my side when I looked up. He ripped off his shirt and wrapped it around the mutilated form of Dallas. He tightened it hard around the injury, trying to prevent as much bleeding as possible. Would it really help much?

"Fuck you," Bishop muttered. "You're not making me look bad by dying a heroic death, you got that, you piece of shit? I'm onto you. You're gonna make it out of here."

He was fast. He wrapped Dallas and scooped him into his arms within moments. Now he had Gascoigne, the bag, and another body. And a bite mark on his bicep. But Bishop gritted his teeth and then gave me a smile. Like he always did.

"Please," I whispered. "Please let us make it through this."

Together we ran up the stairs. Trucks screeched to a halt in the hyperloop tunnel, but by then I had slapped the last of the explosives on the exit. After we entered the topside building, Bishop set them off, crushing the stairway with already cracked concrete from the earlier explosion.

I didn't even see the details of the building we ran through. I couldn't focus on them. Only running.

We couldn't stop.

I hit the door to the exit and slammed through it hard, breaking something on the doorframe in the process. We exited into the desert, the sight of sandy dunes, A-grass, and lifeless shrubs in every direction. The overcast skies blanketed Earth in an icy quilt, a steady wind washing over us, but the heat of my pulse and panic refused to be chilled.

How much time had gone by? It would be soon. No turning back.

Two trucks with six soldiers each drove over the broken roads of the forgotten civilization, heading straight in our direction. The Iron-Blooded hadn't taken any risks. Some went through the tunnels; others went over land. They were coming for us from every angle.

I grabbed Bishop's arm and forced him back toward the subway station building. We had to take cover. Bishop stopped, pulled out the last EMP grenade, and threw it as hard as he could in the enemy's direction. The weapon landed in one of the truck beds and pulsed, wrecking the electronics in the engine and the nanites of the Iron-Blooded soldiers.

Old-world soldiers before the bombs had protections against such EMP tactics—medications, defibrillator-style recovery tools, and protective gear—but judging by the panic of the Iron-Blooded, none of them had any recourse to what had been done.

The second truck peeled away in the opposite direction, no doubt fearing we had more EMP grenades.

But we didn't. No more grenades. No more explosives. Just a handgun and ammunition.

And before the second truck got too far, I spotted a familiar sight. Commander Dannik. He pulled out a sniper rifle and braced it on the cab of the vehicle. To my shock, he aimed and fired within a matter of seconds. His shot missed and exploded a mound of sand next to me.

Bishop ducked around the side of the building and set Gascoigne down. She balanced on her only functioning leg and ripped Bishop's handgun from the waistband of his pants. Without asking to engage, or even giving us warning, she leaned around the corner and fired.

Although her aim wasn't the greatest, she never flinched or recoiled whenever enemy bullets came close. Almost like she didn't give a fuck if she got shot at all. Such disregard wouldn't land her a long life, but it did add a killing edge to her combat. The panicked Iron-Blooded, some of whom were still trying to solve the EMP problem, weren't the most competent of opponents given the situation. She shot four of the Iron-Blooded, and the last ducked behind the trucks on wobbly legs. They never emerged afterward.

Dannik shot again, grazing the building and leaving a long furrow through the cement. Gascoigne shot at him, but he was much too far away for her handgun.

Bishop gulped down air.

"What're we doing?" he asked between pants. Chelsy hung on his arms, staring at her father's trembling body. "If we stay here . . . they'll send more."

"It's almost time," I said, breathless. "Stay here. And don't look."

In that moment the wind died down, like even the world was holding its breath.

The flash happened first.

The light was so bright and brilliant, if we had been looking straight at it, we would've been temporarily blinded. It lit up the area for miles around, casting harsh shadows across the landscape—some so black they'd scar the area for days to come. Even though the Thompson Space Force Base was a good eight miles away, it didn't matter. We could still see it.

Fission bombs were *that* powerful.

I had left the bomb on the spaceship and estimated a period of time for us to escape the blast radius. I had hoped to be farther away, not out in the dunes of the Mohave Desert. Still, it would work. Hopefully.

A wave of heat washed over us.

Thermal radiation.

If we had been a couple miles closer, we probably would've suffered first-degree burns.

"We need to go now," I shouted. "So they won't be able to follow!"

Gascoigne wrapped her arms back around Bishop's neck. He took in a few deep breaths before running with me away from the building. I picked a direction—one with lots of dunes, twists, and rocks—and I didn't look back.

"Everyone," I said. "Close your eyes."

They did as I said, but not before Bishop covered Dallas's face for him.

A rush of air blasted over us. The bomb sent sand everywhere, some of which scratched across my skin, stripping away outer layers of my flesh. I kept as covered as possible, my jaw clenched and my eyes shut tight. The winds lasted far longer than I thought they would, but I never let up or stopped running.

Finally, the wind stopped and a tremor shook the ground afterward. When Bishop slowed, I turned around and grabbed his arm.

"Not now," I said. "You have to keep going."

I didn't know from where Bishop summoned the last bit of strength but he nodded and continued again at my pace, running alongside me, his focus on the path ahead of us.

I ran behind a large sand dune and slid into a crouching positioning, hiding myself as much as possible. Bishop followed suit, along with Chelsy. We hid among the sand, our trail hidden by the blast of wind. And it wasn't like the Iron-Blooded were watching us, not when a fission bomb had gone off in the middle of their base.

And those who had looked would be blinded.

When I finally felt safe enough to glance up, I spotted the massive pillar of dust and particles—the mushroom cloud of destruction and ruin. It reached into the atmosphere itself, poisoning everything with its nuclear touch.

But it had to be done.

Without a spaceship, the architect couldn't leave Earth. And thus, Architect Riven and the rest of the Teth were trapped.

I didn't even need to speak to the architect to voice my solution. I knew the problem with the satellites would be solved, even if I destroyed the plexus at the space force base.

Architect Riven wouldn't allow anything to happen to the rest of the Teth, after all.

The remaining Iron-Blooded obviously felt the explosion was more pressing than finding me. Commander Dannik's truck sped away from the subway station, leaving us to the chill of the sands. When I had planned my escape, I almost thought about vindictively killing Dannik somehow, but I avoided such urges to give us the best chance of success. I wondered if he would ever attempt to find me again.

Bishop threw off the duffel bag and sat back against the sand, his eyes half-lidded, every bit of him coated in sand and sweat. I rubbed at my ears, the sand deep enough it scratched my eardrums.

Chelsy threw off the covering on Dallas's face, her only concern her father.

For the second time in a short while, no one seemed to breathe.

Dallas was alive, but only technically. Sure, people could live from having a limb violently rent from their body, but not in our condition. We had no doctor. No medicine. No way to give him blood. He bled into Bishop's fatigues, his skin pale, his lips white. Even the nanites couldn't prevent his impending death.

I almost hated that we'd brought him because of the grief it would cause, but I knew that leaving him wouldn't be right. We had to be there for him in his last moments. It was the least we could do.

Chelsy, tears streaming down her face, kept him close. To my surprise, he opened his eyes halfway, draining the last of his strength no doubt to see his daughter one last time.

She stroked his blood-matted hair, her fingers shaking.

Dallas coughed and attempted to move his mangled arm, but he couldn't.

Bishop placed a hand on his chest, his touch gentle. "You're a good man, Dallas. But you don't need to keep fighting anymore. You did it. You saved her."

Dallas exhaled, a tear running across the bridge of his nose.

With unsteady hands, Chelsy reached into her uniform pocket. I supposed the Teth must have been merciful—they'd given her back her notebook and pen—and she struggled to flip through it to reach the empty pages. When she found one, she placed the pen down, the tip wobbling as she forced herself to write. Each letter shakier than the last.

The words: I love you.

She showed him the paper, but Dallas could barely keep his eyes open.

"I promise she'll be safe," Bishop said. "You don't have to worry about anything else."

Chelsy drew a heart and placed it on Dallas's chest. Dallas's breath came out slower and gentler than before. So Chelsy drew another one. And another one. And continued to place them on him until he finally stopped breathing.

It shook me.

I stood and walked away, my own memories of family members haunting the edge of my thoughts. I needed deep breaths. Lots of air. I hated that my decisions could have such consequences. It was on me when people died, but I had to shoulder the responsibility and learn to move on.

Logically I knew it was true, but repeating such things in my head didn't seem to quell the distress in my heart.

I couldn't revert to doubting. I had to trust what I'd done. I hadn't forced Dallas into anything, nor would I abandon his wishes now that he was gone. I would be there for Chelsy, and I would see humanity brought out of the depths of hell.

But it still took me a moment to grapple with the reality.

CHAPTER FORTY

We buried Dallas in the desert. Not because that was ideal—far from it—but because we needed the catharsis of doing something for him and for Chelsy.

She used all of her notebook to make paper flowers while we dug and wrapped his body. Then she placed the makeshift bouquet down and stayed next to the mound. But we couldn't stay long. We left afterward and walked for hours away from the grave. Only at night did we rest between red rocks jetting from the Earth.

The Iron-Blooded never followed us. I suspected they didn't know where we were, and they were much too busy scrambling with their losses.

In less than a day, we spotted signs for a town called Searchlight. All the graffiti about the place mentioned houses, plants, and bright lights. A placed called Trouble's Roadhouse was open to all passersby, apparently, and without much discussion, we headed for it. Bishop, on the verge of collapsing, asked me to carry the duffel bag, and I happily did. I kept it close to my chest, cradling it.

Chelsy held my hand the entire way, her father's dog tags clinking against her chest as she walked.

Searchlight had a chain-link fence and men with guard dogs, but they let us in without many questions. Trouble's Roadhouse, the largest building in the center of town, wasn't difficult to find. We traded our ammo and handgun for a couple weeks' stay in one of the second-story rooms. The moment we arrived and spotted the two twin beds in the room, everyone breathed a sigh of relief.

Bishop set Gascoigne down on the edge of the mattress before leaning back against the wall and sliding into a sitting position on the floor. Chelsy took the second bed, her melancholy expression unchanged the entire trip.

A small table with two lawn chairs was the entirety of the furniture provided to us. I took a seat and the chair legs wobbled, but I didn't have much energy to stand. The silence that followed weighed heavy.

"You blew up the spaceship," Gascoigne said, cutting through the thick atmosphere with her gruff voice. "That's what happened, isn't it?"

I nodded.

"You had a fission bomb? And that was how you used it?"

Again, I nodded.

"If that was what you were hoping to do all along, why destroy the crèche? We could've been long gone without anyone knowing if you had left the crèche alone."

Maybe. I had thought about it over and over. I opened the duffel bag and inhaled deeply. "I have two reasons. First, the most obvious, is I wanted the panic. If we left, and someone found the fission bomb, it would be disabled and I would've failed. But after the crèche was destroyed, I knew they'd send every drone and soldier after me. There wouldn't be any time to accidentally discover my bomb."

"What's the second reason?" Gascoigne demanded.

"I wanted them to think the eggs had been destroyed. I wanted that report to get out first, before the rest of the ship was nuked."

I withdrew the crèche canisters from the duffel bag one at a time.

An architect egg. A warrior egg. An innovator egg.

The canisters, mostly metal with some thick glass windows, made it through the escape. I silently thanked my luck—or whatever forces controlled such outcomes—that I still had them. Without them, I couldn't complete my plans.

"Are those alien eggs?" Bishop asked. "I saw them when I rummaged through the bag, but I figured they had to be something else. No way you would be crazy enough to take alien eggs."

Chelsy turned her attention to us, staring intently at the canister. She lifted her eyebrows and fidgeted with the blankets on the bed.

"I took the eggs," I said. "This one here is an architect."

"You think the aliens won't know those are missing?"

"Weren't you listening?" Gascoigne snapped. "That was one of the reasons she destroyed the crèche. So the architect would think the eggs were lost. And they probably didn't have any time to investigate, either. Not when the ship became ground zero for a fission bomb."

If I only used the fission bomb, the architect—distraught over the loss of its last egg—may have sent people after me on the off chance I took it. Just on the off chance. I knew it in my gut. But if I gave the architect reason to doubt, like the crèche exploding, the aliens would likely classify me as someone who hated their kind and totally unlikely to have stolen their eggs.

I closed my eyes and exhaled. "I'm sorry I put you all in danger, but this was the only way I could think to force the architect to change the satellites and leave the space force base with the crèche eggs undetected."

No one said anything. I hoped they believed me. If I could've used a different solution, I would have. But it was the only one that made sense.

I feared Chelsy's interpretation of the situation the most. She was a child, I knew that, but that didn't mean she wouldn't blame me for her father's death. What if, just like with Tamura, she hated me?

Bishop and Gascoigne turned to Chelsy as though they could read my mind. I didn't look. I didn't want to see the same expression my sister had given me all those years ago.

When Chelsy did nothing, Gascoigne returned her hard look to me. "Why?" she demanded. "Why do any of this? What could you possibly hope to gain from having a bunch of alien eggs? Are you going to sell them back to the Iron-Blooded? Is that it?"

"Never," I said. "I hate the Iron-Blooded."

Chelsy scooted to the edge of the bed and nodded along with my words. Although I was elated to see she wasn't actively upset, she still didn't look right. She watched, rapt, and waited for me to continue.

I ran a hand through my hair and stared at the eggs. "Life since the Forever Winter has been hard. Ex Cathedra wants to unite everyone by force. United California wants to remain separated from everything. The marauders in the lawless lands just want to do whatever they want. All these societies . . . even places like Richfield . . . they want to make a better future, but I don't think they're doing it right."

Gascoigne huffed a laugh. "Oh, yeah? You think you can do better?"

"Yes," I said without hesitation. I held the eggs close.

In my moments of deep contemplation, I'd thought of a solution. Something better than anything else offered by the world. Something to save both humanity and the Teth.

"Architect Riven was right," I muttered. "Too many of the aliens are mindless beasts. I need to fix that if I'm going to help humanity."

"We could kill them," Gascoigne said. "That's Ex Cathedra's rule on the book. Eliminate any and all aliens."

"I could. But I want to make a new way of life. Something better than before. The aliens—the Teth—they're like us in a lot of ways. And they can be just as talented. They were a spacefaring race before us. They value science and cooperation."

"The Teth architect was gonna treat us like animals," Bishop interjected.

"That's why we needed a new architect," I said. "With this one, we can start over. We can build something new, without carrying the baggage of the past. Imagine if we could clear the drone nests and actually make parts of the wasteland safe again. Wouldn't that be something great?"

Gascoigne sneered. "People will hate that. Even in Boulder City, they hated Theon and his drones, simply because he had aliens. It'll never work."

"And some people say Ex Cathedra will crumble to its own bloodthirst," I said. "But you still believe in them, don't you? You think they're helping humanity? Well, this is what I think will help. And I'm not going to be a passive participant in life anymore. I'm going to create things. Better things. To help people."

My hatred of the aliens stemmed from cowardice, much like most of my old decisions. I needed to move past it if I were going to lead a new architect into cleaning the world of drone nests and violent alien locations. I knew what needed to be done, and I had the conviction to do it.

No doubt in my mind.

"Bishop," I said. "You've taken me so far already, but I can go on my own now. You don't need to stay."

"What're you trying to say?" he asked. "You want me to leave?"

"That's not what I said. I'm just saying . . . you can do whatever you think is right for you."

He laughed and rested his head against the wall. "Oh, I see. Puttin' me on the spot. Well, I already made up my mind. I want . . . to honor my family. I've avoided the place of their death so long, but I know some things there still remain. I want to get them and take them with me to a place I can finally call home."

"And where is that?"

"I don't know. Some place with aliens, apparently."

I smiled, if only because I had been worried. I didn't want Bishop to leave. I wanted him to stay close. I . . . wanted him, period. His strength and mirth could lift me out of any dark place in my life.

Bishop turned to Gascoigne. "What about you? Still thinkin' about puttin' a bullet through your head?"

She shot him a glower. But before she could say anything, Bishop lifted his hand.

"I've been meanin' to thank you, by the way. For helpin' us with the Iron-Blooded. You're not the best shot, but I'm glad you took a few assholes down. Ever seen my tally marks? You might be interested in making some of your own."

"I'm used to heavy weapons," Gascoigne drawled. "The type used while in a judge exoskeleton."

"Didn't answer my question, though."

The long pause afterward made me think Gascoigne would take him up on his offer for the bullet.

"I'm weak," she stated. "Without my suit, I'm nothing."

I knew the words well. And I knew nothing I could say would ever change her mind.

"Still didn't answer my question," Bishop said as he snapped his fingers. "Come with us. I promise I won't bite. Well, actually, *you* better promise not to bite. And if you do, I won't mind carrying you."

She huffed and turned away, her stony expression rigid. "You won't be able to stop Ex Cathedra."

"Maybe if we found our own suits," I said, touching the connector on the side of my head. "And maybe, with the help of an architect, we'll have our own army."

Gascoigne said nothing afterward, but I knew she didn't want to die.

Chelsy leapt from the bed and walked to my side. I didn't know what to say to her. She had to come with us, because she was my responsibility now. It was my decisions that cost her Dallas's life, and even though Bishop made a promise to look after her, the weight of such actions fell on me.

Despite not having any paper, and without a common language between us, Chelsy touched her chest, just above the dog tags, starting a sentence.

Then she pointed to Bishop, and then Gascoigne, and then to the eggs. She hugged herself afterward and then motioned to the room. Finally, she out turned her pockets—empty—and touched her short, black hair.

We were her family now. She had nothing else.

At first I thought these facts were made apparent in anger, but then she touched my own short hair before wrapping her arms around me. Her hot tears dropped onto my shoulder, and I knew she realized that I had given up just as much to be here.

I didn't have anything else, either. The people in the room—the eggs in front of me—I had nothing else. But that was okay.

Together we would create something better than before. Something grand and epic.

To save Earth from the darkness that engulfed it.

ABOUT THE AUTHOR

Shami Stovall is an award-winning fantasy and science fiction author. Previously, she taught history and criminal law at the college level and loved every second. When she's not reading fascinating articles and books about ancient China or the Byzantine Empire, Stovall can be found playing way too many video games, especially RPGs and tactics simulators. She loves John, reading, and writing about herself in the third person.